A Scandalous Past

AVA STONE

Night Shift Publishing

AVA STONE

ISBN: 1517270782
ISBN-13: 978-1517270780

Dedication

For my amazing critique partners:
Jane Charles
Tammy Falkner
Lily George
Samantha Grace
Suzie Grant
Julie Johnstone
Jerrica Knight-Catania

One

July 1814 –Avery House, London

CORDELIA Avery was certain she hadn't heard her mother correctly. It wasn't even possible that her mother had changed her opinion about attending the Staveley ball. "I beg your pardon?"

Lady Avery dropped her napkin to the breakfast table and narrowed her light green eyes on her youngest daughter. "I said the only reason we're even attending Lady Staveley's ball is because Sally Jersey expressly asked us to be present."

Cordie nearly dropped her fork onto the table, but that would only earn her another lecture on comportment, so she grasped the utensil tighter. Ever since her dearest friend Olivia, the newlywed Duchess of Kelfield, had hastily married a rather scandalous duke, Lady Avery's entire demeanor had changed. Not only was Cordie not allowed to see Livvie, she might as well have been shackled to her mother for all the freedom and spare time she enjoyed.

Cordie nodded, but didn't say anything. Her mother had agreed to the ball. If she opened her mouth, Lady Avery might very well change her mind, and she couldn't risk that. Livvie was certain to be at the Staveleys', as they were relations, and it would be the first time since her wedding that Cordie would have the opportunity to see her dear friend.

"I do want you to promise me not to associate with either Olivia or

1

Kelfield."

"Of course, Mother. You've been very clear on the subject," Cordie lied, her fingers crossed beneath the table. She didn't really think the crossed fingers made the sin any less, but it was the best she could do at the moment. After all, she couldn't tell her mother that she had every intention of speaking with both Livvie *and* Kelfield, if the latter happened to be present.

Since they were children, she and Livvie had been inseparable, growing up in a village that bordered Sherwood Forest. Until Livvie's recent marriage, they'd seen each other every day of their lives. The forced separation twisted Cordie's heart and left her feeling strangely alone.

"Thankfully no one outside the family knows you jilted the man, but between that unfortunate situation and Olivia's scandalous actions your reputation is dangling by a thread. And now since you've rejected Captain Seaton's offer, you'll have to be on your absolute best behavior if you want to catch a *proper* husband."

Cordie resisted the urge to roll her eyes. She hadn't *jilted* Gabriel Seaton, not technically. After all, they weren't officially betrothed. He'd never gotten the opportunity to speak with her brother, Gregory, on the matter. It was a narrow escape in Cordie's mind, and she was grateful that she learned just what sort of a dictatorial prig the captain was before their betrothal could be finalized. Not that she should have been surprised. He was a captain, accustomed to giving orders and being obeyed. But that sort of life wasn't for Cordie. She was looking for a little more freedom.

She feigned an accommodating smile for her mother and placed her fork on her plate. "Catching a *proper* husband is, of course, my goal." And truly it *was*, though Cordie had a feeling that her idea of a proper husband and her mother's were quite different.

Lady Avery frowned, and Cordie wondered if her mother could read her thoughts. "One wouldn't know it. Your sister was already married with one babe by the time she was your age."

Cordie suppressed the urge to scowl. Her mother made it sound as if she were on her deathbed. At twenty, it was true she was far from the youngest debutant in Town, but neither was she the oldest. And she'd had plenty of offers the three previous seasons, but until the captain, no one had turned her head—and what a colossal mistake *that* would have been.

"You'll be fortunate if any decent man will look past your association with Olivia."

She wouldn't tolerate a husband who wouldn't. Neither would she tolerate a husband who wouldn't allow her to continue her friendship with Olivia. This breakfast discussion made one thing perfectly clear. She needed to find a husband—quickly—but one *she* could live with the rest of her days, her mother be hanged. A husband who would give her the freedom she craved. A husband who would let her make her own decisions. A husband who would love her like Kelfield obviously loved Olivia.

But where was she to find a paragon like that?

Almost to his Mayfair home, Brendan Reese, the Earl of Clayworth, stifled a yawn. The last bloody place he wanted to be was London, and yet he'd raced here from his Derbyshire estate after receiving a summons from Caroline Staveley. Apparently Caroline's young cousin Olivia had gotten herself into a bit of trouble with the Duke of Kelfield and had been forced to marry the notorious scoundrel. The new duchess was being accepted less warmly than a leper in the midst of the *ton*. So Caroline, a meddlesome but lovely woman to be sure, was determined to change the tide of opinion in her cousin's favor and was hosting a ball in honor of the duke and his new duchess.

This was the sort of thing Brendan normally could care less about. He had enough of his own problems, and had anyone else summoned him with the words, "Your stodgy presence is required to lend Livvie an air of respectability," he would have told the author to go jump in the Thames. But he could rarely refuse Caroline. Not only was she the sister of one of his closest friends, but she was also one of the few people who had been kind to his late sister, Flora. That generosity could never be repaid.

Still, now was not the best time for him to leave Derbyshire. His youngest sister, Rosamund, was becoming more and more difficult to manage and his nephew, Thomas, was in desperate need of some male guidance. And he still hadn't found those damning letters that could get them all sent to Newgate. Perhaps he could search again in London, as if he hadn't already done that more than a dozen times already.

Of course, he'd already looked every place he could think of, more times than he could count. Brendan had methodically searched his ancestral home, Bayhurst Court in Derbyshire, from top to bottom, gone over every inch of Clayworth Hall in Kent, he'd gone through every nook and cranny of his hunting lodge in Yorkshire, and he'd gone over his Hertford Street home with a fine-toothed comb more than once. But the letters detailing his mother's crimes against the crown were nowhere to be found, and the only clue he had was the memory of his late wife's cryptic taunt. "The Lion holds your secrets." He didn't know what the devil that meant.

The coach pulled to a stop in front of his Mayfair home. Brendan exited the carriage then climbed the front steps to be greeted by his butler, Higgins.

"Lord Clayworth, Lord Masten awaits you in the blue parlor."

How odd. Brendan raised his brow in question at his butler. He hadn't realized Masten was in Town. Even so, it was unusual for his friend to await him here, especially as *he* hadn't yet arrived.

He strode down the hallway until he reached the blue parlor, a tacky room that his late wife had decorated—a room he should scrap and start all over, if for no other reason than he hated to be reminded that Marina had ever entered his life.

Brendan found Robert Beckford, the Earl of Masten, staring out one of the room's grand windows. His friend's hands were clasped behind his back and he was grumbling to himself.

"Robert?"

His friend spun on his heel and offered a curt smile. "I see she's roped you into this nonsense as well."

Robert could only mean his sister, Caroline. Brendan shrugged. "When Lady Staveley beckons, we all fall in line."

"Like the pack of fools we are," Robert agreed. "What Aunt Jane thought she was doing, leaving Olivia with Staveley and my sister, I have no idea."

"If it's any consolation, Rob, when I saw them in Derbyshire, Kelfield seemed like a man besotted. I wouldn't have believed it myself if I hadn't seen it with my own eyes."

"Bloody wonderful. My sweet, young cousin has married one of the

4

most depraved men in all of England."

To say the very least. Brendan could commiserate. If it had been one of his sisters or cousins who ended up with Kelfield, he'd be as irate as Robert. "It could be worse," he offered, shrugging again.

"Oh?" His friend's brown eyes flashed with indignation.

"It could have been Haversham."

⚜

Marcus Gray, the Marquess of Haversham, left Madam Palmer's establishment sated, but not completely satisfied. Though professional whores were fairly proficient at their trade, they often left something to be desired. What he *needed* was a mistress, though that was a touchy subject at the moment. Right before his wedding, Kelfield had cut his pretty actress loose, and Marc had hoped to snatch up the sweet little number in his stead. Unfortunately, Sarah Kane had already found a new protector, so Marc was still in the market.

As it was too early for most of his usual entertainments, Marc headed over to White's, which was, admittedly, a little tame for him. But ever since Kelfield had married, his old friend was playing at being respectable. It was truly a sight to cherish—and place bets on how long it would last.

After entering the hallowed halls of the club, it didn't take Marc long to find his old friend Alexander Everett, the Duke of Kelfield, in the library, sitting in an over-stuffed leather chair, perusing *The Times*.

Marc quietly shook his head. Though he had witnessed the wedding himself, it was still hard to believe the old devil had actually married the chit. No land, no fortune was gained—just the girl. It didn't make one bit of sense. Not for a man like Kelfield anyway.

"I have seen neither hide nor hair of you since Macbeth," Marc drawled as he looked down on his friend.

"What does that tell you, Marc?" Kelfield didn't bother to look up from his paper, which brought a wry grin to the marquess' face. It must be terribly tedious, pretending to be so respectable.

"Well, you can't be avoiding *me*. So I can only assume you're keeping that pretty little wife of yours tied up at Kelfield House. Has she asked about me?" Marc dropped onto a settee across from the duke and smirked.

Kelfield scowled over the edge of his paper. "Only to berate me for

5

my poor choice of friends."

"Browbeaten already, are you?" Marc cheerfully baited him.

The duke folded his paper in half and narrowed his eyes, clearly allowing Marc to see the true Kelfield, hiding just beneath the surface. "I'm certain you know me better than that, Haversham. Now what do you want?"

"To curse you for leaving Miss Kane so well positioned."

"Turned you down flat, did she?"

"Bastard," Marc answered with a nod. "She's attached herself to Haywood. Can you believe that?" It was certainly hard for *him* to swallow. The penniless baron wasn't in the same league as Marc. It shouldn't have been a contest, and wouldn't have been if Kelfield hadn't left the girl a small fortune as a parting gift.

The duke shrugged. "I told you, Sarah is free to make her own choices."

"I still can't account for you just giving her up. Doesn't seem like you at all."

"Well, times change."

"Ah, Kelfield, there you are," came the deep voice of Commander Simon Greywood from behind them. "Ready for tonight?"

That sounded promising. "What's tonight?" Marc asked, rising from his seat to shake Greywood's hand.

"Nothing," Kelfield answered, though he was drowned out by the commander's reply.

"Caroline Staveley's ball, of course."

Marc fell back on the settee with a laugh, beaming at the duke. "You? A ball?"

"It's for Olivia," Kelfield growled.

Marc's laughter echoed off the walls of the club. "God, Kelfield! You've turned soft. Married a fortnight, and she's already wrapped you around her little finger." Which was something Marc had never allowed to happen to himself. Not even his late wife ever attempted to dictate his entertainments.

It would be vastly amusing to watch the new duchess lead Kelfield around by his prick. Though Marc hadn't received an invitation to Caroline Staveley's ball—most likely an oversight on her part—he wouldn't miss it for the world.

Two

CORDIE could hardly believe her good fortune as she entered Lady Staveley's ballroom. She'd managed to get through the entire day without her mother scolding her. Of course, she'd been on her best behavior — actually she'd been better than her best. After all she couldn't miss this opportunity.

Thankfully the Staveley ball was a huge success. Lords and ladies of all shapes and sizes were crammed into every conceivable spot. None of her mother's events had ever been considered a crush, not compared to *this* anyway. Apparently all of the *ton* was curious about Livvie and Kelfield.

Lady Staveley in all her brilliance, or perhaps dumb luck, had several game rooms set up, right off the ballroom. Thank heavens! Loo was her mother's particular weakness, and Cordie felt confident Lady Avery would sit down at one of the tables, leaving her free to find Livvie.

Her mother glanced around the room and smiled. "Apparently it's a good thing we've come. Everyone is here."

Cordie nodded her head. "Look, Mama, there's Miss Greywood and Lady Felicity. May I go see my friends?"

After glancing at one of the gaming parlors, Lady Avery turned her eyes on Cordie. "No Olivia," she ordered

"You wound me, Mama. I gave my word," she said with feigned sincerity.

Her mother's gaze raked her up and down. Finally she nodded her head. "Very well, Cordelia. I think I'll play a little Loo, but I'll check on you periodically."

Once her mother got sucked in to a table, she'd be lost for the rest of the night. Cordie had no doubt. So, she smiled serenely and nodded. "Do enjoy yourself, Mama."

Lady Avery started for the closest parlor, but Cordie stood rooted to the spot until her mother's bobbing, plum ostrich feather had completely disappeared from view. After that she silently counted to ten, then nonchalantly strode across the floor, peeked into the room her mother had entered, and watched her take a seat at one of the tables.

Victory was at hand.

Her mother wouldn't emerge until it was time to go home—she never did. Cordie's hopes for the evening soared. With a sly grin, she quickly crossed the room to Olivia's side.

Olivia Everett, the Duchess of Kelfield, looked exquisite. She was wearing a copper gown that shimmered under the chandelier light, complementing her auburn hair and hazel eyes perfectly. Married ladies got to wear gowns such as this. Cordie needed to get married and get rid of her own wardrobe, which consisted entirely of simple dresses, like the fern green one she wore this evening.

As soon as they were in arm's length of each other, the two embraced as if they'd been separated a lifetime. "Livvie!" Cordie gushed, squeezing her tightly. "I feel like it's been forever. How are you? Is Kelfield treating you well?"

Livvie blushed at the question, but nodded her head. "I couldn't be happier, Cordie. Truly. Alexander is—"

"Alexander is what?" Kelfield asked as he came up behind his wife, resting his hand on her shoulder. His sinful grey eyes twinkled as they landed on Olivia, and from where Cordie stood she could feel heat radiating off the two of them. What she wouldn't give to have the perfect man look at her like that.

Livvie turned to face Kelfield, beaming up at him, and linked her arm with his. "Alexander is perfect, of course."

The duke chuckled and laid his free hand on his wife's. "Sweetheart, don't tell *everyone*. I've a reputation to protect, you know."

Cordie nearly sighed. They were so in love. Deeply. Completely. She smiled at the happy couple, wishing that someday she could be as lucky as they appeared. Though she would like to skip the scandal part. Her mother would kill her on the spot were she caught in the compromising position Olivia had been. But she wanted everything else.

"Alexander," Livvie began softly, "Cordie and I never get any time alone anymore. Do you mind terribly?"

The duke removed his hand from his wife, stepped away, and winked at her. "Of course not, sweetheart." Then he smiled at Cordie. "I'm only leaving her in *your* care. Don't let any blackguards or scoundrels near her."

Livvie giggled. "Go on with you. I only have a fondness for *my* scoundrel, as you well know."

After Kelfield disappeared into the crowd, Livvie turned her attention back to Cordie, smiling. "I am so glad to see you. But won't your mother be furious if she learns you've been associating with *that scandalous duchess*?"

"Of course she will," Cordie answered honestly. "So we'd best make it worth our while."

"Oh bother!" Livvie whispered with a frown. "Don't look now, but Lord Brookfield is headed our way. His eyes are on you, as usual."

Cordie groaned. Viscount Brookfield was a fortune hunter, nearly twice her age, and he smelled like the inside of her brothers' house slippers. Unfortunately, he'd set his sights on Cordie at the end of last season, or rather on her increased dowry, since her mother was concerned she would never find a proper husband. Brookfield, however, did not qualify as proper husband material in either Lady Avery's eyes or her own.

"My darling girls!" came Lady Staveley's voice from behind them. "I am so happy you're both here."

Cordie adored Caroline, Viscountess Staveley, and had for years. She was everything Cordie aspired to be. Clever. Confident. Constant. And doggedly loyal.

"Caro," Livvie whispered behind her fan, "you must get rid of Lord Brookfield. He'll try to monopolize Cordelia."

Lady Staveley frowned at the approaching viscount. "I don't even recall inviting him. No matter, I'll take care of it."

As the man reached them, Lady Staveley smiled beatifically. "My darling Brookfield," she gushed. "Lady Astwick, the dowager that is, was just asking me about you."

"Indeed?" The viscount gulped.

Cordie almost felt sorry for him. Almost. No one ever wanted to deal with the dowager Lady Astwick. A more frightening dragon didn't exist.

"Oh, yes!" Lady Staveley assured him. "In fact, my lord, I promised her ladyship that I would send you right over to her as soon as I saw you."

"You did?" he squeaked.

"I did. She is there in the corner." Lady Staveley gestured to the other side of the room where many widows lined the wall. "Do you see her?"

Brookfield's face turned white. He'd most assuredly seen the widowed marchioness, and he nodded sullenly. "Indeed, I do."

"Splendid." Lady Staveley clapped her hands together. "Do go on, my lord. I would hate to keep her ladyship waiting."

Brookfield spun on his heels and started across the room, his head hung low, like a man headed to the gallows.

Triumphantly, Lady Staveley turned back to Cordie and Livvie. "Well, that's over. Now then—" she looked Cordie up and down— "no Brookfield for you, darling. I shall endeavor to find you a handsome gentleman by the end of the evening."

Cordie found herself laughing. "Lady Staveley, that is not necessary in the—"

"Caroline." A rich, baritone voice floated over Cordie's shoulder.

She turned, instinctively, to see Lord Clayworth standing behind, and Cordie sucked in a surprised breath. The earl was exceedingly handsome with sandy blond hair lying perfectly in place and blue eyes so dark one could mistake them for a twilight sky. He had a perfect aristocratic nose and a strong chin.

Lord Adonis.

That's how many women of the *ton* referred to Clayworth, generally followed by a sigh. But not Cordie. His beauty was only skin deep. She knew all about the gorgeous earl, and thought it a shame such a striking man should be as unfeeling as a granite statue. No one, however, seemed to know how miserably Clayworth had treated his late wife. They all thought he was a devoted husband, still mourning Marina long after her death, but Cordie knew better.

Cordie knew the truth.

She would be surprised if Clayworth ever thought about his wife or their daughter, both of whom died in childbirth, while the earl had been somewhere else.

Throughout her volatile marriage, Marina had often complained about the earl to Cordelia's older sister Eleanor, and Cordie had often eavesdropped on the conversations. Though all of that was many years ago, when she was still in the schoolroom.

"Brendan!" Lady Staveley's smile grew wide as her eyes fell on the earl. "Darling, I am so glad you found time to attend my little ball."

Clayworth raised one golden brow mockingly. "You didn't really give me much of a choice."

Lady Staveley laughed and tucked her hand around Clayworth's arm. "Darling, you know my cousin, the duchess, of course. But have you met Miss Cordelia Avery?"

More than once, Cordie thought miserably.

"No. I don't believe I've had the pleasure," Clayworth drawled. Though his voice seemed less than pleased.

Cordie frowned. He didn't recall her? Honestly, they'd been introduced many times over the years, her sister being his wife's closest friend and all.

Lady Staveley positively glowed. "Then allow me the honors. Lord Clayworth, Miss Cordelia Avery of Nottinghamshire."

"I am pleased to make your acquaintance, Miss Avery."

"The pleasure is all mine," she replied airily. There was no point in letting the man's rudeness destroy her evening. Not when mother was playing Loo and she could spend time catching up with Livvie.

She started to reach for Livvie's arm, when Lady Staveley tapped Clayworth's chest with her fan. "Darling, you never dance. Might I persuade you to take to the floor this evening?"

The earl glared, momentarily, at Lady Staveley. Then the look of irritation vanished, as if it had never been there. "Yes, of course,

Caroline." His eyes swept across Livvie and then Cordie. "Miss Avery, may I see your dance card?"

Her dance card? Lord Adonis wanted to dance with *her*? All eyes were on Cordie, so she raised her wrist for the earl, where her dance card and small pencil dangled. Then he scribbled his name for the next song — which, unfortunately, happened to be a waltz.

~⚬~

Brendan only selected Miss Avery due to her proximity to Caroline, when she very politely demanded he dance, and the fact that the pretty, dark haired girl was *not* the Duchess of Kelfield. He'd seen the possessive look on the duke's face just moments before, and he had no desire to deal with the girl's depraved husband. That bit of melodrama he could avoid.

So by default, Miss Avery would have to do.

Brendan was surprised that, when the girl frowned at him, her pert little nose scrunched up as he scrawled his name on her card. He stared at her, trying to figure out why her pretty, green eyes darkened to the color of a forest at dusk as she looked at him.

Then the music began and he offered her his arm, which she took grudgingly. How odd. Most girls and their mothers generally tried to grab his attention, not that he ever wanted it, but he didn't remember any young miss ever scowling at him before.

He noticed immediately Miss Avery fit nicely in his arms, which was a strange thought. Probably any woman would fit nicely in his arms. It had been so long since he'd danced with one, he just couldn't remember.

"Why the quizzical look, Miss Avery?" he finally asked.

She tilted her head to one side and the golden flecks in her green eyes sparkled with an emotion Brendan didn't understand. "You really *don't* remember me?"

On his life, he'd never met the girl before. She was either daft or quite confused. "Should I?"

"My sister was *Eleanor* Avery, before she married," she remarked with exasperation, as if that answered his question. It did not.

Brendan shook his head at the pretty girl. It was too bad that she was obviously deranged. "I see. And is that supposed to mean something to me?"

Miss Avery's face turned a bit pink and she opened her mouth a few times, like a fish, as if she was going to say something but thought the better of it. Finally she shook her head. "I suppose not, my lord."

Brendan raised his brow in question. There was something else she'd wanted to say, he was sure of it. As he led her in a turn, he studied her pretty face, certain he'd never laid eyes on the girl before in his life. She was very lovely. He would have remembered her. "You are close to the duchess?" he asked casually.

Green fire shot from her eyes. "She's my dearest friend, and no one would ever have to *force* me to attend a ball in her honor, if that's what you're asking."

"Are you under the impression that *I* was forced?"

"You made the fact perfectly clear when you said Lady Staveley hadn't given you a choice."

She was intent on not liking him for some reason. Well, that was fine with Brendan. He hadn't even wanted to dance with the chit, and wouldn't have if Caroline hadn't *forced* him into it. Both attending and dancing, that is. Brendan decided not to waste any more conversation on the surly Miss Avery, to wait out the rest of the dance in silence. Unfortunately, that left him staring at the girl. It was a shame she was so pretty. She'd probably fool some fellow, blinded by her beauty, into marrying her. The chap wouldn't even realize such a harridan resided under her lovely skin until it was too late.

She did have the most remarkable eyes. Each golden fleck was mesmerizing in its own way, even as she looked annoyed with him. They didn't speak, just glided across the floor, perfectly in sync with each other. Finally the song ended, and Brendan wasn't sure if he was elated or saddened by the fact. If nothing else, Miss Avery was intriguing.

He offered her his arm and then escorted her back to Caroline's side. He bowed stiffly and briefly met her eyes. "It was indeed an honor, Miss Avery."

"Thank you, sir," she responded just as stiffly.

Wanting to avoid Caroline and any other dance partners she thought to thrust in his direction, Brendan quickly made his way to the corner of the room where Robert was talking with their mutual friend. Chester Peyton, the Marquess of Astwick, a large, gregarious fellow was always too loud. When Astwick spied him, his grin grew to the size of his face.

"Well, look, Rob, it's ol' Romeo in the flesh," his voice boomed.

Brendan glowered at the marquess.

Robert simply shook his head. "You've always been too irritatingly cheerful, Chet."

Astwick brushed off the rebuke. "I just don't know the last time I saw you dance, Bren. Miss Avery will be the talk of the Town tomorrow, successfully getting Lord Adonis to waltz with her. Every other girl and her mother will want to know her secret."

"It's obvious," Robert began, "that my sister forced it on him."

Brendan glanced at Masten. Though his words were true, it was a bit annoying he was so easily read. He certainly didn't want them figuring anything else out. He tilted his head to one side. "On the contrary, I found the girl quite delightful," he replied, hoping it made him appear a bit more enigmatic.

"Bloody hell," Robert grumbled. "Now she's beckoning *me*."

As Robert started off towards Caroline, Brendan turned his attention back to the peculiar Miss Avery. Lord Brookfield, a fellow more than twice the girl's age, took Miss Avery's hand in his and led her back to the dance floor. Brendan shook his head. Even she didn't deserve Brookfield's attention. She must have a sizable dowry.

"Oh, Brendan!" gushed Astwick's Scottish bride, Hannah, coming up behind them. "I dinna realize ye were in Town."

"Just arrived this afternoon."

"Well, it's so nice to see ye. How is Rosamund?"

Troubled. Angry. Hard to reach. "Fine, thank you."

Miss Avery caught his eye, across the room. She was miserable, with Brookfield leering down at her. Though why he should concern himself with the annoying chit, he had no idea. "Chet," he began, his eyes still on Miss Avery, "does the name Eleanor Avery mean anything to you?"

"Hmm." Astwick rubbed his chin. "Not really."

"Eleanor Avery?" Hannah asked, with an edge to her voice. "She came out the season I was in London. Doona ye remember, darling?"

That would have been fourteen years ago. Astwick furrowed his brow, and then shook his head. "I seem only to remember *you* from that year, my love."

To the casual observer, one might think the marquess was simply flattering his wife, but Brendan knew better than most that the words were sincere. The two had been reunited the previous summer, after spending more than a dozen years apart. In all that time, Astwick had never stopped loving Hannah.

Since Hannah knew Eleanor Avery, Brendan turned his attention to her. "What do you remember about her?"

The marchioness' blue eyes darkened and she bit her lower lip. "There was nothing particularly special about her. Though she was a bit full of herself. At least she and Marina Winston made sure I knew they were better than me — a silly Scottish lass who dinna know anyone."

Brendan didn't hear much else after Marina's name was mentioned, and his mouth went dry. His eyes flew back to where Miss Avery was still dancing a minuet with the ancient Brookfield. "Marina?" He softly echoed his late wife's name.

Then Astwick's ham hock of a hand slapped his back. "I do remember now. A rather typical brunette. She and Marina were the best of friends. I think she married some sort of diplomat and lives abroad."

A rather typical brunette. That was fairly nondescript. Brendan closed his eyes and tried hard to remember the girl. He'd blocked out so much of the first few years of his marriage, and apparently Eleanor Avery as well. *She and Marina were the best of friends.* Perhaps this Eleanor, wherever she was, might have an idea of what Marina had done with those damned letters, or what the devil she meant by *the lion holds your secrets.*

Across the room, Miss Avery looked quite bored with Lord Brookfield's attention. Brendan smiled at the girl. She had just given him the best lead he'd had in years. He just had to figure out what to do with it.

Three

WHERE was Livvie? Cordie had to suffer through an awful minuet with Brookfield, and then she couldn't spot her friend or Kelfield anywhere. So she strolled the perimeter, past couples dancing, matrons gossiping, and friends clustered together laughing and talking with each other. At one point she caught Clayworth watching her, though why he was doing so she couldn't imagine. Though she tipped her nose further in the air, his eyes never left her. Infuriating man!

"Cordelia Avery!" came a familiar voice behind her.

Cordie turned and was instantly embraced by an old friend. Henrietta Scutchings, a fair haired young matron, smiled sweetly.

"Hen, I didn't know you were in Town."

Henrietta quickly linked her arm with Cordie's and led her towards group of women. "I insisted that Edward return me to London when I heard Lady Staveley was hosting this ball."

She was quickly surrounded by a number of other young matrons, all discussing the unseasonably warm summer. Cordie realized as she looked around her that each of the women present had all come out the same year she and Olivia had. She was the only one left unmarried. Why had that not bothered her before now? Heavens, what if her mother was right? Cordie pushed that thought away almost as quickly as it entered her mind. She refused to believe her mother was right about anything.

"You were at the Prestwick house party, weren't you?" May Lismore asked.

The house party where Livvie met Kelfield. The reason for their rather quick marriage. The crowd around them quieted when Cordie nodded.

Henrietta nearly squealed with delight. "Oh, Cordelia, do tell. What precisely happened with Olivia and the duke? I'm dying to know."

Cordie frowned. They didn't honestly think she'd talk behind her dearest friend's back, did they? In the first place, she would never do such a thing. Besides, Livvie was going through a hard enough time as it was. She would never add to it. "They fell in love. Isn't it obvious?"

May pursed her lips, obviously annoyed with the answer. "I heard they fell into *something*, but I don't know that I'd call it love," she replied cattily.

Cordie's back stiffened and she leveled the matron with her iciest stare. "Well, as I was there, and you were not, I suppose you'll have to take my word for it. They fell quickly in love and Kelfield, who is quite an impatient man by the way, did not want to wait for the banns. And when one is as powerful as His Grace, one doesn't have to. I think it's wildly romantic."

"I suppose she must have forgotten she still had a fiancé," Henrietta whispered loud enough for the entire group to hear.

Well there was that. But Livvie hadn't gone out of her way to fall in love with the duke. It had just happened. "I'm certain Major Moore would want her to be happy."

The women all tittered behind their fans at her and Cordie thrust out her chin defiantly. At one time she and Livvie would have considered each of these women to be friends. How wrong they'd been. Without another word, she spun on her heels and walked back through the crowd.

Then she spotted Livvie, in the main entry way, standing with her husband. She caught her friend's eye and in no time, the duchess waded through the crowd until they were finally together again. "Was that Henrietta?"

Cordie nodded. "She's positively vicious tonight. I'd forgotten that about her."

"They were talking about me, weren't they?"

Cordie hated to see the hurt in Livvie's eyes, so she shook her head.

Her friend had already been through so much, and there was no point in adding to it. "Of course not," she lied. "They ripped my dress apart. It's terribly plain, as I well know. But I can't get away with wearing bold dresses like you married women do. I think I shall have to get married, just to be fashionable."

Livvie hugged her. "You don't have to protect me, Cordie. I can well imagine what they think of me."

They did know each other better than anyone else. Cordie hugged her back fiercely. "They're harpies. Pay them no attention. I don't intend to."

Marc brushed past the Staveley footmen, daring them with his eyes to ask for his invitation. They did not. Where was Kelfield? Then he spotted him across the ballroom talking to Lord Staveley, a recluse of the studious variety. Marc never quite understood the friendship between those two. They had nothing in common—nothing he could see on the surface anyway.

"I'm certain my sister didn't invite *you*," came the voice of an old friend. Luke Beckford, a reformed rake of the first order, glowered at him. "Caroline's gone to a lot of trouble to smooth things over for our cousin. She won't want you creating some havoc."

Marc chuckled. "Relax, Beckford. I've only come to watch the proceedings. This whole Kelfield marriage is quite entertaining."

Then he crossed the room to the duke's side, only to find his friend scowling at him. If he let all the nasty looks go to his head, he'd start to feel unwelcome. "Beckford has certainly gotten priggish since he's married," he said in way of greeting.

Staveley chuckled. "Something my wife thanks God for every night."

Marc looked Kelfield up and down. "And where is your lovely duchess?"

"Talking with a friend of hers," the duke drawled.

Marc stared out at the sea of people. "Ah, there she is. *Who* is that delightful creature she's talking to?" he asked, with an appreciative grunt. The duchess' companion was nothing short of stunning.

"Miss Avery," Alexander answered. "But she's not your sort."

"Funny. She looks exactly like my sort," Marc replied. From her silky brown hair, luscious curves, slender delicate neck, and speaking green eyes—she was dazzling.

"Then I suggest you stop looking." Kelfield's voice interrupted what was starting to be a very nice erotic daydream. "Lady Avery is a high stickler and won't appreciate your attentions towards her daughter. She hasn't even let the poor girl talk to Olivia since our wedding."

"They're talking now," Marc said, his eyes still fixed on the pretty Miss Avery.

"You are truly happy?" Cordie asked for at least the tenth time.

Livvie smiled and replied quietly, "You know that old adage about reformed rakes making the best husbands? Very true."

"Is he truly reformed?" Kelfield didn't seem reformed. He seemed like he'd enjoy devouring Livvie right there in the ballroom.

"Mostly," her friend answered with a blush. "But enough about me, Cordie. Tell me what you've been doing."

"I've taken to walking Rotten Row with mother on a daily basis." She rolled her eyes heavenward. "Then she drags me along to all sorts of charitable teas and luncheons, and lectures me nearly non-stop about my comportment."

"All because of me?" Livvie asked softly, as the first chords of a waltz began.

She hated to see the look of remorse on Livvie's face, so she shook her head. "All because I refused Captain Seaton. Honestly, Livvie, I so envy you. Kelfield would never dream of dictating who you could visit, who your friends were. I was glad to know that about the captain before I accepted him. What a dreadful life that would have been. And in watching you and Kelfield, I think I know exactly what sort of man might suit me."

"What sort?" Livvie asked, her hazel eyes wide.

"The sort who won't restrict me. The sort who will give me free reign. Someone like your Kelfield."

A shadow fell over them, and Cordie looked up into the dancing, light blue eyes of the wicked Marquess of Haversham. He was tall, with ebony hair that curled at the nape of his neck. His broad shoulders made him appear strong, as did the shapely muscles of his thighs. Though Cordie'd never met the man, she'd seen him at Livvie's wedding. His presence was one of the things that had so scandalized her mother. Good heavens he was handsome! And precisely the person she would conjure up, if given the opportunity.

"My lord," Livvie coolly greeted him.

A roughish smile lit his face. "My darling duchess, I have already asked you to call me Marc."

Marc? Cordie sighed.

Livvie shook her head, a false smile plastered on her face. "But that would imply that we are intimates, Lord Haversham, and we are not."

Though Cordie didn't know why they couldn't be friendly. After all, Haversham was a known compatriot of Kelfield's. Any scandal attached to one of them over the years was attached to the other as well.

"My loss," he replied with a wink. Then he focused his icy blue eyes on Cordie, and she felt breathless under his gaze. "*We* have not had the pleasure."

Livvie straightened her back and pursed her lips. "If you're looking for a proper introduction, then I suggest you find Miss Avery's mother."

An anguished squeak escaped Cordie's lips. How could Livvie suggest such a thing? Especially as mother was occupied quite nicely at the moment, and the marquess was looking at her like *that*.

The briefest smile touched his lips, though Cordie felt it wash over her body.

"I'm rarely proper," he confessed with a wink. "So I think I'll forgo speaking to Lady Avery. I'm sure she'd only tell me no, and I have no desire to be turned away from you, my dear."

Cordie sighed. "That's not the least bit conventional, my lord."

He took her hand in his, raising it to his lips. A spark of *something* raced down her arm, settling in her belly. "Conventional is boring. Might I entice you to stand up with me?"

"Cordie," Livvie whispered, "your mother will have an apoplexy."

"Let her," Cordie whispered back. She wasn't about to let the marquess step away from her. She accepted his arm and allowed him to lead her onto the dance floor.

Almost immediately, Cordie realized she might be in over her head. The marquess held her a little too closely, and his smile was a little too wolfish. At the same time, being in his arms was the most daring thing she'd ever done, and after being sequestered and made to be her mother's constant companion over the last fortnight, Cordie relished the stretching of her wings.

"Cordie is an unusual name," Haversham said, splaying his hand across her back.

She swallowed hard, making up her mind to play coy. "That, my lord, is because we were not properly introduced. If we had been, you would know that my name is Cordelia Avery. Only my friends call me Cordie."

"Hmm. We weren't introduced, were we? I suppose that means I can call you anything I want. Venus or Aphrodite, maybe?"

"Not Freya?" she asked with a flirtatious smile.

Haversham threw back his head and laughed. "You didn't strike me as an expert on Norse mythology, angel."

Angel. She let the endearment flutter around her heart.

"I confess I only know of her since one of my brothers spent quite a bit of time in the Scandinavian countries."

"*One* of your brothers?" he asked quietly, letting his masculine voice rumble over her. "Tell me I won't be called out on account of this dance, not having been properly introduced and all."

Cordie giggled. "You are perfectly safe at the moment, my lord. Gregory is watching after the estate in Nottinghamshire, and Russell and Tristan are in Toulouse with the 45th Foot."

When his hand moved across her back, Cordie was in heaven. Every place he touched came alive, and he pulled her closer to him, scandalously. "So—" his gravelly voice nearly made her stumble—"they've left you unprotected for any scoundrel to scoop you up."

She swallowed nervously. "No scoundrel's ever tried."

His wolfish smile deepened. "I'll have to remedy that."

"You flatter me, my lord."

His hand moved again, stroking her back. "I'll do much more than flatter you, angel. Do you think you're prepared for that?"

Yes! She wanted to scream, but she forced herself to remain calm, at least on the surface. "That depends on what you have planned."

He stroked her palm with his thumb, sending shivers racing up her arm. "Well, I've never actually *planned* a seduction before. They just seem to happen."

"A seduction?" She giggled softly. "You do seem terribly sure of yourself."

"When I want something, I go after it."

"And do you want me?" It was a brazen thing to ask, but who knew when she might get another chance.

He stared at her for a moment, his light blue eyes flaming every spot they touched. "More every second."

Suddenly, a shrill scream echoed from across the room, and the music stopped. Cordie's heart stopped beating as well. She knew that scream, and now she'd never know what the marquess planned to do with her. A plum ostrich feather bobbed over the heads of other guests. So Cordie knew it would only be seconds before she was ripped from Haversham's arms.

She smiled an apology. "I did enjoy our dance."

"Unhand my daughter, you blackguard!" Lady Avery screeched, yanking Cordie backwards and beating the marquess' chest with her fan.

Her mortification was now complete. Cordie braved a glance at the marquess to find his light eyes dancing with amusement. "Angel, the pleasure was all mine." Then he winked at her and turned on his heel, leaving Cordie, her hysterical mother, and the rest of Lady Staveley's guests behind him.

As Lady Avery threw her arms around Cordie's shoulders, letting out another horrific squeal, Lord Staveley, thankfully, stepped forward. "Lady Avery," he began, with a calm, clear voice. "Your coach is being brought around."

⸎

Brendan stared after the departing forms of Miss Avery and her mother, just like everybody else in Staveley's ballroom. He'd never witnessed a scene such as that before, not that he could blame Lady Avery for her outburst. If it was his sister, he'd have ripped her out of Haversham's arms too—though he thought the high-pitched wailing and theatrics could have been avoided. As a rule, *he* never tried to bring attention to himself.

One thing was certain—Miss Avery had left quite the impression. Assuming they'd met before, he wouldn't ever forget her again.

"Well," Astwick said under his breath, "no one will be talking about Kelfield after tonight, but I don't think Caroline had *this* outcome in mind."

"No," Brendan replied. "Excuse me." Then he started after the Averys, following their path from the ballroom, down the long corridor, and out the front door—just in time to see them step into their coach.

The door shut behind the baroness, and then Brendan saw it…

The Avery crest, emblazoned on the door. A roaring lion, golden against green.

He stumbled backwards, steadied by a Staveley footman. "Are you all right, my lord?"

No. Maybe. *A lion.* Marina was close to the Averys. Was the answer that simple? "Yes, thank you. I-I need my coach."

"Of course, my lord."

As he patiently waited for his carriage, he was pushed aside from behind.

"Apologies, Clayworth," Haversham threw over his shoulder as he bounded down the steps.

Brendan watched the marquess stride down the street, swinging his cane like a man without a care in the world. Did he even realize the position he'd put Miss Avery in this evening?

Four

WHEN Brendan entered Mrs. Lassiter's gaming hell in Covent Garden, the last fellow he expected to find was Haversham. Not that he should have been surprised. Both of them were fairly skilled at the gaming tables. In fact these sorts of establishments were where the two of them generally rubbed elbows. Caroline Staveley's ballroom was the exception.

The marquess was frowning at the cards in his hands. Brendan didn't have to see the table to know Haversham's hand was a winner. He always frowned in that precise way when he was about to win.

Interesting. Brendan never realized that he'd noticed anything about the marquess before. To be honest, he never thought he'd paid much attention to Haversham. They shared the same vices, both were widowers, and they were of an age. Society saw them differently however. In Haversham, they saw a devil-may-care rogue who lived on the fringe of polite society. And in Brendan, they saw a heartbroken, noble widower who'd buried his wife and daughter years before their time. It was all a lie. The wife was his, the daughter wasn't—though the child's death was the one that still haunted him. No, he hadn't sired her, yet if she'd lived he'd have given her his name. No matter the sins of her mother, the little girl was innocent—just as he'd been.

So if society was wrong about him, were they wrong about Haversham as well?

Somehow he didn't think so. It was one thing to present oneself in the best possible light, to try to appear better than one was, but no one who was noble would wear the mantle of scoundrel willingly—and certainly not as well as Haversham did.

One of the whores Mrs. Lassiter kept on staff dropped onto the marquess' lap and he kissed her neck. Brendan shook his head. No, society was right in regard to Haversham, he had no doubt. What was Miss Avery thinking to stand up with the scoundrel? Was she trying to ruin her good name? He didn't even know the girl. Maybe she didn't have a good name. Why did he even care?

Because of Marina. If those letters were with the Avery family, he couldn't afford for them to hang their head over their daughter's shame and return to their country estate—wherever that was. Nottinghamshire. Caroline said she was from Nottinghamshire. He had no connections there, no reason to be in that county. No, it was best if the Averys remained in London, at least for the time being.

A spot opened up next to Haversham and Brendan crossed the room, claiming it. The marquess raised his brow in way of greeting.

"How odd to keep bumping into you," Brendan said, then nodded to the dealer.

Haversham smirked, shifting the girl on his lap to look at his card. "Indeed, Clayworth. It's been an age and now twice in one night."

Brendan looked down at the upturned nine of spades in front of him. Could have been better. Haversham had the queen of hearts. "You made quite a scene with the Avery girl this evening."

The marquess met his eyes. "Rebuking me? You never struck me as that sort."

"Hardly," Brendan drawled. He glanced at the dealer. "Fifty." Then he tilted his head to one side, studying Haversham. "I've an interest in the girl's family, is all."

"Her *family*?" Haversham threw back his head and laughed. "Are you blind or a eunuch?"

It had been some time since Brendan had taken a woman to bed, but he still had all his parts, and he was fairly certain everything still worked. His eyesight was also fine, but apparently Haversham was blinded by Miss Avery's beauty. Her outward appearance was delightful, but he could do without her sharp tongue and less than scintillating personality.

"My wife was close with the Averys," he replied, as if he'd always known that fact. "I'm just looking out for the girl."

"Hmm," Haversham responded, though his eyes were on what there was of his companion's *décolletage*. "One would think that one of her brothers could do that."

She had brothers? Brendan hadn't realized. Whoever they were, they'd been remiss in their duties tonight. "As they weren't in attendance this evening, I'm speaking in their stead." How many were there? Hopefully none of them had been at Staveleys. As Lady Avery and her daughter were the only ones to leave, he felt fairly safe in that estimation.

Brendan looked at his face-down card. Two of clubs. That wasn't awful.

"Are you, indeed?" the marquess asked. "Funny, she didn't mention you during our dance."

"She is a bit headstrong."

Haversham grinned. "She knows what she wants. Just like you do, I suspect."

"I beg your pardon."

"You obviously are after the girl, same as I am. So why don't we play for her?"

Brendan blinked at the man. Play for her? How un-chivalrous. "I don't think that's proper at all."

Haversham laughed. "Come now, Clayworth. You'll need all the help you can get in regards to my little Freya."

"Freya?"

"Which of her brothers was it that spent time in Scandinavia?"

The blood drained from Brendan's face. Which brother? He had no idea. "Um, the oldest of course."

Haversham's grin spread across his face. "You're an awful liar, Clayworth. Your interest is with the girl, not her family. And I must say, your interest in her has sparked an even stronger one in me. So we'll play for her. Whoever has the better hand will get a fortnight's advantage. The loser can't call on the girl until the fortnight is up."

Brendan wasn't sure how he'd gotten himself into this situation, but he couldn't really back out now either. He looked at his nine and

Haversham's queen. He had a two, and could tell by the frown on the marquess' face as he looked at his down-turned card the man had a good hand. "Very well."

Haversham turned over his card, revealing the king of hearts. That was going to be tough to beat. Brendan turned over his two and nodded for the dealer to give him another card. The four of diamonds. He nodded again. The three of spades. He'd most certainly lost, but he could hold his hand and lose for sure or take another card and press his luck.

The table quieted and all eyes were on him. Brendan nodded for another card. The three of diamonds landed before him.

Haversham's mouth fell open. "God, Clayworth, you took your own sweet time winning the round."

Brendan was dumbfounded. He couldn't believe he'd won either. The odds had not been in his favor.

"Well," Haversham finally drawled, now seeming bored with the turn of events, "enjoy your advantage. When the fortnight is over, Miss Avery will be mine."

He'd won two weeks with the sharp tongued Miss Avery. Now he just had to figure out what to do with her.

⚜

"My lord," Higgins greeted Brendan, as he held open the front door.

"You do know, Higgins, it's not necessary to wait up for me. I'd hate to disrupt your schedule."

The butler shut the door behind him and held out his hand for Brendan's hat and cane. "You have a visitor, sir."

A visitor? It was the middle of the night! Hardly a time for social calls. No, not social calls — but perhaps something else. Had something happened in Derbyshire to Rosamund or Thomas in his absence? "Who is it?" he asked in a hoarse voice.

"Lady Staveley, sir. She insisted she be allowed to wait."

Brendan took a sigh of relief and handed his cane and beaver hat over to Higgins. What was Caroline up to? "Where?" he asked with a frown.

"Blue salon, my lord."

The blue salon. He hated that damned room. Brendan stalked down the corridor, his heart still racing from his earlier scare. He pushed the door open and found Caroline waiting for him, seated at a small desk, writing on some foolscap.

At his entrance, she looked up from her work and smiled radiantly. "Brendan Reese," she chastised him as she stood, "would you care to tell me just why exactly you left my little ball so early?"

He rubbed his brow. It had been a long day. Traveling, attending balls, gambling. He wasn't in any mood to rehash the Spanish Inquisition. "Does your husband know you're here at a most unfashionable hour?"

She had the audacity to wink at him. "Don't think you can distract me, Brendan. And, yes, Staveley is well aware of my location. He'll be so pleased you're concerned for my reputation."

He resisted the urge to snort. Though Caroline was meddlesome and could make an overall nuisance of herself, her reputation was spotless — a grande dame of the *ton*.

"I did not beckon you all the way to Town so that you could leave at the first sign of trouble."

This time he couldn't hold back his snort as he fell into a high back damask chair. "The first sign of trouble?" Lady Avery's scene could more readily be called a travesty of epic proportions.

⋘⋙

Cordie awoke with a smile on her face — perhaps the biggest one ever. After spending the last fortnight in abject isolation, the fog of doom and gloom seemed to have lifted from her soul. She sighed happily, remembering her glorious dream about a certain scandalous marquess.

She rolled over in her bed, towards the window and the light of day, wishing her dream hadn't ended. Would she ever see Haversham again? Not if her mother had anything to say about it. Lady Avery had ranted and raved the entire ride home from the Staveleys', certain Cordie's future was a complete loss.

Though, she'd turned a deaf ear to her mother's ravings, choosing instead to bask in the glow of her body's reaction to Haversham. She'd tingled everywhere he'd touched her. She sighed at the memory of his hand stroking her back. He was heavenly — exactly what she was looking for. Handsome. Wicked. Perfect. *He* always did exactly what he wanted, so certainly he wouldn't begrudge her the same freedoms.

Without a doubt, she was head over heels in love with the man.

She'd never felt this way. Giddy. Silly. Wanton. Not even with

Captain Seaton. Cordie closed her eyes again. In her mind, she could still see his wolfish grin and soft blue eyes, promising delicious wickedness.

A determined knock came from the door. Cordie closed her eyes tighter, not wanting her daydream to end.

"Cordelia!" her mother's voice hissed through the door.

Cordie groaned and rolled over, burying her face in her pillows. It was too early to deal with her mother, so she said nothing, pretending to still sleep.

Then her door was thrown open and the counterpane was unceremoniously stripped away from her. "Cordelia!" her mother barked. "Get up quickly and get dressed. You have a guest."

Cordie didn't move, wishing desperately that her mother would leave her in peace, but then the bed dipped down as Lady Avery sat next to her. "Get up, you silly girl. By some stroke of luck, you may just survive this scandal."

Cordie blinked her eyes open. "What are you talking about, Mama?"

"I knew you weren't sleeping. Why didn't you tell me you waltzed with Lord Clayworth?"

Ugh! Clayworth! She'd nearly forgotten about him. "Because you spent all evening berating me for dancing with Haversham. There wasn't time to tell you anything else."

"Don't even utter *that* man's name." Her mother shuddered dramatically. "I've been beseeched with visitors all morning long. Evelyn Greywood, Nicola Dearden, and Beatrice Peake, just to name a few. Everyone wants to know what you did to capture the earl's attention. He *never* dances, Cordelia. Did you know that? I never realized it. After poor Marina, I never paid Clayworth any attention at all—but he might be your savior in disguise. Everyone is much more interested in your dance with Clayworth than anything else that happened last night."

How was that even possible? She'd danced scandalously close with one of the most notorious gentlemen in Town. Then her mother had created a huge scene by screaming and hitting the man with her fan. But all of Mayfair was abuzz because of her dance with *Clayworth*? That was simply ridiculous. Haversham was much more interesting than Clayworth.

"Anyway, I'll send Bessie in to get you dressed. You have a guest waiting downstairs. So do hurry."

"Who?" Cordie asked, sitting up in her bed.

"The earl himself. Lord Clayworth is in the yellow parlor waiting for you."

Cordie's mouth fell open. What was *he* doing here? He didn't like her any better than she liked him.

Five

BRENDAN paced around the Avery parlor, cursing himself for a fool. What the devil was he doing here? What if the Averys were not only in possession of his mother's letters, but they'd read them as well? What if they threatened to turn them over to the Home Office? Something told him Cordelia Avery would like nothing better than to see him dangling from the gallows. It would certainly explain her cool demeanor towards him.

The night before, she'd laughed gaily with many people and had bestowed an earth-stopping smile on Haversham of all people. If anyone deserved the scowl she'd saved for Brendan, it should have the Marquess of Haversham. So the Averys must know the contents of the letters. It made perfect sense. She thought he was a traitor.

Technically, he was.

Every voyage to France. Each visit to his mother's family. The countless trips he and his sisters had taken with their mother. He now didn't believe that even one of them had been a simple trip to visit family. All of them lies. If he hadn't taken her to Paris time and again, she couldn't have passed off sensitive information to the enemy. He was just as culpable as she was. His ignorance of her crimes did not excuse his guilt. He should have known. He should have realized where her loyalties laid.

Brendan glanced down at his pocket fob. One o'clock. How long did

Miss Avery intend to keep him waiting?

Ever since he'd won his fortnight advantage, he'd been bombarded with thoughts. He couldn't just ask Lady Avery for the damning letters. That would be the quickest way to get a dark, dank cell in Newgate. Young Lord Avery was in the country — that he'd learned from a fellow over hazard the night before. So he couldn't strike up a friendship with the chap. And his two younger brothers were apparently in France among a small troop of soldiers who had yet to return home from the war. Even if Russell and Tristan Avery were in the country, associating with someone they considered in league with the French wouldn't be high on their list. Since it wasn't likely that the baroness would invite him to join her sewing circle or some such nonsense, the only conceivable person he could visit at Avery House was the lovely Cordelia.

Astwick had been correct the night before. Word was already spreading around Town, thanks in large part to their waltz, that he was interested in courting Miss Avery. It was another lie.

His whole life was a lie.

What was one more? Not that in his younger years he might not have been interested in the girl. She was pretty — but then so was Marina all those years ago, and that had been an abysmal union. It was best to keep one's mind sharp when dealing with beautiful women — truly the most dangerous of all God's creatures. Brendan couldn't afford to let his guard down. His family's future depended on him finding those letters, destroying them.

He blinked when Miss Avery entered the parlor, finally deigning to meet him, and he immediately caught his breath. She was stunning in a gauzy, pink dress, which brought a pleasing color to her pretty cheeks. It annoyed him that he noticed such things, but she was nothing short of a vision — something she was obviously well aware of. He'd never done much courting in his younger years, but waiting over an hour for some chit was something he'd never done before. She was apparently used to wrapping men around her little finger.

He wouldn't be one of them. He couldn't be.

"Lord Clayworth," she said crisply, "what a surprise."

Brendan bowed. "You are looking lovely today."

"As opposed to what?" she asked with narrowed eyes.

He grimaced in response. Was there nothing he could say that she wouldn't take offense to? Even after years of watching over his two fairly emotional sisters, he'd never encountered a more petulant woman. "As opposed to most foolish girls who court scandal on a regular basis," he shot back at her. He probably shouldn't have said that. If he was going to somehow get free reign to search Avery House from top to bottom, being on the outs with Miss Avery wasn't the best idea. Still, he'd had all of her impertinence he intended to take last night. They wouldn't continue in that vein.

The pink in her cheeks darkened, which made her even lovelier, though Brendan pushed that thought from his mind. Miss Avery was a harridan, and it was best not to forget it.

"I do not *court* scandal, sir," she replied haughtily. Then she eyed him suspiciously from the corner of her eyes as she sat on a gold brocade settee.

Brendan dropped into a chintz chair across from the aggravating chit. With any luck he could have his mother's letters back in his hands before the fortnight was up, and then Haversham could do whatever he wanted with the spoiled little girl. However, that sudden thought irritated him to no end. As infuriating as Miss Avery was, it turned his stomach to think of her in Haversham's arms. Really. Had she no sense? Someone should take a firm hand with the girl.

The door opened again, and Lady Avery bustled inside, trilling anxiously, "Oh, Lord Clayworth, we are so pleased you have come to call." She settled next to her daughter and batted her eyes.

Miss Avery looked the furthest thing from pleased, as she toyed with the pink velvet ties on her dress. She looked bored. Fidgety. Restless. But no less stunning.

"The pleasure is, of course, mine," Brendan replied smoothly. "I was hoping, Lady Avery, that you would allow me to escort your lovely daughter in my phaeton through the park this afternoon."

Miss Avery looked as though she'd just been sentenced to hard labor in Australia, but her mother beamed. "Oh, my lord, Cordelia would be honored. Wouldn't you, my dear?"

Miss Avery's green eyes flickered to meet Brendan's gaze. "Yes, honored," she dutifully replied. If he didn't know better, he'd think she truly meant it. Cordelia Avery was as good a liar as he was. He made a mental note of the fact and smiled back at her.

"Shall we then?" he asked, offering her his arm.

⚜

As soon as they were outside Avery House and away from her mother, Cordie glared at the earl. What was he about? It wasn't as if she'd charmed him the night before. *That* had been the furthest thing from her mind. However, he didn't spare a glance for her, as if he knew she was frowning at him.

They stopped before his conveyance, and Cordie gaped openly. The high perch phaeton was shiny black and sleek, looking like the sort of thing reckless men used for racing, not leisurely rides in the park. "Where exactly do you plan on taking me?" she asked in wonder.

Clayworth chuckled. "Relax, Miss Avery, I have no plans to kidnap you."

"This is stunning."

"Thank you. Driving is a particular interest of mine. I'm afraid I do over indulge sometimes," he replied, a look of devotion in his eyes as he stared at his conveyance. Then without further ado, he offered her his hand, helping her into the phaeton.

The bench was padded nicely and smelled of expensive leather. Cordie glanced around the phaeton with appreciation. Through the years with three older brothers, she'd heard more about gigs, barouches, chaises, coupes, landaus, and phaetons than she'd ever cared to know. Those old conversations, however, did make her well aware of the excellent craftsmanship of the light four-wheeled carriage.

Before she knew it, Clayworth went around the other side and propelled himself into the seat beside her.

Heavens, he was agile. She hadn't realized that before. In addition to having the body and face of a god, Lord Adonis apparently was quite graceful. Quite a feat for a man of his age.

When she smirked to herself, he caught the look out of the corner of his eye. "Something humorous, Miss Avery?" he asked, directing his bays down South Audley Street.

"I was just thinking that you are in marvelous shape for a man of your many years." There, that ought to be offensive enough to make this sojourn end quickly.

Unfortunately, the earl chuckled in response. "I'm younger than

34

Haversham," he informed her.

Was he? Cordie shook her head and refocused on her escort. "Indeed? One wouldn't know it. You're so stuffy, making you seem older — almost ancient."

He quirked a grin. "No, my dear, you have it all wrong. In comparison to your Haversham, I'm simply an adult."

She frowned at her failed attempt to irritate him as they turned down Curzon Street. He'd been much easier to annoy the night before. What had changed? And why was he seeking her out anyway? He never courted anyone. He never danced. He never drove girls around the park in his exquisite phaeton. None of this made any sense.

"Nothing else, Miss Avery?" he asked.

"Nothing else?" she echoed.

"You don't have any other ruthless comments to make? Old and stuffy. Is that the best you can do?"

Cordie's mouth fell open. He knew she was trying to insult him? And he thought it was amusing?

When they turned on to Park Lane, Cordie caught sight of Kelfield House — Livvie's new home. She'd never even been allowed inside. The imposing mansion towered above them, reminding her of her goals. She needed a lenient husband who would love her and allow her freedom. She was wasting her time with Clayworth.

She glanced up at her escort, knowing with all certainty he was the last sort of husband she wanted. He'd given Marina all sorts of freedom, which was a plus, but he had never shown her an ounce of affection. *Cold and unfeeling* — she remembered hearing his late wife's long suffering complaints. It was good that she knew that aspect of his personality, or she might be flattered by his attention.

Just as they entered Hyde Park, many sets of eyes focus on the pair. Cordie glanced around at the other open carriages, pedestrians, and those on horses. It was easier to count the number of people *not* looking at her. She sucked in a surprised breath.

At her side, Clayworth seemed amused. "It appears you are indeed quite popular, Miss Avery."

Her mother's words echoed in her mind. "I don't think it's me who's caught their interest."

"Of course it is. You caught everyone's attention last night. Mine.

Haversham's. All of the *ton*."

As if conjured up by Clayworth's words, Cordie spotted Haversham just a few feet away, atop a magnificent grey hunter. He tipped his head in greeting and his light blue eyes twinkled devilishly. She had to catch her breath.

Beside her, Clayworth grumbled something about a fortnight's advantage and dishonorable men. Whatever that meant, Cordie had no idea. She smiled at the marquess and her heart leapt as he pushed his hunter forward, stopping at her side.

"You are even more radiant out of doors, angel," Haversham drawled smoothly.

Six

MARCUS Gray was even more devastatingly handsome in the light of day. A blush settled on Cordie's face when she met his gaze. He looked at her with the same wolfish grin Kelfield always wore whenever he spotted Livvie. Her heart raced. Thank heavens her mother hadn't scared the man away. "Thank you, my lord."

At her side, Clayworth sighed. "Haversham, how surprising."

"Indeed," the marquess replied, "I don't believe I've ever seen so much of you, Clayworth."

"I think I preferred it the other way."

Haversham tossed back his head and laughed. "Afraid of a little competition?"

"Hardly. I would simply rather deal with *honorable* men. Those who are as good as their word."

The marquess quirked a grin at Cordie. "Pity. I believe Miss Avery prefers me just the way I am."

Cordie looked from one of them back to the other. Were they really quarreling over *her*? The saintly Lord Adonis and the devilish Lord Haversham? Two days ago she never would have believed it. In the park, everyone's eyes were on them, and they must all appear to be participants in a poorly acted play. If her mother heard about this, Cordie would never be allowed to leave her room again. "Actually, I'd prefer not to have these sorts of conversations out in public," she replied.

Private conversations are my favorite," Haversham replied with a wink.

"Cordie!" came a friendly squeal from across the park.

She turned in her seat, spotting Phoebe Greywood racing across the park towards them holding a blue bonnet to her head, with her brother, Matthew, quick on her trail. It had been weeks since she'd seen Phoebe—well, she'd spotted her at the Staveley ball, but hadn't gotten the chance to speak to her. Cordie was relieved when Phoebe finally reached them—her silly friend was creating even more of a scene.

While Phoebe tried to catch her breath, Matthew hissed something in her ear, but she paid him no attention. Her eyes were focused solely on Clayworth. Cordie glanced over her shoulder at the earl, who met her gaze with a frown. How could she have forgotten Phoebe intended to set her cap for Clayworth? This was perfect. Or it could be, if she had the chance to think the situation through.

"Phoebe, Mr. Greywood, have you met Lord Clayworth? Or Lord Haversham?"

Phoebe's azure eyes sparkled when she shook her head.

"We're truly sorry to interrupt," Matthew Greywood apologized. "Phoebe saw you and was anxious to—"

Suddenly, Phoebe found her voice. "Mother just told me the news. Please tell me you'll ride to Norfolk with *me*. We'll have so much fun catching up."

Norfolk? Cordie shook her head. "What news?"

"I'm sorry?" Phoebe looked confused, which wasn't all that different from her usual look.

"You said your mother just told you the news. I don't know what news you're speaking of."

"Oh?" Phoebe frowned. "Well, Lady Avery said you'd both visit us at Malvern Hall for the next fortnight."

Cordie's mouth fell open. Mother had told her of Mrs. Greywood's visit this morning, but she'd neglected to mention the invitation to Norfolk. What was this about? If Phoebe knew, she'd tell her for certain. Cordie glanced back at Clayworth with what she hoped was an innocent smile. "My lord, do you mind if I walk with my friend for a moment?"

The earl's dark blue eyes assessed her, then he nodded tightly. "Don't go too far, my dear."

She nearly groaned. *Don't go too far?* Did he think she was a child? She was a full-grown woman of twenty and didn't need his directives. "Of course not," she answered with a fraudulent smile.

Matthew Greywood stepped forward and lifted Cordie in the air, placing her safely on the ground. "There you are, Miss Avery."

She smiled a thanks to the man who was now too busy to notice her, his interest suddenly enraptured with Clayworth's flashy phaeton. Before she could link arms with Phoebe, a strong arm snaked around her waist. She turned and smiled up at Haversham. How had she not noticed him dismount? "My lord," she whispered, "there are too many people about."

"I'll have to figure out a way to get you all alone." He slowly released her, and offered her his arm. The promise of his words made her giddy and breathless all at once. He turned his heart-stopping smile on Phoebe. "May I escort the two most beautiful ladies in the park?"

Phoebe giggled, and quickly took his empty arm. "A pleasure to make your acquaintance, my lord."

"Just think of me as an old friend of the family. Commander Greywood is an old companion of mine."

Phoebe grinned. "Mother thinks Uncle Simon is too reckless."

Haversham laughed, a rich sound that made Cordie's heart flutter. She was completely smitten with the man. What a glorious feeling. He towed her closer to him, and she reveled in the feel of the muscles of his arm. He was perfect.

The marquess glanced down at her and winked before turning his attention back to Phoebe. "So, you are taking my Miss Avery to Norfolk?"

"Y-your Miss Avery?" Phoebe squeaked.

Cordie flushed, too embarrassed to look at her friend.

"Mmm," Haversham answered as they stepped towards a copse of trees. "I don't know how I'll go on without her for an entire fortnight."

"Oh, my," Phoebe replied breathlessly.

He smiled down at her, a charming rogue in every way. "You don't mind allowing me a few moments alone with her, do you?"

He was good, or wicked, depending on one's view of him. There was no way romantically minded Phoebe would turn him down. They stopped walking and her friend gaped, open-mouthed. "Cordie?"

This was her one chance. Who knew when she would see the marquess again? "Please, Phoeb?"

Phoebe nodded her head and looked back around the bend they had just taken. "I don't think they can see us from here. But don't go too far."

Phoebe had barely finished her sentence before Haversham whisked Cordie behind a tree. She blinked up at him, an appreciative smile tugging at her lips. In less than a second, his hands were planted on her waist and he loomed over her. "What," he whispered in her ear, "are you doing with Clayworth, angel?"

Cordie swallowed nervously, placing her hands on his firm, powerful chest. "I wasn't given a choice in the matter."

He grinned at that. "Not your cup of tea, is he?"

She shook her head.

"Too stuffy?" he asked, slowly lowering his head.

She nodded.

"Too noble?" he whispered across her lips, and Cordie was certain her heart was about to pound right out of her chest.

"I don't want to think about him," she admitted, desperately wanting Haversham's lips to touch hers more than anything.

He apparently read the need in her eyes, as his smile vanished and he leaned closer. His cheroot scented breath washed over her, and Cordie closed her eyes, more than ready for his kiss.

An instant later, his hands left her waist and his chest disappeared from beneath her fingertips. "Agh!" came his masculine complaint.

Cordie blinked her eyes wide. Haversham was on the ground five feet away from her with Clayworth standing over him, fire in his twilight eyes. Then the earl scowled at her. "You, back to my phaeton!"

She hated being ordered about. Over the last few weeks she'd had to follow every stricture from her mother. She'd been kept from her dearest friend. She'd been made a prisoner in her own home. She hadn't enjoyed one moment of freedom — except for those few moments she'd spent in Haversham's company. The Earl of Clayworth would not dictate to her.

Hands on her hips, she glared back at him. "You're not my keeper."

He stalked towards her, tightly grasping her arm in his hands. "You are under my care until I return you to your mother's doorstep. If you want to throw yourself at every scoundrel in Town, you'll have to do so on your own time."

Clayworth pulled her back through the copse and into the open park. Cordie struggled to free her arm. The earl only increased his pace, and Cordie couldn't catch one glimpse of Haversham or Phoebe. In no time, they reached Clayworth's phaeton and he tossed her into the seat, anger rolling off him.

After he took his spot on the seat and began directing his bays out of the park, Cordie chanced a glance at him. Clayworth's sculpted lips were drawn up tight, his eyes focused on the path ahead of them. A muscle twitched in his jaw, and Cordie felt unexplainably guilty, which was hard to understand. She didn't owe the earl anything. She didn't even like him. She never had. What did she care that he was angry?

"Are you going to mention this to my mother?" she finally asked as they crossed Park Lane.

Clayworth's head whipped towards her, fury flashing from his eyes. "Am I going to mention that *I* allowed the most depraved man in the country to abscond with you? I'd rather not."

"I don't think he's depraved at all."

Clayworth shook his head and refocused on the street. "I don't believe you're thinking at all."

They rode the rest of the way in silence, neither of them looking at the other. Cordie had never been more relieved than when she entered her house and Lord Clayworth said his goodbyes. Thankfully, he didn't mention Haversham, which was a blessing.

***

Brendan tossed the reigns to a footman before bounding up the steps of his Hertford Street home. He'd never been so close to throttling a woman in his life. He would have liked nothing better than to tell Lady Avery what a fool she had for a daughter, but figured that wouldn't help his case to search Avery House. If they were indeed going to Norfolk for a couple weeks, perhaps he could search the place without anyone ever knowing. He had always been a master at maintaining his control, but every second he spent in Cordelia Avery's presence tested that control to its extremes.

His large, oak door opened before his foot even landed on the last step, and Higgins met him with questioning look. This was odd. His butler generally hid behind an unflappable façade.

"Yes, Higgins?" he asked with a raised brow.

"Lord Clayworth, you have a *guest*," the butler replied as he shut the door behind him.

Another one? He'd never been particularly social. When had he become so popular? "Well?"

"Lady Staveley is in the blue salon, my lord, and she..." His voice faded.

Brendan shook his head impatiently. "Spit it out, Higgins. She what?"

"W-well," the old man stammered, "she's taken over. Ordering everyone about."

With a sigh, Brendan shook his head. He wasn't remotely surprised. Whenever Caroline went anywhere, she took over. "Well, that's what she does, Higgins," he replied, dismissing his butler, and he started down the corridor. What was Caroline doing *here* of all places? Didn't she have someone else's life to manipulate and manage? Her pariah of a cousin, for example?

Brendan opened the door of the blue salon, and his jaw dropped open. The room was completely barren. No chairs, no settee, no writing desk. The faded portraits had been removed from the walls, leaving dark spots where they'd once hung. All that was left was an Aubusson rug and dull draperies, which Caroline was examining. "This will have to go too," she said to a harried young maid. Brendan didn't know the girl's name, but she was disheveled from top to bottom, a weary expression across her rather plain face.

After the day he'd had so far, *this* was beyond the pale. Brendan stepped over the threshold and slammed the door behind him, causing the glass in the windows to shake. He'd never known such impertinence in all his days. What did she think she was doing?

Undaunted, Caroline spun around to greet him with a welcoming smile.

He glared at her, then nodded curtly at the maid. "You're excused."

When the maid bustled out of the room, Caroline beamed at him. "Brendan Reese, I absolutely adore you!"

Seven

CAROLINE quickly crossed the room and threw her arms around Brendan, hugging him tightly before releasing him and grinning unrepentantly. "And to think I was so certain that you would be the most difficult one in the bunch." Words flew from her mouth with lightning speed. "Even more so than Robert, and you know how difficult *he* can be. I must admit, I was worried about the situation last night—but you pressed forward, didn't you!"

"Caro—"

She paid him no attention and continued to gush, "I did of course have an ulterior motive in calling you down from Derbyshire, as you've probably realized by now. I was beyond anxious when that awful scene broke out at my ball. And then when Livvie said she was looking for a man like Kelfield... Well, I thought for certain it had all been for nothing."

"Caroline—" he tried again.

"A man like Kelfield! Can you believe it? Nothing could be further from the truth. But you didn't let him have her, did you? Wonderful! Marvelous. You have exceeded my expectations, darling! I knew at the end of last season she was perfect for you. Not a shrinking violet. A girl that could hold her own against *you*, when needs be. But when it seemed she was about to be engaged to that naval captain, it broke my heart. Not that he didn't seem like an all right sort, but... Well, he isn't *you*."

43

"Caroline!" he bellowed. What the devil was she going on about?

She blinked at him, a frown settling on her pretty face. "Yes, darling?"

"What have you done to my salon?" That was as good a place as any to start. After all, he was fairly accustomed to her ramblings. Whenever she was excited, she always gushed until she ran out of strength. Though he had no idea what had her so giddy today.

Caroline's hazel eyes twinkled mischievously. "Well, after visiting with Gladys Avery this morning and she told me the wonderful news, I thought I would come and congratulate you in person. A note is too informal, don't you think?"

Gladys Avery? A cold chill crept along Brendan's spine, as the reason for Caroline's visit began to sink in. "Too informal?" he echoed.

"I'm so glad you agree," she gushed. "So, that butler of yours, who is quite a disagreeable fellow by the way, brought me in here after I insisted on waiting. And honestly, darling, if this is the best room in the house you have for entertaining, you are in desperate need of a refurbishment. Stuffing was actually coming out of the settee. Did you know that?"

He didn't know that, actually. It was so rare that he was in London, or that he entertained. But that was neither here nor there. What the devil was he doing listening to this anyway? "For God's sake, Caroline, you can't go around tearing people's rooms apart."

Caroline pouted. "I'm not tearing it apart. I'm *fixing* it. If you're going to entertain the Averys you can't do so in this room. It just wouldn't do. And since Juliet has so meticulously refurbished Prestwick Chase, I know just the right people to help with this mess." Her hands gestured in a wide sweeping motion to encompass the whole room.

"It wasn't a mess until you touched it… And I have *no* intention of entertaining the Averys." The less he saw of them the better.

She pursed her lips. "Blast you, Brendan. You *are* going to be difficult, after all."

He raked a hand through his hair and began to pace around the desolate salon. "What are you after, Caroline?" he asked, though in his heart he already knew the answer. Caroline Staveley liked nothing better than matchmaking. He'd watched her over the years, always in awe at her abilities in this realm. She rarely, if ever, failed.

"You need a wife, Brendan."

There it was.

He groaned, stopped his pacing, and leveled her with his iciest stare. "I had one, and I have no intention of ever replacing her." Honestly, with everything else he had to worry about, the last thing he needed was to marry some girl. Not even a girl who made his pulse race or his breeches embarrassingly uncomfortable, though finding Miss Avery in Haversham's arms had certainly dashed a bucket of cold water on *that* problem.

Caroline crossed the room in just a few strides, an understanding smile upon her face. "You don't have to pretend with me, you know. I remember Marina and I know what she put you through."

She was one of the few who did. But Brendan didn't want to have this conversation, so he shook his head. "Get my salon back the way it was, Caro. Settee missing its stuffing and all."

"Be reasonable," she pleaded. "Livvie is beside herself with worry for Cordelia — something she doesn't need at the moment. And — "

"I am not going to marry or even court some foolish girl simply to put your cousin's troubled mind at ease," he interrupted, narrowing his eyes on her. Then he started for the door. "I trust you can put this room to rights and then see yourself out."

Just as he opened the door, just as he was almost free of her, Caroline's words stopped him in his tracks. "I don't want her to end up like Flora."

Brendan's breath whooshed out of him. He rarely thought about his sweet, naïve sister, ruined by a handsome rogue, who lost her will to live once the bastard used her. After the birth of her son, Flora didn't have any fight in her, and she simply withered away until there was nothing left of her. He growled as he looked back over his shoulder at Caroline. "I'm not Miss Avery's guardian. She has brothers of her own."

"None of whom are in Town. Gladys keeps her locked up in Avery House. She won't even allow her to correspond with Livvie, for heaven's sake. She is so convinced her daughter's future will be marred, she doesn't allow her any freedoms at all. But Cordelia is clever and determined. If she thinks that scoundrel is her version of Kelfield, she'll flee the nest and she'll be forever ruined, Brendan, and you know that as well as I."

Cordelia Avery did seem intent on ruining herself. He'd seen evidence of it with his very eyes. But what was he to do about it? She wasn't anything to him except a lovely irritant. "I don't meddle in other's lives, Caroline."

She crossed the room to his side, reaching out her hand to him. "Haversham is fickle. He'll lose interest in her as soon as some pretty lightskirt crosses his path, but by that time it could be too late for Cordelia."

A muscle twitched in Brendan's jaw. Miss Avery was so full of life, just as Flora had been. Damn Caroline for bringing his late sister into this.

"You took her riding in the park today. If not to court her, what was your intent?" she asked, her hazel eyes assessing him.

All he needed was Caroline looking into his motivations. He almost winced, but kept his features relaxed. She would notice that, and he couldn't risk the questions that would surely follow. "She caught my interest last night," he replied honestly.

A relieved smile lit Caroline's lips. "I knew it. I could tell the way you looked at her when you danced. Oh, darling, I will be happy to help. Whatever you need."

"My salon back in its original state?" he asked, hoping to lighten the mood.

She smacked his chest. "Not on your life. It'll be perfect in no time."

Brendan rolled his eyes. At least he wouldn't have to think of Marina whenever he walked in here, and if Caroline was busy refurbishing his salon, perhaps he could keep her from paying too much attention to his *courtship* with Miss Avery. There wasn't a way around *that* situation. Not that he could see anyway.

~❦~

Cordie stared up at the yellow canopy over her bed. She still couldn't believe that Clayworth hadn't told her mother. Not that she wasn't grateful—she was. She just couldn't understand it. He'd been so furious with her. Very strange. What did he care anyway?

Was he serious about courting her?

Because she could never accept him. Perhaps if she didn't know how abysmally he'd treated Marina, perhaps if she didn't know he was incapable of affection, perhaps if Marcus Gray hadn't stumbled into her life… But she did know what an awful husband he'd been, she did know he was cold and unfeeling, and Marcus Gray had swept her off her feet. It was pointless to continue worrying about Clayworth or spend any more time thinking about him.

What she needed to do was focus on Haversham. Correspondence was out. Her mother was already keeping an eye on letters coming and going, preventing her any contact with Livvie. The only time she'd been allowed out of the house without her mother in the last three weeks was the ride in the park with Clayworth. But Haversham was clever. Perhaps he'd think of something.

He knew she was going to Norfolk. What if he truly didn't know what he'd do without her over the next fortnight? What if he came for her? Would he rush her to Scotland? Her mother would be scandalized by a Gretna Green wedding, but *she* would be Lady Haversham by that time. It wouldn't matter.

A knock came at her door. Cordie sat bolt upright. "Yes?"

Her mother bustled inside, wearing the brightest smile Cordie had seen in a very long time. "You are the luckiest girl, Cordelia."

Silently she agreed, though for very different reasons than she thought her mother did. She stared blankly at her mother, intent on not giving anything away.

"I've never seen a man stare so intently at a woman before." She squeezed Cordie's hands tightly. "I don't know what you did to capture Clayworth's attention, but he appears quite besotted."

Besotted? She'd seen the look on the earl's face. He was angry and annoyed. Her mother was simply seeing what she wanted to see.

"Mother, I-I don't care for Clayworth. Not one whit. You know how terrible he was to Marina. How could you want the same thing for me?"

Lady Avery frowned. "Perhaps we were wrong."

Cordie leapt off her bed, scowling at her mother. Of all the things she could say! "Or perhaps you're perfectly content with throwing me to the lions. I heard her with my own ears, Mother. Marina was miserable with him. And I must say, I see her point. He is void of emotion—" *if one discounted anger,* "—and I will never accept him. There is nothing you can do."

Her mother's lips pursed in anger. "Cordelia, I have been too lenient with you in your formative years. I see that now, but no longer. If—

when — Lord Clayworth asks for your hand, Gregory will accept him. And you will do your duty."

When. Cordie scowled. She would simply have to make sure he never offered, then.

"We are going to dinner at the Astwicks', and I'll expect you to be on your best behavior."

"The Astwicks?" They weren't part of the Averys' set. The dowager was one of the most powerful women in London, a dragon, and an idol of sorts to her mother.

Lady Avery's bright smile returned. "Isn't it wonderful? Your association with Lord Clayworth has opened many doors."

Doors Cordie would be just as happy if they'd remained closed. Clayworth. Did that mean the earl would be there too? She didn't think she could look at *him* again.

⚜

Brendan walked into the Astwick drawing room, quickly spotting Chet through the small crowd. He crossed the floor in a few strides and nodded to his old friend, who had his arm around his wife's waist. Chet beamed when their eyes met. "So you're being social after all."

Brendan shrugged. "It's so rare that your mother sends a complimentary note, I didn't dare refuse."

Chet's booming laugh attracted a few eyes, but the other guests quickly went back to their conversations, all of them accustomed to Astwick's always too-loud demeanor. Hannah smiled, stepped out of her husband's embrace and touched her lips to Brendan's cheek. "Her ladyship is simply ecstatic about your courtship. She says you were in mourning far too long."

"Sweetheart," Chet began with a frown, "you know better than to quote *my* mother. She's been hounding poor Clayworth for years." Then Chet quirked a grin at Brendan. "But since she brought it up, I was completely surprised by your attention to the Avery girl, both last night and today."

This was what came from years of celibacy and attending to his duty. At the first sign of interest in a woman, the Town went wild with speculation. "What about today?" he asked cautiously.

"Hannah and I love the park, as you know, and we were a bit off the beaten path this afternoon, and...Haversham will be sporting a shiner

48

for at least a sennight." Astwick grinned with a conspiratorial wink. "That bastard had it coming."

"Chester!" his wife complained.

Chet focused on his wife, the look of an unrepentant boy across his face. "You know I'm right."

Hannah shook her head, her pretty golden curls bobbing back and forth. "Just watch your language around the boys."

Chet chuckled. "Yes, I'm certain they never heard that particular word in the army camps."

Hannah heaved a sigh. "That is no' the point." Her blue eyes suddenly grew wide. "Heavens."

"What is it, sweetheart?" Chet asked, all amusement gone from his voice. "Are you feeling all right?"

She blushed slightly. "It's no' *that*, darling. It's just Miss Avery has arrived."

Brendan immediately turned from his spot to see the enchanting Cordelia Avery step into the drawing room. *Enchanting*? Troublesome, was more fitting. Obstinate, was apt as well. But somehow enchanting was the word that came to mind when his eyes landed on her. Cordelia's dark hair was piled high on her head and though her pale yellow gown might be described by some as plain, on her it was breathtaking. She wore a simple row of pearls around her neck, and tiny white rose buds in her hair

He swallowed nervously, aching to remove those flowers one at a time.

God! What had come over him?

Eight

CORDIE immediately felt Clayworth's gaze on her and she swallowed nervously. He'd been so angry with her after their ride, and yet the look in his eyes spoke of something else. If she didn't know better, she'd think he was glad to see her. In that moment, it was easy to see why so many women over the years had dreamed of him. There wasn't a man more handsome than Lord Adonis. His jacket matched his eyes, so dark blue it was almost black, making his snowy white cravat even more dramatic. His golden hair nearly shined under the warm chandelier light. This was a man whose mere presence stripped women of their breath.

Clayworth tipped his head and quirked her a crooked grin. From across the room, he almost seemed charming.

Cordie mentally shook her head. Such thoughts were foolish. Just then, the dowager Marchioness of Astwick crossed the floor towards them. Honestly, the tiny old woman with grey hair, heavily adorned in jewels, didn't look like a dragon, but Cordie had witnessed her vicious tongue in action before. She was suddenly much more nervous about greeting the dowager than she was about spending the evening in Clayworth's company.

"Gladys!" the old woman barked in greeting. "Why have you been keeping this delightful creature hidden away?"

"I-I," Lady Avery stuttered.

50

The dowager waved her hand in the air, successfully shushing the baroness. "Never mind." She stretched out her frail hand to Cordie. "Walk with me, Miss Avery."

She didn't really have a choice. Cordie linked her arm with the dowager and was surprised with the agility the woman possessed. "Thank you, my lady."

The dowager's pale eyes flashed to hers, and when she smiled, it seemed as if her face might crack from the exercise. In fact, Cordie had never seen the woman smile before. She hadn't even heard rumors of the possibility before. She glanced over her shoulder to see if the Four Horsemen of the Apocalypse had just arrived.

"What are you looking at?" the dowager boomed loudly.

"Nothing."

"I should say not. Clayworth is in front of us, not behind."

Cordie lost her footing and the warmth of a blush crept up her neck.

"Stand up straight. Women didn't slouch in my day," the old woman directed.

"I...um...sorry."

"And don't stumble around with your words. If you're going to handle a man like Clayworth, you need to be firm."

"Yes, of course, my lady." She hoped that seemed firm enough, not that she wanted to handle a man like Clayworth, but she didn't want the woman to bite her head off.

"So," the dowager began, "you've caught everyone's attention, Miss Avery. And now that you have it, what do you intend to do with it? Which of the two handsome devils bandying for your attention do you intend to choose?"

"My lady, you flatter me. I—"

"My intent is not to flatter you, but to get a straight answer. That fellow over there has been a friend of my family for years, though he doesn't visit enough for anyone to know it. The best sort of man there is. I wish my son was a bit more like him."

Across the room, her son, the Marquess of Astwick, silently toasted her with his glass of champagne, completely unaffected by her cruel words. Cordie's eyes flashed to Clayworth's, realizing that the dowager could be heard in every corner of the room. His twilight eyes danced as if he was truly entertained by this highly improper conversation. Not that anyone would ever rebuke the dowager marchioness, but Cordie was mortified just the same.

At that moment, the dinner chime rang and she'd never been more relieved to be granted a reprieve.

"Brendan Reese!" the dowager bellowed loudly. "Come and escort my delightful Miss Avery into dinner."

He was at her side in the blink of an eye, an arm outstretched, and a playful grin on his lips. "Miss Avery."

A spark of awareness jolted through Cordie as she accepted his arm, and she almost pulled back her hand. She looked up into his handsome face and the fluttering in her stomach began anew. "You have quite the champion," she whispered, trying to bring her heart rate down to an acceptable level.

"Me?" His smile grew. "I've never heard her call anyone delightful before," Clayworth whispered to her. "What could you have possibly have done to garner such praise?"

Cordie shook her head. "I don't know. I've always been terrified of the woman."

Clayworth chuckled and placed his free hand over hers, sending a fresh wave of tingles racing up her arm. "So you do have *some* sense."

She didn't find that remotely humorous and stiffened her back in response.

"Oh, now," he began soothingly, "my dear, don't be so serious."

That *he* would say those words to her was suddenly quite funny, and Cordie had to stifle a giggle. "Coming from you that does mean something."

"I had no idea that *anything* I said meant something to you."

She grinned at him. "True, I generally choose to ignore you."

"You have a saucy tongue, Miss Avery."

"It's one of my better qualities."

"Not from where I stand." The crooked smile returned to his lips.

She didn't know what he meant by that. Before she could find out, Cordie was surprised to discover the dowager had assigned her to be seated between Lord Astwick and Lord Clayworth at the table. As the youngest daughter of a mere baron, she was generally at the other end of the room when it came to gatherings such as this. But the dowager had raised her ancient brow and said in a crystal clear voice that *she* could do whatever she wanted in her own home.

Once seated, Lord Astwick chuckled and inclined his head towards Cordie as everyone else started in on their turtle soup. "Don't look so frightened, Miss Avery. I know it's difficult to tell, but I've never seen mother take to anyone so quickly before."

She nearly choked. "She likes me?"

The marquess' smile widened. "You don't know how rare that is."

Actually, she had a fairly good idea. The widowed Lady Astwick, one of the pillars of society, could make or break someone if she was of a mind. It was a pity the dowager hadn't taken to Livvie. No one would dare disparage the scandalous Duchess of Kelfield if Lady Astwick were her champion. She wished she knew what she'd done to capture the dowager's attention so she could pass the information to her friend.

Cordie felt Clayworth's eyes on her and she tilted her head to one side to see him better. The intensity of his stare startled her. His twilight eyes deepened even more and the flutters in her stomach increased when he quirked her the smallest of smiles.

"Miss Avery," Lord Astwick began in a voice that was much too loud for normal dinner conversations. "I understand Clayworth drove you 'round in that flashy phaeton of his today."

"Chet!" Clayworth growled on her other side.

The marquess paid his friend no attention, but continued in his booming voice. "My dear, you should make him take you along the Bath Road and give you a real ride. The wind through your hair, no pedestrians to watch out for."

Clayworth placed his spoon back on the table, a little harder than was necessary, and glared at his friend. "I can't even believe that you would suggest such a thing, Astwick."

The marquess waved him off with a flick of his wrist. "Honestly, Brendan, I'm having a conversation with Miss Avery. No one has included you." Then he turned his light green eyes on Cordie, a mischievous smile on his face. "As I was saying, my dear--"

"That you would even suggest that I would risk her safety," Clayworth interrupted, then he grumbled something unintelligible, though Cordie thought it sounded like he thought she risked her own safety more than enough and didn't need any help from him.

She scowled in response. She was perfectly safe and had been her whole life, before their paths even crossed.

Astwick chuckled, completely unmoved by his friend's irritation. "Brendan, you're an excellent driver. Miss Avery seems like an adventurous sort to me. I'm certain she'd be perfectly safe in your hands and would enjoy the ride immensely."

"I think that sounds like an excellent idea," the dowager barked from her spot several people down. It was quite improper for the old woman to talk over so many people from so far away, but no one would ever consider rebuking her. "Lady Avery," she called even further down the table, "I suggest you allow Clayworth to take your delightful daughter for a spirited ride."

Cordie's mother's eyes widened, as though trying to sort out the proper protocol for this bizarre conversation. Finally she nodded. "If you think that's wise, my lady."

"I'm always right," the dowager confirmed, then turned her attention back to wherever it was before she bellowed across the room.

Clayworth glared at Astwick. "Are you happy now?"

"Quite," the marquess replied as he dipped his spoon into his bowl.

The idea of racing along the Bath Road in that exquisite phaeton made Cordie's heart leap. That particular conveyance was made to go fast. It sounded exciting. Would he really take her? If so, would he drive at breakneck speed or like an old farmer with a horse cart? She chanced a glance at the earl, who was frowning at his bowl.

"You don't have to take me, my lord," she said, with a mischievous smile of her own. "I'm certain I can find someone else who is willing."

⚜

Brendan's eyes shot to her pretty green ones in an instant. *Someone else who is willing.* He knew exactly who she had in mind. He should throttle Chet for even bringing the subject up. Damn interfering friends. "On the contrary, Miss Avery, nothing would please me more."

Taking her for a spirited ride. He wished the image that flashed in his mind at the phrase had been of his phaeton and bays on the Bath Road. Unfortunately it was a different sort of ride altogether he envisioned. Cordelia Avery beneath him. Her soft breath on his lips. Her green eyes tinted with passion. Her breasts bared for his touch. Her legs spread waiting for him. For the love of God! This wasn't like him at all.

Perfectly safe in his hands. Bollocks. At the moment, he wasn't certain she was any safer with him than with Haversham.

"You don't look very pleased." Her quiet voice interrupted his thoughts.

Of course he wasn't pleased. Brendan always prided himself on his excellent control of any situation, but he didn't seem to be in control of anything in her presence. Not of her, certainly, but not of himself either. When he'd found her in Haversham's embrace that afternoon, he'd wanted to kill the man in his spot. He wasn't prone to violence and he didn't have uncontrollable, lascivious thoughts. At least he hadn't until Cordelia Avery entered his life.

Brendan took a calming breath. He needed to remain focused, find his mother's letters, and keep Miss Avery safe until Haversham lost interest in her. Then his life could go back to normal. He could go home, to his duties that awaited, to his nephew, Thomas, who needed his guidance, as well as to figuring out what to do with his sister, Rosamund.

Miss Avery's pretty brow was furrowed and Brendan winced. Why should her emotions matter to him one way or the other? If she was having this effect on him after only one day, what sort of state would he be in after weeks of her acquaintance? Months? How long would it take to find those damned letters?

Then he smiled, remembering a comment from their afternoon ride. He might just be saved. "Are you indeed going to Norfolk, Miss Avery?"

She nodded, still frowning at him. "We leave on the morrow."

Thank God!

He could try to get his mind straight in the interim. "And you'll be gone a fortnight?"

"Yes."

Relief washed over him. He could return to Derbyshire and check in on Thomas and Rose while she was away, while she was safe from Haversham. He could use the time to get himself under control. Then when he returned to Town, he'd search for the letters, and keep Miss Avery safe from herself. As far as plans went, it was filled with holes, but for a man who suddenly found himself drowning, it was like grabbing on to floating balsa wood.

Brendan flashed her his most charming smile. "I suppose we'll have to wait for your return before we schedule our ride then."

When the women finally left the men to their port, it couldn't have been a moment too soon. Brendan's last hold on his control was dangling by the tiniest of threads. All throughout dinner he'd had to endure Chet boasting about Brendan's every accomplishment to Miss Avery, rattling off his estates and properties. It was as if his friend thought he was incapable of courting the girl on his own. Of course he wasn't courting her, not really. But if he was, he wouldn't need any help, and certainly not from Chet of all people. His friend didn't even know the meaning of the word subtle.

"You can thank me now," the gregarious bastard said with a smile when it appeared the other gentlemen were engaged in a rather uninteresting political discussion.

Brendan glowered at Chet, but kept his voice low to keep the others from overhearing. "I'd like to thank you right into the Thames. That was the most bloody awful dinner I've ever had to sit through."

"Oh, that's Hannah's fault," Chet said as he raised his glass to his lips. "She stumbled across some unemployed army cook and hired the man on the spot. I'm still trying to get accustomed to the fellow's idea of what passes for fine dining."

"It wasn't the bloody food," Brendan bit out. Though the meal wasn't a highlight either. "I can do without your help where Miss Avery is concerned, and I'll thank you to keep that in mind."

Chet shrugged, unconcerned as always. "Someone needs to help you. I saw the blackguard abscond with her this afternoon, Brendan. Miss Avery is tempted by adventure and excitement, neither of which are your best qualities. If you're going to win her, you're going to have to go about it differently."

"Since when did you become an authority on young ladies?"

With a brilliant smile, Chet had the audacity to wink at him. "Oh, *I'm* not. But Caroline is, and she thinks you need a little guidance. I'm inclined to agree with her."

He was going to slowly kill them all. Caroline. Chet. The dowager. Every blasted last one of them. He pushed his glass aside and rose. "Thank you for a delightful evening," he replied mordantly.

"Bren!" Chet frowned.

But he didn't look back. He waved his hand over his shoulder and started for the corridor. He stalked down the hallway, past the drawing room, and was just about to turn the corner towards his escape when he heard her voice behind him.

"So, are you really the best swimmer in all of Derbyshire?" she asked with a hint of amusement.

Brendan spun on his heel to find her standing quietly in the doorway of the Astwick library. How he'd missed her a moment ago, he had no idea. The soft glow from the wall sconces bathed her skin in golden hues, complementing her gown. One dark curl had escaped her coiffure, and rested temptingly on her shoulder. He couldn't help but smile at her. "I'm sorry about all that in there."

"Do you really need that much help, my lord?" A soft giggle escaped her, and Brendan was entranced by the sound.

"No." Against his better judgment he walked towards her. His heart pounded so loudly, he could hear it in his ears. *Miss Avery is tempted by adventure and excitement.* Dear God, somewhere in the last day he'd completely lost his mind.

Nine

CORDIE'S eyes widened when Clayworth suddenly stood before her. There was something different in his eyes, something she hadn't noticed until now. Desire. She'd seen that look on Captain Seaton's face before she broke their engagement, but it had never left her as breathless as she felt in this instant.

The earl touched her fallen curl and wrapped it around his pinkie, staring at it as if her hair held the answers to the world's greatest questions. Then his eyes flashed to hers. "Do you crave adventure, Cordelia?" he asked softly, his hand gently caressing her cheek.

Cordie stood paralyzed, staring up at him in amazement. Her name had never sounded so sensual as it did on his lips.

Clayworth's free hand was suddenly on her waist and he backed her further into the library, holding her closely against him. "Is that why you surround yourself with dangerous blackguards? For the adventure?"

She still hadn't found her voice, which was something that never happened. Cordie should ask him to stop, or yell for someone to help her, or slap sense back into him. But she couldn't do any of those things as his mesmerizing dark blue eyes bored into hers. His gaze dropped to her lips, and she swallowed nervously.

"If I was a wicked scoundrel, could I capture your heart?"

She managed to shake her head. She wasn't after adventure. Where had he come up with that idea? She craved freedom to do what she wanted, to be loved and desired. He apparently desired her, but he was incapable of love, and she shouldn't forget…

His warm mouth covered her lips, and Cordie lost all thought. Her eyes fluttered shut. She staggered slightly, but his muscled arms steadied her, drawing her to his strong chest. She inhaled the heady scent of rich, spicy port on his breath as he sucked on her bottom lip. Clayworth's tongue lightly touched the corner of her mouth, and Cordie gasped. He deepened his kiss, surging inside her.

Tingles raced across her skin. She wouldn't be able to stand at all if he wasn't holding her.

"Kiss me back," came his guttural plea.

Her hands, of their own free will, cupped his jaw, and she tentatively touched her tongue to his. Clayworth moaned at the contact and his arms tightened around her, nearly robbing Cordie of her breath. Even still she'd never known the wanton feelings that were flooding her. Captain Seaton had kissed her, of course, but not like this. Not like he was a starving man, and she a platter of delicacies. Each time his tongue entered her mouth, she was certain she would melt away into complete nothingness.

"Cordelia!" came her mother's voice, somewhere off in the distance.

Clayworth slowly raised his head and stared down at her with such an intensity Cordie thought she might burst into flame.

"I think you're dangerous for me," he told her before dropping his arms and stepping a few feet away.

A moment later, her mother stood in the doorway, smiling when her eyes landed on the earl. "Oh there you are, Cordelia. I thought I'd lost you."

Clayworth stepped forward and smiled at the baroness. "My apologies, Lady Avery. Your daughter was simply helping me look for a book."

Her mother frowned at the innocent explanation. "A book?" she asked dejectedly

"On Scandinavia," he lied smoothly. How could he speak so calmly after that kiss? She couldn't form a sentence if her life depended on it, but his cool façade was firmly back in place.

Lady Avery's face brightened instantly. "Oh, Lord Clayworth, Cordie should have told you that we have dozens of books on the Scandinavian countries. My youngest son, Tristan, spent quite a bit of time there."

The earl's smoky eyes settled on Cordie and she couldn't help but stare back at him, at his perfectly chiseled jaw, his slightly swollen lips that had so recently touched her skin.

"She didn't mention it," he drawled easily, though his baritone voice made Cordie's knees weak.

"Silly girl," her mother trilled, stepping further into the library. "My lord, I insist you visit us at Avery House to peruse our library."

"I will be anxiously awaiting your return from Norfolk."

The ride to Norfolk was painful in many ways. In the first place, Cordie had hoped she and Phoebe could talk openly on the journey, but unfortunately, at the last moment, their mothers decided to change coaches and ride with them. They certainly couldn't discuss anything important with those two harridans listening to their every word. Worse than that, however, was the fact the ride was exceedingly bumpy and she couldn't even drift off to sleep, which she desperately needed as she hadn't gotten a wink of sleep the night before.

All night she'd gone over and over Clayworth's kiss. From start to finish. It was the most uncomfortable night she'd ever spent. She'd tossed and turned this way and that, trying to forget every touch of his tongue to hers, how large and imposing he felt surrounding her in his muscled arms, the urgency in his voice when he'd demanded she kiss him back.

Sitting next to Phoebe, she shifted uncomfortably in her seat as the memory flashed again in her mind.

"Are you incapable of sitting still?" her mother finally wondered aloud.

"Sorry. I suppose I'm just anxious to arrive," Cordie replied and stared out the window at the passing Norfolk countryside. Honestly, how much longer would it be? And could she retire immediately upon their arrival? Even if she did so, would sleep continue to elude her?

Her mother smiled at her, the first smile Cordie had seen on her face in quite a while. "Don't worry, dear. I'm certain he's awaiting your return just as anxiously as you are. But time apart is good, too. Absence makes the heart grow fonder and all that."

Phoebe's mouth dropped open, then she recovered with an innocent smile. "Oh, I'm so relieved that you know, Lady Avery. I was feeling so guilty. Mother would never let a man like him court me."

Haversham. Cordie's eyes flashed to her friend and at the same instant her heart sank. How could Phoebe say that to her mother, of all people?

Lady Avery frowned and turned her attention to Mrs. Greywood. "Evelyn, is there something unfavorable about Lord Clayworth that I'm unaware of?"

Phoebe's face flushed red when she met Cordie's eyes, apparently just now discovering her error in opening her big mouth.

"Clayworth?" Mrs. Greywood echoed, then shook her head. "He's a paragon in everyone's eyes."

Though Haversham's name wasn't mentioned, it didn't take her mother long to figure him out. Cordie could tell the exact moment Lady Avery's mind reached that conclusion, because her face turned a perfectly horrid shade of puce. The Greywoods presence in the carriage was the only thing preventing her from suffering a sore backside and bleeding ears.

Lady Avery glared at her daughter the rest of the journey, two more excruciating hours, until they finally reached Malvern Hall. Cordie wasn't certain which was worse — the anticipation of dealing with her mother's rising ire or the actual event.

⚜

Brendan arrived at Bayhurst Court shortly after dusk. His nephew, Thomas, raced down the grand staircase upon his arrival and threw his arms around Brendan's middle. "Uncle! You've returned," the boy gushed.

Brendan ruffled his nephew's shaggy, light brown hair, then took a step back to get a good look at the boy. "I was barely gone at all."

At ten years old, Thomas was more like a son than a nephew. When Flora died weeks after the boy's birth, Brendan immediately took over the infant's care. At the time, he had hopes his new wife, Marina, would make a good mother to the child, but the circumstance of Thomas' birth was not something Marina could get past.

"Well, we weren't expecting you," Thomas explained with a shrug. "We thought once you got to London you'd stay for a while."

"Actually," Brendan began, gesturing for Thomas to follow him as he went to his study, "I'm only home for a bit, I'm afraid. I'm working on something in London."

"Then why are you here?" Thomas asked. The boy was always inquisitive. It was one of his better qualities, in Brendan's opinion. Always trying to figure out how things worked and why things happened.

Brendan clapped his nephew on the back. "I hadn't planned to be gone for long and I wanted to get things in order before I abandon you and Rose for a period of time."

"How long will you be gone?" the boy asked, a hint of sadness in his voice.

He had no idea. At least not until he had searched Avery House from top to bottom. But how long would that take? He could find the letters in a day if he was extremely lucky, or it might take months. "I'm not sure, Tom." And then there was Cordelia. When he'd foolishly taken her in his arms, the last thing on his mind were those blasted letters. Would he even be able to focus on the job at hand if she was around, tempting him with her very presence? And if she was gone, he didn't have an excuse to visit Avery House. It was a quandary indeed.

As they reached the study, Brendan held the door open, then followed his nephew inside. He quickly poured himself the brandy he desperately needed after his journey. Then he took a second snifter and poured just enough for a swallow. He handed Thomas the dash of brandy and seated himself opposite the boy in one of the room's overstuffed leather chairs.

Thomas looked at the glass with a frown. "For me?"

Brendan shrugged. "You're growing into a man, Tom. Be careful with the first sip, it will burn a bit on the way down." He threw back his own glass and downed the velvety oak brandy in one swallow. He would generally prefer to nurse such an exceptional drink, but tonight he was tired and sore, and had lots on his mind he wanted to forget.

Thomas peered into his cup and sniffed, crinkling up his nose.

The sight made Brendan laugh. "Thomas, if you don't want to drink it, you don't have to."

"No, no." The boy frowned. "I'll try it." He tentatively tipped the snifter back and took just a sip. He squinted and moved his tongue around like a dog trying to get rid of a bad taste.

"All right," Brendan said with an indulgent smile. "You're not ready for it yet. We'll try again next year."

Pleased, Thomas placed the glass on a side table. He tilted his head to one side, looking intently at his uncle. "What are you working on in London?"

"A little family business. Something your grandmother left undone."

Thomas nodded, as if he understood, though he couldn't possibly fathom what Brendan was trying to accomplish. He hoped to keep it that way. Thomas' life as a bastard would be hard enough over the years. He didn't need to know he was the grandson of a traitor as well. "How's Rose?" he asked, hoping to change the subject.

"The same," Thomas answered quickly.

It would have been a surprise if he'd answered differently. Rosamund had been *the same* for more years than Brendan could remember. She seemed to be perpetually ten or eleven years old, never advancing mentally. In the past, Brendan had invited all sorts of doctors to examine his sister, but no one could ever come up with a reason for her strangeness, nor a cure. One fellow suggested sending her off to live in a hospital in Scotland, but Brendan wouldn't hear of it and tossed the man out. No one would love Rose and care for her like her family. He couldn't possibly trust her care to someone else. Whatever was wrong with Rose, she deserved better than that.

"Are you all right, Uncle?" Thomas asked.

Brendan nodded. "Of course, Tom. Why would you think otherwise?"

Thomas pursed his lips and furrowed his brow. "I don't know. You just seem different."

If a ten-year-old boy could tell he was different, Brendan didn't have chance of fooling anyone else. He wished he knew what *seemed* different about him, so he could try and mask whatever it was.

"This business," Thomas continued, "of grandmother's. If it's waited this long, will it hurt to let it wait some more?"

Brendan shook his head. "I'm afraid so, Thomas. The sooner I take care of this situation, the sooner things can go back to normal."

As soon as the words left his mouth, Brendan wasn't certain he wanted things to go back to normal. What if he courted Cordelia in earnest? God, he couldn't get her off his mind. The way she tasted like sweet summer berries, the way her rounded breasts felt pressed against his chest, the way she made him harder than he'd ever been in his life.

He had to find the letters. If by some miracle he could convince the girl to marry him, her future would be forever tied to his. He couldn't risk bringing her into his family if the letters dangled out there, ready to ruin everything in their life with no notice.

No, everything hinged on finding his mother's letters.

Ten

WHEN Cordie was five, she made the mistake of telling her father over dinner that she wasn't going eat her "bloody" squash. Her mother and sister's mouths had dropped open and all three of her brothers sucked in surprised breaths. Her father, an imposing man, had pushed away from the table, snatched her up with one hand, and returned her to the nursery, where he blistered her backside. He hadn't even asked where she heard *that* word—he hadn't needed to. The next day, both Russell and Tristan walked with the same painful limp she did.

Her father's punishment was a blessing in comparison to what her mother had doled out in the years since. Cordie wasn't quite certain how, but her mother's blows always seemed more powerful than she remembered her father's being all those years ago. And while Lord Avery quietly went about his business with a steely determination, Lady Avery ranted and wailed the entire time.

Cordie went without dinner the first night in Malvern Hall. She couldn't possibly sit down if she wanted to. Lying down hurt as well. So she leaned against a heavy armoire in her guest room and tried to convince herself that the pain would subside soon. It always did. Her situation was desperate, more so every moment she remained at home. She needed to marry quickly. It was her only way out of the situation.

She was so confused now. Haversham or Clayworth? The two men couldn't be more different. Days ago, the choice would have been easy.

Haversham desired her and would offer her the freedom she most wanted. He was sinfully handsome and his very presence spoke of untold pleasures that awaited her. Her mother would hate him, and that was definitely a plus in his favor.

Clayworth, on the other hand, was more difficult to figure out. He was a dichotomy. For years she'd heard Marina complain about her loveless marriage. Clayworth was cold, cruel, passionless. She knew each complaint by heart. But she was having a difficult time rectifying those words with the man who held her and kissed her with a fierce passion. Was he like that with Marina in the days before their marriage? And then did it just go away? She didn't think she could take his defection. Her heart couldn't withstand the pain of losing his affection. After one kiss, she knew this with absolute certainty.

A knock interrupted her thoughts, and Cordie stepped away from the armoire. "Come in," she called as brightly as she was able.

Phoebe quickly stepped inside and spun to face Cordie, anguish marring her pretty features. "I am so sorry, Cordie. I-I...Well, I'm the biggest fool there is."

Though she currently agreed with her friend, it wouldn't help to stay angry at Phoebe. She shook her head and feigned the sweetest smile she could manage. "Don't be silly. I'm fine."

Her friend's face fell even more. "Don't pretend. I heard her. I heard the things she said, and then you didn't come to dinner..."

"I'm not really hungry."

Phoebe threw her arms around Cordie. Pain radiated through her body and she couldn't help but suck in a steadying breath. Phoebe jumped back quickly. "Good heavens! Are you *hurt* too?"

"It's not that bad," Cordie answered. Over the years she'd been subjected to her mother's punishments more often than she'd like, but this latest bout was the worst ever. However there was no reason for Phoebe to know that. There was no reason for anyone to know.

Her friend's face scrunched up as if she was going to cry. "I'll have Millie take a look at you."

"Please don't." All she needed was for everyone at Malvern Hall to learn of this.

"Cordie, if I hadn't opened my mouth you wouldn't... Well, you're obviously in pain. Millie won't tell a soul. And she's real good with ointments and such… If you need that."

It would be nice to sit down. She nodded her head once, mortified that anyone knew what had happened to her.

~~~~

Phoebe easily found Millie, a maid, in the dressing room off her grandmother's suite of rooms, sorting through stockings. The maid greeted her with a smile and tucked a grey curl under her cap. "Miss Greywood, you look like you've gotten into to some sort of trouble again."

Truly, she generally was in some sort of trouble whenever she sought Millie out. A scrape here, a scratch there. A ripped seam here, a torn flounce there. She didn't enjoy being accident prone, but since she was, she'd had no choice but to stay in Millie's good graces. This was the first time she didn't need Millie's expertise for herself. An image of Cordie's pain-stricken face flashed in her mind, and a fresh wave of guilt washed over her.

"Millie, I need your help and your silence."

The maid frowned at her, punching her hands to her hips. "What sort of trouble are you in, Missie? And if it has anything to do with that Wilkins boy, you better tell me right now."

Warmth rushed up Phoebe's cheeks. How could Millie think *that*? "Of course not! Heavens, Millie, is that your opinion of me?"

The old woman sighed, then shook her head. "You certainly wouldn't be the first woman to make foolish choices because of a man. Most of us have done so one time or another. But that *particular* trouble isn't something I could help with. I wouldn't have a clue what to do."

"I'll keep that in mind," Phoebe replied in an appalled whisper. "My friend, Miss Avery, has been hurt. No one can know, but I need you to look at her."

"Hurt?"

"I haven't seen the injury myself. I came right to fetch you."

"What were the two of you up to that no one can know?" the old woman asked suspiciously.

Phoebe's face heated up again. Millie was generally much easier to deal with. "We weren't up to anything. I think her mother hurt her. Will you please come look at her?"

Millie frowned, but nodded her head.

Once inside Cordie's room, Millie took immediate control. She barely greeted Cordie, before she unbuttoned her dress and pulled it over her head in one fluid move. Phoebe took the gown and draped it over a chintz chair. When she heard the maid's gasp, Phoebe spun around. She couldn't quite believe what she saw. Cordie's entire back and bottom was raw and red. There were even some spots with dried blood.

"Oh, my!" Phoebe stared in shock.

"Miss Greywood, find one of Miss Avery's nightrails. Help her get it on. I'll be back," the maid ordered softly.

"Please," Cordie begged.

The maid held up her hand. "I know. I won't tell anyone."

As Millie left, she briefly met Phoebe's eyes, and she knew she'd done the right thing in going for the maid. Phoebe found a soft silk nightrail in the armoire and turned back to Cordie. Silent tears were streaming down her friend's face, and Phoebe's heart ached at the sight. Cordie was always composed—the most confident and self-assured of all her friends.

She rushed forward, holding out the nightrail. "Let me help you."

Wordlessly, Cordie nodded and together they slid the soft material over her head and down her battered body. Once that chore was done, Phoebe felt completely helpless. There was nothing for her to do, and she didn't want to gape at her friend.

"Mother said everyone expects Lord Clayworth to offer for you."

"It's possible," Cordie whispered. "I'm sorry, Phoebe, I know you'd decided to set your cap for him. I promise I didn't encourage him."

That Cordie could be worried about hurting her feelings when she was in so much pain herself, Phoebe couldn't believe. She waved her off. "I don't even know the man. But I thought you didn't like him. I thought you couldn't even abide him."

Cordie sighed. "I don't know what I think anymore, Phoeb. My heart says one thing and my mind says something else."

"Tell me," Phoebe pleaded. Talking was better than the silence that made her remember her friend's injuries.

Cordie looked forlorn. "My heart says Clayworth. He kissed me, and I felt like his soul touched mine. I know that sounds foolish."

"No. It sounds heavenly." Phoebe couldn't even imagine how that would feel, but the words were lovely. "So, it's Clayworth, then." If a man made her feel like that, it wouldn't be a contest.

Cordie shook her head. "As women we're so ruled by our hearts, and I think we end up getting hurt because of it, making foolish mistakes. We should think with our heads. Make wise decisions. My head says Haversham."

Phoebe softly giggled. "You do realize that sounds ridiculous."

She was glad when Cordie smiled back. "He's a scoundrel, Phoebe. He doesn't care what anyone says, what anyone thinks. He does whatever he wants. He's like Kelfield. Can you imagine the duke keeping Livvie prisoner? Or not letting her do what she wanted?"

"No." Kelfield was besotted with Livvie. Anyone who saw them knew that. Phoebe wasn't so certain it was because he was a scoundrel, though. It could just be that he was so in love with her. But then, maybe Cordie was right. Maybe it was because she was a woman and thought with her heart that she believed the romantic version.

Millie returned that moment, carrying a pitcher of water and a satchel of supplies. "All right, Miss Avery, lay on your stomach. This will sting a bit."

Cordie slept better than she'd expected. Of course, Millie had given her a sleeping drought which helped immensely. She was stiff and sore, but after bathing, she felt much better. When her maid, Bessie, came in for her, Cordie was already dressed. The fewer people who knew of her injuries the better. Not that Bessie would be surprised, but Cordie wanted a little privacy.

She found her way downstairs and stopped a footman for directions to the breakfast room.

"Miss, you follow this hall, and —"

"I'll show her," interrupted a voice Cordie could have gone the rest of her life without hearing again.

She took a deep breath and looked over her shoulder at Captain Gabriel Seaton, handsome as ever in his blue naval regimentals. His light brown eyes assessed her and he nodded in greeting. "Cordelia."

Cordie hadn't seen him since she'd broken off their engagement and his presence here was most surprising. "Captain," she answered stiffly. It would have been nice to know *he* was here.

The captain offered her his arm, which she grudgingly took, not seeing a way around the situation. "I am surprised to see you here."

He sighed. "As I was surprised to find myself seated next to your mother at dinner last night. Are you feeling better this morning?"

"Yes, thank you."

He directed her down a long corridor, before making a turn. "I have missed you," he said softly as they continued.

She couldn't say the same, not even to be polite. Escaping life as his wife had been a lucky stroke. "Aren't naval captains supposed to be at sea?" she asked amiably. At one time he'd promised to take her with him on his voyages. While that fate would remove her from her current predicament, it would only be trading one jailer for another. There was also the fact that Clayworth's kiss made her forget every single one the captain had ever given her.

"I've come at the Admiralty's request. Commander Greywood has retired, but his advice is still in demand."

She nodded at the explanation, wishing he'd come to visit the commander at another time.

"I'm certain you've now seen the error of your loyalties."

Cordie looked up at him. "I beg your pardon."

A disbelieving smile curled his lip. "I mean, she's now raising his bastard daughter. No gently bred woman would agree to such a thing. Your loyalties are misplaced in her, Cordelia."

He was talking about Livvie? She hadn't known that fact. It was shocking. "Are we speaking about the Duchess of Kelfield?" She hoped Livvie was all right. Did Kelfield expect that of her?

"Who else?" he scoffed angrily. "You broke our engagement due to my lack of support for her situation."

Cordie drew herself up to her full height and released her hold on his arm. "We were never technically engaged. And I ended our *association* due to your lack of support for me."

He looked at her, hurt in his eyes. "I never saw this side of you before."

"Then aren't you fortunate to have escaped?" She then stalked down the corridor, ignoring the soreness in her back.

"Cordelia!" he called after her. "You don't know the way."

"I'm certain I can find my own way." The words meant much more than he would ever know.

Eleven

CORDIE followed the soft sounds of a harpsichord until she stumbled across Phoebe in the music room. Her friend's eyes were closed as she focused on plucking the strings of her instrument. Cordie must have made a noise, because Phoebe's eyes flew open and she smiled brightly. "Oh, you're up? Millie thought you might be out for a while."

As her friend rose from her seat, Cordie smiled nervously, the events of the night before embarrassing her all over again. She cleared her throat. "I ran into Captain Seaton before breakfast."

Phoebe winced. "Oh, I'm so sorry. I meant to tell you last night..." Her voice trailed off. Then she frowned. "Are you all right?"

Cordie nodded her head firmly. "Nearly perfect." She didn't want to talk about what Phoebe had witnessed. No one knew about her mother's punishments, not even Livvie, and she hoped to keep it that way.

"So," Phoebe said, as she carefully linked her arm with Cordie's, "you've decided on Haversham?"

She supposed she had. He was the logical choice, after all. "Yes." Even as she said the word, her heart ached.

"Well," Phoebe began, "I thought about that quite a bit last night. How much do you know about the marquess?"

Now Cordie felt foolish. What did she know about the marquess? She knew about the scandals he'd been involved in over the years. She knew that he was wickedly handsome. She knew he was a friend of Kelfield's, which was quite important. "Not much I suppose."

Phoebe nearly bounced on her toes. "Excellent. Follow me."

Her friend excitedly towed her back upstairs, to the family's wing and into Phoebe's set of rooms. Books were scattered across the bed as well as foolscap with jotted notes. Cordie followed Phoebe's lead and sat on the edge of the bed. "What's all this?"

"We'll get to that. But first, I do have two unmarried uncles. Both are younger than Haversham. You could be my Aunt Cordelia."

Cordie couldn't help but grin. That was the second time someone referred to the marquess as old. How old was he? "Are either of them scoundrels?"

Phoebe shook her head. "Only Uncle Simon has ever been referred to as such, and he's already married."

"I'm afraid I can't consider either of them then."

Phoebe heaved a sigh. "Well, it was worth a try."

Then a thought occurred to Cordie. She really should test her theory. "Your Aunt, the one who married the scoundrel..."

"Aunt Liberty?"

Cordie nodded. "Is she happy with him?"

"Ecstatic, especially since he's retired from the navy."

That was good news. "And is he ever controlling or demanding with her?"

Phoebe fell back on the bed with peals of laughter. "I'd like to see him try."

Relief washed over Cordie. She was on the right path. Her resolve strengthened, she picked up a piece of foolscap with splotchy writing. "What's this?"

Oh!" Phoebe shot back up and snatched the foolscap from Cordie's hands. "You're going out of order. Now I did a lot of research on Haversham last night. I thought if you're dead set on him, that you should know as much as possible."

It was a fairly good idea, actually. Cordie positioned herself on the bed, ready to learn.

"He was born in '77. An only child. His family seat is in eastern Yorkshire outside Driffield. He attended Eton, started at Oxford, but didn't complete his studies."

"How do you know all this?" Cordie gaped at Phoebe. She'd never considered her friend to be this organized. She always seemed the silliest of the bunch.

"Oh, I just went through Debrett's last night, and I talked a little with Matthew. He's been to some of those clubs and gaming hells Haversham frequents. I couldn't get him to tell me a lot, but I did get some useful information from him."

Cordie gasped. Did Matthew Greywood know what they were up to? "You didn't tell him —"

Phoebe rolled her eyes. "Please. He was with Clayworth when you and Haversham snuck off. He's worried about you falling in with the wrong sort, by the way. So, that's what I told him I was doing — gathering information on the marquess to make you see straight. Men deny it, but they gossip just as much as we do."

Relieved, Cordie took a steadying breath. It appeared Phoebe'd thought of everything. "What did he say?"

Well, the marquess is most definitely a rake, along the same order as Kelfield — but then we knew that. He was married for quite a while until his wife passed away three years ago. It was apparently a loveless marriage as the marchioness never left Yorkshire, and Haversham rarely left London. They have one child, a daughter – Lady Callista, who is, according to Debrett's, seven years old. So no male heir, at least not a legitimate one, and that's something you could use to your advantage."

No gently bred woman would agree to such a thing. The captain's words echoed in her mind. "Phoebe, do you know what's happening to Livvie?"

At once her friend looked panicked. "No, what?"

Cordie shook her head. "Someone mentioned that Kelfield has a daughter and Livvie is acting as the child's mother."

Phoebe took a breath, the smile returned to her face. "Oh, that. Mother is scandalized over it, not that she can say so out loud. My cousins Kurt and Kitty were born on the wrong side of the blanket, and since they live here and my grandparents dote on them, Mother has to bite her tongue."

"So, it's true?" Cordie couldn't imagine Livvie having to experience such an ordeal.

Phoebe shrugged. "Such are the perils of marrying a scoundrel. If you want a saint, Clayworth's your man."

Clayworth. His name made her heart beat faster. Cordie shook her head. It was best not to think of him. It would only make this harder. "What else?"

"Something terrible, but I'm not sure what it was."

"What do you mean by that?"

Phoebe frowned. "I'm not sure. Matthew said that the marquess did something truly terrible years ago. He said it was never spoken about, but that everyone knows it, or everyone does who was around at the time. Since my brother's your age, none of his friends know what it is either."

How terrible must it be to not even be spoken of? Cordie stared towards the window, trying to think of the worst thing possible anyone could do. Had he killed someone? What was worse than that? "Someone must know. I certainly can't ask my mother."

"Nor mine," Phoebe replied with a sigh. "She'd think I'd set my cap for him."

Cordie sat up straight. "What about one of your uncles? The commander must know."

Phoebe paled instantly. "*Uncle Simon.* That would be worse than asking my mother."

But someone must know. Someone she could trust to tell her the truth, no matter how awful.

Lady Staveley.

The answer made her smile. Lady Staveley was the most trustworthy person of her acquaintance. As soon as she returned to London, she'd find some way to speak with the viscountess and find out what awful thing the Marquess of Haversham had done.

༒

Marc left Mrs. Palmer's establishment with a frown. The girl who'd entertained him wore the cheapest of perfume, and now he smelled of the awful stuff. He might not have cared if she'd satisfied him, but she hadn't. She was more concerned with his coin that his cock. Perhaps he was just losing his interest in this sort of thing. No one would ever have believed that.

His coachman pulled open his door, and Marc barely met the man's eyes. "Mrs. Lassiter's."

"Of course, my lord."

As he settled against the leather squabs, he realized what he'd known for some time. This predicament he was in was all Cordelia Avery's fault. She looked at him with her passion-filled, green eyes, making him nearly lose all control. She was full of life, spirited, stunning, but best of all — ready to be seduced. A lethal combination. Ever since he'd met her, he'd been obsessed with having her. No one since had satisfied his cravings.

She was the perfect solution to his ennui, or she would be if she was in London. How much longer would she be in godforsaken Norfolk?

When his coach finally rumbled to a stop at his favorite hell, Marc threw open the door and bounded up the steps. At least he could while away the time here. The double front doors opened and Marc's eyes widened in surprise when two burly men actually tossed Lord Brookfield out on his arse. He'd heard of such things happening before, but he'd never actually witnessed it.

With a raised brow, he stepped over the fallen viscount into the hell. Raucous laughter and billows of smoke assailed him as he entered. "Lord Haversham, welcome back," Peters, Mrs. Lassiter's brawny butler, greeted him.

Marc tipped his head in acknowledgement. "Peters." He brushed past the man into the closest drawing room on the right. Thankfully there was a spot open at a table of *vingt-et-un* on the far side of the room. It was the perfect thing to lift his spirits.

He took a spot beside Lord Ericht, a young, Scottish earl, and nodded to the dealer.

"It's no' a verra lucky spot."

Marc raised his brow at Ericht. "I beg your pardon?"

"They just tossed out the last chap in that seat."

Marc waited for his hand to be dealt, then looked back at the loquacious Scot. "Brookfield?" he asked the man.

"Aye."

After glancing at his upturned seven of clubs, Marc hoped the unlucky streak ended with Brookfield's departure. "What happened?"

Ericht gaped at him as if he'd just escaped Bedlam. "He's insolvent. No' a farthing to his name. Surely ya heard."

Was that all? Marc shrugged. Brookfield wouldn't be the first peer to lose everything. He glanced down at his down turned card. The Ace of Diamonds. That was more like it.

Now that the Scot was talking, he seemed incapable of shutting up. "Kept going on about the lass he's going to marry. Says her dowry will more than pay his debts. But those oversized footmen wouldna listen."

Really, Marc couldn't care less. He'd like to focus on the game. "Lucky girl," he replied, hoping to end the conversation.

Ericht chuckled. "No' that anyone believed Miss Avery will have the dolt. He's delusional, if you ask me."

Marc's head snapped to the Scot. "Miss Avery? Miss *Cordelia* Avery?" His Freya wouldn't look twice at that nasty, unkempt Brookfield.

"Do ye ken the lass?"

Not as well as he'd like, but Marc nodded anyway.

"She is a bonny little thing. I might've been interested in her myself if... Well ye ken. 'Tis a shame."

Marc simply stared at the man. What did he know?

The Scot gulped, suddenly uncomfortable with the intensity of Marc's glare. "I mean, there's only one reason why a girl's family increases her dowry to such a level."

Marc's eyes opened wide as realization struck him. In truth there were only two reasons for a girl's increased dowry—her lack of success on the marriage mart, or her lack of a maidenhead. It wasn't even possible that Cordelia Avery hadn't entertained offers of marriage.

Everything else suddenly made sense. No innocent miss would waltz with him in the middle of Caroline Staveley's ballroom. No innocent miss would engage him in conversations about seduction. No innocent miss would take off with him in Hyde Park. Cordelia Avery was no innocent miss.

Thank God!

It was the best news he'd had in a very long while.

He wouldn't have to play coquettish games. He wouldn't have to take it slowly with her. He wouldn't have to wait to bed her at all. What an incredible stroke of luck.

It was obvious Clayworth wanted to marry the girl, and that was fine with Marc. As long as she was in *his* bed at night, he didn't care where or with whom she spent the rest of her time. In fact, that might be the best solution. After all, that sissy Clayworth never stopped his first wife from cuckolding him. Why would he care if Cordie did? She could have the respectability of marriage to that paragon, but the pleasure of warming Marc's bed.

He could hardly wait for Miss Avery to return from Norfolk. Already he planned how he would welcome her home. His cock twitched in anticipation.

"Ericht, do you by chance have your calling card on you?" he asked as an idea formed in his mind.

"Aye," the Scot replied, reaching inside his jacket.

Naïve fool. Marc resisted the urge to smile.

Twelve

CORDIE hoped she sounded pitiful as she tossed and turned in her bed with her mother looking on. If she could avoid attending Lady Dixon's charity luncheon and could manage to slip away to Lady Staveley's, she knew she could discover Lord Haversham's secretive past. Of course, Lady Staveley would try to warn her about the dangerous path she was on and Cordie would listen dutifully, as long as she gathered the necessary information.

Standing above her, Lady Avery pursed her lips. "You seemed perfectly fine yesterday."

Cordie sighed weakly. "I-I think the journey home was too much for me."

Her mother folded her arms across her chest, the sunlight catching her large ruby ring. "Get your rest then. Lord Clayworth will be by tomorrow and I want you looking your best."

Cordie moaned in response, this time in earnest at the thought of having to see Lord Clayworth. How could she even look at him after that kiss? How could she look at him knowing they had no future?

Her mother's frown deepened at the more genuine sound of anguish. "Perhaps I'll send for Doctor Watts, too."

As if that old man could fix what was wrong with her. Cordie grunted noncommittally and rolled to her side, patiently waiting until she knew her mother had left the house.

As soon as she felt it was safe, Cordie retrieved a pale green muslin dress from her wardrobe. After returning from Norfolk the night before, she'd decided on this particular day dress, as it was one of the few she wouldn't need assistance with. Kid slippers weren't the best for walking all the way to Lady Staveley's, but her half-boots would make too much noise as she left the house, and *that* she couldn't risk.

She quickly ran a brush through her tresses and fashioned them in a simple chignon. Staring at her reflection the entire time, she worried what would happen if her mother learned of her excursion. If she got caught, she'd say she went for a walk to get a bit of fresh air. As if the air in London was fresh. Unfortunately, she couldn't think of a better excuse. Therefore she just had to make certain she didn't get caught.

Cordie quietly opened her door, crept down the hallway, and silently descended the servant's staircase. She pressed her ear to the door at the bottom of the steps, listening for any activity in kitchen. All was silent, and she sent up a grateful prayer.

After peeking through the door, she hurried across the kitchen floor and out the servant's back entrance. She'd made it. She was safe. So far. Without hesitation, she scampered down the mews and around to the front of the house.

She could almost taste victory, but as she neared the street a man grasped her arm and stopped her in her tacks.

Catching her breath, Cordie stared numbly up into the Earl of Clayworth's startling twilight eyes. She couldn't help but gasp. The fortnight she'd spent away from him didn't prepare her for the intensity of his stare. "Y-you weren't supposed to call until tomorrow," she stumbled.

His eyes narrowed, and she felt a cold chill creep up her spine. "Where are you sneaking off to, Cordelia?"

Cordie heaved a sigh. Arrogant man. She didn't owe him anything. It was easier to dislike him when he showed her his cool, controlling demeanor. It was easier to keep in mind everything Marina had ever said about him.

She wrenched her arm out of his grasp and leveled him with her most haughty look. "I have not given you leave to call me by my first name."

He didn't even blanch. "Don't evade me, *Cordelia*. Where are you going without an escort?"

Demanding, difficult, self-important men! She'd had her fill of that particular breed in Norfolk, as the captain had remained in residence throughout their visit. Now that she was free of him and her mother, she wasn't about to let Clayworth assume the role. "Who do you think you are, sir? I don't answer to you."

"I'm only going to ask you one more time," he threatened.

"Or what?" she shot back. How dare he accost her on the street and demand answers?

He stepped closer to her and lowered his voice to an intense whisper. "When I said you'd have to throw yourself at every scoundrel in Town on your own time, I didn't really mean it."

She'd never *thrown* herself at anyone. She wanted to slap him. She truly did. She settled, however, for simply glaring at him. "Once again, my lord, you are not my keeper."

"Perhaps I should to be."

She felt his gravelly voice all the way in her bones, warming her from the inside out, but she ignored her body's response to his words. He wasn't offering what she wanted. She needed a lenient husband. It was obvious he could never be that. "I don't need a keeper, nor do I want one. Now, excuse me, sir."

Cordie turned on her heel and started towards Curzon Street, which was pointless. Clayworth was right on her trail. "If you're going somewhere, at least allow me to escort you."

"I have hordes of scoundrels to throw myself at. You'll simply be in the way."

He grasped her arm again, forcing her to stop on the path. Cordie stared at the mother-of-pearl buttons on his waistcoat rather than look up into his all-knowing eyes. Still she felt his gaze on her. "I'm sorry, I shouldn't have said that. But when I saw you sneaking from the mews, I let my imagination get away with me." His voice softened, as did his old on her arm. "Where are you going, Miss Avery? And in such a hurry?"

Slowly her gaze lifted to his eyes. Concern was etched upon his godlike brow, and her heart lurched in her chest. Why did he have to look at her like that? As if he was truly worried, truly cared? Cordie mentally shook the thought off. "I was just going to pay a social call, my lord. There's nothing nefarious."

"Where's your maid?"

She frowned at him. Really, it was none of his concern. "I'm not going far, and you are delaying me."

The tiniest smile cracked his lips. "You have an awful habit of trying to avoid my questions, Cordelia."

Not well enough, or he wouldn't realize it. And why did he insist on calling her by her given name? It was making it quite difficult for her to think straight. "You *are* delaying me," she repeated.

Truly, who knew how long it would be before her mother returned.

"You should have your maid with you, or some unscrupulous fellow might try to snatch you up, and then where would I be?"

In that instant, there was nothing Cordie could do to escape him. He would never let her continue to Lady Staveley's unescorted and she couldn't keep arguing with him in the middle of South Audley Street. One of the neighbors was sure to notice that, and with all the attention Clayworth attracted, someone was bound to mention it to her mother. Cordie's shoulders sagged. The best laid plans.

Then an idea occurred to her. She didn't have to get answers from Lady Staveley. Lord Clayworth seemed determined to save her from herself. He must know what awful thing Lord Haversham had done. She could probably charm it out of him.

⚜

A look of *something* flashed in Cordelia's beguiling eyes. The gold specks seemed to twinkle. Brendan didn't know what the look meant, but something told him it didn't bode well for him.

"My lord," she said softly, "I think I've decided not to go out after all. Would you like to come inside and join me for some tea instead?"

The words sounded innocent enough, but there was something going on in her mind. She was plotting, he just couldn't figure out what she was after. There was only one way to find out. Brendan offered her his arm. "My dear."

When she linked her arm with his, Brendan suddenly didn't care what she was after. She felt *right* at his side, like she was supposed to be there, like she was supposed to be his. He knew she felt it too, because of her quick intake of breath and expression of utter confusion on her angelic face.

81

A smile tugged at his lips. He affected her just as much as she affected him. It was a heady emotion he'd certainly never experienced before. Then a wild idea flashed in his mind. What if he didn't need to search for the letters at all? What if he could convince the Averys to return them to him as a…wedding gift? It could save him tons of time—time he could be spending on his honeymoon. Besides, they wouldn't want Cordelia painted with the same traitorous strokes he would be if the contents got out.

Apparently the time he'd spent away from her had done nothing to dull the need he had for her. Truly amazing. He would never have believed it possible.

Brendan guided her towards the front steps of Avery House, noticing everything about her. How she shyly watched him from the corner of one emerald eye. How her pert little nose scrunched up a bit, as if she was trying to figure something out. How softly the breath escaped her mouth, which brought his attention back to her perfectly shaped, rosebud lips. The memory of their kiss radiated through his body and he would have given anything at that moment to taste them again.

"Miss Avery!" screeched a voice from behind them, breaking the mood entirely.

Cordelia's grasp tightened on his arm, and Brendan looked over his shoulder, discovering the rumbled Lord Brookfield closing in on them.

"Miss Avery!" the viscount called again. "It's so fortunate our paths have crossed."

Brendan frowned at the man. "Brookfield."

The viscount's eyes widened in that instant, as if he hadn't noticed Brendan until that very second. True, in Cordelia's presence everything else did dim. However, how the man missed seeing Brendan before now was a mystery. "Oh, Clayworth."

Cordelia's hand tightened again on his arm like a tourniquet, causing him to glance back at her. To look at her, one would never know she was upset. Her features were perfectly in place and she even gifted the viscount with a pleasant smile, but her death grip on Brendan's arm spoke of something else.

Brendan frowned at the fortune hunter, as an overwhelming need to protect Cordelia rushed through his veins. "I'm afraid Miss Avery and I are in a bit of a hurry."

The viscount blinked at Brendan. "But it looks like you're just arriving. I only need a minute of the lady's time."

"Perhaps another day. As I said, we're pressed for time at the moment." Brendan turned Cordelia back towards her front door.

"Please!" the man's anguished cry halted them in their steps.

Brendan looked back at Brookfield, now on his knees. "Get up, man!"

But the viscount's eyes were locked on Cordelia's. "Please, Miss Avery, please marry me. I'll be the best of husbands. Whatever you want is yours."

She sucked in a startled breath and Brendan wrapped his arm around her waist. "I think that's enough, sir," he said, leveling the man with his iciest stare. What was wrong with Brookfield? Had he no dignity at all?

Cordelia's brow furrowed as she looked at the crumpled man before them. "I am truly sorry, my lord, but my affections lay elsewhere."

Brendan's mouth went dry. With whom did her affections lay? With him? Or with that bastard Haversham? After their kiss, he wanted to believe that is it was with him. At the same time, however, she was sneaking out of her house. Was she late for a rendezvous with the marquess?

The door opened and the Averys' butler, an older man with a tuft of white hair, stared at the scene before him. "Miss Avery! I thought—"

"Yes," Cordelia began pleasantly, "I did go for a short walk after all, Sanders."

The butler frowned at her, but opened the door wide. "Lord Clayworth."

Brendan ushered Cordelia over the threshold and directed the butler to close the door behind them, and noticed that an entire conversation transpired between Cordelia and the servant with their eyes. He'd love to know what that was all about.

"That was dreadful," she said softly.

That was an understatement. Did men fall on their knees before her on a regular basis? She had handled herself well, despite Brookfield's production. She'd been kind to the dolt, who wasn't the least bit deserving, in Brendan's opinion. Dropping on his knees before the girl with all the world to see! What sort of man did such a thing?

A desperate one.

Everyone knew Brookfield was penniless, but perhaps the situation was even worse than Brendan had imagined. He looked at the pretty girl still on his arm. If he hadn't happened upon her when he did, what might Brookfield have done to her if he'd stumbled across her first? He cringed at the possibilities that flashed in his mind.

"Are you all right?" she asked.

Brendan frowned at her. "You asked me to tea, did you not?"

"Yes, of course."

Thirteen

AFTER adding one sugar to Lord Clayworth's tea, Cordie handed him the cup and took her own spot on the lavish, gold settee across from him. The earl's earlier smile was gone, and he appeared like a man with much on his mind. She heaved a sigh. It would be much more difficult to charm answers out of him now. It was also hard to remember why she wanted to know anything about Haversham when Clayworth's twilight eyes landed on her. He truly could take her breath away with just one look.

"You do realize if I hadn't been there, you could have ended up in quite a bit of trouble?"

Trouble? From Brookfield? She giggled. The fortune-hunting viscount was far from her favorite person, and she would never consider marriage to him—but the man was harmless, if a bit odiferous.

"I do wish you'd take this seriously," he said, his frown deepening.

Cordie took a sip of her own tea, hoping to cover her grin. No one could take Brookfield seriously, except it seemed for Lord Clayworth. Then again, Lord Clayworth took everything seriously, so she shouldn't be surprised. "Have you been well?" she asked, hoping to lighten the mood.

The earl's face softened a bit. "You're changing the subject. Don't you realize it's dangerous for a pretty girl to go around unchaperoned?"

"Yes, I had a lovely time in Norfolk. Thank you so much for asking," she replied, then took another sip of tea.

He rubbed his brow and closed his eyes, as if to stave off a headache, but Cordie knew she was charming him. A small smile tugged on the corner of his lips and her heart raced at the sight. He was always a striking man, but when he smiled, no one was more handsome. Lord Adonis was a most appropriate moniker.

Clayworth opened his eyes, piercing her with his stare. "I've never met a lady less concerned for her own personal safety before. Does your mother know the chances you take?"

Not if she could help it. Cordie toyed with one of the ties from her dress and shook her head. "You won't tell her, will you, my lord?" she asked, hoping she sounded coy.

He heaved a sigh. "I should, you know. Someone needs to keep you out of trouble."

Cordie flashed him a charming smile and could actually see his resolve melt away.

"Just promise me you'll be careful," he said, his baritone voice rumbling over her.

This was perfect. They were negotiating. There would be no reason to sneak off to Lady Staveley's if he'd just tell her what she wanted to know. "I'll promise, on one condition."

"Yes?" He narrowed his eyes on her.

"I'll promise to be more careful and take a maid out with me in the future, if you'll tell me something."

"What do you want to know?" he asked as he slid to the edge of his seat, his desire-filled eyes drinking her in.

Cordie swallowed. If she didn't ask now, she'd lose her nerve and get caught up in the emotions of being with him. "I—um—well, you must know whatever horrible thing Lord Haversham did years ago. The thing no one talks about. What was it?" The words flew out of her mouth.

Clayworth deflated before her eyes. A frown marred his too handsome face and he slumped against the back of his chair. He looked as if he'd just been punched. His eyes slowly rose to meet hers. "Haversham."

Her heart aching, she nodded. It was one thing knowing she was ignoring her own heart, and another to know she'd hurt him. That certainly hadn't been her intent. "I am sorry." It was impossible for the simple words to convey just how sorry she was.

He steeled his features and shook his head. "The particulars aren't for an innocent lady's ears, Miss Avery. I'm not willing to barter your safety. Promise me you'll be careful. If you ended up hurt I— Just promise me."

His sincere plea was almost too much for Cordie, and she found herself nodding in agreement.

"I'll hold you to that." Clayworth stood up and placed his cup with the tea service. "Until next time, Miss Avery."

He was leaving? Cordie suddenly felt like crying. "You'll return tomorrow, won't you?" she asked before she could stop herself. He shouldn't come back. It was too hard to see him.

Clayworth heaved a sigh. "I am supposed to take you for a ride, Miss Avery, but under the circumstances, if you'd rather not—"

"Oh, please do," she said, even though she should let him go. But it was just *one* outing. One ride in his exquisite phaeton. No one but the two of them. She'd have to live the rest of her life without him. Shouldn't she get at least one ride to remember through the years?

"As you wish." Clayworth nodded and then strode quickly from the room, taking Cordie's heart with him.

She was making the logical choice, wasn't she? Clayworth was too intense. He'd never let her have the freedom she desired. She was making the right decision. She just wished it didn't hurt so dreadfully.

Cordie had no idea how long she sat staring at her tea, but when Sanders entered the room to announce Lord Ericht, the cup had grown cold.

Ericht? The handsome Scottish earl? She'd never met the man. She'd seen him before, but they'd never been introduced. Cordie couldn't imagine what he was doing here, but she nodded to her butler. "Show him in, Sanders. And—um—fresh tea, if you don't mind."

She placed her cup next to Clayworth's discarded one and wished again that he'd never left.

"The Earl of Ericht," Sanders intoned.

Cordie slowly turned to face the man, but found instead the laughing, soft blue eyes of the Marquess of Haversham. He winked at her. "Miss Avery, so nice to see ye again," he drawled in a fake Scottish accent that was surprisingly well done.

It was hard not to smile at that. He was inventive, if nothing else. "Please, Lord *Ericht*, do have a seat," she replied, waiting for Sanders to leave them.

When the butler left, Haversham sauntered to where she sat on the settee and planted himself next to her. A roguish smile lit up his face. "Sorry for the subterfuge, but I didn't think the old man would admit the wicked Marquess of Haversham," he explained, as he took one of her hands in his.

The marquess' lips pressed to her knuckles, and though it felt rather nice, he didn't send jolts of heat racing across her like Clayworth did. Cordie shook her head. She was being foolish. Lord Haversham was the logical answer to her problems. And here he was. He'd found a way past her mother's guard. She should be ecstatic.

"Are you really wicked?" she asked, wondering briefly if *he* might tell the terrible thing he'd one. She rather supposed he wouldn't.

He ran his hand along her bodice and grinned. "How badly do you want to know?"

"Well," she began, moving out of his reach to pace the room. "I think I should know everything about you, my lord."

"Marc," he prompted.

Weeks ago the idea of calling him that had sent shivers racing across her, but not now. It was good, she supposed, that he was still so interested in her. She wanted an affectionate husband as well as a lenient one, after all. An idea flashed in her mind. She hadn't really seen Clayworth differently until he'd kissed her. What if the same was true for Haversham? It would be a relief not to pine away for another man her whole life. She stopped pacing and gifted the marquess with what she hoped was a seductive smile. "Marc." She let the name drip off her lips. "Would you like to kiss me?"

He was at her side in the blink of an eye, wearing a devilish smile. "And much more," he promised silkily.

Cordie bit her bottom lip.

Marc tipped her chin up and lowered his head, but before his lips could touch hers, an ear piercing wail came from the doorway. Cordie's shoulders slumped forward. Why did her mother have to return *now*?

"Out!" Lady Avery screeched at the top of her lungs. "Out!" Then she raced toward the marquess, beating him with her reticule. "Get out of my house, you blackguard!"

Marc raised his brow at Cordie, paying no attention to the beating he was receiving. "Soon, I will have that kiss, Miss Avery." Then he looked down at her mother and growled, "Take your hands off me."

Lady Avery winced and backed up immediately. The sight made Cordie's heart soar. With Marc to protect her, her mother would never lay another hand on her. Kiss or no kiss, she needed a plan to become the man's marchioness. Sooner rather than later.

He tipped his head in farewell and then spun on his heel, leaving them in his wake.

Fire shooting from her eyes, her mother wailed, "Cordelia, have you lost your mind?"

"I didn't invite him here, Mama," Cordie tried to explain, not that she wouldn't have if he hadn't thought of it first.

The answer only increased her mother's hysteria. "Do you think I want you following in Olivia's scandalous footsteps, young lady?"

"Livvie is happy, Mama!" Cordie shot back. How could her mother, after knowing Livvie her whole life, be so vile to her now? "And a duchess! A *duchess* for heaven's sake! They're not generally denigrated, you know."

"They don't generally behave in such ill fashion either."

"You should want as much for me. And Haversham is a marquess! Loads better than a puffed up naval captain."

"Captain Seaton was a decent man," Lady Avery's voice rose even louder as she puffed out her chest.

It had grated on her nerves to see the captain cater to her mother over the last fortnight, still trying to get in her good graces. "Gabriel Seaton was a dictatorial prig and I'm glad he's gone."

"Well, I..." her mother began, interrupted by a loud scraping at the door.

Then Sanders entered the room, a look of confusion on the old man's face. "I'm sorry to interrupt, my lady, but your sons have returned."

The air whooshed out of Cordie. Her *brothers* were here? She'd been praying for their safe return for what felt like a lifetime. The anger drained immediately from her mother and they exchanged smiles of relief and happy squeals of joy at the same moment. Lady Avery pushed past Sanders to get to the doorway, Cordie right behind her.

They didn't have to go far. Standing in the hallway were her brothers Russell and Tristan, and behind them a dear old friend, Major Philip Moore. Both women squealed again. Russell embraced their mother and Cordie threw herself into Tristan's awaiting arms. She hadn't realized how scared she was that they wouldn't return until she felt Tristan's strong arms hold her. She had missed them both dreadfully. After a long moment, they switched partners and Russell held her tightly.

Thank God they were safe. Thank God they were home.

"Philip Moore!" Lady Avery finally rushed towards the major, arms outstretched. "My dear boy, I can never thank you enough for keeping Tristan alive."

Tristan groaned nearby. "Mother, I wish you wouldn't say it like that."

"Into the parlor, all of you," her mother demanded, directing everyone inside the nearest room. "And, Sanders, tea, if you will. Who knows when these boys have had decent fare. You're all too thin, the lot of you."

Tristan slid his arm around Cordie's waist. "You are a sight for sore eyes, sis."

"Oh, Tris," she whispered back. "You don't know how worried I was. When Russell said you'd been hit—"

Her youngest brother blushed. "He exaggerates. You know that."

"Oh, I'm just so glad you're here." She pressed a kiss to his cheek. Tristan was her closest sibling in age, and he'd always been her favorite brother. Kind hearted and honest, she'd adored him her entire life.

Their mother hooked her arm with Tristan's and steered both her sons into chairs near hers. Cordie settled next to Philip on the settee and smiled at him. In so many ways he was like another brother. They'd all grown up together in Nottinghamshire. "It is good to see you, Philip. We have been so worried about all of you."

"Indeed we have!" Lady Avery seconded. Her eyes filled with tears as she looked at her youngest son. "Tristan, my heart stopped when we got the news you'd been injured."

"Mother, it was nothing," Tris almost growled.

"Don't listen to him, Mother," Russell interrupted, a mischievous grin on his face. "The battle was intense. Loud. Sound was everywhere. If it hadn't been for Philip knocking Tris to the ground, he'd have taken a ball in the chest."

"It wasn't that bad," Tris grumbled.

Russell raised his brow, like only an older and irritating brother can. "All he ended up with was a broken arm. That time."

"Thank you, Russell," Tris replied fiercely.

Philip gently touched Cordie's hand, and her eyes flew to his. "I didn't mean to eavesdrop, but you were yelling when we arrived."

Cordie blanched. She hadn't realized everyone heard their argument. That was a bit embarrassing. The entire room fell silent.

Philip pressed on, "Were you talking about *my* Olivia?"

He didn't know about Livvie? Cordie wished the floor would swallow her whole. How did he not know? No one had told him? Livvie and Philip had been engaged for years. She would still be waiting for him if Kelfield hadn't swept her off her feet.

"See here," Russell cut in, leveling her with his soft green eyes. "I'll not have *my* sister falling prey to Marcus Gray. What was he doing here?"

"I'll put a ball in his skull if he returns," Tristan threatened.

"And a blade in his chest," Russell added.

"Charming!" Cordie frowned at her brothers. All she needed was their interference. "It's so wonderful to see that the two of you are still so civilized after your stay in the army."

Russell shook his head. "You can't bait us like that, Cordie. Have you gone and lost your mind? I mean, Haversham for God's sake? Do you have any idea of his reputation?"

"I know that he'd grant me the freedom to do as I pleased," she shot back. "He wouldn't dictate who my friends could be. Or what I could say. Or what I could do. And he cares about *me*, Russell. So both of you—" she paused, gesturing wildly to both her brothers— "had better keep your pistols and swords to yourselves, or I'll never forgive you."

Lady Avery smiled wistfully. "It is good to have you home. Perhaps you can talk some sense into her. Ever since Olivia…"

Philip's eyes flew to the baroness. "Pray continue, my lady. Ever since Olivia what?"

She looked away from him, so he turned his attention to Cordie. "Ever since Olivia what? Please tell me."

Cordie couldn't look at him either. Philip was devoted to Livvie. He always had been. He *was* owed the truth, however. "I-I suppose that means you don't know."

"Know what?" he demanded, which really wasn't like him at all. He was normally so softly spoken.

Cordie glanced up at him, her heart aching for him. "I don't think she meant for it to happen, Philip. It just did."

"What happened?" he nearly bellowed.

She took a deep breath. Perhaps if he knew *how* it happened, it would help. "Well, you see, we'd gone to a house party in Derbyshire at the home of the Duke of Prestwick—"

"She married the Duke of Prestwick?" he asked, confusion on his face.

"No," Cordie quickly replied, "His Grace of Prestwick is just a boy, but *his* sister is married to Livvie's cousin Lucas Beckford. It was the worst house party I've ever been to. There were no entertainments to speak of, and surly naval captains, and we were dreadfully bored."

A muscle twitched in Philip's jaw and he rubbed his forehead. "For the love of God, Cordelia, pray get to the point," he barked impatiently.

Before she could continue, her mother interrupted. "The Duke of Kelfield was in attendance as well, Philip." She frowned at Cordie as she spoke. "The girls returned early from the country and two days later Olivia was Kelfield's duchess. I'm unsure of all that transpired as Cordelia had gone alone to keep Olivia company. I entrusted Cordie would be safe in Lord and Lady Staveley's care, a mistake I won't make in the future."

Cordie leapt off the settee, awash in anger all over again at the injustice. "I've done *nothing* wrong, Mama. And yet you insist on keeping me locked up here like some villain."

"Nothing wrong?" her mother echoed. "Then just what would you call allowing Haversham to call on you?"

Cordie didn't have time to answer as Philip leapt to his feet beside her. "I'll kill him!"

That was the worst possible turn of events. She had to stop him. Philip started for the door and Cordie chased after him, wailing, "Philip, no! Please stop! Listen to reason."

But he didn't stop, and Cordie turned around to see her mother and two brothers staring at her in disbelief.

Fourteen

CORDIE lay on her bed staring up at the canopy above her, having been banished to her room after Philip Moore stormed out. Her mother was still furious over finding her, once again, in Haversham's arms. She was fortunate that Russell and Tristan had returned, or her punishment would have been more severe. However, that was the least of her worries at the moment.

A few streets away, Livvie's life must be falling apart. Cordie's heart ached for her friend. It ached for Philip too. How horrible for him to find out the love of his life had married another. It reminded her of the look of utter devastation Lord Clayworth wore in her parlor that very afternoon when she'd mentioned Haversham's name. Though the two men handled the situations quite differently.

Upon learning of her continued interest in Haversham, Clayworth hadn't stormed off ready to kill the man. Instead he'd made her promise to be careful with such a sincere plea, Cordie hurt just remembering it. Guilt washed over her again. Was she doing the right thing? Why did she keep coming back to that? She knew in her mind that she was, but her heart seemed unable to give up.

A knock interrupted her thoughts. "Come in," Cordie called.

The door opened and Tristan stood at the entrance, shaking his head, wearing a crooked smile. "You always were the most rebellious of us all."

He stepped inside her room and crossed the floor in just a few strides. Then he flopped down on the bed, next to her. "I don't agree with Mother often, Cor, but Haversham? What are you thinking?"

Cordie shrugged and closed her eyes. "Not you too, Tris. You're supposed to be on my side."

"I'm always on your side," he assured her, dropping a very brotherly kiss to her cheek. "And I'm ready to listen."

He would listen, she knew that, but he wouldn't understand. He was a man and couldn't possibly comprehend how difficult her choice was. He'd always had his freedom to do what he wanted. No one ever told him he couldn't be friends with his friends or he couldn't go wherever he pleased. She could try to explain, but it would end up being a very frustrating conversation, and she wasn't up for that just now. "Tris, what did Philip do?" she asked, changing the subject.

His body tightened next to hers and she took in a sharp breath. Certainly he didn't *really* kill the duke. "That's men's business, Cordie."

Men's business, indeed! No. Her brother, dear as he was, would never understand her predicament. Irritating man! She sat bolt upright and glared at him. "Tristan Randolph Avery, Olivia is my dearest friend. Now you tell me this instant."

He chuckled, his weight shaking the bed. "You sound just like mother."

It was the worst thing anyone had ever said to her. Her mouth fell open. Stunned by his words, Cordie didn't even realizing she was crying until her tears dropped to her hands and Tris' face contorted with concern.

He sat up in an instant and smoothed her tears away. "Dear God! What is it? What did I say?"

Words wouldn't come out of her mouth. She sounded like *Mother*? The very last person she wanted to be like in any way was their mother. He couldn't have hurt her more if he'd thurst a knife into her belly with that accusation.

"No, no, no," Tris tried to soothe her, though he sounded quite panicked. "Don't cry, Cordie. I'll tell you whatever you want to know.

Just stop looking like that."

She was never emotional like this. She put her hand to her heart and took one big calming breath after another. How silly of her. She'd never realized that her tears were a tool to get things she wanted. How unfortunate to discover so late in life.

When she could speak, she pierced Tristan with her most pleading look. "What *did* Philip do?"

He frowned and wiped away the last of her tears. "He challenged Kelfield."

"He *what*?" she asked, shocked and angry all rolled into one. What was wrong with men? This was how they thought to solve problems?

"I shouldn't have said anything." Tris started to slide from the bed.

Cordie grabbed his lieutenant's uniform and held tightly. "Has he lost his mind? Doesn't he realize what this will do to Livvie?"

"Kelfield dishonored him, Cordie. In Philip's spot, I'd do the same."

"Stupid, foolish men, all of you."

"Thank you," her brother replied with a furrowed brow.

Cordie leapt off the bed, pacing a path in her rug. "Russell's his second, I suppose."

Philip and Russell were the closest of friends. It wasn't even possible he'd picked someone else. If she had the chance to think through this clearly she might be able to do something to fix the mess these men had created.

"Cordie," Tristan said warningly.

"They could *delope*," she said hopefully. "Philip's honor could be preserved and neither of them would have to die." How could Kelfield even compete with a trained soldier in such a realm? Poor Livvie, it would destroy her.

"They can't *delope*," Tristan said the word as if it left a bad taste in his mouth. "How do you even know such things?"

She gaped at her brother. "I've listened to you three my entire life."

He massaged his temples. "We had no idea you were such an apt pupil. Anyway, even if they wanted to *delope*, which Philip would not, they're not using pistols. Kelfield chose swords."

Swords? She shuddered. How terribly gruesome. Unless...an idea began to form in her mind. "At dawn tomorrow?" she asked. These sort of things were always at dawn, usually the next day, before the participants had time to think about how incredibly stupid they were.

"Philip won't change his mind and Kelfield *can't* back out. So whatever you're thinking, put it out of your mind. None of this concerns you."

It was a concern of hers, however. People she loved were bound to get hurt one way or the other. Livvie. Philip. She didn't know Kelfield particularly well, but she did like him. The whole thing was a terrible situation. "It concerns Livvie," she said evenly.

"Cordie." He shook his head. "I didn't come to discuss any of *this* with you."

Then she remembered. Tristan's first words chastised her involvement with Haversham. Cordie closed her eyes. There were much more pressing things to worry about at the moment. "I'll not discuss the marquess with you, Tris."

"Good," he said cheerfully.

Cordie opened her eyes, only to narrow them on her brother. Why did he sound so happy? "What then?" she asked suspiciously.

Tristan shrugged. "Mother seems convinced you'll receive an offer from the Earl of Clayworth. It's a good match, Cordie."

She winced at the name, remembering once again the look of pain she'd caused on his handsome face. She didn't want to think about Clayworth. It hurt too much. But Livvie... If Cordie could focus on helping her friend, she wouldn't have to think about the earl. "Mother's mistaken. He won't propose."

"You can't possibly know what goes on in a man's mind, Cordie."

She scowled at him. "Probably not, because you all make such foolish, idiotic, ridiculous decisions. No one with a clear mind could sort you all out."

Tristan chuckled. "You haven't changed one bit, sis. I'm so glad."

Brendan climbed the steps to his Mayfair home, cursing himself the entire way. What the devil was wrong with him? He'd known since the very beginning she was infatuated with Haversham. Did he think that his one kiss would change all that? Just because the kiss was the most intense he'd ever had, just because the kiss made him forget what he was after, just because the kiss made him hope for the impossible did not mean it had the same effect on her.

But he would have sworn it had.

His butler opened the door and smiled tightly. "Lord Clayworth."

"Higgins," Brendan responded, handing his cane and hat to the man. He started off towards his study. So Cordelia Avery had rejected him. It wasn't the worst thing in the world. It just felt like it. Unfortunately, he still didn't have his mother's letters, so he was caught in the awful circumstance of having to see her again, over and over, until he finally had the evidence of his mother's crimes in his possession. The torture this situation presented should be punishment enough to absolve him of whatever sins he'd committed in his life.

"Ah, Brendan, there you are," came Caroline's ever cheerful voice.

He cringed as he came to a stop. The last bloody person he wanted to see was Caroline. Who knew what trouble she had in store for him? Brendan shook his head. "Sorry, Caro, I'm in a bit of a hurry at the moment."

"The parlor's done, darling. I just wanted you to have a look."

There wasn't a polite way around it. He heaved a sigh and turned on his heel. Caroline Staveley met him with a beatific smile, arms outstretched. "I'm certain you'll adore it."

Brendan stepped towards her and when she wrapped her arms around him, he felt the first peace he'd had in hours. As irritating and meddlesome as Caroline could be, she really was a warm and generous lady who genuinely cared about those fortunate enough to have earned her loyal devotion. For some reason he was one of those people.

She stepped out of his arms and frowned at him. "Darling, what is it?"

He could tell her, most of it, anyway. She would understand, commiserate even. However, that would make him appear weak. Brendan smiled tightly and lied, "I'm just worried about Rose is all."

Caroline nodded, linking her arm with his. "She wants a season in London."

She did, actually, but how Caroline knew that he had no idea. "Yes."

"I understand your reluctance. Part of her is growing up, but the other part is so…"

"Immature," he offered.

Caroline smiled. "I was going to say innocent."

That worked too. "You were trying to gloss over the fact that she is completely ill-suited for such a thing. But making *her* understand it is something else."

They'd reached the blue parlor, but Caroline kept her hand on the knob. "Perhaps she simply needs something else to focus on. If you were to remarry, think of the excitement Rose would enjoy."

"I'm not marrying anyone, Caroline, to keep Rose entertained or otherwise."

"You are stubborn," Caroline said without heat. "All right, I'll warn you. Your parlor is a bit different, and if you don't like it you won't hurt my feelings at all."

Brendan nodded, just wanting to get it over with.

Caroline opened the door, holding it wide for him to step inside. The room was beautiful. No longer blue, it was green—the exact shade of Cordelia's eyes. How had Caroline managed that? Even the large mirror and portraits were in new golden frames that reminded him of the flecks in her eyes. There was a new damask settee, a shade darker than the walls and two ornate chairs with soft, golden accents. A cherry wood writing desk and tables had been added, giving the room a warm feel it had lacked before.

"So?" she asked hopefully.

Cordelia had never been here, but it felt like her. "It's beautiful," he whispered. He'd have to avoid this room like the plague, to keep from thinking of her.

"Oh, I'm so glad you like it," Caroline gushed. "And now, do you have plans for tonight?"

Immediately, he was suspicious. "Why?"

She frowned at him. "Well, I thought if you were free you might enjoy dining with Staveley and me tonight. It's been forever since you've visited."

"Who else is going to be there?" He didn't need to see Cordelia Avery just yet. Tomorrow was already too soon, and blindsiding him was something Caroline would do without any qualms.

Her hazel eyes narrowed. "Just us. What is *really* wrong, Brendan?"

"I just have a lot on my mind." That was an understatement.

She studied him, her mouth pursed, and he was afraid she might see through him. "I see. So, will you join us or not?"

He could go to one of his clubs and get foxed. That would take

Cordelia off his mind, at least for the night. Or he could go to a hell and get sucked into a game of Hazard. Astwick had his box at Drury Lane. That was a possibility as well. Nothing really appealed, however. He shrugged. Why not? "I'd be delighted."

Fifteen

IT WAS unfortunate Philip chose Russell as his second. Tristan would be much easier to manipulate. Cordie paused outside the library and prepared herself. At least it was Russell. Gregory would be near impossible.

She slowly pushed the door open and found Russell sitting in an over-stuffed leather chair, relaxing with a book and drinking some brandy. Perfect. Her middle brother was always the easiest to influence when he was drinking. She flopped down in a chair across from him and smiled sweetly.

He looked up at her and raised his brow. "You want something."

"I do not." She feigned innocence.

Russell grinned at her. "I've not been gone all that long, Cordelia. When you want something your nose scrunches up just a bit."

Blast her brother for knowing her as well as she knew him. Not that she was going to let that deter her. "Russ, about—"

He roared with laughter. "Russ? You only call me that if you've exhausted all other options. What is it, Cordie?"

"Very well," she said, sitting forward in her chair, disbanding all pretense and cutting to the chase. It would have been so much easier with Tristan. "This duel between Kelfield and Philip. It's to be swords?"

"How do you know that?" he asked, narrowing his green eyes on her. "Tristan."

Russell sat back in his chair with a humpf.

"So it's to be swords. Will it be first blood or to the death?"

"Haversham hasn't shown up to discuss the terms. And," he said, pinning her with his gaze, "no, you won't see him while he's here."

"Oh for heaven's sake, Russell, the marquess is the last thing on my mind at the moment." She sighed, shaking her head. "Olivia loves her husband. You would only have to see them together to know that. Please make it First Blood. It would destroy Livvie if Kelfield died. Injured she could live with."

"This is not something that concerns women, Cordie."

There it was again. Obnoxious brothers. She frowned at him. "Spoken like a pompous man."

He chuckled. "Tristan should be shot for even telling you in the first place."

"Well, I suppose since you're all intent on killing each other, he can be next on the list." Then she touched her brother's leg. "Please. Livvie is my dearest friend, Russell. I don't want to see her hurt. If either of them died, she would be devastated. You grew up with her, same as me. I know you don't want that."

Russell sighed. "I'll agree to it if Haversham will. But if you tell anyone that you talked me into this, I'll deny it and put snakes in your bed again."

Cordie's mouth fell open. "That was *you*?" Then she smacked him. "Russell Avery! On more than one occasion you and Gregory both told me Tristan was the culprit. I threw a rock at his head."

He threw back his head and laughed. "You always had awful aim."

He could laugh at her if he wanted to. One down, one to go. She kissed Russell's cheek, then excused herself and made a beeline to the front parlor so that she had a good view of South Audley Street. The Marquess of Haversham wouldn't get past her.

⋘⋗⋙

Marc was still in awe by the turn of events. Kelfield had genuinely seemed reformed. For years he wouldn't have been surprised to have been informed he was the duke's second. The two of them had cut quite a swath through Town. But now? He couldn't imagine what the happily married Kelfield had done to get himself into this sort of trouble. Not that it mattered. Kelfield had been his second in the past. Duty dictated he return the favor.

How fortunate Major Moore's second was Captain Russell Avery and the two of them were to establish the parameters of the duel. A legitimate reason to be at Avery House. With any luck he could get his hands back on the delightful Cordie while he was there, though that seemed like a long shot. Twice he'd tried to kiss the girl, only to be interrupted. His patience was wearing extremely thin.

When his coach rumbled to a stop in front of Avery House, Marc didn't wait for the steps to be lowered. He threw open the door and hopped out, but before he strode up the steps, a strange movement from the corner of the house caught his eye. For a moment, he thought he saw Brookfield's unfortunate form lurking there, but after blinking a few times, he decided it was the moonlight and darkness playing tricks on his mind.

Shaking his head, Marc turned back towards the front door and purposefully climbed the steps. Before he could knock, the door wrenched open. Standing before him was the exquisite Cordelia Avery, who flashed him a cheeky smile. "My lord, we meet again."

Sweet Lucifer, she was a vision—one he could barely wait to get his hands on. He grinned back. "Butler duties? What other talents are you hiding, Miss Avery?"

She grabbed his arm and pulled him inside. Marc almost stumbled but pulled her sweet little body against his. She sucked in a surprised breath. "Not here," she whispered, pulling out of his grasp and tugging him towards the front parlor.

If she wanted to be alone with him, he'd go anywhere she deemed.

Once inside the parlor, Marc swiftly shut the door behind them and wasted no time in pulling her back into his arms. He wouldn't be denied this time. Before she could speak, he pressed his lips to hers. His cock instantly sprang to life. She tasted like heaven, sin, and sweetness all rolled into one. She sighed softly and he splayed his hand across her back, pressing her closer to him. This was what he'd been waiting for.

An instant later, she pushed at his chest and staggered backwards. "My lord, I need to speak with you."

"I much prefer what we were just doing," he replied, barely touching the side of her neck. Though to be honest, he'd prefer a bit more than just kissing her. His breeches were already straining at the seams.

Her cheeks heated and she shook her head. "Please, I don't have much time."

"What are you concerned about, angel?" he asked smoothly, kissing her fingers.

"This duel—"

"You know about that?" He dropped her hand. Her brothers should be shot for telling her. Women never understood this sort of thing. What were they thinking?

"Please make it just to first blood drawn, my lord," she begged quietly.

First blood drawn? Marc shook his head. "Kelfield made it quite clear he wanted it to the death."

Cordie frowned at that, then she touched a button on his waistcoat. An invitation if he'd even seen one. "But as seconds, *you* and my brother set the stipulations."

"You do realize that neither gentleman would be happy with your interference?" he asked, towing her a bit closer. Her dress was simple, but from where he stood he had an exce

"Please," she whispered, placing her hand on his chest.

Marc's pulse quickened at her touch and he couldn't resist holding her against him, relishing the feel of her breasts, the gentle slope of her hips, and wishing she was bare before him. "I suppose I could be convinced to see things your way," he replied in a gravelly voice.

Cordie tipped her head back and began to play again with one of his buttons. "What would it take, my lord?"

The naughty chit was making it most uncomfortable to remain fully clothed. Marc's grin widened. "What are you offering?" As if he didn't know. He just wanted to hear her say the words.

She smiled coyly. "A kiss."

A kiss? She was a tease. Marc stroked her neck, dipped his head toward hers and whispered in her ear, "You've already kissed me, Cordelia. I want something else."

"A kiss is all I can offer," she replied softly.

"But you'll *kiss* me again. Right now, if I wish it, because you enjoy my kiss. That's not a bargaining chip, my beautiful temptress."

She sighed. "I do enjoy your kiss, but I can go forever without having it again."

The little minx knew she had him. She had to feel his straining cock against her belly. Marc stared at the pretty girl in his arms. What game was she playing? They both wanted the same thing. He could barely think straight.

Someone scratched on the other side of the door. Cordie frowned. "One moment, Sanders," she called.

Marc ran his finger along her lower lip. God he wanted to take her right now. "A kiss, then," he finally said with a wicked grin. "But I choose where." He'd make her strip down before he decided where his lips would start.

"As long as it's not out in the open for anyone else to see."

What a strange thing to say. Of course no one would see. What sorts of things did she have in mind? "My gorgeous girl, you can rest assured that no one but I will see where I plan to kiss you."

The scratch at the door came again, more insistent this time. "Coming, Sanders," Cordelia said, slipping out of Marc's grasp. Then she opened the door and rushed into the hallway.

He found the Avery's elderly butler glaring at him. "Lord *Ericht*," the man said with obvious distaste.

Marc growled at the butler. He was going to need a few minutes alone before he met with Captain Avery. The idea of meeting the army officer in his current state did put a damper on his immediate problem. When he felt he was in a sufficient condition to see the man, he stepped into the hallway and allowed the surly butler to lead him to the Avery study.

Captain Russell Avery stood when Marc entered the room. An imposing man in his regimentals, the captain frowned when he met Marc's eyes. A thought occurred to him almost immediately – it would have been much easier to seduce Cordelia Avery before this giant of a guard had returned from the battlefields. The lingering effects of the man's sister immediately evaporated.

Marc strode across the floor and offered his hand. "Captain Avery."

"Lord Haversham, please have a seat."

Marc dropped into a seat across from the captain, assessing the officer as he sat back down behind the heavy mahogany desk.

"We each have a duty to our friends, my lord, but after this situation is over we will deal with your attention to my sister. Unless you'd like to meet me or one of my brothers on a similar field of honor, you'll keep your distance from Cordelia."

Marc hadn't imagined they'd start off the conversation with threats, and he couldn't help but smirk at the man. He was an officer in Wellington's army, but Marc was a peer of the realm. They weren't on the same level, not even close. "I'll keep that in mind, Captain." Then he slid forward in his chair, leveling the man with his iciest stare. "What do you say we make this quick, sir? I imagine emotions have run high to get His Grace and the major intent on killing the other. I have no idea what precipitated the disagreement, and frankly I don't care. As I have many other places to be tonight, I propose we make the duel to first blood drawn and call it an evening. What say you?"

The captain's eyes widened in surprise, but he nodded slowly. "If that's what you think is best, my lord."

Marc rose from his spot and slapped the desk. "Excellent. See you at dawn on the north side of the park?"

The captain nodded again. "I had no idea this would be handled so efficiently."

"As I said," Marc replied, starting for the door, "I do have many other places to be."

Sixteen

WHEN the door to Staveley House was pulled open, Brendan smiled at the ancient butler who stood before him. Most butlers in Mayfair were elderly, but Merton looked as if he'd actually participated in the crusades. How the man had the energy to breathe truly was a mystery.

"This way, my lord," Merton said, and slowly ambled off down the corridor.

Brendan had no choice but to follow the old man, excruciatingly slow as he was. Finally, the butler stopped before Lord Staveley's library and pushed the door open. "My lord, the Earl of Clayworth has arrived."

David Benton, Viscount Staveley, was at the doorway in a heartbeat. His hand extended, Staveley smiled amiably. "Ah, Brendan, good to see you. Come on in."

The library was not an unusual place to find the viscount. In fact, Staveley spent most of his time in this room, perusing old books and researching something, though what that was Brendan didn't have a clue. It was one thing Staveley never spoke about.

"I'm certain you'll be glad to have Caroline back here, now that she's finished overseeing the refurbishment of my parlor."

Staveley chuckled and motioned for Brendan to find a spot in one of his leather chairs before taking a seat himself. "She'll find some other project to occupy her time. In fact, it'll just be you and me for dinner. She ran out of here not half an hour ago."

Good heavens, that was odd. Caroline could be tiresome, but she'd never abandoned a dinner guest before, at least not that Brendan knew about. "If you'd rather I come back later, Staveley —"

The viscount shook his head. "Don't be ridiculous. She's just a little scatterbrained ever since she got home this afternoon."

She'd seemed fine when she left his home. "Why? If you don't mind my asking?"

"Oh, she hadn't heard about the duel until she walked in the door. I'm afraid it put her in a frightful mood."

"Duel?" He hadn't heard about it either. He couldn't imagine who was involved to get Caroline upset. Robert was safely in Dorset, and he believed Luke had returned to Derbyshire.

"Major Moore returned today," Staveley replied, as if that answered his question.

It did not. He didn't even know the name. "Major Moore?"

Staveley nodded. "The young man was Olivia's intended. He arrived in Town this afternoon and went straight to Kelfield House."

Ah, that did explain everything then. Had Brendan been in Moore's position, he'd have done the same thing. He chose not to voice that thought, however, as Kelfield was one of Staveley's oldest friends and now a cousin by marriage. Still, there was nothing even the intrepid Caroline could do about the situation. Then his stomach tightened. "Certainly, Caroline doesn't think she can *stop* the event."

Staveley barked with laughter. "Honestly, Brendan, even my wife isn't that foolhardy."

Well, that was a relief. Brendan sat back in his seat, relaxing a bit. "Where did she run off to then?"

"I'm not sure," Staveley replied, rubbing his chin. "She got some note from Miss Avery and she tore out of here."

Miss Avery! Brendan's heart lurched. Was Cordelia in some sort of trouble? "You don't know where she went?" he asked, not even bothering to hide his panic.

The viscount shrugged. "She didn't say. I'm sure she'll tell me when she returns, she always does...well, most of the time."

Brendan leapt from his seat. "For God's sake, Staveley! How can you just let her gallivant around Town the way she does?"

"Let her?" the viscount echoed with an amused look on his face. "Have you *met* my wife? No one lets her do anything, Brendan, and I wouldn't want it any other way. She wouldn't be Caroline otherwise."

That was the most ridiculous thing he'd ever heard. He didn't even say good-bye to the viscount as he stormed from the library and out of Staveley House. South Audley Street wasn't that far. If Cordelia was in trouble, he could make it faster on foot than wait for his carriage to be brought around.

⋘⋙

A smash could be heard coming from the yellow parlor. Cordie winced at the closed door, wondering what Philip had just broken. He had taken the 'first blood drawn' stipulation rather badly. Though he was suffering, she couldn't feel guilty about her actions. Both he and Kelfield might get injured, but they'd live to see another day.

She had hoped Philip would begin to see reason. If she could just have a few minutes with him, he'd see things her way. Unfortunately, he'd holed himself up with Russell, of all people.

"I'd like to run *you* through with my sword, Avery," Philip's voice came through the oak door.

"You do now, Moore. But you'll see I was right. We just arrived in England. Do you want to be exiled in less than a day? And what if you did kill him? Do you think Olivia would thank you for making her a widow? By all accounts she loves him."

Philip said something Cordie couldn't quite make out. It sounded like a growl.

"Cut your losses," Russell advised. "She's just a girl, Philip. There are a million others out there. You're a war hero, for God's sake, they'll be lining up to set their caps for you."

"She's not *just* a girl! She was *my* girl, Russell."

Cordie closed her eyes. Even if her brother couldn't feel the pain that rolled off Philip, she could. It was a terrible situation. Truly, he deserved better, and she wished she could help him. Not that she regretted her actions. She'd saved a life, maybe two, and she wouldn't feel badly about that.

She was concerned about the deal she'd made with the marquess however. He'd had a strange look in his eye when he agreed to her kiss.

108

At the moment she'd been in such a hurry, with Sanders growing impatient on the other side of the door, Cordie hadn't clarified where he wanted to kiss her. The park again? Or maybe the gardens at Vauxhall? Somehow she wasn't certain that's what he meant at all.

This could certainly be a problem. After all, she wanted to marry the man, not be ruined by him.

The dinner chime rang, bringing her back to the present. She glanced quickly at the door that sheltered Philip and Russell, then darted for the dining room. Heaven forbid they find out she was eavesdropping.

Tristan was waiting just inside the dining room, and quickly offered her his arm, one eyebrow raised. "I can't believe you actually pulled it off," he whispered. "What did you say to Russell?"

Cordie smiled at him, allowing him to lead her to the table where their mother was already seated. "I don't have any idea what you're talking about." Until the duel was over, she wasn't about to talk about the particulars on the off chance something might change.

Tristan winked at her. "I've missed you."

"I missed you too," she said, sliding into her seat. "I'm so glad you're home, Tris."

He took the spot next to her. "Please. You haven't even had time to miss me. Betrothals, jilted naval captains..."

Cordie rolled her eyes. "He never spoke with Gregory. I was never technically betrothed."

"I was," Philip Moore remarked from the doorway, with Russell right behind him.

Cordie flushed red. She hadn't intended to say that. Poor Philip. It would be best for her not to say another word all night.

"Oh, Philip," her mother trilled, "ignore her. She's such a foolish girl and doesn't have any idea what she's saying."

Cordie let the insult roll off her. With a little luck, she could bring Haversham up to scratch, then she could avoid her mother until the end of time. Showing her anger wouldn't further her goals and would only make evading her mother more difficult in the coming days.

Russell and Philip took seats across the table, and Cordie stared down at her empty plate. Philip looked more miserable than anyone she'd ever known.

"Why is Greg holed up in Papplewick?" Tristan asked, ending the awkward silence.

"It is August, Tristan," Lady Avery replied with a frown. "I can barely drag him to Town for the season."

Sanders approached the table, confusion etched across his brow. "Lady Avery," he whispered loud enough for the entire table to hear, "Lord Clayworth is demanding to see Miss Cordelia."

Cordie's heart stopped beating. Clayworth was here? To see her? All eyes focused on her and she swallowed nervously.

"What did you do, Cordelia?" her mother asked.

She shook her head. "Nothing, Mother." Did he have a guilty conscience for not revealing her escape earlier? Was he still trying to keep her out of trouble?

"Show him in, Sanders," the baroness directed.

A moment later, the Earl of Clayworth burst into the dining room. His eyes were wild and his face flushed. He looked as if he'd been through quite an ordeal, and Cordie couldn't imagine what would have him so upset. When his eyes landed on her, he took a deep breath and began to rub the lines of worry that marred his handsome brow.

"My lord," Lady Avery began with a frown, "we were not expecting you."

Clayworth then glanced around the room, as if now noticing that everyone was gathered at the dining table. "I'm very sorry to intrude."

Her mother's face softened to a smile. "Have you dined yet, my lord?"

He shook his head. "I couldn't possibly impose on — "

"Nonsense," Lady Avery interrupted him, pointing to the open spot next to Cordie. "I insist you stay."

Clayworth's eyes flashed to Cordie's, and she sucked in a breath. His very gaze sent tingles racing across her skin. How could she possibly manage an entire meal beside him?

Tristan stood and gestured to the spot. "I'm certain my sister would prefer your company to hearing more of our tales from the battlefield."

He didn't want to stay. It was obvious in how stiffly he stood, but he inclined his head. "Of course. Thank you for your generosity."

Tristan held his position until Clayworth reached his chair, then he offered his hand in greeting. "Lieutenant Avery. The ugly fellow over there is my brother, Captain Avery, and of course our very good friend

Major Moore."

"Clayworth."

Tristan's eyes dropped to Cordie and he smiled. "Yes, I know, my lord."

He slid into the spot next to her and Cordie chanced a glance at him. "My lord," she said softly.

His twilight gaze nearly made her melt. "I'm relieved to find you well, Miss Avery," he replied as a footman quickly set a place in front of him.

Relieved to find her well? What did he expect to find? He'd seen her that very afternoon. How reckless did he think she was that she couldn't stay out of trouble for a few hours? It wasn't particularly complimentary. Her ire began to build.

"I understand," Russell broke in, "that you intend to take Cordelia for a ride along the Bath Road in your phaeton."

"On the morrow," Clayworth agreed.

"Is it particularly fast?" Russell asked

Clayworth nodded his head. "I've been told so."

"Of course," Cordie said to her brother. "Lord Clayworth does everything faster and better than anyone else."

"Cordie!" Tristan muttered under his breath.

She ignored her brothers and flashed a cheeky smile at the earl. "Or so Lord Astwick has led me to believe."

⚜

Brendan raised his brow at the lovely lady at his side. She was clearly annoyed with him, and he couldn't blame her one bit. What a fool he was! Running through Mayfair on foot, convinced she needed to be rescued, only to find her safely surrounded by her family. Army officers, for God's sake! Neither Haversham nor Brookfield would get past these men.

He was losing his bloody mind.

He somehow managed to get through dinner, answering question after question about his phaeton and horses. Though he'd be hard pressed to relay the conversation, his attention was focused solely on Cordelia, who was breathtaking even when angry at him.

When dinner came to an end, Lieutenant Avery stood with the women. "I'll forgo port, gentlemen. It has been too long since I've enjoyed female company."

Brendan rose from his seat as well. "I should be leaving."

Beside him, Cordelia took a staggered breath, and he couldn't tell if she was relieved by the fact or bothered by it. He imagined it to be the former, as she'd barely spoken three words over dinner.

"Do stay, Clayworth," Captain Avery replied. "I'd like to speak with you, if you don't mind."

Somehow Brendan kept himself from groaning. He could just imagine the warning the captain would give him, not that he could see a way out of the situation, and not that he didn't deserve it after barging in to their dinner. "Of course."

Brendan reclaimed his seat while the others left, even Major Moore. God, this was going to be more painful than he thought. He imagined the captain would quickly ask him to keep his distance from Cordelia. No brother wanted an obsessed fellow calling on his sister. Who knew what such men were capable of?

"I need to ask you a favor, Lord Clayworth."

Here it was. *Stay the bloody hell away from my sister.* He steeled himself for the words. "Yes, Captain?"

"I'm afraid I was a bit negligent in my duties this evening. I need to arrange for someone to officiate a duel between the Duke of Kelfield and my friend Major Moore."

Brendan kept his mouth from dropping open.

"It is something Lord Haversham and I should have agreed upon, but he was in and out so quickly, I'm afraid this detail slipped past me. You are known for your honor, sir, and you would be doing me a great service if you would perform the duties."

Certainly not what he was expecting. Relief washed over him. He would have agreed to just about anything if that meant he wasn't barred from Cordelia. Doing Captain Avery a favor was the least he could do. "Of course."

The captain took a long swallow of his port. "Thank God. I didn't have the heart to tell Moore I'd flubbed that last bit up. He's already furious I agreed to first blood drawn."

"First blood drawn?" Was he joking? That essentially made the duel not even worth fighting. Moore had every right to be furious. Kelfield had stolen the man's fiancée and the worst he could do was a little nick?

"Why would you agree to such a thing?"

The captain's eyes widened in surprise. "I don't know really. It seemed the thing to do. We've just returned from France. I'd hate to see my friend exiled. But I couldn't imagine it would be the first thing out of the marquess' mouth, and before I could think clearly, I'd already agreed."

"It was the first thing out of Haversham's mouth?" That didn't seem right at all. Kelfield wouldn't be happy with this turn of events either. No man would willingly agree to first blood drawn, especially when one's wife was the prize. The duke would want the major dead.

"I was a bit surprised."

That little sneak. What had Cordelia done to arrange this outcome? "Tell me, did your sister have anything to do with this?"

The captain blanched.

Dear God, she was trouble. He just hadn't realized how much until this moment.

Seventeen

CORDIE crossed the floor to Philip's side. In all the years she'd known him, he'd never seemed this distraught. She smiled. "How are you holding up, Philip?"

His frown deepened. "Have you seen her?"

Livvie. Cordie shook her head. "I've not been allowed. Did you see her?"

He nodded, pain marred his face. Cordie linked her arm with his. Poor man. She wished she could wave a magic wand and take away all his misery.

"She was there when I challenged him, begging him not to accept, then begging me to withdraw."

How awful for Livvie. She couldn't imagine what she would feel if she'd witnessed such a scene with Clayworth. She closed her eyes. It wasn't the same thing at all. Philip had been Livvie's fiancé and Kelfield was her husband. Clayworth would never be either to Cordie, and she really shouldn't think of him in such a way—it was already too hard to see him.

"I just can't believe she loves him," Philip muttered.

"Did she say that?"

Philip nodded. "I saw her face in my mind every night I was away. I only got through the war, knowing I was coming home to her."

"Oh, Philip," Cordie said softly, "you got through the war because you're a soldier and you were trained to do so."

"Many trained soldiers didn't make it home, Cordie. And I hate war. Only now I wish I was still there. I wish there was an enemy I could tear apart with my hands."

That was a bit gruesome. Cordie sucked in a breath. Before she could find words to respond to Philip, the Earl of Clayworth stood before her, wearing his usual frown. Though she couldn't imagine what he had to frown about this time. He was the one who burst through her dining room doors uninvited, acting like she couldn't be trusted more than a few hours in her own care. "My lord," she muttered.

"Major, do you mind?" Clayworth asked, offering his arm to Cordie at the same time.

"No, of course not," Philip replied.

Cordie glared at Clayworth before accepting his arm. What was he about?

"Miss Avery," he began smoothly, "I'm afraid something has come up, and we'll have to postpone our ride."

Something came up? What could possibly have come up since dinner? Cordie shrugged. She should probably keep her distance from him anyway.

"My dear, would now be a good time for you to show me those books on Scandinavia?"

A blush crept up her neck at the memory those words brought. The last time they were in a library together, the way he'd kissed her. She couldn't be alone with him again, not like that. It was already too hard to be in his presence. Besides, she was quite annoyed with him at the moment.

"No need, sir. Tristan lived there for a year. I'm certain he'd be happy to tell you whatever you'd like to know."

He squeezed her fingers meaningfully. "But your brother seems otherwise engaged at the moment, and I am very interested now."

Cordie narrowed her eyes on him. Irritating man. "I'm sure I can convince him to share his memories with you."

"Cordelia," her mother barked, "why are you being difficult? Show Lord Clayworth to the library."

She'd like to show him right out the front door. "My lord," she almost growled.

When he calmly raised his brow, she wanted to jump out of her skin. She allowed him to lead her to the corridor, but once they were alone, she dropped his arm and stalked down the hallway. Clayworth said nothing, but he was right behind her the entire time. She turned one corner, then another, finally stopping at the library door.

"There you are, my lord. I believe Tris' books are all on the top of the first shelf. Do help yourself."

She turned to leave, but he grasped her arm, forcing her into the library and sending jolts of awareness through her. Blast him for making her heart race when she was so angry with him. Cordie tipped her head back and looked up into his twilight eyes.

"What did you promise Haversham to garner his support for your little plan?" Clayworth asked evenly.

Her mouth fell open. How could he possibly know what transpired between herself and the marquess? Was he spying on her? "How dare you?"

"How dare *you*?" he countered, towering over her. "Did you *not* promise me this very afternoon you'd be careful?"

She blanched. "It was for a good cause."

"A good cause?" he echoed menacingly. "There is *no* cause that is worth your safety, Cordelia. For God's sake, the haphazard way in which you go through life is enough to put me in an early grave."

"I take offense to that. I do not go through life in a haphazard way. I think things through logically and make sound decisions."

"Indeed?" Clayworth asked, arching one golden eyebrow. "What did you promise Haversham?"

Cordie wrenched her arm out of his grasp and stalked further into the library, putting distance between them. "I don't owe you any answers, sir."

In the blink of an eye, he was before her. "Tell me, Cordelia, or I swear I'll call Haversham out myself."

Her heart seized at the image of Clayworth facing the marquess on a field of *honor* over her. What a horrible thought, especially after all she'd done to make sure Philip and Kelfield didn't kill each other. She didn't want to contemplate such an event. His dark eyes remained fixed on her and Cordie shook her head. "A kiss."

"A kiss?" he echoed. At her nod, his jaw clenched. "You let *him* kiss you?"

Cordie nodded. He had kissed her that evening. She decided it was best, however, not to mention that the terms of her agreement with the marquess had yet to be filled. With the blue fire in his eyes, it seemed the logical thing.

Despite his fierce look, Clayworth gently touched her cheek, and Cordie swallowed nervously. He closed the small gap between then and lowered his head. "Did he make your heart beat faster? Did his touch make your knees weak? Did the feel of his lips make you forget everything?"

No. "It was a very nice kiss," she whispered. If she'd never have been kissed before, it would have been a magnificent kiss. If she'd only been kissed by Gabriel Seaton, it would have been a magnificent kiss. The marquess was quite talented, but his lips, his hands, his presence only made her yearn for Clayworth, which made no sense at all. *He* was the exact wrong sort of man for her.

"My kiss is not nice," his gravelly voice rolled over her. His hands moved to her waist and he quickly pulled her against him. Clayworth kissed her neck and jaw, searing heat wherever he touched her. "*Ma minouche dangereuse*" he whispered across her lips, staring at her with such intensity, Cordie lost her breath.

Before she could speak, his demanding lips claimed hers. Cordie's mind spun. She'd longed for this for weeks, needed it, craved it. His tongue touched her lips, searching for entry. Cordie opened for him, and she relished the taste of port when his tongue touched hers. Shaking, she ran her hands up his muscled chest and wrapped her arms around his neck, pulling his weight against her.

Clayworth moaned and backed her into a wall lined with books. His lips, his tongue never stopped moving on her, and a welcome heat pooled deep in her belly. Cordie kissed him back, nipping at his lips and mingling her tongue with his. She'd never felt so wanton in all her days.

If he'd just touch her breast or her bottom, she was certain she could assuage the desire that was raging through her. But his hands remained securely at her waist. She shimmied against him. "Please."

His lips left hers and trailed along her jaw to her ear. "I can't, *ma minouche*, or I'll never stop."

She didn't want him to stop. She wanted him to touch her everywhere, to hold her forever.

Clayworth's tongue touched her ear lobe, sending new waves of desire washing over her. No one had ever done such a thing. She was barely breathing. "I want you, Cordelia." His raspy voice tickled her ear.

Oh, she wanted him too. "Then touch me," she begged.

"Marry me," he countered.

He'd somehow said the wrong thing. Cordelia pulled out of his arms and took a staggering breath. He wanted her right back where she was, and took a step towards her. She raised a hand to stop his advance.

"I-I can't," she finally said.

Fury built inside Brendan. "Why the devil not?" Never in his life had he felt such need, such fire for a woman. He knew she felt it too. Whenever he held her, she nearly melted into him.

"You're not right for me," she whispered.

"I beg to differ," he couldn't help but growl.

Her pretty brow furrowed as she fumbled for an answer. "You, well, you're *you*, and — well, you couldn't possibly understand."

True. He *couldn't* understand a word she was saying. "You're not making any sense, Cordelia."

"I know," she whispered.

"Do your affections lay elsewhere?" he asked, echoing her words to Brookfield.

She turned away from him and her shoulders sagged forward. "Please don't ask me that."

It was the first ray of hope he'd felt. She couldn't answer him, because her affections lay with him. He knew they did. So whatever was keeping her from him, whatever Haversham held over her, Brendan would have to find out. Holding Cordelia Avery in his arms was the first real joy he'd known in forever. "I'm not giving up on you," he vowed.

She looked over her shoulder at him and frowned. "I wish you would. You're making this very difficult for me."

"Good," he answered. If she was intent on pushing him away, he wanted it to be difficult. He wanted it to be damn near impossible.

Eighteen

ALL of Avery House was silent. Philip and Russell were already gone and the sun was barely on the horizon. Though the outcome of the contest, one way or the other, didn't matter to Cordie, she still paced a path around her room. She wished she could be at Kelfield House with Livvie. Hopefully, Lady Staveley was with her. Hopefully, she'd shared the contents of Cordie's letter with Livvie, informing them of the first blood drawn stipulation. Hopefully, her friend was experiencing some peace, knowing that neither man would perish because of her.

A soft knock sounded on her door, startling her. Quickly, Cordie threw on her wrapper, then rushed to door. Tristan stood before her, two cups of tea in his hands.

"I knew you were awake. Here," he said, offering her one of the cups.

She opened her door wide and her brother strode inside, collapsing in one of her chintz chairs. "What a night."

That was an understatement. She couldn't sleep at all with thoughts of Clayworth popping up in her mind just as she was about to doze off. Why was he making things so difficult? Why couldn't he just be the cold, heartless man she'd always thought him to be? If she wasn't distracted by him, she'd have already found a way to bring Haversham up to scratch.

"They're gone?" she asked, knowing the answer and sinking into a chair opposite him.

Tristan nodded. "So, will you still not discuss Haversham with me?"

"I'd rather not. You'll tell me I'm making a huge mistake, and I'd prefer not to hear that if you don't mind."

He raised his brow and quirked a grin at her. "Is that what I'll say? Have you had the entire conversation in your head?"

She sipped her tea, avoiding his question.

"And what about Clayworth? Is he off limits as well?"

"Most definitely."

"What a shame." Tristan tried to hide a smirk behind his cup. "I was dying to know what you did to get him so...excited."

"Excited?" she echoed. What was he talking about, for heaven's sake? "I don't think he gets excited about anything. Angry, irritated, yes. Excited, no. He's far too serious and intense for that."

Her brother choked on his tea. "The man I saw last night was excited, and you'll have to take my word for it." Then he laughed to himself, obviously at her expense.

Cordie rolled her eyes. Brothers could be the most aggravating of all creatures.

"I think mother's right, by the by. I think he will offer for you. He appears quite the besotted man."

She winced at his words. All night she'd thought of Clayworth's passionate proposal, how her heart ached to accept it. She needed a plan to bring Haversham up to scratch. "Tris, I know I said I didn't want to talk about the marquess..."

Her brother's jovial expression vanished immediately. "He's dangerous, Cor."

He couldn't possibly be as dangerous as Clayworth was to her. "He doesn't seem like it," she replied quietly.

"Well, that's just something else you'll have to take my word for."

He knew. He knew whatever awful thing Haversham had done. She could see it on his face. But how could she get him to tell her? By feigning complete innocence, perhaps? Convince him that telling her was the only way to keep her safe. That might work. If not, she could always resort to her newest weapon against her brother — tears.

She giggled. "Oh, Tristan, I'm certain you're mistaken. He has a wicked reputation, I know, but he seems harmless to me."

Her brother narrowed his eyes on her.

"And I daresay I've spent more time in his company than you have." With any luck, she'd spend a lot more.

"Cordelia," he began.

"I think men see things differently than women," she went on, as if he hadn't spoken at all. "I mean, look at Kelfield. All you men think he's wicked and dangerous, but I've seen him with Livvie, Tristan. I don't believe a more gentlemanly man exists." That wasn't entirely true, but she figured it would get her brother's ire up.

"I meant it when I said I'd put a ball in his skull, Cordie. You're my little sister and I'd die before I let him touch one hair on your head."

"Oh, Tris," she said, rolling her eyes. "Surely, you're overreacting. I mean what could he have done that is *so* bad? He's always acted the perfect gentleman with me." That was far from the truth, but Tristan didn't need to know the particulars.

With a frown, he placed his cup on the small table. Then he turned his attention back to Cordie, studying her. Finally he heaved a sigh. "I love you more than anything, Cordie. You know I'd never want you to be hurt, and I'd kill any blackguard that tried."

"No brother is ever happy with the man his sister sets her cap for. Matthew Greywood has made Phoebe's life miserable. And —"

"That's hardly it," he interrupted. "Russell and I both like Clayworth just fine."

She smiled sadly at that. "But I haven't set my cap for the earl."

Tristan rubbed his brow. "Why not, Cordie? He's wealthy, well respected, seems besotted with you."

Cordie took another sip of tea. When she lowered her glass, she frowned at her brother. "Don't you remember how miserable he made Marina?" At Tristan's nod, Cordie continued, "I don't want that to be me."

"But you're not like Marina, it might not be the same."

"Please, Tris, we were talking about Haversham. Why do you think he's dangerous?"

Her brother grasped her hand and squeezed. "I became friends with a cavalry officer from Sussex during the war. Lieutenant Colonel Oliver Burke," he began as Cordie listened patiently. "A decade ago, Burke's older sister was betrothed to Haversham. The marquess did something, I'm not sure what it was, but Miss Burke called off the wedding on account of it. Apparently, Haversham didn't take kindly to being jilted and made to look like a laughingstock before the *ton*, so he plotted revenge against the girl."

"Revenge?" Cordie echoed, caught up in the story. After all, she'd jilted Captain Seaton. Would he plot revenge against her? The idea made her shudder.

"Burke says he set out to destroy her, one way or another. He forcibly absconded with her from a house party and no one could find them for days. The act alone ruined her, which was Haversham's plan. She jilted him, and he was going to make sure no one would have her afterwards."

Cordie's mouth dropped open. The poor girl. She blinked at her brother. "What happened to her?"

Tristan sat back in his chair, a bit more comfortable now. "Well, everyone was searching for her, naturally. A friend of Burke's older brother was the one who found her. Chivalrous chap married her to keep the gossip down. Not that it mattered. She never quite recovered, socially speaking, from the ordeal. She and her husband live quietly in the country somewhere."

It was quite a story, not that it affected her terribly. She had no plans to jilt him at all. In fact, the faster she could get him to the altar the better. However it was good to know what he was capable of, the way his mind worked. That could be useful in the future. Cordie smiled at her brother. "Tris, thanks for telling me."

"So you see how dangerous he is." Tristan's frown deepened. "Don't give me heart palpitations. Stay away from the scoundrel, will you?"

Cordie nodded. Another lie. Once she was Lady Haversham, everything would turn out all right and Tristan would forgive her.

Cordie's three brothers were all fairly different from each other, but the only thing they apparently all agreed on was their abhorrence of attending societal affairs. Since Gregory was safely ensconced in Nottinghamshire, he was the only one excused from attending the Sunderland ball. The other two were not so fortunate.

Upon entering the festive room, Russell made his way directly to the refreshment table, while their mother sequestered herself in one of the gaming parlors. Tristan grimaced at Cordie. "So I suppose you're left in *my* care."

"Sorry to be such a burden," she replied tartly, looking over the sea of people, hoping to catch a glimpse of Livvie. It seemed unlikely that a society stickler like Lady Sunderland would invite the scandalous duke and duchess to her ball, but Cordie still held out hope.

"Miss Avery," came the stern voice of the dowager Marchioness of Astwick. "My darling girl, it has been forever."

Cordie turned around, gracing the dowager with a smile. It was so strange that the woman had taken to her, not that she was about to do a thing that would change the situation. The astonished look on Tristan's face was priceless, however, as he stepped backwards and inhaled sharply. If Cordie didn't know better, she'd think her brother had swallowed his own tongue. "Good evening, Lady Astwick," Cordie greeted her with a curtsy.

"It is now," the dowager stated matter-of-factly. "Where have you been keeping yourself the last few weeks?"

"I've been in Norfolk visiting friends, my lady."

"Norfolk? Who would ever live in *Norfolk*?" the old woman barked.

Cordie stifled a laugh. A good many people lived in Norfolk, but the dowager made it sound as if was the end of the world. "Lord Malvern's family, my lady."

The dowager made an unpleasant face as if she smelled something awful. "That silly Greywood chit?"

Phoebe was silly, but Lady Astwick shouldn't say so with such a derisive tone. "Miss Phoebe Greywood is one of my dear friends. I would hardly call her silly."

The old woman's light eyes danced merrily. "I do like your spirit, Miss Avery. Loyalty is a rare trait in this young generation, even when it's misguided."

"Am I misguided?" Cordie asked, raising her brow.

"You and I both know that Greywood girl is a simpering fool."

"Lady Astwick!" she chastised.

The dowager squeezed Cordie's hand. "Your loyalty is commendable, Miss Avery." Then she turned her attention to Tristan and narrowed her icy eyes. "And who are you?"

Tristan gulped and then squared his shoulders.

"Lady Astwick, this is my brother Lieutenant Tristan Avery. He's just returned with the 45ᵗʰ Foot from Toulouse."

The dowager's expression lightened incrementally as she assessed him. "I assume, Lieutenant, that you showed more bravery on the battlefield."

"I don't believe my adversary was as formidable as you, my lady," Tristan replied, blushing just a bit.

"Ah," the old woman began, looking over Cordie's shoulder, "just the gentleman I wanted to see. Brendan Reese!" she bellowed.

A heartbeat later, the earl stood before them and offered a slight bow to the marchioness. "Lady Astwick, always a pleasure."

"Clayworth, why are you wasting your time trying to charm *me*? Miss Avery is right here, or have you lost your eyesight?"

His twilight eyes flashed to hers and Cordie's mouth went dry. He was so startlingly handsome and she couldn't look at him without remembering his passionate kiss and heartfelt proposal.

"My eyes are always on Miss Avery, my lady, but thank you for your concern."

The dowager's eyes actually twinkled, a miracle in itself. "Would you care for some advice, Brendan?"

If he was trying to suppress a grin, he failed miserably. "I don't believe you've ever asked that of anyone before."

"You may only dance with Miss Avery twice without raising eyebrows. So I suggest you wait for waltzes and make the best of your time in between."

"What if I want to raise eyebrows?" he asked, now grinning from ear to ear, making Cordie's heart leap in the process.

"You've already done so, with your attention to the girl, Brendan. There's no point in appearing gauche."

"Wonderful words of wisdom," Clayworth replied, merriment evident in his voice. Then he refocused his dark blue eyes on Cordie. "Miss Avery, would you care to take a turn about the room with me while I wait for the next waltz?"

It wasn't even possible for her to refuse. Not with the dowager essentially forcing them together. "Of course, my lord."

When she took his arm, tingles raced across Cordie's skin. Touching him should be avoided at all costs. As they stepped away from the dowager and Tristan, Cordie noticed a mortified expression on her brother's face. Apparently Clayworth noticed the look too and he chuckled. "He'll be all right. She's not as frightening as she seems."

"She's downright terrifying," Cordie replied.

"She adores you, which is easy to see." His gloved fingers squeezed her hand on his arm.

Cordie glanced at the other couples in the middle of the room enjoying a spirited reel. "On the contrary she seems to adore *you*, my lord, and by extension me."

He shrugged. "Such is the case when someone has known you your entire life."

Or not. Her mother had known Livvie since infancy, and now she wouldn't acknowledge her if they were the only two in a room. "I had no idea your families were so close."

"She apparently formed an attachment for my mother when she first arrived in England. I'm certain mother would have had a much more difficult time navigating the *ton* without Lady Astwick's council." He frowned when he said that and looked out above the sea of people, seemingly lost in another time and place.

Cordie had never seen him look so forlorn before and she couldn't help stepping a bit closer to him. Everyone knew the late Lady Clayworth had doted on her children. "Do you miss your mother?"

"I think about her every day," he answered in a cold voice that sent icy shivers up her spine.

Perhaps Lady Clayworth wasn't as doting as she appeared in public. Perhaps it was all for show. Cordie was familiar with that breed of mother, and she squeezed the earl's arm.

"I understand Major Moore has returned to Nottinghamshire," he said evenly, changing the subject.

Cordie nodded. "He left right after the duel. Do you believe Kelfield was hurt badly?" Russell had refused to tell her a thing.

He looked at her out of the corner of his eye. "You do seem overly concerned with every scoundrel in Town."

She scowled at him. "I promise not to throw myself at Kelfield. He is married to my dearest friend, which is why I'm concerned for him."

"He'll live. The injury was minor, and not as deep as I'm sure Moore would have liked."

"Barbaric behavior, duels." She shuddered. "I'll never understand the male of our species."

Clayworth laughed. "We're not that difficult to understand, *ma minouche*."

"Why *do* you call me your kitten, my lord?"

He stopped walking and stared down at her, a lighthearted smile on his lips. "Because you're adorable and you make me want to play with you."

Cordie's heart stopped beating. She knew it did. When he looked at her in such a way, it was as if time stood still and no one but them existed. She almost sighed.

Clayworth dipped his head towards her and whispered, "Among other things."

What *things*? Her breath caught. The way he said the words sent spirals of desire straight to her core. It really was too dangerous to spend an inordinate amount of time with him.

The first chords of a waltz began and Clayworth grinned at her. "My dance, I believe."

He whisked her out on the floor with smooth elegance. Cordie felt lost as she stared up into his eyes, so dark, so piercing. It would be so easy to give in to him, to accept his proposal, to follow her heart. If she wasn't careful, she'd do that very thing. It was imperative that she remember who he was.

Controlling. He'd never allow her the freedom she so craved. After only five minutes in his company, she'd realized that.

Cold. How many times had she listened to Marina bemoan his cool indifference? More times than she could count. If she lost her heart to him, it would destroy her when his interest turned elsewhere.

"Why do you look so serious, *ma minouche*?" he asked, as he spun her into a turn. "Of the two of us, you're supposed to be the carefree one."

Cordie forced a smile to her face. "Just woolgathering, my lord."

His twilight eyes narrowed. "Do you think I can't tell the difference between your genuine smiles and your fraudulent ones?"

Cordie gaped at him. How was it even possible he could know such things about her? Her own mother couldn't tell the difference.

"It's all in your eyes," Clayworth answered her unasked question. "They sparkle with life when you're truly happy. What's troubling you,

Cordelia?"

She shook her head. "You wouldn't understand."

"You've said that before. Explain it to me, and I'll try my hardest."

What could she possibly say to him? *I want to accept your proposal, but I'm afraid.* That wouldn't do. "I'm in a quandary, my lord," she finally said. "I don't even understand it myself. So I have no idea how to explain it to you."

He frowned at that, but said nothing else. Clayworth continued to lead her around the room, never pulling her closer than was proper. Never moving his hand along her back. Never whispering scandalous suggestions in her ear. And still she wanted him more than ever. The more time she spent with him, the more she wanted to be with him.

He was dangerous to her plans.

As the waltz came to an end, Clayworth wasted no time, and led her out onto a balcony away from the prying eyes of the *ton*.

Nineteen

BRENDAN wanted just a bit of privacy. Something was going on in Cordelia's head, and he'd never get a straight answer out of her with an audience. It would be hard enough with just the two of them. He'd never met a woman who was so evasive in his entire life. Marina had always ranted and raved, hollering at the top of her lungs. Her motives and thoughts had never been a secret.

He directed her to an area of the balcony, hidden in the shadows. The perfect place for a lovers' tryst. While that would have been a nice distraction and his body hungered for it, she was already skittish and he couldn't risk her bolting at the moment.

"Why did you bring me out here, my lord?" she asked, her green eyes reflecting the moon above.

"There are too many ears in there," he replied evenly. "And I wanted to talk to you."

"Talk?" She sounded suspicious.

"Cordie?" Lieutenant Avery's voice came from the entry to ballroom. "Are you out here?"

"Here, Tristan," she said, stepping away from Brendan. "Lord Clayworth was allowing me a breath of fresh air."

The lieutenant grunted. "Honorable intentions or not, Clayworth, I do wish you wouldn't put my sister's reputation in jeopardy."

"Oh, for heaven's sake, Tris!" she whispered.

But he was right. Brendan sighed. "Of course, Lieutenant, my apologies." He walked to where Cordelia stood. She was glaring at her brother and Brendan bit back a smile. She was so full of life. He absolutely adored her. "Miss Avery," he said, offering her his arm.

For the first time ever, she took his arm without pause, and Brendan's heart expanded in his chest. If he could only get her to agree to his proposal as easily.

"We were just talking, Tris," she said tartly.

The lieutenant winked at his sister. "Well, you can just *talk* in there, with everyone's eyes on you."

If her brothers had returned from France just a few weeks earlier, he would never have put himself in the position to protect her. He'd have never gotten close to her. He would never have fallen for her independent spirit and youthful naïveté. He would never have lost his heart to her. "He's right, Cordelia," Brendan whispered.

She tugged on his arm and pulled him back through the doors, past her brother into the light of the ballroom. "It's not enough I have *her* watching my every move. Now I've got those two hovering like vultures," she muttered under her breath.

Brendan touched her chin and tipped her head back, so she had to look at him. "He's doing his duty as your brother. I might very well have ravished you back there."

She rolled her green eyes. "You are all that is proper, my lord. I'm certain you would never consider doing *that*."

Only every night since he'd met her. "Don't be so sure," he replied quietly, still gazing into her eyes.

"Cordie!" came a girlish squeal from behind them.

She let go of his arm, turned around, and embraced a raven-haired chit. The same girl from the park, if Brendan wasn't mistaken. Miss Greywood.

"Phoebe!" Cordelia gushed. "I didn't know you'd returned to Town."

"How are you?" Miss Greywood asked, with more feeling than Brendan could understand. The intensity of the girl's stare sent chills down his spine, as if there was a deeper, more sinister meaning in her words.

Cordelia blushed slightly and shook her head. "I'm fine. Really."

Something was going on. The two girls looked at each other, conversing silently with only their eyes, and Brendan wished to hell he knew what it was. After he convinced Cordelia to marry him, he'd sit her down and have a long talk about her proclivity of keeping secrets. Though to be honest, he did have a few of his own, didn't he? Of course, after they were married, he wouldn't need to keep those secrets from her. The Averys would give him his mother's letters and there would be nothing left to hide.

Above Cordelia's head, Brendan spotted Lieutenant Avery looking sheepish. Poor fellow, he was simply doing his duty by his sister. Brendan nodded at him. In the lieutenant's shoes he'd do the same, or should have done it better with Flora all those years ago. The officer started towards their small group.

"Tristan," Cordelia said coolly, eyeing him up and down.

"Cor," he said softly.

She turned her attention back to Miss Greywood. "Phoebe, you've never met my brother, have you?"

The girl shook her head, her pretty black curls bounced against her alabaster shoulders.

"Phoebe Greywood, my brother, Lieutenant Tristan Avery," Cordelia introduced, gesturing from one to the other.

"A pleasure, Miss Greywood," the lieutenant offered with a bow.

Miss Greywood giggled. "Lieutenant, I've heard so much about you. How nice to finally meet you."

The officer groaned and glanced at his sister. "I'm certain I'm much nicer than whatever she said."

Miss Greywood giggled again. She had a pleasant laugh, if one liked giggly girls. It was apparent, however, that Lieutenant Avery did not and he frowned just a bit.

Their small group increased by one when Captain Avery joined them, draping an arm over the lieutenant's shoulder. "Keeping Cordie out of trouble, Tris?"

"Trying," the younger officer admitted.

Miss Greywood's giggle evaporated as she stared at the army captain, and her blue eyes sparkled with wonder.

"Very amusing, Russell." Cordelia leveled the captain with her most haughty look. "Phoebe, this is unfortunately another brother of mine—Captain Russell Avery. Russell, this is my very good friend, Miss Greywood. Do try to be your most charming."

The captain took Miss Greywood's hand and pressed a kiss to her gloved knuckles. "I'm always charming."

"Or so he believes," Cordelia muttered so quietly only Brendan could hear.

"Oh, dear!" Phoebe Greywood squeaked.

"What is it?" Cordelia asked, stepping towards her friend. Phoebe whispered something in Cordelia's ear, then both girls straightened.

"It'll just take a needle and thread, Phoeb," Cordelia offered with a smile, not a genuine one. She then turned to her brothers, her pretty green eyes narrowed to slits. "We're going to mend a torn flounce in the retiring room, in case one of you wants to stand guard."

The captain shook his head, oblivious to her irritation or immune to it. "I'm certain you can handle that all on your own."

The two girls took off, vanishing through the doorway. In the pit of Brendan's stomach, he felt something wasn't quite right. He glanced at the two officers who groused about their forced attendance at this particular event. Neither of them seemed concerned about Cordelia at the moment. Was he overreacting again, like when he sprinted through Mayfair only to find her safely in the company of her family? Most likely. He *was* losing his mind.

⚜

"What is it, Phoebe?" Cordie asked as soon as they were out of the ballroom.

Phoebe grabbed her hand, pulled her down the corridor and around a corner, finally stopping in front of a quiet salon. "Lord Haversham," she whispered. "I bumped into him when I arrived tonight. He wants to see you."

Cordie sucked in a breath. The marquess was here? "Where?"

Phoebe's eyes shot to the doors of the salon. "I promised I'd bring you. Are you still sure about this?" She looked back towards the ballroom. "Lord Clayworth seems so…"

"I'm sure," Cordie assured her, though she wasn't quite convinced herself. She had made this decision, however, when her mind was clear. It had to be the right course. After all, her mind was much more rational than her heart. The marquess represented everything she wanted in life. She needed to keep the ultimate goal in mind.

Phoebe frowned.

"Phoeb," she said quietly, "if my brothers see you, they'll wonder where I am. Can you hide out in the library or something until I find you?"

Her friend nodded. "But don't take too long. I would like to dance tonight."

"Of course," Cordie answered with a smile.

Phoebe blushed. "And your brother—Captain Avery, is he...?"

"Unspoken for," Cordie finished. "I'll see what I can do."

Phoebe pushed her towards the parlor door. "Do hurry then."

Cordie pushed the door open and stepped inside. Haversham leaned against the side wall with a generous amount of whiskey in his glass. When his light blue eyes fell on her, a roguish smile lit up his face.

"I was starting to lose my patience, angel," he drawled placing his glass on the mantle and pushing himself away from the wall.

Cordie shut the door behind her and started toward the marquess. "I couldn't let anyone note my absence, my lord."

"Marc," he reminded her.

"Marc," she echoed softly, closing the gap between them.

He touched her cheek and smiled. "So there is the little matter of our deal, Cordelia."

"A kiss," she replied. "But not here. There are too many people about." Clayworth, in particular. It would be terribly difficult to kiss the marquess knowing the earl was so close. She didn't know if she could do it. Distance was a necessity.

His smile deepened and he ran his fingers along the column of her neck. "My thoughts exactly. We'll need to go somewhere else."

"Somewhere else?" Cordie blinked at him. "But my family, my brothers are in the other room. I can't leave now."

"Your brothers." Marc frowned. "Did you know Captain Avery threatened me?"

"Russell *threatened* you?" Her voice rose an octave. The interfering, overprotective lout!

"He said he'd call me out if I came near you again, but I can't seem to help myself."

How dare Russell think he could take control of her life in such a manner? She was perfectly capable of making her own decisions. How was she going to get Haversham to propose if he wasn't allowed near her? Not that she was allowed near him, but that was another matter altogether. Russell could cost her the only chance she had at becoming the Marchioness of Haversham. Blast him!

"Where do you want to take me?" she asked, her mind made up.

"Somewhere quiet." His gravelly voice washed over her. "Somewhere we can be alone."

Twenty

HOW long could it take to repair a bloody flounce? Brendan kept his eyes glued to the entryway, his unease growing with every minute that passed. He shook his head. He was being ridiculous. What sort of trouble could she have gotten herself into?

Viscount Brookfield strode through the door, wearing a rather threadbare jacket and a desperate look. Brendan's wariness doubled. Cordelia couldn't be alone with Brookfield about. Who knew what he was capable of? Brendan doubted Phoebe Greywood could hold off the fortune-hunter.

"You're making a mistake," the lieutenant warned his brother. "That chit's giggle is enough to make one jump off the cliffs of Dover."

The captain chuckled. "She seemed delightful to me."

Brendan cleared his throat, garnering both officers' attention. "Your sister has been gone quite a while."

Lieutenant Avery smirked at him. "Watch it, Clayworth, you're in danger of revealing your hand where Cordie's concerned."

"She's awful with a needle and thread," the captain added. "Consider yourself warned, though you didn't hear that from me."

"I have a bad feeling," Brendan admitted, certain the two fellows would think he'd lost his mind.

Captain Avery sighed. "Very well, Clayworth, if it will make you feel better I'll track her down." Then he added as an afterthought, "And the pretty Miss Greywood."

The lieutenant rolled his eyes. "It should be quite the campaign for you to locate the retiring room, Russell. Good luck with your endeavors." He then turned his attention back to the dancers just a few feet away, grumbling something about stupid societal affairs.

Brendan watched the captain leave the room and took a calming breath. He was being foolish. He knew he was. He just couldn't shake the uncomfortable feeling that something was wrong. He considered going after the captain, but figured the officer had the situation under control. The man was Cordelia's brother, and at the moment Brendan didn't have any claim to her.

It felt like a lifetime before Captain Avery re-entered the ballroom, his face ashen white. Brendan and Lieutenant Avery noticed him at the same moment and quickly crossed the room.

"What is it?" the lieutenant asked.

"I can't find her," the captain admitted. "Lady Sunderland has four retiring rooms. Two on this level and two above. No one has seen either her or Miss Greywood in any of them."

"We'll split up," Brendan ordered. "They've got to be here somewhere." At least he prayed they were.

~~~

Phoebe paced the library for what felt like the millionth time. How much longer would she have to wait? Cordie had said the library, hadn't she? Phoebe pulled out an ancient tome with a dark, red spine with golden lettering. Ancient Rome. Not even remotely interesting. She slid the book back in place and began her pacing again.

The door opened and she sucked in a breath. Who, besides her, would go traipsing about the library during a ball?

"Cordie?" a male voice called.

Oh, no! Oh, no! Oh, no!

Phoebe bit her lower lip and started to back towards the far side of the library. There was a nice little alcove she'd noticed earlier, and it would be the perfect place to hide. But then something caught her at the back of her legs and she stumbled backwards, falling on her bottom. "Oh!" she cried, as the wind whooshed out her. Immediately, she covered her mouth in horror.

How stupid could she be? Now he, whoever he was, would surely find her.

At that moment, Lieutenant Avery stepped around the corner of a shelf and stared down at her, relief washed across his face. "Thank God!" He rushed forward and helped her to her feet. "Are you all right, Miss Greywood?"

Unable to find her voice, Phoebe nodded.

"Where is Cordie?" he asked, his golden brown eyes boring into her.

"Cordie?" she squeaked. What was she supposed to do now? She couldn't tell them where she was? That was sure to land them both in trouble.

His eyes suddenly narrowed. "Yes, my sister, your friend. Where is Cordelia?"

Phoebe gulped, shaking her head.

"Answer me!" he nearly growled.

Phoebe backed away from the lieutenant. He seemed fairly dangerous and she didn't want to be too close to him. "I-I'm not certain."

"You're not certain?" he asked with a frown. "Why didn't you return to the ballroom?"

"I-I was looking for a book."

"A book?"

"On Ancient Rome. I find the era fascinating."

He stalked towards her, disbelief etched across his brow. "And I'm Julius Caesar. Where is my sister, Miss Greywood?"

"I've already told you. I'm not certain." She turned on her heel to escape the officer. Every moment spent with him, his ire seemed to rise and she'd rather not be around should he explode like Mount Vesuvius.

"Where do you think you're going?" he demanded.

"Back to the ballroom. It was your suggestion, Lieutenant, and I believe a very good one. So nice making your acquaintance." Just as she started for the door, she tripped again. Blast her clumsiness! She stared at the angry, upside down face of Lieutenant Avery, hovering over her.

"You seem to be in quite the hurry, Miss Greywood."

Phoebe swallowed nervously. "No, just accident prone, Lieutenant." She scrambled back to her feet and started towards her exit, when the officer snared her about the waist and pulled her against the wall of his chest.

"Where is my sister?"

"Un-unhand me," she begged, prying at his fingers.

His grasp tightened. He was too strong for her. "You tell me where Cordie is and you'll gain your freedom," he hissed in her ear.

Phoebe shook her head. Cordie needed time to bring the marquess up to scratch. She couldn't tell anyone where she was. "I-I already told you. I don't know."

"I think you know exactly where she is."

"She's probably still in the retiring room." This was perfect. This was her escape. "I'll be happy to search the room for you."

"You little liar," he growled. "I know damn well neither of you were ever in any retiring room. Now start speaking or I'll get out my horsewhip."

Having seen the scars on Cordie's back, Phoebe believed him instantly. Her heart pounded and she took a steadying breath. Why hadn't Cordie come back for her? "Sh-she's in one of the parlors at the front of the house."

The lieutenant did not release her as promised. Instead he pushed her towards the doorway, maintaining his position of half a step behind her. "Show me."

Phoebe nodded. There was nothing else she could do.

In the corridor, they bumped into the handsome Captain Avery and Phoebe's heart leapt to her throat. He looked just as panicked as his brother, and she saw her chances with him dwindle away.

"Miss Greywood, where have you been? Where is Cordie?" the captain asked.

"Don't listen to a word she says," the lieutenant advised. "She's going to *show* us where Cordie is." He pushed her forward a bit. Obviously, the man still thought he was on the battlefield and hadn't adjusted to life in the civilized world. Phoebe felt like a prisoner of war.

"Do you really think it's necessary to manhandle her?" The captain's voice came from behind them.

"She's already tried to run off twice. I'm not taking any chances."

Phoebe led them to the parlor where Cordie and Haversham were holed up and tried to wrench herself free of the lieutenant's hold. "Please, you're bruising me."

"Tris, let her go," his brother directed.

The lieutenant freed her to throw open the door, but the room was empty. There wasn't a sign of Cordie or the marquess anywhere. Both officers' eyes bored into hers. Phoebe shook her head in confusion. "But this is where I left them."

"Them?" Lieutenant Avery barked. "Who was with her?"

"Tris!" the captain growled. Then he focused his startlingly green eyes on Phoebe. "Who was with her?"

Cordie should be here. Was she in some sort of trouble? Phoebe shook her head. She had to tell the truth. If something happened to Cordie, it would all be her fault. "Lord Haversham," she whispered.

Both men's mouths dropped open, and Phoebe felt like the biggest fool.

"God in heaven!" Captain Avery blanched.

"You *left* her with him?" the lieutenant demanded.

"It's not Miss Greywood's fault, Tristan," the captain replied quietly.

"What has she done?"

"Ruined herself completely."

⌒⌒⌒

Brendan could hardly believe his ears. He'd just happened to stumble upon the brothers Avery and Miss Greywood when he overheard their conversation. His adorable Cordelia had gone off with Haversham? His heart ached at the thought of her in the marquess' clutches. As worldly as she made herself appear, she was actually a very innocent, naïve girl. But she wouldn't stay that way for long, if someone didn't do something.

Memories of Flora after her lover had abandoned her, rushed into Brendan's mind. He'd rather be hung for treason than let the same thing happen to Cordelia.

There had to be something he could do. If he could just find her. Years ago when the marquess had taken Ella Burke, he'd fled to his Yorkshire estate. Of course, they'd started out in the county, and Brendan didn't think he'd go that far away. So the lout's Mayfair home seemed the place to start. It was the closest place to look anyway. He prayed he'd make it there in time.

Twenty-One

IT WAS only a short distance from the Sunderland's to Haversham's enormous home in Upper Grosvenor, so it wouldn't take long to arrive. Cordie sat back against the leather squabs, immediately second guessing herself. Had she made a foolishly impulsive decision?

Letting him compromise her was the quickest way to the altar.

The marquess sat across from her with a devilish twinkle in his light eyes. The sight made Cordie swallow nervously. What had she gotten herself into?

"You look nervous, angel," he said silkily. "There's no need."

"I'm fine," she lied and forced a smile to her face.

"You're stiff as a board. One would think you've never done this before."

Cordie frowned at him. What was he talking about? Escaping from a society ball or kissing a man to fulfill the terms of a bargain? Either way she was nervous enough and didn't need his scrutiny. "That's not very complimentary."

His rakish grin widened. "My apologies. I promise to be extremely complimentary in the future."

The future. They *had* a future. Well, that was something. It was what she wanted, after all. Cordie ignored the twinge of pain in her heart and smiled in return. Haversham was exactly the sort of husband she needed. He was devilishly handsome and he'd leave her to her own devices, while his name and position would protect her from her mother. She couldn't possibly ask for more.

An unwanted thought niggled in the back of her mind. *She did want more.* It wasn't Kelfield's status of scoundrel that had initially set her on this quest. It was the look of love and devotion on his face that he reserved only for Livvie. Being married to a scoundrel had its own benefits, but what she'd truly wanted was for the man she loved to adore her the way Kelfield did Livvie. Was it possible Haversham could become that man?

Though in her heart she knew the answer to that, she refused to acknowledge it even to herself.

The coach rambled to a stop, and Cordie's heart froze. Haversham climbed out first into the foggy night and offered his hand to her. Shaking slightly, she allowed him to help her to the ground.

"You're as skittish as a kitten," he said with chuckle.

Dread washed over her. *A kitten?* Why did he have to say that of all things? An image of Clayworth flashed in her mind and she snatched her hand back from the marquess. "I—um—I don't think I can do this."

His smile vanished. "I beg your pardon?"

"I mean, I—um—I'm not ready, my lord." Anger flashed in his eyes, and she gulped. Was *this* the look Miss Burke had seen all those years ago? Would he try to take revenge on her as well?

"Marc!" a man's strangled voice interrupted them from a few feet away.

Haversham looked over his shoulder and straightened in an instant. "Kelfield?"

Cordie stepped away from the marquess and stared into the mist. It was Kelfield. He staggered a bit and came to a stop before them. He blinked when his eyes fell on her. "M-Miss Avery?" the drunk duke slurred. "Wh-what're you do-doing here?"

"She's my guest." Haversham answered for her, frowning at his friend. "What the devil is wrong with you?"

Kelfield tried to straighten up, but wobbled a bit. "I need a place to stay, Marc."

Haversham waved him up the stairs. "Stay as long as you want."

The duke furrowed his brow, trying to focus on Cordie. "Olivia wouldn't want you to be here."

Olivia wouldn't want him walking the streets deep in his cups either, but Cordie kept that thought to herself. "Thank you for your concern."

"*I'll* thank you to mind your own business," the marquess growled at his friend's departing form. Then he turned his attention back to Cordie. "*We* had a deal."

They did have a deal. She'd risked everything to save the man who'd just stumbled across Haversham's threshold. Cordie closed her eyes, praying for strength. "Very well, my lord."

"Inside," he barked at her. "I don't need a bloody audience."

She climbed the stairs and was shown into an elegant salon, remodeled in the Greek style. What was she doing here? This was a terrible mistake, but one she couldn't see a way out of. The marquess poured himself a liberal amount of whiskey and swirled the amber liquid around his glass before downing it in one gulp.

"My lord," she began softly.

"Quiet!" he ordered, rubbing his brow.

So much for her theory that he wouldn't be controlling.

Finally he sank into a gold and white brocade chair, closing his eyes and massaging his temples. "*You* are a tease, Cordelia."

She said nothing to defend herself. He was right, after all.

"I thought you wanted this as much as I did."

"So did I," she whispered.

He opened his eyes and pierced her with pained look. "And what do you want now?"

She gulped, afraid to tell him. "I—um—well, I'd like to go home."

Haversham pinched the bridge of his nise between his fingers. "Come here, Cordelia."

She stepped towards him and swallowed when his eyes never left her. Cordie stopped before him and took a deep breath. "Yes, my lord?"

"I don't think I'll get over you." He sighed. "It's Clayworth, isn't it?"

"Yes," she admitted quietly.

Haversham sat forward in his seat and grasped her hand in his. "I'm at least owed my kiss, am I not?"

Unable to speak, she simply nodded. They had agreed to a kiss and she did owe him a debt.

The marquess raised her hand to his lips and pressed a soft kiss to the inside of her wrist. Then he squeezed her fingers and dropped her hand. "There. I'll have Anderson take you home. You'll understand if I don't accompany you."

Relief washed over her and Cordie swiped at a tear. "Oh, thank you, my lord." She leaned forward and kissed his cheek. "You are a gentleman."

He scoffed. "I'd rather you didn't tell anyone."

A gurgled laugh escaped her at the same moment they heard an angry voice yell from the corridor.

"Where is she? Cordelia!" Clayworth bellowed, his voice echoing throughout the house.

Haversham leapt to his feet, nearly knocking Cordie to the floor. He caught her elbow and sat her in his vacant seat. The marquess bolted to the salon door and hauled it open. A split second later, his face met with Clayworth's fist.

Cordie screamed as Haversham dropped to the floor.

The earl's eyes flashed to where she sat on the chair. Relief spread across his features and he wasted no time stepping over the marquess, crossing the room, and hauling her into his arms. "Tell me you're not hurt," he begged.

Cordie choked on a sob. In his embrace, she'd never felt so safe. She managed to shake her head. "I'm fine."

Clayworth held her back a bit and examined her face, as if to tell if she were being truthful. "You're not fine," he told her, a frown marring his too handsome face. "You're completely ruined, Cordelia. Your brothers, Miss Greywood, your mother, and others are searching the Sunderland's from top to bottom. Surely you didn't think your absence would go unnoticed or that Miss Greywood wouldn't be concerned by your disappearance."

She hadn't been thinking at all. Cordie fell back into her seat and gaped at him. *Ruined*? Oh, good heavens! What was she to do now? Her mother would kill her.

Haversham staggered back to his feet, holding a blood soaked kerchief to his nose, glaring at Clayworth. "That is the last bloody time you're going to hit me unaware."

Cordie jumped from her seat at the sight of him. "Oh, my lord, are you all right?"

"Do I look all right?" he snapped back.

She rushed towards him. "Lie down on the settee and tilt your head back."

⚜

Brendan's mouth dropped open as he watched Cordelia hover over the bastard, propping pillows under his head. Her reputation was in tatters and she was concerned about Haversham's bleeding nose? She was the most infuriating woman he'd ever...been in love with. Of course, she was the only woman he'd ever been in love with, so he didn't have anyone else to compare her to, but still he was on a quick path to Bedlam because of her.

"For the love of God, Cordelia," he barked, "we don't have a lot of time. How long do you think it will take someone else to come looking for you here?"

She turned away from Haversham to face Brendan, anguish alighting her face. "There's nothing to be done, my lord."

"Of course there is," he stalked towards her. "You'll marry me. We'll leave for Scotland right now, before anyone realizes we're gone."

She staggered slightly, and he grasped her elbow, steadying her. Cordelia's mesmerizing green eyes were wide with surprise. "Marry you?"

Not exactly the way he'd planned on convincing her, but there wasn't a lot to be done about it now. "I know," he said with a self-deprecating smile, "I'm not right for you. But you don't really have any other option at the moment."

He hated that her eyes flashed to Haversham, so he quickly pressed his case. "You'll send a letter to your mother at the first posting inn, saying I convinced you to run off with me. I'll send a similar one to the Astwicks, asking them to turn the tide of opinion in our favor. Your family will know the truth, but it won't matter. Your reputation will be safe, for the most part. Scottish wedding notwithstanding."

"I'd marry you," Haversham said from the settee, "but I think your brothers wouldn't stop 'til they caught up to us. Somehow I don't think they'll try too hard if it's Clayworth."

The marquess shot Cordelia a meaningful look that Brendan couldn't interpret. His jaw clenched at the sight. What was the bastard saying to her? He sincerely hoped he'd broken the scoundrel's nose.

Cordelia glanced back at him and nodded. "All right, my lord."

Brendan heaved a sigh. Thank God. He'd make sure she never regretted her decision. "We'd best be on our way."

Haversham laughed to himself. "I'll tell them you hit me when I tried to stop you. I should get to play the role of hero just once in my life." Haversham could tell them whatever he damn well wanted, as long as Cordelia was safely in Brendan's arms, he didn't care.

Twenty-Two

CORDIE was relieved it was dark in the coach as they traveled out of London. She didn't think she could take Clayworth's scrutiny at the moment. Of course, his eyes were probably on her anyway, but since she couldn't see them, it didn't unnerve her like it would have in the light of day. Somewhere along the way, she had completely lost control of her life. She could spend the long trip to Scotland going over the events of the last month in her mind and try to pinpoint the exact moment it all stopped making sense, but really what good would that do her? The past was over and didn't matter nearly as much as the future.

Her future.

Thoughts about where she went from here kept her eyes wide open as the London landscape vanished from the coach windows behind them. What did her future hold? She would be tied for life to the Earl of Clayworth. While he wasn't exactly the tyrant she'd always supposed he was, the idea was still a frightening one.

As a young girl she had always looked up to her sister Eleanor and her friend Marina. With three brothers closer in age to her, Cordie gravitated to the older, more sophisticated females whenever they were around. Marina had been beautiful. Curls the color of spun gold, eyes like a warm spring sky, and the perfect figure that left most men panting.

She had been elegant and graceful—all good things a countess should be. It wasn't even possible for Cordie to fill her shoes.

Which was only part of the problem. If *Marina* had been miserable in the role of Clayworth's wife, how poorly would Cordie fail? Perhaps she would have been better off married to Captain Seaton or even the Marquess of Haversham—not that his belated proposal had been sincere, but it was a nice gesture all the same.

"Are you awake?" Lord Clayworth whispered.

As if it was possible for her mind to relax enough for her to drift off. For a moment she thought about feigning sleep, not terribly keen to begin a conversation with him. Whatever he had to say could be put off. They had a long trip ahead of them, after all. However, she was rarely a coward. "Yes," she said, clearing her throat.

"I know you don't want this, Cordelia. I am sorry it had to be this way."

She was too. Sorry they had to race from London to Gretna Green in the middle of the night, with her family worried sick about her. Sorry her friends and family wouldn't be with her when she married. Sorry she would marry a man whom she could never make happy. Would Russell and Tristan really chase after them? Or was Haversham right? When they learned she was with Clayworth would they simply let her go?

There didn't seem to be another solution that would protect her reputation, however. And as Clayworth's countess, she would be out of her mother's house. She supposed she would always be in debt to him for both those things. "Thank you for making this sacrifice for me, my lord."

He sat forward on his bench and took both of her hands in his. "It's not a sacrifice, *ma minouche*. I want you for my wife, as you well know."

It was the *why* she couldn't understand. She wasn't any prettier than any of the girls who had tried to catch his attention over the years. She wasn't more accomplished or better connected. She *did* have that grotesquely over-sized dowry. "Are your funds in order?" As his wife she had a right to know that sort of thing, didn't she?

The earl chuckled, and the rich baritone sound filled the coach with warmth. "Get some sleep, Cordelia."

❧❧❧

Cordie awoke rather suddenly when their coach found a hole in the road. She sat up and blinked her eyes into the brightness that spilled inside the conveyance and stretched her arms. Sleeping in a carriage was not the most comfortable thing in the world. Every muscle was sore. Ball gowns were not the most practical of traveling apparel either.

She clutched a quilt that was draped over her more closely and looked across the coach at her husband-to-be.

Cordie screamed.

Who was that? The man sleeping on the other coach bench was not the Earl of Clayworth! Scraggily beard and mud splattered clothes notwithstanding, no one in their right mind would mistake this man for the earl. Had she been abducted?

The man's eyes flew open in a panic at the same time the coach slowed to a stop.

"Who are you?" she demanded.

"W-Wilson," he stuttered. "Sorry to frighten you, milady."

She wasn't anyone's *lady* yet, though she opted not to correct the man.

The coach door jerked open and Clayworth's popped inside. "Are you all right, Cordelia?"

She pointed at Wilson, whoever the devil he was. "Who is this man?"

A smile tugged at the earl's lips. "This is my coachman, Wilson. We've been trading off on the driving all night."

"I can take the box now, milord," Wilson said, moving towards the door.

"Have you had enough rest?" Clayworth asked, getting out of the man's way.

"I don't think I could go back to sleep now if I wanted to," the coachman said with a shudder. "That scream's rattled me nerves."

"Let me know when you start to get drowsy."

"You'll be the first to know."

Clayworth climbed inside the coach, shut the door behind himself, and settled in Wilson's vacated spot. "You never struck me as the screaming sort."

Cordie sat back against the squabs, folding her arms across her chest. "How was I to know you traded places with your coachman? I thought I'd been abducted or something."

His golden brows shot upwards and he bit back a smile. "Abducted?

You are the adventurous sort after all."

Wonderful, now he was mocking her. Cordie glared at him. "As I was frightened, I hardly find the situation humorous."

He sobered up immediately. "There's no reason to be afraid. I've waited my whole life for you, Cordelia. I'm not about to let someone snatch you away."

He'd waited his whole life for her? What an incredibly romantic thing to say. She grinned at him, despite herself. Could his words possibly be true?

"How did you sleep?" he asked after a moment.

Cordie tried to suppress a yawn. "Awful. Coach travel is not conducive to a good night's sleep, my lord."

"Sore?"

She nodded.

"Come here," he said, patting the seat beside him.

⚜

Cordelia's eyes grew wide, but only for a second, then she joined him on his bench. Brendan was playing with fire, he knew it, but he couldn't help himself. She looked as if she'd been delightfully tumbled already. Her pretty brown curls had slipped from the perfect chignon she'd worn the night before, and her pink gown was crushed beyond repair, or at least until someone pressed it again.

Brendan had never seen a more beautiful sight.

He adjusted his position so that he sat sideways, and then turned Cordelia so her back faced him. When his hands brushed her shoulders, she shivered, and Brendan smiled to himself. He affected her as much as she affected him. It was a good indication they would have a passionate marriage. Thank God. "Relax," he told her and began to massage her shoulders.

The soft moans and sounds of ecstasy that escaped her lips as he ran his hands along her back and shoulders made his cock stiffen in response. It had been forever since he'd bedded a woman. Perhaps if he'd done so more frequently, he wouldn't be about to explode out of his breeches now.

Brendan leaned forward and barely touched his lips to the slender column of Cordelia's neck, eliciting a soft gasp from her. He didn't stop. He ran his lips along her shoulders, squeezing her arms in the process.

Her skin was so soft, like sweet clotted cream and he wanted more of her. He wanted all of her.

But not now. Not yet.

She would be his wife in just a few days' time. He could wait. At least he thought he could. She deserved much more than a quick tup in his coach. She deserved a soft bed with fresh linens, pillows, and a silky nightrail.

Brendan managed to pull himself away from Cordelia and shook the images of her naked and waiting for him from his mind. Perhaps Wilson would get tired soon.

Cordelia looked over her shoulder and smiled at him. "That was very nice. Thank you."

She didn't move to the other side of the carriage, instead she leaned her head on his shoulder and Brendan's breath caught. He lifted his arm and cradled her against him. It was easier to resist her when she was sleeping. "Are you still tired?" he asked hopefully.

"No. But you must be exhausted after driving."

"We'll stop in Stamford soon. You can post a letter to your family and we'll get some breakfast. Wilson will probably need a break by then."

"You don't need to press too hard, my lord. I'm certain Haversham is right. My brothers won't follow when they learn I'm with you."

Brendan could go forever without hearing Haversham's name, and he frowned. The night before, a lot of questions had gone unanswered. At the time he was focused on convincing her to leave with him, but now… "Why did you go to Haversham's last night?"

She tipped her head up to look at him. The golden flecks in her green eyes didn't sparkle like they usually did. "I—um—well, I suppose I wasn't thinking clearly."

"Don't you know what could have happened to you?"

"He was a perfect gentleman."

Brendan's blood began to boil. She could not possibly be defending the scoundrel. "Perfect gentlemen don't abscond with young ladies from balls and take them to their homes."

Cordelia placed her hand on his chest and frowned. "Are you going to berate me the entire way, my lord? If so, it is going to be a very tedious trip."

Berate her the entire way? "Cordelia, I know you're accustomed to running around Town and doing whatever you want, but not anymore. You're going to be my wife and..." His voice trailed off when a look of abject misery settled on her face.

She pushed away from him. "I'll have to follow your every dictate. Your every order," she whispered. "Yes, I know."

He'd never seen her look so dejected and his heart constricted. Still he couldn't let her go around like she had been. It was a miracle she hadn't gotten herself into worse trouble than this before now. "I only want to keep you safe."

"I'm not a child."

As the creamy swells of her breasts rose with her every breath of air, Brendan's blood raced to his groin. "I am well aware of that."

She narrowed her beautiful green eyes on him, then reclaimed her spot on the opposite side of the coach, turning her back on him and snuggling back under the quilt he'd draped over her the night before. "Do I have your permission to go back to sleep? I find I am suddenly weary of this conversation."

He groaned and rubbed his brow, exhausted from having driven half the night. Caroline Staveley's words about Cordelia from weeks earlier echoed in his mind. *A girl that could hold her own against you, when needs be.* Oh, God! Would the rest of his life be this struggle? He'd be lucky to make it to Scotland.

Twenty-Three

A YOUNG stable boy gaped at Cordie when she stepped out of Clayworth's carriage into the yard at the coaching inn, muttering something about strange habits of the gentry. Unconsciously, her hand flew to her unkempt hair. She must look a fright. A glance down at her crumpled ball gown confirmed that her appearance was worse than she thought. No one in their right mind would travel in such an ensemble.

Wonderful!

Not that she was particularly vain, but every bride wanted to look her best—even if she was to say her vows over a blacksmith's anvil with no one she knew anywhere in sight... Well, except for the groom. At the moment she didn't even want to look at her groom, however. They weren't even married yet and he was already telling her what she could and couldn't do. This did not bode well for the future.

Blast him for touching her soul too! For making her want him. He said such sweet and heartfelt words, and the way he touched her always made her melt. She longed for him to take her in his arms again and kiss her as passionately as he had in the past.

But *not* at the moment!

Still smarting from their earlier conversation, she now had to go sit in the taproom to write a letter of explanation to her mother. How could she write a flowery letter, professing her desperate love for the sainted Clayworth, when she'd like nothing better than to strangle him? Still it had to be done. Who knew how many people Lady Avery would have to show the letter to, excusing her daughter's absence from Town? It would have to be a good letter.

As she entered the coaching inn, her eyes adjusted to the darkened taproom. Then she felt a hand at her waist and looked beside her, up at her intended's handsome face. He looked just as ridiculous as she did. Formal wear in broad daylight and wind-tousled hair from having driven his coach. She hated that her pulse raced with his touch.

"I've rented a private room, darling, so that you can write your letter. Breakfast will be served soon. After I help Wilson change horses, I'll join you."

His lips barely touched her cheek in the most chaste of kisses. Then he left her in the care of the innkeeper's wife, a portly woman with a large nose and a matron's cap.

"This way, Lady Clayworth," the woman said, hobbling toward a pair of doors at the far end of the room.

Lady Clayworth. Good heavens! She was already playing the role of countess? Cordie caught her breath then quickly followed the rounded woman, who opened the doors and gestured her inside. Of course Clayworth would have presented her as his wife. She couldn't very well travel the country as an unmarried miss in the company of a gentleman.

"His lordship said you need some foolscap and ink?"

"Yes, please. I need to post a letter to London."

The innkeeper's wife smiled, revealing a mouth missing many teeth. "We'll do the best we can, milady."

She was alone then, looking around the private parlor. It was dark, with a heavy wooden table in the middle, an old sideboard against a far wall, and the whole place smelled of stale ale. Still, it was nice not to have her bones jostled back and forth as they had been in the coach for the last several hours, if just for a little while.

"Here ya go, milady," the portly woman called happily as she entered the parlor, with some parchment, an ink well, and an old quill. She placed the items on the table and then bustled out to retrieve her breakfast.

Cordie stared at the blank foolscap. What was she going to say? Some fabricated tale of romance and adventure. If she was going to lie... She might as well make it a good one. She might as well make it what she wished the truth was.

Dear Mother,

I am certain my disappearance has worried you, and for that I am sincerely sorry. My intent was never to cause you grief. I have no excuse for my rash actions except for my undying love for Lord Clayworth and my impatience to become his wife. When he suggested we set off for Gretna Green, I couldn't possibly refuse. I do hope you will find it in your heart to forgive your impetuous daughter.

Please be happy for me. In Clayworth, I have found all I have ever wanted in a husband and am thrilled at the prospect of being his wife. He is warm, considerate, and he understands me. He loves me, encourages me to be myself, and promises me the freedom I have always craved. I am quite fortunate to have found such a paragon.

While we should have taken a more traditional route, received Gregory's approval and waited for the banns to be read, we were simply too eager to delay any further. We are quite anxious to start our life together, and I'm certain you'll wish us your every happiness. When we return to London, I will call on you upon my earliest convenience.

Your devoted daughter,
Cordelia

She put the letter aside, rereading it a half dozen times. As far as absolute fiction went, it wasn't bad. She did wish, as she lingered on the words, that they were true. How different this excursion would be if that was the case.

Breakfast consisted of a meat pie, currants, and fresh tea. Not the most glamorous meal for a countess-to-be, but since she was starving, Cordie wasn't about to complain. Flavor danced on her tongue and in no time, she had finished everything set before her.

She was fairly surprised that Clayworth hadn't yet joined her. How long could it take to change horses? Not that she was in a hurry to see him. She needed to find a way to deal with him, to keep him from being too controlling. There had to be a way.

Then the solution to her problems popped in her head, and a genuine smile spread across her face. *Lady Staveley* enjoyed free reign. Certainly there was some way to achieve the same for herself. If asked, the viscountess would share her secrets, Cordie was certain. She took a relieved breath. It was still possible for her to have everything she ever wanted.

"You look happy," Clayworth said from the doorway, looking every inch like Lord Adonis, if one discounted his dirty evening wear.

Cordie's heart leapt in her chest. To have the freedom she desired *and* this man as a husband. Life couldn't possibly be better. She beamed at him, rising from her seat. "Oh, I am." Crossing the floor, she rose up on tiptoes and pressed an innocent kiss to his lips. He felt warm and heavenly.

Clayworth's arms tightened around her waist, and his intense twilight eyes stared down at her. "What was that for?"

She playfully cocked her head to one side. "You are very suspicious, my lord. Isn't a wife allowed to kiss her husband?"

⚜

Except that he wasn't that yet, and she'd been fairly annoyed with him most of the morning. She was the most confounding woman he'd ever met. Hot then cold then back again. How long would this appealing Cordelia last? Pressed against him and heating his blood, Brendan wished it would be forever, but he knew better than that. "Indeed. But what has changed your outlook, my dear?"

She rested her hands on his chest, making his heart beat faster and his pants a bit tighter.

"I'm about to get everything I ever wanted. Why wouldn't I be happy?"

"You're about to marry me," he reminded her. She hadn't been happy about that prospect earlier. Something was going on in her pretty head. Some devious plot, he could tell. Did she have plans to run off and leave him here?

Cordelia's smile widened. "Upon reflection, I think I'll enjoy being a countess."

"*My* countess?" he asked skeptically.

"Who else's?" she asked, drawing light circles with her fingertips across his chest.

Dear God, he wanted her. She was going to undo him, unless... His eyes flew to the table. A reprieve. "Your letter is finished?"

Cordelia nodded.

"I'll get it posted right now," he released her from his arms.

She frowned at him. "Are you afraid of me, my lord?"

In more ways than she would ever know. "Of course not," he lied, retrieving the letter in his hands. "Do you mind? We should make certain our stories are similar."

Cordelia sat back at the table while he scanned the letter for Lady Avery. He tried to keep his eyes from bulging out of his head. Where had she come up with this drivel? "No one who knows me will believe any of this." He rubbed his brow. "I promised you the freedom you crave?" Had she lost her mind?

She scowled at him. "Then we are at an impasse, my lord. No one who knows me would believe I would run off for less than that, and I'm not writing another letter."

Dear God she was willful. What did she need freedom for anyway? He would take care of her the rest of her days. Give her everything she desired. Love her with his every breath. What was this drive for something else, something that was impossible?

"Here ya are, milord," the portly innkeeper's wife said from the doorway with his breakfast. "I'll put ya down right there next to her ladyship."

It didn't matter. She could want the impossible, for all the good it would do her. After they were married, he'd set her straight. There was no point in arguing about it now. The tempting smell of meat pie made his stomach grumble, and he took the spot next to Cordelia.

As he took his first bite, he realized she was looking at him strangely. "What is it?" he asked after a swig of ale.

"You look exhausted," she said. "It's not really necessary to move at this breakneck pace, is it?"

Brendan narrowed his eyes on her. Did she have some plan to run off and leave him here? Something was going on in her mind. He shook his head. The faster they got to Scotland the better. The faster they said their vows, the faster he could bed her. Delaying wasn't an option. "One doesn't slowly elope, Cordelia."

"At this pace, you'll be falling asleep over the anvil."

A smile tugged at his lips. He wouldn't fall asleep over the anvil. After their vows were said, he'd scoop her off to the nearest hotel and make her his countess in the most meaningful of ways. "You don't need to worry about that, *ma minouche*."

"Why are you doing this, my lord? Why did you come to my rescue? Why are you so intent on marrying me?"

If he could alleviate her concerns, it wouldn't hurt to tell her, would it? The letter to her mother, written in her own hand, professed her undying love for him. If only that were true, the words would be much easier for him to say. Brendan sat back in his chair and stared into her mesmerizing green eyes. She was a vision. His vision. Full of life, if a bit stubborn, but his all the same—or she would be in a day and a half. "Because I'm in love with you, and I couldn't allow Haversham or anyone else to ever hurt you, Cordelia. I'm far from perfect, but I'll be a good husband and see that you never want for anything."

Her face lit up at his words, and she looked every inch the raving beauty who owned his heart. "You're in love with me?"

"Deeply," he admitted, with what he hoped was his most charming smile. "So, I'm afraid we'll have to continue at this breakneck pace all the way to Scotland, because I can't stand to wait any longer than is necessary to make you mine." At least that part of her letter was true.

"Oh, my," she said quietly as a pretty blush settled on her cheeks.

Twenty-Four

OUTSIDE the inn in Stamford, Clayworth resumed his spot on the coachman's box and Wilson climbed inside the coach with Cordie. At first, the coachman eyed her warily, as if he expected her to scream again at any moment. That wasn't particularly complimentary. She didn't go around screaming on a regular basis—just when she thought she'd been kidnapped. That was quite an acceptable reaction under the circumstances.

Somehow Clayworth had managed to find her a copy of Maria Edgeworth's *The Absentee* to occupy her time. She and Livvie had both read the book two years ago when it was first published, without her mother's knowledge, of course. Lady Avery had not found Ms. Edgeworth's view of the *ton* to be flattering, therefore the book was off limits. The story was still fresh, and Cordie was grateful for the diversion from her musings. She could go mad trapped in this coach, wanting to see and talk to Clayworth, especially after his admission back at the inn.

They had stopped briefly for lunch, but Wilson was always present, and she had been unable to say another private word to the earl. Though what she would say was lost on her. She probably should have told him that she was just as in love with him, but the words hadn't come at the inn. She'd simply been too stunned to say much of anything.

As the light slowly faded to darkness, Cordie put down her book and rested her head against the squabs. Clayworth was in love with her? It was almost impossible to believe. She hadn't even allowed herself to hope for such good fortune. She really could have everything she ever wanted, especially if she could somehow gain his leniency. Lady Staveley's advice would be priceless.

Besides, she didn't want to worry about any of that at the moment, too swept up in the heady feeling that Clayworth was in love with her. It was amazing, as if she was floating in the clouds, despite the fact that they were racing to the Scottish border to keep her from ruin. Even so, niggling thoughts crept in every now and then. Did being in love mean something different to Clayworth than to herself? He must have felt that way about Marina at one point, but it hadn't lasted. How was she to keep from going down that treacherous path? Was it even possible? Was it inevitable that they would wake up one day and just not love each other anymore?

The coach began to slow, and then it finally came to a stop. Loud, raucous sounds began to seep inside the carriage, then the door opened and Clayworth offered her his hand. "Welcome to Doncaster, my dear."

Wilson sat up with a jolt, blinking his eyes into the darkness. "Doncaster, milord?"

"Do you mind changing the horses alone and grabbing a bite, Wilson? I'd rather not leave my lady unattended here."

Cordie looked past Clayworth's shoulder towards the coaching inn. Two barrel-chested fellows were singing at the top of their lungs, while others littered the yard, staring at the earl's coach with covetous eyes. A stab of fear went through Cordie. This was not the sort of establishment she'd ever been before.

Clayworth must have read the look on her face because he tightened his grip on her hands. "You're safe with me, Cordelia."

"They look rather dangerous."

He raised her hand to his lips and pressed a reassuring kiss to her fingers. "I had hoped to make it to Pontefract, but with the horses we got in Newark-on-Trent we were lucky to make it this far."

Clayworth looked like a man possessed. His face was red from the wind and his eyes were bloodshot. Cordie hated to see him like this. The trip back from Scotland would not be at such a pace. "I'm sorry," she offered lamely. "I'm so sorry to put you through this."

A smiled spread across his face. "It's a small price to pay, when you're the prize at the end, *ma minouche.*"

He led her into the establishment and quietly ordered a private room and dinner. Though they were quickly attended to and the roar of the noise was drowned out some by closing the doors, Cordie still felt ill at ease. They quickly ate a bit of stringy mutton, some carrots, and over-cooked broccoli before heading back out to the carriage. "I promise," Clayworth told her, "our next meal will be better."

Cordie smiled at him, relieved they were departing Doncaster. "Don't make promises you can't keep, my lord. Who knows what is in store for us tomorrow."

Wilson was already waiting for them atop the coachman's box with four fresh horses ready to carry them through the Pennies. Clayworth helped Cordie into the dark carriage and then followed her inside. Before she could sit back onto her bench, the earl scooped her up and settled her on his lap, cradled in his arms. "I know exactly what is in store for us tomorrow, my love."

Cordie sucked in a breath and stared at him, though he was hard to see in the dark. She shook her head. "You can't rest with me on your lap."

His lips touched her neck and Cordie swallowed, as tingles raced across her skin. Liquid fire pooled deep in her belly and she clutched his arm that lay across her middle. He was powerful and intoxicating, and she struggled to catch her breath. Still it wasn't enough. She wanted him to touch her everywhere, to never stop.

But he did.

Clayworth sighed deeply and raised his head. Though she could feel his eyes on her, she couldn't see him in the dark. "You are almost impossible to resist."

"Then don't," she whispered. They'd be married in a day or so, anyway.

"Not like this," he answered. Clayworth kissed her hair and Cordie rested her head on his chest. "Why did you think I was wrong for you?"

Though she was startled by his question, the soothing tone in his voice put her at ease. There wasn't a place for secrets between them. Life was going to be difficult as it was. It would be best to get a fresh start.

"Your marriage to Marina was not a happy one," she began.

"No, it wasn't," he replied evenly. "How did you know?"

That was a bit embarrassing, but she had started down this path. "I—um—well, when I was younger, I would eavesdrop on conversations between my sister and Marina."

"You were an unrepentant hellion even then, *ma minouche*?" he asked with a touch of mirth in his voice.

"I hardly find the situation amusing, my lord. Marina complained for years about your cool indifference. You weren't even there when she died along with your child. That is not the sort of future I want." His body tightened against hers and Cordie winced. She'd probably said too much. Would she never learn to keep her mouth closed?

"You're right. I should have been there," he acknowledged. "But I hadn't laid eyes on Marina in well over a year. The child, as you can deduce from that, wasn't mine and I wasn't at all anxious to see her."

The revelation was shocking. Cordie was glad it was dark in the coach, so he couldn't see her stunned expression. Marina had been unfaithful? She would never have imagined that to be the case. She'd never even hinted at anything like that to Eleanor. Then again, Marina might not have necessarily wanted to discuss her own sins so freely either. Still, she was astonished. What else was she wrong about? "I—I didn't know," she said feebly.

"But it won't be like that with us," he told her softly, tightening his embrace.

"How can you be so certain?" Something had obviously gone wrong in his first marriage. How could he know they weren't fated for the same end?

"You're the only woman I have ever loved, Cordelia. Our future lies on a different path."

Cordie stared at him, wishing for a little light. She couldn't see his eyes, and could only make out darker shadows on his face. "You *never* loved Marina?" How was that possible? She was perfect, or at least Cordie had thought she was. She still couldn't get over the fact that Marina had cuckolded Clayworth. It was unfathomable.

"I don't like to speak ill of the departed."

"Please, my lord. I need to know how things were."

He sighed, and his hand stroked her neck, until Cordie relaxed against him again. "We didn't suit. Not from the very beginning, and I'm afraid the situation between us never improved."

"What happened in the beginning?" She needed to know what sorts of things to avoid.

Clayworth took several breaths, and Cordie thought he wouldn't answer her at all. He was tired. Perhaps she shouldn't push him —

"Marina made up her mind that I was the husband she wanted, and she went about making certain that happened," he finally began. "I'm not particularly social, you may have noticed. But I'd gone to Town that Season, to escort my sister, Flora." His voice cracked a bit on his sister's name, but he continued. "I wasn't of a mind to court anyone. That wasn't my purpose in attending the events of the *ton*. Of course, I noticed Marina. She was beautiful, but so were dozens of others, and as I said, escorting Flora was my top priority.

"One night I got distracted, which is easy to do when you're conversing with Astwick. Of course he was simply Lord Chester Peyton at the time. Anyway, I was remiss in my duties, and I couldn't find Flora."

Cordie could actually hear him wince with the admission. Had she made Russell and Tristan feel the same? Guilt slowly seeped over.

"Marina came from nowhere and said she knew where my sister was. Fool that I was, I believed her. As soon as we were in the corridor, she screamed at the top of her lungs and threw herself at me. The ballroom emptied to find her shaking, in my arms. Later she said she'd seen a mouse and had been frightened. I was foolish enough to believe that too, at the time, and felt horrible for compromising her in such a public way, unintentional as it was. We were married by special license two days later."

That was how they'd married? "I had no idea."

"It wasn't how I'd hoped my life would go, but I thought to make the best of it. The problem was, we didn't suit. We saw the world differently, and some things can't be overlooked or ignored."

"What things?" she asked before she could stop herself. She'd already intruded enough.

"Family, for one. Marina was an only child, and could never understand my devotion to my sisters."

"I could do with a few less brothers," she said, hoping to lighten the mood.

"No, you couldn't," he said with certainty. "As repressive as you find them, I've seen the love in your eyes when you talk to your brothers."

"You haven't met Gregory," Cordie said with a mock shudder. "He's nearly as stodgy as you."

Clayworth's arms tightened around her again and he softly kissed her temple. "There's more I should tell you."

"You don't have to."

"You'll find out anyway, and I'd rather be the one to tell you."

Well, that sounded positively ominous, and Cordie tilted her head back again, wishing she could see his face.

"Flora thought herself in love with a scoundrel who ended up abandoning her when she discovered she was with child. A few weeks after the birth of my nephew, she lost all desire to live and faded away. Thomas is twelve now, the light of my life, and he lives with me in Derbyshire."

Cordie sucked in a surprised breath. The Earl of Clayworth was the last sort of man she expected to raise a bastard. "But he..." Her voice trailed off, as she couldn't finish the statement.

"Looks like his mother," Clayworth finished for her. "How could I not love him? And then there's Rosamund."

Lady Rosamund Reese. Cordie had seen her once at a small country ball while she and Livvie were staying at Prestwick Chase in the spring. "I remember her. She is stunning."

"She's afflicted," he informed her with less emotion than she would have expected at such a pronouncement. "They don't know with what. She has grown into a lovely, young woman, but her mind is that of a child's." He heaved a sigh. "So there you are, Cordelia. I'm afraid you're getting the raw end of the deal. My family is filled with bastards and simpletons."

Even so, she could hear the love his voice, and loyalty was something she understood to the depths of her soul. Cordie snuggled against him and kissed his chest. "But I get you."

Twenty-Five

THE next day was tedious as they continued their journey. Cordie awoke somewhere outside Penrith when the light streamed inside the coach, and she found herself once again in the company of Wilson and his light snores. The night before seemed like a dream. Despite the misgivings she'd had about Clayworth in the past, she considered herself quite fortunate to be his soon-to-be bride. He was honorable, honest, loyal, devastatingly handsome, and he made her heart race.

Married life seemed promising.

It was late in the afternoon when their coach finally rambled over the Scottish border into the sleepy, little village of Gretna Green. When the carriage door opened, Clayworth helped Cordie to the ground and everything seemed more real. This was it.

With a crooked grin, he offered his arm. "My lady."

Cordie allowed him to escort her to the entrance of a white stone blacksmith's shop. A small child was playing with a doll and glanced up at their footfall. "'ere ye here fer a weddin'?"

Clayworth smiled at the child. "We are indeed."

The girl scampered towards the steps before disappearing into the establishment. "Papa!"

A moment later, a man dressed in all black and looking more like a vicar than a blacksmith appeared in the doorway. "Ye lookin' tae get married?"

"With great haste," Clayworth answered.

The man nodded. "Come in, come in, sir. Have ye go' a ring?"

"I do."

Cordie glanced up at her intended as they stepped over the threshold. *He had a ring?* They hadn't stopped anywhere along the way to get one.

The man spoke to the child, "Fetch me two bodies, Bonny." Then he turned back to Cordie and Clayworth. "Step forward. Tell me yer names."

"Brendan Reese, and my bride is Cordelia Avery."

"Well, Mr. Reese, aboot the payment..." The man's voice trailed off.

"Will one hundred pounds suffice?"

"More than enough, sir," the man said, eying them now from top to bottom. "It is sir, isn't it? Yer no' some lord or somethin'?"

"The Earl of Clayworth," he informed the man.

At that moment, two brawny fellows stepped from the attached house into the blacksmith's shop. "Angus, Hamish, will ye witness fer Lord Clayworth?"

Both men agreed with nods of their beefy heads.

"Verra well, step forward, m'lord, Miss Avery," the blacksmith said. He grasped Clayworth's right hand and Cordie's left, and began to wind a golden cord around their wrists, binding them together. "Repeat after me, m'lord. I, Brendan Reese, take ye, Cordelia Avery, tae be my wife before God an' these witnesses."

Clayworth's twilight eyes sparkled as he repeated the words. Never in her life would she have thought these surroundings would have been romantic, but the man staring at her made her knees weak and her heart pound.

"All right, Miss Avery, yer turn. I, Cordelia Avery, take ye, Brendan Reese, tae be my husband before God and these witnesses."

"I—um," she cleared her throat and swallowed. "I, Cordelia Avery, take you, Brendan Reese to be my husband before God and these witnesses." Chills raced across her skin with these words. They were the most important ones she'd ever said, giving herself to this man.

"Ye've go' the ring, m'lord?"

"Yes, of course," Clayworth said, fumbling around in his pocket, finally retrieving a small golden ring. His eyes flashed to hers, rich with desire, and Cordie nearly lost her breath. Then he slid the ring onto her finger of the hand that was bound to his.

There were words engraved on the band, and Cordie squinted to read them. *Dw i'n dy garu di.* She twisted the ring around her finger with her thumb, before glancing back up at her husband. "What does it mean?"

"I love you — in Welsh. It was my grandmother's."

A laughed escaped her throat. "A French mother and a Welsh grandmother? Honestly, my lord, are you English at all?"

"Don't forget the Scottish wedding," he replied with a wink.

"*Mìle fàilte dhuit le d'bhréid, fad do ré gun robh thu slàn. Móran làithean dhuit   is   sìth, le d'mhaitheas is le d'nì bhi fàs,*" the blacksmith said in Gaelic. He smiled. "Ye may kiss yer bride."

Clayworth pulled her towards him and held her in his arms before dipping his head for the most innocent kiss he'd ever given her. Then he paid the blacksmith, who unbound their hands and suggested a nice inn a few blocks away.

The White Heather Inn was much nicer than any place they had stopped along the way. Swathed in soft shades of purple and white lace, the inn was warm and inviting. After ordering a bath for their room, Clayworth left to see about their horses. She was glad for the time alone with a mirror. Three days of travel in a ball gown had certainly taken their toll.

As she stepped into the brass tub, Cordie sighed as the heavenly water sloshed against her aching muscles. She slid down until her body was covered and closed her eyes, content to never leave the peaceful water. However, she now had a husband, and she was fairly certain that he wouldn't be content to let her stay in the tub forever.

Still it was nice to wash away days of travel from her skin and wash her hair with the lilac soap the inn provided. She almost felt like herself again.

The door creaked, and Cordie's eyes flew open. Her husband stood in the threshold with a simple package wrapped in brown paper. She resisted the urge to scream and hide herself from his view, but... Well, he was her husband now. Besides, she was fairly certain the water covered most of her anyway.

"I didn't mean to frighten you," he said sheepishly, then gestured with the package. "I—well, I thought after three days in a coach you'd want something besides your ball gown."

Cordie was speechless, almost. When? How had he found something for her to wear? "What is it?" she asked, nearly forgetting her state of dishabille and sitting up in the tub. She quickly sloshed back down.

Clayworth placed the package on a small table by the window. "Back in Stamford. The innkeeper easily put together our situation. Most people don't travel in evening wear and have urgent needs to post letters to London." He smiled at her, making Cordie's entire body tingle with awareness. "It's just a nightrail," he explained. "Belonged to her daughter. I hope it fits."

It was one of the sweetest things anyone had ever done for her. Cordie shook her head in disbelief. "Thank you."

"Anyway," he cleared his throat. "I'll give you a few more minutes, order dinner, and be back."

Her escape from reality was over. Cordie nodded in agreement to the plan.

Brendan forced himself to leave the room. He'd never seen a more beautiful sight in all his life, but he couldn't just scoop her up and toss her to the bed like some lecherous bastard, no matter how badly he wanted to. He somehow made his way to the taproom and ordered a meal he had no intention of eating to be brought to their room.

Knowing that his wife was upstairs, completely bare made it nearly impossible for him to focus on the task at hand. He wished there was a freezing loch nearby that he could dip himself in, just to get his mind to return to some sort of working fashion.

"M'lord?" a young maid said, staring at him strangely. Brendan wondered how long she'd been trying to get his attention. From the exasperated look on her face, it had been a while.

"Yes, I'm sorry?"

"I said I'll bring it tae yer room when it's ready."

"Th-thank you," he mumbled before climbing the stairs that led to the room where his wife was waiting.

For a long moment, Brendan stood outside their door, resting his head against the frame, cursing himself for a fool. It had been too long since he'd taken a woman to bed, and his need to have his wife was too great. Above all else he needed to maintain his control. He didn't want to scare her, or go too fast, or hurt her. Why hadn't he participated in carnal activities more often over the years? He'd be much more likely to reign in his desires now if he had.

"M'lord?" an annoyed voice came from behind him.

Brendan turned around to see the maid balancing a tray of food on her shoulder. She gaped at him as if he'd escaped from Bedlam. Not that he could blame her. What sort of fool stands outside his bedroom door, while his wife of less than an hour awaits him on the other side? He nodded. "Yes, of course. Thank you."

He knocked, then poked his head in the room. His eyes nearly popped out of his head. Cordelia was standing by the grate in the nightrail he'd given her. It should have been an innocent ensemble, but apparently the innkeeper's daughter was not as endowed as his wife. The simple muslin hugged Cordelia's curves in such a way he didn't think he could speak.

The maid cleared her throat.

"Yes, yes, of course," he said, finding his voice and opening the door to admit the girl. "Dinner has arrived, my dear."

Cordelia's eyes sparkled when they landed on him, and Brendan took a steadying breath, still not in complete control of himself.

"Do put the tray here, miss," his wife said to the maid, indicting a table by the window. "And could you have someone bring more hot water for his lordship's bath?"

He neither needed nor wanted a *hot* bath, but perhaps the cooler water already in the tub would help him regain his control while he washed away the smell of sweat, horses, and days' worth of travel. "No need," he told the girl, who already thought he was insane. "Thank you for your help."

With a shake of her head, the maid departed, muttering something about the lunacy of Sassenach men.

Once alone, Cordelia's green eyes raked him from head to toe. "I assumed you would want to bathe, my lord. Do you want me to have someone remove the tub?"

He shook his head. "I'm sure the water that's there will be fine." He shrugged out of his jacket, all the while keeping his eyes leveled on his bride in her too-tight nightrail. She *was* the adventurous sort. What where his chances of getting her to bathe him? "Cordelia…"

She frowned. "I do wish you'd call me Cordie. Only my mother calls me Cordelia… Well, and my brothers, but only when they're angry with me."

Cordie. It did suit her. Spirited, reckless, full of life—all the things he'd been missing for far too long. "Cordie Clayworth," he tested the name, smiling when she walked towards him.

"Thank you again for the nightrail," she whispered, stopping directly in front of him. "It was so sweet of you to think of it."

"I want you to be happy, Cordie, and comfortable." He fingered the faded lace edging at the bodice, his fingers brushing against the top of her creamy breasts that he longed to taste. "I'm sorry if the fit isn't right," his voice sounded strangled to his own ears.

True joy shone from her mesmerizing eyes. "Oh, my lord, it's perfect… Well, it's a little tight, but I despaired at the thought of having to put that gown back on, so this is wonderful."

Brendan tsked and shook his head. "My lord? Cordie dear, you are my wife. Must you still call me that?"

She cocked her head to one side, a mischievous smile on her face. "My sincerest apologies, Lord Adonis."

Lord Adonis! He'd hated that moniker for more years than he could remember. He closed his eyes and groaned. "Please don't call me *that*."

Cordie giggled and ran her hands along his chest, searing him with her touch, before lightly setting them on his shoulders. "What shall I call you, then? Do you prefer Clayworth?"

He snaked an arm around her waist and pulled her against his body. "Brendan," he said fiercely.

She looked surprised by his tone, and probably his action, but her smile never faltered. "Indeed? My mother always referred to my father as Avery, even to this very day. She never calls Gregory by that name."

At the moment, he didn't care what Lady Avery called anyone, but he did enjoy watching his wife's lips as she spoke. It gave him the best ideas. Brendan slowly lowered his head and kissed Cordie the way he'd wanted to at the blacksmith's shop, the way he'd wanted to in the coach for days. Her lips were pliant beneath his and she tasted like the sweetest berries. When she sighed against his lips, clutching his shirt in her hands,

Brendan swept his tongue into her mouth. His body tightened with unbridled need

Dear God, she was heaven. All the heaven he could ever want to hold in his arms. She kissed him back, and began to twirl her hands through his hair, nearly robbing him of his breath. Then she giggled against his lips. Brendan pulled back from her. "What are you laughing at?"

Cordie moved her hand from his air and presented him with a twig he must have picked up while steering their coach. "And you taste like horses," she told him, with a charming laugh.

Blast! He did need a bath. Brendan stepped out of her embrace to unbutton his shirt. With a raised brow he asked, "I don't suppose I could convince you to bathe me."

Thankfully, she didn't even look bashful. "Brendan Reese, are you incapable of such a chore on your own?"

He winked at her. "I've been doing it for years, my dear. I just think you'd make it more enjoyable." She did blush at that, and Brendan felt his heart soar. He entwined his fingers with hers. "Come be a good wife, Cordie," he encouraged, tugging her toward the tub.

Twenty-Six

CORDIE couldn't believe she was going along with this, though she was curious to see where it would lead. Her husband was so strong, like steel, whenever she touched him. Seeing him would be an adventure all on its own. Did he really want her to bathe him, though? She couldn't imagine the stuffy earl wishing for such a thing. Of course he didn't seem quite so stuffy anymore. He'd loosened up a bit, or perhaps she was just accustomed to him now. Either way, it didn't matter.

Brendan dropped into a wooden chair and pointed his booted foot at her. "Will you do the honors, my dear?"

She raised one eyebrow haughtily. She hadn't agreed to be the man's valet. Still that meant she would get to touch him. Cordie dropped to her knees and tugged at his first boot.

"Pull up from the heel," he advised.

"Is this why you married me?" she asked tartly, though she followed his instructions anyway. Almost at once, the boot flew off his foot and she fell backwards, landing on her bottom. When her husband laughed, she scowled at him. "I'm so glad you're enjoying yourself. Remove your own boots."

Brendan laughed even harder and pulled her up from the floor. "You are delightful." He winked at her, then he tugged off his other boot.

Cordie's eyes widened when he unbuttoned his shirt and slid it over his head. She stared at him in awe. As startlingly handsome as Brendan always was, unclothed, her husband was a work of art. His sculpted chest was lightly dusted with dark golden hair and rippled muscles. Cordie swallowed and a fine tingle of anticipation played at her nape when he slipped the first button through its hole.

Brendan stilled his hands and took in her anxious expression. "Cordie, you didn't use all the soap, did you?" he asked softly.

It was obvious he was trying to put her at ease, and Cordie sighed. Even in this, he was a gentleman. Her heart swelled at the realization. By some amazing stroke of luck, she'd married him and he was...perfect. She managed to shake her head in answer.

He smiled at her as he finished with his buttons and stepped out of his trousers and small clothes. Cordie turned her head, suddenly unable to look at him or to let her eyes drop to that part of him. Her face flushed red and she started to walk away, but he clutched her arm. "Don't go," he pleaded, pulling her back to him.

She stared up into his twilight eyes, and shook her head. "I—I don't know what you want from me, what I'm supposed to do."

His arms encircled her, and she felt *that* part of him through her nightrail, firm and hard. She now realized she'd felt it many times before—whenever he held her, kissed her, sat her on his lap—but she'd never realized what it was. How embarrassing. How could she not have realized it? He was exceptional in size.

She wished she'd had the chance to talk to Livvie before this point. So she'd know what to expect, what was expected of her. She should have pressed for this sort of information when they last saw each other at Lady Staveley's ball, not that it would have been appropriate, but she'd at least have some idea as to how to go from here. As it was, she was completely lost.

"You use soap and water," he said, interrupting her thoughts, grinning at her.

Cordie blinked at him. "I beg your pardon?"

"You asked what I wanted. You're supposed to bathe me, remember? Use soap and water." He released his hold on her and sunk into the tub. "Oh, and if you don't mind, my dear, could you place all our clothes in the hallway? The innkeeper said he'd have them washed and pressed for us."

Collecting their clothes was the perfect distraction, and Cordie set to the task immediately. However, they had very few articles and the chore was soon finished. She chanced a glance at her husband, eyeing her from the tub. He smiled at her and held up the bar of soap in his hand. An invitation.

Cordie swallowed nervously, but gathered her courage and crossed the floor towards him. "You do realize, Brendan, once we return home, someone else will have to play the part of your valet. I'm not going to make a habit of collecting your clothes or pulling off your boots or…bathing you after this."

His deep chuckle instantly disarmed her. "You may like bathing me."

She dropped to her knees beside the tub and reached for the soap in his hands. His fingers closed around hers, and his gaze caught her before he released his hold. Cordie took a steadying breath and dipped the soap into the surprisingly warm water. She worked up a slippery lather, and gingerly touched her fingertips to Brendan's chest. His muscles contracted and she pressed her hand against the firm ridge, skin to skin. A ripple of desire spread through her and her eyes flashed to his. Dark, intense with emotion.

"If you don't want me to smell like horses, my dear, you're going to have to do better than that." He guided her hands with his own, up and down the panels of his chest, sloshing soap and water everywhere. Brendan's golden hair tickled her fingers and sent hot flashes to her core. Touching his bare skin, learning the feel of his body, made her very aware of his strength and power—and how very much she wanted him.

"Use the pitcher for my hair, if you don't mind," he said, breaking into her musings.

Cordie stood and retrieved a porcelain pitcher from the washstand, hoping to gain some sort of control in the process. When she turned back to Brendan, his eyes were still focused on her, pupils dilated with potent desire. An answering response hardened her sensitive nipples.

The overwhelming need to tell him of her heart washed over Cordie. She knelt beside him again, and filled the pitcher with bath water. "Close your eyes," she whispered. When he complied, she poured the water over his golden hair and rose higher on her knees to run the soap though his locks. "Brendan," she began as she ran her fingers through his hair, glad his eyes were closed. This would be much easier to say if he wasn't looking at her. "I should have told you this already, and I feel awful I haven't done so before now…"

He said nothing, but furrowed his brow.

"It's just that when you told me," she said quickly, hoping to relieve the look of concern on his face, "I was so surprised, I couldn't really think, which is not an excuse, I know." She was rambling, but she couldn't seem to help herself. She refilled the pitcher with water and rinsed the soap from his hair. "But the truth of the matter is, I've felt this way for quite a while, even when I didn't want to, even when I tried not to."

She blotted a towel against his eyes, and he opened them, piercing her with his stare. "What are you trying to say, Cordie?"

"I—" she gulped, then continued with a whisper, "Brendan, I love you."

In the blink of an eye, he'd hauled her into the tub with him. She didn't even have time to gasp at being soaked completely though, as he crushed his lips to hers. His hands were everywhere, cradling her bottom, caressing her back, pulling at the buttons on her nightrail. All the while, his lips never left hers. Water sloshed to the floor at regular intervals and the groans from her husband became more desperate.

Finally, he pulled his head back and stared at her with relief. "Thank God." His wet hand cupped her cheek, sending warmth shooting through her body. "You don't know how badly I needed to hear that."

Cordie kissed his palm, then snuggled against his chest. When Brendan's arms wrapped around her, she smiled. This was everything she wanted in life. "Was it quite necessary to drag me in here with you?" She touched her lips to his chest, reveling in the intimacy as he stroked her hair.

"Um," he answered. "It seemed the thing to do at the time."

She giggled and rejoiced when he laughed along with her, knowing she would never forget this moment as long as she lived. Cordie rested her hand on his chest and looked up into his dark blue eyes. "I don't suppose you have another set of dry clothes for me to wear?"

A smile tugged at his lips as he shook his head. "But I'm certain I can keep you warm enough."

He lifted her in his arms and stood up in the tub, water dripping in rivulets down them both. He stepped out of the bath, and crossed the floor towards their bed. "Let's get you out of this, shall we?"

Back on her own feet, Cordie sucked in a surprised breath when Brendan's hands returned to the buttons of her nightrail.

"There's nothing to be nervous about," he told her, as he peeled the wet material from her body, letting it pool at their feet. "I'll be careful with you."

The cool air hit her body, and her nipples hardened into tight peaks. She was mortified that Brendan noticed this too, then his warm, wet hands gently caressed her breasts, pushed against her nipples, and Cordie thought she'd expire on the spot. The silky smoothness of his fingers on her bare skin was the most intense, exhilarating sensation she'd ever experienced.

His lips captured hers and Cordie couldn't stop the moan of pleasure from escaping when Brendan licked at her nipples, slid his hands around to cup her bottom, and massaged the muscles into taut awareness. Moist heat pooled between her legs, and *that* part of him prodded against her belly. He licked her lips. "I have needed you for so long."

Cordie sighed when he pressed her down onto the mattress beneath him. She stared up into his twilight eyes and swallowed. "Please," she said, when he only looked at her. Shouldn't he be doing *something*?

Brendan nuzzled her neck, and let his fingers trail down her side. "I don't want to rush, and I need to make sure you're ready for me, love."

Ready for him? She'd been ready for him for the last month. Denying it, hiding from it, wishing it away. But now… Now there was no reason not to…

His warm hand caressed her belly, then slid *lower*. Cordie held her breath. What was he doing? Then Brendan's mouth covered one of her nipples and he gently sucked, nipped, and then sucked again. The rhythm was her undoing. "Brendan," she gasped, unconsciously grasping his still wet hair.

A finger trailed through her springy hair and his palm cupped her mound. She tightened instantlysucked in a breath as his finger probed her folds, nudged at her entrance, then slowly pressed inside. She tightened instantly, but relaxed and when he suckled her breast.

Brendan's finger nudged at her entrance, and then slowly pressed forward. Cordie closed her eyes, reveling in the feel of him inside her.

Rhythmically, he pressed in and out of her, over and over, until Cordie was writhing beneath him. It was like nothing she'd ever imagined. Then his thumb brushed against *something*, and she lost complete control. Screaming her husband's name, release engulfed her. Her legs fell open, limp. She struggled to catch her breath.

Brendan's hand left her, moving slowly up her belly, trailing fire wherever he touched. He shifted his position, urging her legs wider, kneeling before her. His lips found hers, and he devoured her, tangling his tongue with hers, marking her as his. "Dear God, I love you," he whispered fervently.

He nudged again at her entrance, this time with something much larger than his finger and Cordie's eyes widened in surprise. Brendan kissed them closed, used his tongue to open her lips, stroke the moist softness of her mouth. He cupped her bottom, raised her slightly off the bed, and slowly, gently pushed into her. She sucked in a breath.

His handsome face looked strained as he pushed forward, and she sucked in a breath. She'd never imagined it would feel like this. Strange, exhilarating, urgent, all rolled into one. She wriggled against him, wanting him deeper, and he gasped. "For God's sake, Cordie. I'm trying to go slowly."

"Please, don't," she begged. "You're torturing me."

He choked on a laugh. "I think it's the other way 'round, my love." But he pressed himself deeper and groaned, his fingers digging into her skin.

Then he took a deep breath. "Please remember that I love you."

Cordie beamed at him. She could never forget that, no matter how many years she—

Brendan thrust forward, and she sucked in a breath, startled by the slight pain.

"Oh!"

He looked at once remorseful. "I'm so sorry."

But the pain was already ebbing, and she touched his cheek, hating to see his mournful expression. "I'm fine. But if you don't continue, I think I shall expire from want."

Relief washed across his face. "Thank God."

He moved deeper inside her, until it was impossible to determine where he ended and she began. Then he pulled out, only to thrust back inside. Over and over he did this, holding her in place with his hands, while strangled need coursed through her veins. Cordie writhed, wanting him closer, wanting him deeper, until he started to rock against that sensitive spot and all the stars in the sky fell from their celestial homes, crashing down on her.

"Oh, Cordie!" her husband growled, thrusting deep, one last time. It felt as if lava gushed inside her.

Brendan released his hold on her and collapsed at her side, holding her tightly in his arms. "My darling wife, I don't think I'll ever be the same."

Sated and exhausted, Cordie snuggled in his embrace, resting her head on his chest. "Ummm, never," she whispered dreamily.

Twenty-Seven

WITH early morning light streaming through the windows, Brendan slowly awoke. His wife was nestled against him, her soft breath tickling the hair on his chest. Last night had been the most amazing of his life. For the first time in so long, he was optimistic about the future.

He was desperately in love with his bride, and her with him—something he hadn't even dared hope for. Their marriage would secure his mother's letters, freeing him from the nightmare he'd been living for too many years.

Cordie stirred in his arms and he glanced again at her beautiful face. Her pert little nose was scrunched up and her hand fluttered toward her eyes. The morning light glinted off the golden band on her finger and his heart swelled with pride. Though this was not the route he would have preferred to take to the altar, or anvil as the case may be, he'd do it all over again.

Cordie's cold foot slid up his leg and his eyes flashed to her face, to find a teasing smile on her lips. "Good morning, husband."

He grinned back, still amazed at his luck that this goddess would warm his bed until the end of time. "Ah, my beautiful wife," he said, rolling Cordie to her back. "Are you sore, darling?" he asked, kissing her collarbone as his hand teased a nipple.

"A little," she admitted. "Though it was well worth it." An innocent blush colored her cheeks as she ran her fingers over his chest. "Must we leave, Brendan? Can't we just stay here forever?"

In other words, not back to their lives or the real world they'd left behind. He rose up on his arms and softly claimed her mouth, caressing her cheek. He'd do anything to make her happy, but they couldn't stay here. "This from the woman who told me yesterday she had no intention of playing my valet? How would we go on *here*, sweetheart?"

She furrowed her brow. "Well, not *here* then. But, well, I'm just not ready to give you up."

He wasn't all that anxious to return to London, either. Now that she was his wife, there was no pressing need for the letters. Her family would certainly hand them over. They didn't need to rush back for them. "Cordie, instead of heading for London, why don't we go to Bayhurst Court instead? I'm anxious for you to meet Thomas and Rose, for you to see my home — *our* home."

She smiled brightly, making his heart leap. "I would like that very much. Besides, I don't think I could take another long coach ride anyway for a while. My bottom will be bruised for months as it is."

"Indeed?" he asked with a grin. "Let me see."

Mortified, she pushed away from him. "I beg your pardon?"

Life with her would never be dull. Brendan tugged her back into his arms. "Now be a dutiful wife and let me see your bottom."

"Absolutely not!"

He kissed her, deeply, relishing the taste of her lips and the warmth of her mouth. Cordie's fingers danced through his hair, and he groaned, wishing madly that she hadn't admitted to being sore. It would be so nice to take her again. With strength, he didn't know he possessed, Brendan pulled out of his wife's hold, smiled rakishly, and flipped her onto her belly.

She wriggled away, trying to escape him, however she was laughing too hard to do so. Although Brendan had only meant to run his hands over her backside and tickle her, the number of healed scars all across her back stopped him short.

It felt as if the wind had been knocked out of him.

"Dear God," he muttered, tentatively tracing one of the longer scars with his forefinger.

Her laughter gone, Cordie looked over her shoulder, panic etched across her brow. "Is it worse than I thought?"

Brendan glanced briefly at her bottom. Though he didn't see any bruising, there appeared to be scars there too. "Who did this to you?"

"What do you mean?" she asked, scrambling out of his grasp and covering herself with the counterpane.

Fear flashed in her eyes, and he was certain his heart stopped. "You know exactly what I mean. You've been injured. Many times." Some scars were older than others. She hadn't acquired them in a carriage accident or something similar. They'd cover her entire body if that were the case.

Cordie's gaze dropped to her lap. "Please."

"Please what?" he nearly roared, but he tried to maintain his anger and it came out more as a hiss. "Sweetheart, who did this to you?" He was going to kill whoever it was. That anyone would hurt his darling wife, so full of spirit and life, made his jaw clench and his muscles tense.

She heaved a sigh and shrugged. "My mother's always found me to be a bit willful, and..." Her voice trailed off.

Her mother? For the love of God! She was one of the few people he *couldn't* kill. A man, he could call out. But a woman? His mother-in-law? As fury and rage faded into despair, Brendan hauled his wife back into his arms, holding her tightly to him. "Cordie my love, no one will ever hurt you again!" he vowed hoarsely.

Her arms wrapped around his neck and she kissed his cheek. "Brendan, I'm all right."

He would see to it that she was better than *all right* the rest of their days. It was good they'd already decided on Bayhurst Court. He would need time to adjust to this revelation, and somehow he'd have to find the strength to behave civilly to Lady Avery. He wasn't certain how much time that would take.

⚜

Cordie struggled to get a brush through her hair. A bird's nest was an apt description. This is what happened when one went to bed with wet hair and participated in vigorous activities. The memory of those activities, however, was like a dream come true, so she couldn't really complain. She could, in the future, make sure her hair was braided before indulging again. This was awful, especially without a maid. She winced, trying to untangle a knot on the side of her head. It was going to take forever.

The door opened to their room and she looked over her shoulder, embarrassed when she saw the confused expression on Brendan's face. She must look a mess.

"Are you all right?" he asked.

Cordie pursed her lips. "I'm just having a bit of trouble with my hair, but I'll be done soon."

He stepped forward and put out his hand. "Give me the brush."

"I can manage on my own."

"You're making it worse, love. And I do so love your hair. I'd hate for you to be bald. Besides, you played my valet yesterday, let me play your maid."

Cordie bit her lip, looking up at him. This didn't fall under normal husbands' duties, did it? She couldn't imagine Kelfield doing such a thing for Livvie.

"I have sisters, Cordie. I've done this a time or two."

She shrugged, but handed over the brush. "Just be careful and don't tug too rough."

Brendan started with one side, and very gently, with the precision of a lady's maid, untangled her hair. Her silky strands fell against her neck, and he moved to the back. "Rose loves to have her hair brushed. She'll probably ask you to do it for her."

"She'll like me, won't she?" Cordie asked, suddenly worried how his family would view her.

"She'll love you," he promised, moving the brush through her tresses with much greater ease than she had done. "Probably too much. If she makes you uncomfortable, you'll have to let me know."

Cordie couldn't imagine the stunning girl she'd only seen from afar could make her uncomfortable. Besides, she was Brendan's sister. They'd have to find a way to make everything work. From what he'd said about Lady Rosamund, she'd be in their care until the end of time.

Brendan finally finished with all the tangles, and then pressed his lips to her cheek. "Apparently I'll have to be more careful with you in the future."

"Don't you dare." Cordie grinned. She didn't want him to be careful. She didn't want any less than what he'd given her the night before. His warm breath against her cheek sent delightful shivers racing across her skin as the memory of their wedding night flashed again in her mind.

Brendan chuckled. "My adventurous wife."

She stood from her seat and lightly touched her lips to his. "Hmm."

His arms wrapped around her waist. "Are you ready, love? Wilson has the coach prepared."

Cordie shook her head. "In a minute. Let me just put my hair up."

He took a handful of her hair and brought it to his nose. "Leave it unbound."

Her cheeks warmed, but she nodded anyway.

As they left the little inn, Cordie's heart leapt. As peaceful and idyllic as she found Scotland, she was anxious to see her new home. Her new family. She climbed inside the coach with Brendan right on her heels. He pulled her onto his lap and nuzzled her neck, making her giggle.

Cradled in her husband's arms, Cordie had never felt so loved or so safe. She was still unsure how things had turned out so well for her, though she didn't want to question her good fortune. She just wanted to enjoy it.

"Sweetheart," he said, "we really should have a talk."

Cordie tipped her head back to see him, as uneasiness spread through her. Why did they need to have a talk? Everything seemed so perfect. "What about?"

"One of the things I most love about you is your adventurous spirit, but... Well, you're my wife now."

She pursed her lips. "And you want to make me a prisoner."

"You have quite a way of looking at things," he answered with a frown. "I only want to keep you safe."

"I am perfectly capable of making my own decisions," she said, scrambling off his lap.

His arms tightened around her and he pulled her back. "Don't run away from me."

"Let me go!"

"Not until you listen to me." Then he kissed her temple and softened his voice. "Back in London, you nearly stopped my heart on more than one occasion. You recklessly went about Town with no concern for your safety, and I can't allow that. If something happened to you..."

Cordie folded her arms across her chest and glared at him. She was not reckless... Well, not most of the time.

He cleared his throat. "We're lucky no one else knows of your antics. If they did, your reputation would not be salvageable."

He sounded just like her mother. Cordie shook her head. "I don't care what people think, Brendan. I'm not going to live my life afraid of what others might think of me. Just so you know, I intend to resume my friendship with the Duchess of Kelfield, and there's not a thing you can do to stop me. Olivia is my oldest and dearest friend, and I'm not willing to give her up."

Twenty-Eight

BRENDAN gaped at his wife. What was that about? He didn't care if she was friends with the Duchess of Kelfield. The girl was Robert and Caroline's cousin, after all. He'd insist Cordie stay away from the *Duke* of Kelfield's friends — the Marquess of Haversham, in particular — but he didn't mind the duchess at all.

"All right," he said cautiously. Who knew what might set her off, and he was intent on calming her. They had a long ride ahead of them, and he'd rather not spend it arguing.

Cordie narrowed her green eyes on him. "All right? That's all you have to say?"

What was he *supposed* to say? What was she expecting? "I don't have a problem with Her Grace. Some of Kelfield's compatriots are a different matter, but I've always found the duchess to be a generous lady."

Whatever retort his wife had planned for him died on her tongue. Then she sagged against him. "You don't care if I'm friends with Livvie?"

"Not if you don't care that I'm friends with Astwick."

A laugh escaped Cordie's throat.

"You laugh. He's quite irritating." Was she worried about the Duchess of Kelfield all along? He wished she'd have said something. He could have put her mind at ease weeks ago. "Cordie, why would you think I'd keep you from your friends?"

She swallowed, then closed her eyes as if she was in pain. "Mother wouldn't let me see her after she married Kelfield, and ever since I've been all alone. Not completely. I mean, Phoebe has been a wonderful friend and I'm thrilled Tristan and Russell have returned from France unscathed. But..." She heaved a sigh. "I've known Livvie since before we could walk. She's always been in my life and I in hers. It's been an awful strain. I felt as if my heart had been ripped out of my chest."

"My love, I am *not* your mother," he said, the memories of his wife's scars fresh in his mind making his words harsher than he would have liked.

"Well, Captain Seaton was adamant I wouldn't maintain our friendship either."

Who the devil was that? "Captain Seaton?"

"He was my fiancé."

Brendan's body tightened and his mouth fell open. "Fiancé?" Why was this the first he was hearing about Captain Seaton, for God's sake?

"Well, not anymore," she quickly clarified.

"I should say not." She was *his* wife after all. "Can I expect to be called out in the same fashion as Kelfield?" He wasn't sure he'd ever get that image out of his mind. Both Major Moore and the duke were emotional disasters over the duchess.

Cordie shook her head. "Not the same thing. Technically, we were never engaged. I determined what sort of dictatorial husband he intended to be before our plans were finalized, and I cried off. He never even spoke with Gregory on the matter."

A moment of clarity engulfed Brendan. All of this was why she'd fought so hard to keep herself from him. The quandary she'd spoken of. She'd loved him, but was afraid he'd treat her the way her mother did and Captain Seaton would have. What a fool the captain was to have lost her, a mistake Brendan wouldn't make.

He caressed his wife's cheek. "If you want to resume your friendship with Her Grace, you have my blessing. You have my name, Cordie. If an association with us helps the duchess in society, I'm more than willing to give it."

"You are?" she asked, looking hopefully into his eyes.

Did she think he was an ogre? "Cordie, I dashed from Bayhurst Court when Caroline Staveley summoned me for her rather impromptu ball in honor of the Kelfields. If I didn't shy away then, why would I do so now?"

"I hadn't thought of it like that," she said. Then she shook her head. "But you said you didn't have a choice. I remember, because at the time I thought it was a rather unkind thing to say in front of Livvie."

Brendan rested his head against the leather squabs. "'Your stodgy presence is required to lend Livvie an air of respectability.' Those were the words my dear friend Caroline Staveley used to beg me to Town. My irritation that evening was directed at her, not your friend."

"Oh," his wife said softly.

"She's a good friend?" he asked, glad his wife didn't seem angry with him anymore.

"Very."

"I'm sorry you were kept from her." He kissed the top of her head. "I love you, Cordie. I would never do that to you."

"Thank you." Then she smiled shyly at him. "I'll try to be a dutiful wife."

She would *try* to be a dutiful wife. Brendan bit back a smile. As far as concessions went, it wasn't much. But where Cordie Clayworth was concerned, it was an enormous coup. "I'm a very lucky man."

"Are you?" she asked quietly.

"Hmm," he answered, winking at his bride. "The first time I met you, I wanted to kiss every inch of you. And now I can do so whenever I want."

She laughed and pushed away from him. "Lady Staveley's ball was *not* the first time you met me."

She had said they'd met before, hadn't she? He'd somehow forgotten that. "When did I first meet you then?"

"At your wedding breakfast. Eleanor was Marina's maid of honor. We were all there."

His eyes widened. That was *thirteen* years ago. No wonder he didn't remember her. "Good God, Cordie, how old were you?"

"Seven. And I remember thinking at the time that you reminded me of a golden haired fairy tale prince."

Seven? Brendan winced. He'd robbed the cradle. Literally. "I'd prefer to think we met at Staveley's, if you don't mind."

"You don't want to think about Marina's connection to my family," she said understandingly.

Marina's connection to the Averys. If she hadn't been close to them, if she hadn't given them his mother's damning letters, he'd have never pursued Cordie. In a strange way of thinking, it was the only gift Marina had ever given him. Brendan shook his head. "No, I'd just prefer not to think that my bride was *seven* when I married the first time. It makes me feel old."

She laughed.

He loved her laugh. The way she sounded so carefree and lighthearted was like a balm for his soul. He would never tire of the sound. Still she was laughing at *him*. "Oh, don't think I've forgotten, my darling wife. I know very well that you think I'm old and stodgy."

"You *are* thirty-five, already with one foot in the grave," she teased.

Brendan slid her from his lap and edged Cordie towards the other end of the bench. Then he stalked towards her before she could bolt, not that there was any place she could hide from him inside their coach. In the blink of an eye, he had her trapped beneath him, ruthlessly tickling her sides until she begged him between squeals of laughter to stop.

His hands stilled, settling on her waist and he kissed her. She opened instantly for him, and their tongues touched, nearly melding together. Cordie's hand slowly slid down, until she cupped his ass, making him groan against her mouth, wanting her, needing her all over again. "How sore are you?" he growled.

She grinned. "Is *that* what you were asking this morning? You should have been more clear, Brendan. I was sore, but not that sore."

A mistake he wouldn't make again. He reached for the hem of her ball gown, and began edging it up her leg, a rakish smile on his face the whole while.

Cordie's mesmerizing green eyes widened in surprise. "Not in *here*." She slapped at his hands.

"Why not?" he asked, ignoring her blows and tugging her skirts to her waist.

"W-well," she gulped. "There's Wilson for one thing."

Brendan chuckled. "Wilson won't hear us, and if he does, he values his employment too much to mention it." He untied her drawers and kissed her neck.

"B-but in a coach?" she continued. "Is that even possible?"

His lips moved to her earlobe, where he nibbled. "I assure you it is."

"Oh, Brendan!" Cordie moaned.

He slid her drawers from her legs and made quick work with the buttons of his trousers. His cock sprang free, hard and straining, anxious for the soft, feminine folds nestled between her legs. With his knees, he nudged Cordie's legs wide, with one of them falling over the edge of the bench.

Gently, he ran a finger along her warm feminine folds, thanking God she was already wet and waiting for him. The heady scent of woman, his woman, filled the space between them and he reached for his cock, guiding himself to her swollen entrance. He pushed inside her and his head fell back. A guttural sound escaped his throat as her warmth closed around him. Her arms slid around his waist, pulling him closer.

Her core melted as he slowly pressed deeper, the warm honey of her essence coating him, pushing him to the edge. It took all of his strength not to pour himself into in her that very instant, but he wanted their pleasure to last beyond just a moment. He braced his hands on the wall of the coach for purchase and started his slow, deliberate torture.

Cordie's eyes fluttered closed until he ran his tongue along the creamy skin of her breast, dipped to tease a rosy nipple out of hiding. Her eyes flew open and she started, clenched her legs around him in response. He covered her face and neck with kisses, whispering words of love and encouragement with each thrust. Her breath came in pants as he rocked them towards climax. He clasped her to him as they found their release, not wanting to leave the intimacy of their joining.

The rocking carriage was more arousing than soothing, and within a short time Brendan found himself as hard and wanting as a man in the first throes of manhood. It was only concern for her newly aroused femininity that had him withdrawing and cradling her while she slept.

∽⚜∾

Somehow, Cordie slept through the remainder of the day, and only awoke when Brendan laid her across a bed at an inn. She'd had the most wonderful dreams all afternoon, each of them ending the same, wrapped in her husband's arms.

"Are you still tired?" Brendan whispered.

She shouldn't be, not with all the sleep she'd gotten. Still, she could barely find the energy to answer him. "Uh-huh," she said dreamily.

He chuckled as he kissed her cheek. "My sleeping beauty. Do you want to stay in your gown? Or sleep in your chemise?"

Cordie blinked her eyes open, trying to adjust to the light in the room. "No more nightrails you've charmed out of innkeepers?"

A smile tugged at the corner of his lips. "I've only been successful at charming *you* today, love."

She returned his smile. "I am glad to hear it. I don't like the idea of maids all across England falling in love with my husband, trying to woo him with their nightrails."

Brendan dropped on the bed beside her, and cradled her against him. "If anyone deserves to be jealous, Cordie, it's me. In the last fortnight, you've received two marriage proposals—both right in front of me, I might add—and just today I learned you had a fiancé. We're going to have to do something about your proclivity for attracting men."

"I received *three* marriage proposals," she corrected him with a giggle. "Brookfield's, yours, and then Haversham's. But the marquess wasn't sincere."

"How do you know?" his voice sounded strangled.

"Because he'd just agreed to take me home before you barged in and punched him in the nose. Poor fellow."

Brendan growled, deep in his chest. "Blackguard deserved more than that."

"He only asked me so that it would seem like I had a choice. But he knew I'd never pick him. He knew I loved you."

"You told *him*?" Brendan asked with wonder.

Cordie shook her head. "He guessed. When I couldn't..." She *couldn't* finish that sentence. What a mistake she'd nearly made. Thank heaven Brendan had found her, had whisked her off to Scotland.

"I'd prefer not to think about the scoundrel. From now on I want to be the only man in your thoughts," her husband whispered in her ear, before rolling her onto her back. Then he made love to her over and over again.

Twenty-Nine

CORDIE stared out the coach window with anxious anticipation, as her new home grew ever closer. Bayhurst Court, a sandstone Tudor mansion, stood proudly against a backdrop of Derbyshire's rolling hills. She looked back at her husband over her shoulder, to see him smiling at her.

"You'll love it," he told her again.

"And you're sure they'll like me?" she asked for the hundredth time.

Brendan nodded. "Why are you so worried?"

How could she explain it to him? "Well, they're your family...and I've never met them, but suddenly I'm one of them, and I..."

"I've never met your brother, Lord Avery."

Cordie shrugged. As if Gregory would care one way or the other. He'd just be glad she wasn't publicly ruined. "It's not the same thing, Brendan. We aren't going to live with *my* family."

"Rose and Thomas are your family now, Cordie. And they're going to love you. I promise."

As if on cue, the carriage rambled to a stop on the drive. Brendan gave her a quick kiss, then she took a steadying breath before Wilson opened the door. Her husband stepped out first and then offered her his arm. Cordie glanced up, stumbled slightly as her knees went weak. An entire household staff littered the front lawn.

"Did they know we were coming?"

Brendan quirked a grin. "I sent a note from Gretna Green. It probably arrived a few days ago, as the mail coach didn't stop along the way like we did."

Cordie blushed, remembering their stops. Each inn where her

husband made passionate love to her. Brendan winked at her, and Cordie felt certain he was remembering the same things she was at the moment.

"Uncle!" a boy shouted, running towards them. He was a handsome boy with light brown hair, and Brendan's twilight eyes. He stopped short before he reached them, furrowing his brow.

"Thomas," Brendan greeted his nephew with a smile. "Allow me to present my wife, Cordelia, the Countess of Clayworth. Cordie love, this is Thomas."

Thomas Reese bowed slightly. "My lady."

She nodded to the boy and smiled. "I've heard so much about you, Thomas. It's very nice to meet you."

"He looked surprised at her words. "Thank you." Then he looked at Brendan. "Uncle, if you have a moment, I need to speak with you."

"Is she here?" screeched a voice from inside the house. Cordie froze to her spot, as she recognized it instantly.

So did Brendan. His handsome face turned at once to a scowl. "Lady Avery is here?" he asked his nephew.

Thomas glanced first at Cordie and then at his uncle before nodding. "And her sons."

Cordie's eyes flew to the front of the manor house. Her mother was here? Her brothers? She felt faint, but Brendan's arm snaked around her waist. "Breathe, love. We knew we'd have to face them sooner or later."

She had been hoping for never, but before she could respond, her mother bolted from the house. "You ungrateful child!" she wailed, causing the staff assembled on the lawn to all draw a collective breath.

"My dear mother-in-law," Brendan called smoothly over the crowd. "We are so pleased you have come to visit."

He really was an excellent liar. Her mother stopped in her tracks, though she glared at Cordie. "Thank you for your generosity, Lord Clayworth," she clipped out.

⁂

The ability to maintain his temper under extraordinary circumstances was one of Brendan's better qualities, or at least he'd always thought so. However, keeping calm in Lady Avery's presence was a test of wills. Between the strained look on Thomas' face and the way Cordie shook at the sight of her mother, his blood boiled. Still he needed the letters from the woman. He couldn't lose his control.

Thomas tugged on his jacket and he looked at his nephew. It was obvious the boy had great need to speak with him, but he couldn't let Cordie go unguarded either—not with images of her scarred back fresh in his mind. He wouldn't leave his wife alone the entire time that harridan was under his roof.

"Fielding," he addressed his butler, who looked rather confused on the lawn along with several footmen, maids, grooms. "Please have tea delivered to the blue salon for our guests. My countess, Thomas, and I will be there shortly. We have a bit of business to attend to first."

His nephew gulped, and Brendan winked at him, hoping to relieve the boy of his anxiety.

Lady Avery harrumphed, but retreated to the house, trailed by half his staff. After waiting a moment, Brendan led his wife and nephew toward the gardens. With everyone else inside, it seemed the safest place to talk. "Thomas, what do you need to tell me?"

The boy frowned, glancing at Cordie, then shrugged, unwilling to speak.

His wife gently touched Thomas' shoulder. "She hasn't been too awful, has she?"

His nephew's eyes lit up. "We were afraid..."

"That I was like her?" his wife supplied.

The boy shrugged again and Brendan ruffled his hair. "Not to worry, Tom. Nothing could be further from the truth. How's Rose? Where is she?"

Thomas smiled. "Well, Richard Lester's come back to the village—"

Richard Lester? Brendan's day just went from bad to worse. When the young man had left Sudbury two years ago, Brendan had despaired for Rose's health. She'd been so desperately in love with the fellow. "Oh, God," he moaned. "What's he doing here?" And what was Brendan going to do when Lester left again?

"Well, he took Mr. Pitney's position at the vicarage."

Richard Lester was the new vicar? Brendan rubbed his brow. The village had been trying for some time to replace the late Mr. Pitney. Never in a million years would he have thought the position would be filled by their old neighbor. "She's with Lester?" he asked, already knowing the answer.

Thomas nodded his head. "Old Mrs. Lester invited her for lunch."

Damn the woman! She knew exactly how badly Rose had handled her son's departure. He heaved a sigh.

Cordie touched his arm, concern etched across her brow. "Is everything all right?"

He scoffed his answer. His immature sister was bound to get her heart broken a second time—not that he could do anything about it— and his offensive mother-in-law was visiting for an indeterminate amount of time. Cordie was right. They should have stayed in Scotland. "I'll tell you all about it later, love."

"Are you home for good?" Thomas asked. "Did you finish whatever business of grandmother's you went to London for?"

He should have already told Cordie about the letters. He'd have to do so soon, but not now. They had too many other things to worry about at the moment. "Not quite. I'm still working on it."

He avoided his wife's questioning gaze.

⚜

Cordie had been anxious about her arrival at Bayhurst Court, but now she was very nearly trembling. Why had her mother come here? Brendan excused Thomas, who was relieved not to have to suffer through tea with Lady Avery. For that, Cordie was relieved too. Who knew what awful things her mother had said to the boy?

Brendan led her into his home and down a corridor. "Don't worry. She can't stay forever."

After a few turns, he directed her into a parlor, and Cordie caught her breath. They were *all* here. Her mother, Russell, Tristan, even Gregory! "Goodness, was all this necessary?"

Her brothers all rose from their spots when she entered the room. "Good to see you too, Cor," Tristan said with a wink.

They all resumed their places when Brendan led Cordie to a settee and sat beside her.

"So, are you married?" her mother demanded from a frilly chintz chair, scowling.

"Of course we are," she replied. What did her mother think? That she'd taken off for Scotland with the earl but had gotten sidetracked?

Her mother shook her head with disapproval. "You are too reckless and willful for your own good!"

Brendan tensed next to her. "Then think how fortunate you are to have her off your hands, Lady Avery."

"I would have expected better from you, my lord," she shot back. "You saw fit to send a letter to Lord Astwick, but neither of you thought to send one to me? I was beside myself with worry."

"Haversham told us what happened," Russell offered quietly from his corner. "So we weren't *that* worried."

"I wrote a letter. In Stamford," Cordie protested. "And it was a very good letter. Clayworth read it himself."

"Indeed," Brendan stiffly added from her side. "We sent both letters from the inn. Cordie's letter to you and mine to Astwick."

Her mother went on as if she hadn't heard a word. "Then we arrived here, and—" she humphed indignantly— "well, my lord, if I'd had any inkling of the sort of household you run, I'd have never let you near my daughter."

"Mother!" Gregory hissed.

"What is that supposed to mean?" Brendan asked, sliding forward in his seat, leveling her with his iciest glare.

"It means, sir," Lady Avery began, her shrill voice echoing off the walls, "that you have some bastard child running around this place and that sister of yours is... Well, I don't even know *what* to call her."

Cordie cringed. Her mother was the most cruel of any person she'd ever met. Brendan didn't deserve this treatment. All he'd done was rescue her from her own folly.

The blood drained from Brendan's face, and Cordie placed her hand on his back, wishing them both away from her family. "Madam," he clipped out. "I'll have your bags packed and you can be on your way."

Lady Avery leapt from her seat, glaring at him. "The sooner, the better." Then she turned her eyes on Cordie. "I always knew you'd end up ruined. I take no pleasure from being right."

"Or you could leave now, and I'll have your bags sent after you," Brendan suggested with a sneer.

Thirty

HIS wife's three brothers gaped at him, and Brendan rubbed his brow, hoping to stave off a headache. He probably should have held his temper better, but the acidic words that spewed from the woman's mouth made it impossible for him to keep his control. For her to speak so disparagingly about Thomas and Rose and then Cordie—he couldn't sit back and listen to it. If she was a man, he'd have throttled her.

The brother he'd never met before, which meant he *had* to be Lord Avery, pushed his wire-rimmed glasses up his nose. "Well, good for you, Clayworth. Someone should have said that a long time ago."

Then the two officers roared with laughter. "I've never seen her turn quite that shade of purple," Lieutenant Avery chortled.

"Or speechless," Captain Avery added, though he tried to bring his merriment under control.

"It's hardly a laughing matter," Cordie chastised her brothers, looking from one to the others. "How could you bring her here?"

Lord Avery shook his head. "You don't honestly think *we* brought her here, do you? She'd already trapped these two in her clutches before abducting me from Pappelwick. I think my ears are still bleeding from her wailing the whole journey."

Captain Avery grinned. "Yes, we had to rush out here, to make sure you were safe, Cordie."

Brendan's jaw clenched. *Make sure she was safe.* Where were these big strapping men when Lady Avery was taking her frustrations out on Cordie? So the captain and lieutenant were abroad, but what was Gregory Avery's excuse?

"Well, as you can see, I am perfectly safe *and* legally married," she replied tartly. "So, love you all as I do, there is no reason for you to stay. Do have a nice trip back."

Lieutenant Avery chuckled. "You do need to work on your hostess skills, sis. I'm starting to feel unwanted."

"Are you saying I should be more cordial to my *uninvited* guests?"

When her brothers dissolved into another peal of laughter, Brendan calculated the odds of his wife being furious with him if he murdered the trio. He somehow thought she might be a bit miffed. Instead, he cleared his throat and leveled Captain Avery with a firm stare. After all, the middle brother did seem to be the most serious of the group. "If Cordie's letter didn't make it to Avery House, what's the word about Town?"

"Am I ruined?" Cordie asked quietly beside him.

The captain shook his head. "Ah, well, Lord Astwick has taken care of that situation. The fellow does have an imagination. Every female in Town is enchanted by his flowery version of your great love story, complete with a spontaneous elopement. Of course, the men would like a word with you for making them all look bad."

Lieutenant Avery added, "And then there's Brookfield. He's furious, says you stole Cordie from him."

Captain Avery snorted. "Please. He's an opium eater. No one pays any attention to him."

Brendan frowned at the statement. He hadn't heard that about the viscount, but now that the captain mentioned it, the viscount did seem odd. He'd had the look of a desperate man when he'd proposed to Cordie on the steps of Avery House, and his eyes didn't quite seem right. At the time, Brendan had only focused on his outlandish behavior. It was indeed fortunate he'd come across Cordie that particular day before Brookfield got his hands on her. The man wasn't even in his right mind.

"An opium eater?" Cordie asked, her green eyes wide.

Captain Avery nodded. "I've seen the look on countless soldiers' faces. They start on the stuff in army hospitals for pain, and then it starts to become something else. I'm not sure what started Brookfield on his course, but I know an eater when I see one."

"But everyone else is appeased?" Brendan asked? He'd owe Astwick the rest of his life for pulling this off.

"What about Haversham?" Cordie asked, causing Brendan to scowl. What did she care what that bastard thought? "Has he said anything?"

Her brothers' smiles vanished instantly. At least they were all of a mind about Haversham. The lieutenant sat forward in his seat, glaring at his sister. "You're lucky Clayworth got to you first. I don't even know what I would have done to you."

"He was right out of his mind," the captain confirmed. "Scared the devil out of poor Miss Greywood. I've never seen Tris so furious. Poor girl was shaking like a leaf by the time he was through with her."

"What did you do to Phoebe?" Cordie demanded.

Lieutenant Avery scoffed. "Nothing she didn't deserve. Annoying little twit. Helping you take off like that. Her brother ought to keep a better eye on her."

The room fell silent, as all three Avery men realized *they* should have kept a better eye on their sister. But for once, Brendan was glad they hadn't. If things had been different, he might never have convinced Cordie to marry him. The ineptitude of the brothers Avery had been a blessing in disguise.

Still there was the matter of the letters. Lady Avery would probably not speak with him, so he'd have to deal with the baron. That was probably better anyway. He wasn't certain he could contain his fury with his mother-in-law for even the smallest amount of time. "I am assuming you're Lord Avery," he said to the dark haired fellow with green eyes hidden behind wire- rimmed glasses.

The man blushed and rushed forward with his hand outstretched. "My apologies, Clayworth. How unforgivably rude. Gregory Avery, your humble servant. I can't thank you enough for...well, for saving Cordie from her own recklessness."

His wife stiffened at his side, so Brendan took her hand in his and squeezed reassuringly. "It was my pleasure. I would like a moment of your time however, Lord Avery. I have something of a sensitive nature I need to discuss with you."

"Of course."

Brendan stood, then eyed the two officers with his sternest look. "If either of you leave my wife alone with *that* woman, I'll have your heads."

The two exchanged identical looks of surprise. "Bit overprotective," Captain Avery replied. "What do you think mother's going to do?"

He'd rather not think about the answer to that question, and he darkened his scowl. "Do I have your word to keep Cordie in your sight?"

"Brendan, that's not necessary," she whispered.

But it was necessary. He hated leaving her himself, but he'd rather deal with Lord Avery in private. Cordie didn't need to know the particulars. "Captain? Lieutenant?" He waited until both officers answered in the affirmative before he led Lord Avery to his study.

The baron tried to relieve the tension by trying to explain that their mother meant well, and she'd just been worried about Cordie's wellbeing. Brendan barely paid attention to the man's words, though he did get the impression Lord Avery felt his mother was harmless. Now was not the time to dispel his thoughts on the subject. At the moment he'd rather not alienate the man, since he needed his assistance. There would be plenty of time in the future to go down that particular road.

He offered his brother-in-law a glass of whiskey when they entered his study, then poured one for himself before sliding into the seat behind his mahogany desk.

"This is about the dowry?" Gregory Avery asked, before taking a swallow of whiskey.

Dowry? That hadn't even crossed his mind until now. He'd be glad to forgo that for his mother's letters. He had no need of her money. "No." Brendan shook his head. "I know you're aware of my previous marriage," he began.

Lord Avery blanched. "Oh, God." He placed his glass on the edge of Brendan's desk, squeezed his eyes shut ran a hand through his dark hair.

Well, it was obvious the baron was familiar with the topic of conversation. The rest should be easy. Certainly Avery wouldn't want his sister's life to be turned upside down from the contents of the letters. Brendan slid forward in his seat. "Well, about that—"

"I didn't know you knew," Lord Avery said with a wince.

Of course he knew. His wife had taunted him with their existence. "Marina didn't exactly make a secret of it."

Apparently unable to remain seated, the baron stood and paced around the room. "I-I... Oh, God!" The man sounded positively tortured.

"There's no reason for all this, Avery. I just want what's mine."

The baron stopped in his tracks and the color slowly drained from his face. "Are you going to make Cordie suffer because of me?"

It was now obvious they weren't talking about the same thing, though Brendan wasn't quite certain what the topic was at the moment. He frowned at his brother-in-law. "Why would I do that?"

"To punish me," the baron answered quickly. "But I've been suffering for years, Clayworth. I lost her, and I lost my child for God's sake. Isn't that enough? Cordie shouldn't be made to pay the price for my indiscretions."

Brendan's mind raced, trying to make sense of Gregory Avery's blathering. Until he hit on the answer, or at least suspected he had a fairly good idea of what the young baron was talking about. He suddenly felt sick. Gregory Avery was the father of Marina's child, or at least he thought he was. The answer was clear as day. Lord Avery thought he wanted to berate him for his past with Marina.

Brendan heaved a sigh. At least he was on the right trail. *The lion holds your secrets*, Marina had said. Gregory Avery was the head of his family. His crest was a roaring lion. Marina had given the letters to her lover for safe-keeping. *Gregory Avery was the lion.* "All I want, Avery, are my mother's letters. Return them to me and all is forgiven."

The man gaped at him. "What letters?"

Thirty-One

WHAT letters?

Brendan shook his head as irritation flooded him. Did this man intend to play him for a fool? More of a fool than he'd already played him for? He clenched his jaw and slowly rose from his seat, keeping his eyes leveled on his brother-in-law all the while. "I'm in no mood for games, Avery. I know Marina gave you letters that belonged to my mother and I want them back. Where are they? London? Nottinghamshire?"

The man shook his head, staring at him in bewilderment. "Marina never gave me any letters, Clayworth. She never gave me anything," he replied sadly.

Brendan clutched the corner of his desk. Damn if the man didn't look sincere. But it didn't make any sense. *Avery was the lion.* Avery was her lover. Who else would she have given the letters to? Had she hidden them somewhere? "Where did your...liaisons take place with my wife?"

Gregory Avery gulped nervously. "I—We... Marina always came to me at Rufford Hall. It started when she would visit Eleanor, but over the years after Ellie was gone, she'd come under the ruse of visiting mother and Cordie."

Dear God! Brendan winced. *Not* Lady Avery. "If she didn't give the letters to you, then she gave them to your mother. I need them."

His brother-in-law narrowed his eyes. "Why? What's in them?"

Brendan stared at Gregory Avery and he clamped his mouth shut. He'd never spoken the awful words aloud to anyone, not his friends, not Cordie, not even to himself. He certainly couldn't say it to one of the men who'd cuckolded him. "Because they're mine," he growled. "And I think you've taken quite enough from me, don't you?"

"I—I," Lord Avery stuttered, then he squared his shoulders. "Look, Clayworth, I know I was in the wrong. I've told myself over the years that, because I loved her and you didn't, that it was all right. I suppose God will decide that in the end. But putting my past indiscretions aside, if you're involved with something nefarious, something that could hurt my sister, I have a right to know."

"Something that could hurt your sister?" Brendan roared, rising from his seat, pounding his fist on his desk. "Would that you were so concerned about her before our marriage."

"Someone should have watched her better, I concede. But—"

"Not *someone*, Avery! You! While you've been licking your wounds over my dead wife, your sister has been subjected to that monster you call a mother. And *now* you're worried about Cordie? A little late for that."

The baron's brow furrowed. "What do you mean by that? What do you mean my mother is a monster?"

Brendan's gaze darkened, while the images of his wife's scarred back flashed in his mind. "Let me be perfectly clear, so there are no misunderstandings, Avery. You have a sadistic mother. And when I saw the injuries she's inflicted on Cordie over the years, I wanted to kill her with my own hands. I still want to, but that would only bring more pain to my wife and I refuse to hurt her, so I'm controlling my temper as best I can. But you'd be wise to limit my exposure to your mother."

"Injuries?" the baron echoed, his frown deepening.

How blind was the man, for God's sake? "More than I can count, all across her back."

"Oh, my God." Gregory Avery's mouth fell open. "I—I had no idea. When we were children mother would...but I didn't think she still was," he added in a horrified whisper. "Why didn't Cordie say something? Why didn't she tell me?"

Most likely because his head was buried so deep in the sand, she couldn't depend on his help. Since Avery looked so forlorn, Brendan kept that thought to himself. Cordie was safe now. It wouldn't do any good to berate the man for a past he couldn't change, and there were no more younger sisters that needed protecting.

He did, however, still need his mother's letters. "Your sister is very independent. Perhaps you've noticed." Brendan sighed. "Listen, Avery, despite our...history, we're family now. Trust me when I say it's important I get those letters back. My future depends upon it. So does Cordie's, since she's my wife."

Gregory Avery's green eyes blinked at him. "That bad?"

Brendan nodded. Once.

"Then you're going to have to tell me what it is, Clayworth. If we don't find them, I'll need to have a plan to take care of Cordie, if whatever this is catches up with you."

"She's my wife. I'll keep her safe." Besides, he'd never entrust her to Gregory Avery's care.

"You can't even keep yourself safe."

Brendan shook his head, then roughly rubbed his brow. Her dowry. He could put it in a trust for her. If he was found out and hung, the title would go into abeyance. The crown would seize all of *his* assets. But Cordie could get by with her dowry. He was sure he could convince her to watch after Rose and Thomas for him. Once she got to know them, she'd love them, he had no doubt. Never had he met a woman with such strong loyalties. She wouldn't let anything happen to Thomas or Rose. Cordie was a strong, willful woman. If he set things up right, she'd survive. With the enormous amount her family had bestowed on her, the three of them could live comfortably — without her ever having to reside under an Avery roof again. Perhaps he could move a sizable amount into a trust for Thomas as well, and then —

A knock on his door brought him back to the present. "Come," he barked.

A lanky, auburn-haired fellow poked his head inside the study. *Richard Lester.* Could his day get any worse? "Ah, Lester. I heard you were back in Sudbury."

The young vicar blushed. Brendan wanted to yank the white collar from around his neck and strangle him with it. Rose did not need *this*.

"Lord Clayworth," Lester said softly. "I was hoping to speak with you. Is now a good time?"

Brendan glanced at his brother-in-law. "Find out from your mother where she has my letters, Avery. We'll finish this later."

The baron nodded, stood, and quietly quit the room.

Brendan gestured to the vacated seat. "Sit, Mr. Lester." He sank into his own chair, arms folded across his chest, leveling the vicar with his sternest look. It was with only the slightest degree of satisfaction that Brendan noticed Richard Lester gulping uncomfortably. "Well?" he asked irritably.

"I understand congratulations are in order, my lord."

Brendan narrowed his eyes on the man. "Two years ago, Lester, you left our fair village to seek your fortune, breaking my sister's fragile heart in the process. Now, it's not your fault she fell foolishly in love with you, but I do hold you responsible for the way in which you left. A terse note and nothing else." The vicar shifted uncomfortably in his seat. "Only to return now, to offer me congratulations on my marriage? You've taken up Mr. Pitney's post and think things can go back to the way they were before?"

"My lord, allow me to explain..."

"Leave Sudbury. Leave Derbyshire, Lester. Leave England, for God's sake. I'll finance the entire thing. But I won't let you destroy Rose like—"

"I want to marry Lady Rosamund," the soft spoken vicar nearly shouted.

"No," he answered coolly.

"But, my lord," the man pleaded, sliding forward in his seat. "Hear me out. I know I made a mistake when I left. I shouldn't have done so. I never intended to hurt Rose—"

"Lady Rosamund," Brendan growled. The collared bastard would at least show his sister the respect that was due her position.

"I never intended to hurt Lady Rosamund," the vicar amended quietly. "I love her, Lord Clayworth. I always have. That's why I left. I knew she loved me too. But nothing could come of it. My father would never have allowed me to..." His voice trailed off.

"Your father was right, Lester. Are you daft? You've spent enough time with my sister to know she isn't...normal. She can't marry you or anyone else. Aren't you concerned about your issue? Do you want your children to have tainted blood?"

The vicar leapt from his feet. "Don't you dare say that about her!"

Truly, Brendan had never seen so much fire in the young man before. Still it was a pointless conversation. Rose wouldn't ever marry. "Go home, Lester. And stay away from my sister. I don't want her heart broken again."

"You're the one breaking it this time," the young man hissed.

"Well, I suppose it's my turn then."

⚜

Tristan left his chair and took the spot next to Cordie on the settee. He draped his arm around her shoulders and squeezed her elbow. "You don't know how relieved I am, Cor. I know you were opposed to Clayworth, but he seems like the decent sort."

Cordie's irritation drained from her and she shook her head at Tristan. He was so concerned about her, it would be difficult to remain angry with him. "He is the decent sort," she agreed.

"Do you think you can be happy with him? Do you want one of us to have a talk with him? Make sure he knows he has to treat you well or else."

Cordie nearly blushed, thinking about exactly *how* well her husband treated her. "There's no need for that, Tris. I'm certain we'll rub along well."

A few feet away Russell frowned. "What do you suppose he wanted with Greg? Something of a sensitive nature? That sounds ominous."

Tris shrugged. "He probably wanted to talk about the dowry. A hundred thousand pounds! What was Greg thinking to increase it to such a level? It comes off as desperate in the worst sort of way."

Cordie cringed. "Mother was convinced I'd never marry."

"It was a foolish thing to do. Probably kept the right sort away," Russell added. "There's only a few reasons a girl has a dowry that size."

Before Cordie could find out what those reasons were, she noticed a pretty, flaxen haired girl standing in the doorway. She'd seen the girl once before and would never forget her beauty. Lady Rosamund Reese. Quickly, she stood and smiled at her sister-in-law. "You must be Rosamund."

The girl barely nodded, looking like a frightened kitten.

Cordie smiled and stepped towards the girl. "I'm very pleased to meet you, Rosamund. I'm Cordelia, and these are my brothers Lieutenant Tristan Avery and Captain Russell Avery," she said, gesturing to herself and the two officers.

Lady Rosamund furrowed her brow and tilted her head to one side as if she was trying to sort them all out. Then she nodded, silently.

Reaching her new sister-in-law, Cordie linked her arm with the girl, who looked to be two years her junior. "I'm certain Lord Clayworth will be back shortly. Would you care to join us?"

Rosamund worried her lip. "I'm getting married," she said quietly.

Cordie's eyes widened. Brendan had made it seem as if his sister would never marry, that she would stay with them forever. Perhaps she was simply confused, since Brendan had just married. "Are you?" she asked cautiously.

The girl beamed a smile, lighting up the room. "Richard said so. He said he was sorry for leaving me before, but he still loves me."

"Oh, I'm sure he does," Cordie said, for lack of anything else to say. It was easy to see why Brendan was so concerned for the girl. She was childlike. Innocent and shy. But she was also stunning. Twinkling twilight eyes and pretty pink lips. It was an unusual combination.

"I am sorry Mr. Pitney died. But now I have Richard again."

The earlier conversation with Thomas came back to Cordie. Someone named Richard Lester had returned to Sudbury, and Rosamund had been with him. Brendan hadn't been happy about the fact.

"And he said he'll never leave again," her sister-in-law continued, now chatting much faster. "Isn't that grand?"

"Grand," Cordie agreed, while her brothers both shrugged.

"Brendan will be so happy."

Not if the way he reacted in the garden was any indication. Cordie led Rosamund around the room, hoping to find out exactly what was going on. "Does Brendan know Richard?"

"Oh, yes," Rosamund happily exclaimed. "Richard lived here before. But his father didn't like me and he made Richard leave. But now he's back, and he said he'll never leave again," she repeated.

"Rose," Brendan's hard voice came from the doorway.

Cordie and Rosamund stopped in their tracks to face the earl. His sister's face lit up once more and she ran across the room, throwing her arms around him. "Oh, Brendan, I'm so happy. Where is Richard? What day am I getting married?"

Thirty-Two

HOLDING his sister in his arms, Brendan's heart ached. He couldn't remember the last time Rose was happy. Damn Richard Lester for returning and filling her head with fanciful ideas. He pulled away from his sister and smiled. "I see you've met Cordie."

Rose scrunched up her nose and shook her head. "Cordie?"

Brendan reached his arm towards his wife and drew her to them. Cordie took his hand, and he smiled. With everything else that was wrong in his life, at least he had her. Maybe nothing would come of his letters. Whoever had them hadn't seen fit to use them in the five years since Marina's death. Maybe he was worrying for nothing. "Rose, *this* is Cordie."

His sister shook her head. "No, Brendan. This is Cordelia. She told me."

He laughed. "Dearest, only her mother calls her Cordelia, or her brothers when they're angry with her."

The two officers both chuckled from their spots. "Too true, Clayworth," Lieutenant Avery added with a grin.

"Where is Richard?" his sister asked again. "He wanted to speak with you."

Brendan's jaw tightened. "Richard had to return home, Rose. We can discuss this later."

She shook her head defiantly. "But he said he wouldn't leave. He told me. What day am I getting married, Brendan? Richard said *you* would pick the day."

His blood was nearly boiling over and he wished the vicar was within sight, so he could unleash his frustration on the man. "Rose," he began with the practiced calm he always used when speaking to her. "We'll discuss this later. Right now Cordie's family is visiting and we are being rude."

Rose shook her head again, just as stubbornly as the first time. "I want Richard."

"I'm sorry, dear, he isn't here."

"I want Richard!" she yelled. "What did you do to make him leave? He told me he wouldn't leave."

Apparently, they wouldn't discuss this later. Brendan squeezed Cordie's hand, hoping for her added strength. Then he released his wife and grasped his sister's elbow. "Calm down, Rose. Let's go to my study, so we can talk."

"Let go!" Rose yanked her arm free and bolted through the doors.

Without looking back at his wife or guests, Brendan chased after her sister. "Rosamund, stop this instant!" he called after her.

She sped down the corridor and out the front door, then slid to a stop. "Richard!" she cried with relief.

Brendan winced when he spotted the vicar on the front drive. A muscle twitched in his jaw. Why was the man still here? "Rose!" he yelled after his sister.

But she didn't pay him any attention. She raced down the steps and threw herself into the vicar's awaiting arms.

Brendan stalked forward. This had gone too far. The man was upsetting his household, which he didn't need at the moment—not that he'd ever need it, but with the Averys in residence now was the worst possible time.

"You said you wouldn't leave," Rose said, tightening her hold on Richard Lester.

The vicar's angry brown eyes pierced Brendan, though he spoke very softly to Rose as he caressed her back. "Shh. Don't get upset, sweetheart. I'm not going anywhere except home."

She looked up at him, tears streaming down her cheeks. "Please don't leave, Richard," she begged.

The pain in his sister's voice was almost too much for Brendan to take. Why had Rose been punished with her childish mind? Why couldn't she have the same life others enjoyed? A hand touched his back, and Brendan turned to find Cordie standing behind him, tears in her own eyes. He pulled her to him and kissed her brow, finding peace in her embrace.

"Brendan, what is going on?" she asked softly.

He shook his head, unable to find his voice.

Cordie leaned her head against his chest and kissed him, then she stepped out of his embrace and walked towards Rose and Richard Lester. "I don't believe we've met," she said sweetly.

Lester nodded and smiled tightly. "Richard Lester," he introduced himself.

"So nice to meet you, Mr. Lester. I'm Lady Clayworth. Won't you come inside and join us for tea?"

Rose hiccupped and Lester brushed the tears off her cheek. His eyes flashed to Brendan and he nodded. "Thank you, Lady Clayworth. That is most generous."

⚜

Whatever was going on, Cordie knew it wouldn't do to discuss it out on the front lawn. Brendan seemed nearly immobile when she turned back to him. "I'm certain you'd rather not have my family witness this, whatever it is. I'm unfamiliar with Bayhurst Court. Where should the four of us have our tea?"

He closed his eyes, as if the process caused him pain. "Cordie, there's nothing to be done. Let him go on his way."

There had to be something. It would help to know exactly what the problem was, however. "Brendan, you can explain this to me on the way. Where should we have our tea?"

He opened his eyes, pain reflecting in his twilight pools. "I thought you were going to try to be a dutiful wife."

"Well," she said, grinning at him, hoping to make him smile, hoping the husband she loved was still in there, "I've been thinking about that. You do realize our vows didn't specify what was expected of me, not like they would have if we'd married in a church. I think that gives me some leeway."

He snorted and rubbed his brow. "I knew it wouldn't last."

Cordie slipped her hand in his. "I love you, Brendan. That will always last. Perhaps something can be done." She glanced over her shoulder at the young vicar and her sister-in-law.

Brendan followed her gaze. "She can't marry. That's what this is all about," he whispered so low only she could hear.

"Why not?" she asked quietly.

"Because it's not responsible."

Responsible? Since when did two people loving each other have to be responsible? She'd learned that lesson well. She had tried to be logical in her choice of spouse, and look how that had turned out. She would have been miserable if she'd gotten her way and ended up with Haversham. "Honestly, Brendan, I'm certain there were many more responsible girls *you* could have married. Now, please tell me where we can assemble for tea?"

Defeated, he shook his head. "The yellow parlor will do."

She rose up on her toes and pressed a kiss to his cheek. "Thank you." Then she turned and smiled at the distraught couple behind them. "His lordship suggests the yellow parlor. Rosamund, will you please direct Mr. Lester there? Your brother and I will join you shortly."

When they were alone on the lawn, Cordie looked up at her husband to find worry marring his too-handsome face. "There's no point in pursuing this, love. You're just going to make it harder on her."

Cordie didn't see how that was possible and she shook her head. "Tell me what you're worried about, Brendan."

"I've already told you. Rose is afflicted. Marriage is not in the cards for her."

She sighed. "Did you not see the way Mr. Lester looked at her? The devotion in his eyes? He does know of her affliction, does he not?"

Brendan frowned.

"But he loves her anyway? He wants to marry her anyway?" she pressed.

"He hurt her once, Cordie. Walked away from her and never looked back. I thought she would wither away and die, just like Flora did. I can't let him do that to her again."

She cupped his jaw and stared into his dark blue eyes. He was always trying to save someone, wasn't he? Her husband was a wonderful man, and she was quite fortunate to have him, as was Rose. Still that didn't mean he had all the answers. "I don't think he'd be able to, if they were married. Leave her, that is."

"It would be worse," Brendan replied. "And if they were married, I wouldn't have any say, any control—just like your brothers lost with you."

"Perhaps," Cordie answered carefully. Her mind spun until she had a solution that would make even Lady Staveley proud.

Brendan couldn't believe he'd let Cordie talk him into this. It was foolhardy on many levels, but he kept going back to the look of pure joy he'd seen on Rose's face that afternoon. If it was possible for his sister to be happy all her life, if she could be as happy as he was with Cordie, he wanted it for her.

As they entered the yellow parlor, Brendan looked directly at Richard Lester. The vicar met his gaze head-on, no longer the directionless youth he'd been when he departed Sudbury. On the settee beside Rose, Lester cradled her hand in his own, and Brendan's worries washed over him anew. What if this man hurt her again? How would Rose go on? He'd watched one sister die of a broken heart and didn't have it in him to watch the same tragedy happen again.

Cordie went directly to the tea service and poured. "Mr. Lester, how do you take your tea?"

"Two sugars, no milk."

"Brendan?" she asked, while she added the sugars to the vicar's tea.

"Nothing for me, love," he answered, sitting in a light yellow brocade chair.

She handed Lester his cup and smiled at Rose, who was still teary-eyed. "And what about you, Rosamund? Would you like tea?"

Rose nodded. "Lots of sugar, please."

Cordie laughed. "My friend Phoebe Greywood is the same way."

Brendan closed his eyes, praying his wife was right about this. The sound of her voice put him more at ease. He took a steadying breath, then opened his eyes, leveling them on the young vicar. "All right, Lester. My wife has convinced me that I should at least hear you out."

The vicar's eyes flashed to Cordie and he smiled at her, then he looked back at Brendan. "Lord Clayworth, thank you." He cleared his throat and sat a little straighter. "I have returned to Sudbury, replacing Mr. Pitney as this parish's vicar. My income is modest, but I can provide for Rose."

"She has a sizable dowry," Brendan said. She hadn't until about five minutes ago, but she did now. After working through the situation with Cordie's dowry, he'd decided it would be best to make sure Rose had a similar trust in case the worst occurred. Making certain she was safe and comfortable was a top concern. Before he was marched off to the gallows and his funds seized, he could make sure Rose would be provided for.

The vicar's eyes widened at the announcement.

Cordie had suggested that instead of Lester taking a spot at the vicarage, that Brendan offer him the rectory on Bayhurst grounds. He would essentially be the man's employer. He could still keep an eye on Rose. In the event his property was seized by the crown, he wasn't sure what would happen to Lester. It would be better to let him maintain his position in the village. "The dowry is in the form of a trust, however. It is in Rose's name, and I am the executor. If I am unable to perform those duties, the responsibility will be transferred to the Marquess of Astwick."

He would have to go to Town fairly soon and have his solicitors draw up this agreement. He did not relish that conversation. These were rather unusual circumstances, with even more unusual stipulations. Solicitors, as a rule, preferred situations that were not unusual.

"Lord Clayworth," Richard Lester began softly, "I am not interested in your money. I love Rose for herself."

That Brendan did not doubt. Lester must truly love Rose to want her as his wife for the remainder of his life. She could be difficult and immature, but Lester had grown up with her. He knew those things. Yet, he still wanted to marry her, as Cordie pointed out. He did know exactly what he was asking for.

Brendan nodded. "You may start the banns Sunday."

"Oh, Richard!" Rose threw her arms around Lester's neck and the vicar kissed her cheek. Then she leapt from her seat and dropped on her knees before her brother. "Brendan, thank you."

He prayed she'd stay this happy throughout her life. And he prayed he'd be around to see it. "You are welcome, dearest. Now, if you and

Cordie will excuse us, I do have something else I need to address with Mr. Lester."

Rose scrambled to her feet and linked her arm with Cordie's. "I am getting married."

Cordie smiled at him, and Brendan felt it in his soul. He was the most fortunate of men to have her as a wife. Having her approval was heady indeed.

After his wife had shut the door, leaving them alone, Brendan narrowed his eyes on the vicar. "Just so there are no misunderstandings, Lester, if you hurt her, leave her like you did before, there won't be a place safe enough for you to hide in all of England."

The man didn't even flinch. "I've lived without her for two years, my lord. I don't want to go back to that existence."

Brendan nodded, rose from his seat, and escorted his soon-to-be brother-in-law from the yellow parlor. In the hallway, he found Gregory Avery waiting from him, a pensive expression across his face. "Mr. Lester, I expect you will call on Rose tomorrow."

"Of course, my lord," the vicar said cheerfully before showing himself out.

Brendan stepped towards Avery, with a raised brow. "Well?"

The baron shook his head. "Mother had no idea what I was talking about, Clayworth. And neither do I."

Brendan's heart sank. "Then they must be at your Rufford Hall. We need to find them."

"I think it's time you told me what this is all about."

Thirty-Three

BRENDAN frowned at Gregory Avery. In the baron's spot, he'd demand the same thing. Still, he couldn't just blurt out the truth. *Well, my mother was a traitor and a spy. I'd like to get her letters back to avoid the gallows myself.* So, he shook his head. "They're of a personal nature and could be quite embarrassing for my family, of which your sister is now a member."

Avery scoffed. "You truly are the heartless bastard Marina always said you were."

His body stiffened at the insult, and he wished he could throw the baron from his house. However, that wouldn't help his quest, so he reigned in his temper. He and Avery could sling insults back and forth at each other, or they could work towards a solution. There certainly was no point in doing the former. "Do you know of a place she might have hidden them?"

Avery shook his head in disgust. "How dare you pretend an interest in my sister — marry her for God's sake, when all you really wanted were letters Marina never even gave my family! Cordie deserves better than you."

On that they could agree. Cordie deserved a husband whose past didn't threaten her future. However, he wouldn't give her up for anything in the world. Brendan rubbed the bridge above his nose, hoping to avoid a headache. With the way this day was going, he didn't hold out a lot of hope. "This isn't helping anyone, Avery, least of all your sister. Now we need — "

"What's not helping me?" Cordie's voice came from the end of the hall. With a concerned look, she started towards them.

Gregory Avery's eyes challenged him to tell her the truth, which Brendan had hoped to avoid, though that didn't seem possible any longer. He would, however, not do so with an audience. "Cordie love, I am so sorry things have been in disarray ever since we've arrived. Allow me to take you on a tour of Bayhurst Court."

"Are you going to tell her or shall I?" the baron demanded, making Brendan want to punch him right in the mouth. His wife wouldn't thank him for that, however.

"Stay out of my affairs, Avery," he warned, with only the slightest edge to his voice.

"What is going on with the two of you?" Cordie asked, stopping next to Brendan and linking her arm with his.

Her green eyes, so filled with worry, made Brendan's heart lurch. What if she believed, as Gregory Avery did, that he'd only married her to get his hands on the letters? That thought had never entered his mind until this moment. True, the possibility of reclaiming the letters had piqued his interest initially, but not for very long. Cordie had captured his heart so early on, the letters had ceased to be a motivation where she was concerned. "Dear, there's something we need to discuss."

The baron snorted.

Cordie frowned at her brother. "Greg, I don't know what has gotten into you."

"Your husband has something to tell you, and if you want to leave him when this is all over, I'll do everything in my power to help you."

***

Cordie gaped at her brother. Why on earth would he say something like that? The words were just as surprising as the source. Gregory was always so involved with his own life, he paid very little attention to hers. Brendan tightened his hold on her arm and she glanced up at him. Her husband's face was white as a ghost. "Brendan?"

He glared at her brother. "How dare you! She is *my* wife."

"How dare you!" Greg countered.

Something was terribly wrong. Her brother was never belligerent. Cordie's stomach tightened. "Will one of you *please* tell me what is going on?"

Brendan glowered at her brother, but spoke very softly to her, "Allow me to show you to your suite of rooms, love. We can talk there. Alone."

She felt sick. Whatever this was, it was truly awful. She nodded, clutching his arm tighter, wishing they'd never left Scotland, wishing the real world hadn't come crashing back in on them. Her family. Brendan's sister. Whatever *this* was.

Her mind was numb, searching for possible scenarios, as he escorted her down the corridor, around a corner, and up a flight of stairs. She had no idea where she was going and doubted she'd remember her way back at the end of this. Jaw clenched, Brendan said nothing, and she had the feeling he was trying to find the best way to tell her something dreadful. All of it making her much more anxious.

Finally they stopped in front of a large oak door and Brendan pushed it open. "Mrs. Webb has apparently been working tirelessly on getting your rooms in order ever since my instructions arrived."

She took no note of the room other than the fact that it was yellow, as she was too upset to focus on anything in particular. "Mrs. Webb?"

He smiled sadly. "Our housekeeper. I'm sorry my plans fell apart at the seams. I'd intended for you to meet the staff, tour the estate, but…"

"My family," she responded quietly. Glad as she was to see Tristan, she wished none of them had come. "Brendan, what is going on between you and Greg? The two of you looked ready to tear each other apart. That is not like my brother at all."

"I'm afraid Lord Avery and I see many things differently." He then grumbled something that sounded like, "And he seems to make a habit of taking my wives away from me."

Though she must have misheard him. "You're not making any sense, Brendan."

He pulled her into his arms and kissed the top of her head. "I don't want to lose you."

There was no danger of that. They were married. Their marriage was well and thoroughly consummated. They couldn't even get an annulment if they wanted it—which she wholeheartedly did not. "My place is with you. What has you so upset?"

His hold tightened around her and he his voice shook, "I'm at a loss as to how to tell you this. Which is ridiculous. I had the entire trip to Scotland to do so. I just didn't think it would turn out like this."

It was worse than she thought. He'd never shied away from telling her anything. Cordie pulled back and looked him in the eyes. His twilight gaze was more intense than she could ever remember. "Please, you're worrying me."

"I've never spoken these words aloud, Cordie. Give me a minute."

She looked around her room and spotted two chintz chairs near a large window. "Perhaps we should sit."

He nodded and followed her to the chairs, sinking into his after she took her seat. "I've been... Well, my mother... Marina found..."

"Brendan, you know *my* darkest secret. You're my husband. You can tell me anything."

He sat forward in his seat, grasping her hands in his, a desperate look across his face. "You do believe I love you?"

She nodded. "And I love you, too."

Brendan closed his eyes. "After my mother died, Marina went through her belongings..."

Cordie patiently waited for more. This had to do with his mother and Marina, but not them. Whatever it was, they'd find a way to sort it out.

"It was stupid, foolish of me. *I* should have done the chore."

"I'm sure you were grieving."

"I've grieved a lot more over the last seven years," he grumbled.

"Why?" she asked quietly.

He pierced her with a pained look. "Mother was a traitor, Cordie. A spy for the French. I didn't know. Marina found some letters, correspondence she'd saved from her contacts in Paris. What they wanted from her. Thanking her for supplying other information. Things of that nature."

Cordie couldn't stop her mouth from falling open. A traitor? A spy for the French? She couldn't imagine such a thing. Not after the countless soldiers who'd died fighting on the continent. Not after the thousands who'd been injured. Not after Russell and Tristan had both risked their lives in the war. This was why Greg thought she'd want to leave her husband.

Though apparently, her oldest brother didn't know her well at all. She'd never just abandon her husband. Especially as he'd done nothing wrong.

Brendan wasn't a spy. He didn't even have to tell her, for her to know the truth. She knew him. He was honorable, noble. "You're innocent."

He rubbed his brow. "*I* took her to France, Cordie. Her and my sisters, time and again, to visit family. In the eyes of the crown, I'd be just as culpable."

That was ridiculous. He couldn't be responsible for something he didn't know about. She shook her head. "Don't say that."

"It's with a heavy heart that I do so. I am so sorry to have attached your name to mine—"

"How dare you?" Cordie interrupted. "Brendan Reese, I am happy to be your wife, and I would not want it any other way. I can't believe that you do."

"You know that's not what I meant." He stood and began to pace the room. "I'd just hoped to have this resolved before we married, or shortly thereafter."

What did their marriage have to do with any of this? "How so?" she asked with a frown.

Brendan stopped mid-pace, his twilight eyes boring into hers. For the longest time, she thought he wouldn't speak at all. Then he took a deep breath. "I believe your family is in possession of the letters. I think Marina hid them somewhere at Rufford Hall."

Cordie gaped at him. "Rufford Hall?" Her stomach dropped and she felt the room start to spin. "That's why you courted me," she whispered, realization setting in. "That's why you married me."

"No!" he hissed, rushing to her side. "You can't believe that. Tell me you don't."

She didn't want to believe that. But somehow it made sense. Why he'd suddenly been interested in her. Why he'd insisted on courting her, even when she fought him every step of the way.

Brendan knelt at her feet. "Cordie, tell me you don't believe that."

She shook her head, unable to find her voice.

He squeezed her hands, begging her with his eyes. "I fell in love with you, Cordie. With your spirit and love of life. Your blind loyalty and devotion to those you love. Your beguiling green eyes and sharp tongue. You take my breath away every time I look at you. From the very first, you captured my heart. Please tell me you know that."

She didn't realize she was crying until Brendan brushed away her tears. "Why do you think my family has the letters?" she asked so softly she could barely hear herself.

Brendan wrapped his arms around her. "Forget the letters, Cordie.

We'll deal with them later. Do you know that I love you?"

Ten minutes ago she did, and she wanted to believe him now. A memory of him smoothly lying to her mother about looking for a book on Scandinavia flashed in her mind. At the time, she'd been astounded that he could recover so deftly from their kiss and innocently converse with her mother.

He loved his family fiercely. She'd seen that first hand with Lady Rosamund this afternoon. Certainly he wouldn't hesitate to marry her in order to protect the ones he loved.

It would be in his best interest for her to believe he loved her. If he wanted his letters, he would need her support in dealing with her family. Especially as Greg didn't seem willing to give them to him. Well, that was ridiculous. They belonged to him. Greg shouldn't withhold them. "Brendan, please let me go."

His arms fell from her, and he looked as if she'd punched him. "Cordie."

She stepped around him. "If you need your letters, I'll make sure Greg gives them to you." Focusing on the task at hand would keep her mind off her breaking heart.

He called out just as she reached the door, "Wait!"

Cordie's heart leapt and she turned to face him. "Yes?"

"He doesn't think he has them. He doesn't know what's in them."

Cordie closed her eyes, willing her heart not to ache. "We'll have to tell him, Brendan. With the animosity between the two of you, if he finds them, he'll read them anyway. I don't believe he'll want to hurt me anymore than I already am. Greg can be trusted."

Her husband snorted at that.

"Despite his distance, my brother does love me. He wouldn't do anything with your letters, because it would reflect badly on me. I suppose your choice of wife was wise after all."

Before he could utter a protest, she quit the room.

Thirty-Four

CORDIE smoothed her skirts back in place, hoping that none of her brothers noticed how upset she was. Over the years she'd had lots of practice in disguising her feelings, this was just more of the same. She stepped inside Bayhurst Court's blue parlor with a fraudulent smile plastered across her face.

Russell and Tristan were involved in some deep conversation, barely noticing her arrival, but Gregory's brow was furrowed and his green eyes followed her into the room. Cordie swallowed, gathering her strength. "Greg, may I have a word with you?"

She didn't particularly want to have this conversation in front of Russell and Tristan. It didn't seem wise to discuss her late mother-in-law's treasonous activities in front of soldiers who'd recently returned from the front lines, brothers or not. Though Tris would forgive her anything, she'd really rather not put him in that position.

Gregory inclined his head. "Of course."

He followed her out to the corridor and Cordie wished she knew the layout of her house. "How long have you been here?"

"A few days. Are you all right? Do you want me to take you back to Rufford Hall?"

She shook her head. "Do you have any idea where another parlor is?

I'm sadly unfamiliar with my own home."

"This isn't your home, Cordie," he said with a frown as he led her down the corridor into an empty room, done mostly in white. He shut the door behind them. "Did he tell you the truth about these letters he's after?"

Cordie nodded. "I need you to find them, Greg. Clayworth believes they're at Rufford Hall for whatever reason. It is imperative."

"Whatever it is he's done, you don't have to stay here. I may not be as well connected as the earl, but—"

She held up her hand, silencing her brother. "He's my husband, Greg, no matter how we arrived at this point. And as my brother, I need your help. I don't know why Marina would hide these letters at Rufford Hall, or even where—but retrieving them is most urgent."

"Why? After all these years?"

Cordie choked back a sob. "He's been looking for them all this time. If someone gets their hands on them—"

"Then what?" her brother demanded.

"Please keep in mind if anything hurts Clayworth, it will affect me as well. I may never recover from this."

"That thought has been foremost in my mind, Cordie. Now, tell me what is so damned important."

"Promise not to tell Russell or Tris," she whispered.

Greg shrugged. "I promise."

Cordie leaned in closer to her brother on the off chance someone in the hall could hear them. "Clayworth's mother was French," she began quietly, searching Greg's face for a reaction of any sort. When he nodded for her to continue, she did. "Well, apparently her loyalties always remained with her home country. For years, it seems, she was spying for the French and passing off sensitive information on trips to visit family. I'm not—"

"And Clayworth?" Greg asked with a frown.

"Is innocent," she defended. "But the letters detail his mother's traitorous acts. If they're found out..." Her voice trailed off. What would happen in that event? She hadn't thought that far ahead. It wouldn't be good, but—

"He'll he be sent to the gallows," Greg finished for her. His face went white. "Dear God, that's what she had planned," he whispered just loud enough for Cordie to hear.

She blinked at her brother, not understanding at all what he meant. "Greg?"

He shook his head. "She said she had a plan to leave him so she'd be free."

"Marina?" she asked quietly.

"I couldn't imagine what she meant by that. She was the man's wife. She'd never be free of him. But if she was a widow…"

Prickly chills raced up Cordie's spine at the thought and she shivered. She didn't want to envision Brendan in any state except alive. Marina had planned to have him executed? She thought she might be sick, so she dropped into a chair. "That's awful."

"She was very unhappy."

That was not new information. Cordie shook her head. "*I* have no desire to be a widow, Greg. You need to scour Rufford Hall."

"You'll come with me. I don't want to leave you here with him. The way he went about all of this…"

Her heart ached at the truth of her brother's words, but she smiled as brightly as she was able. "Despite everything, I'm his wife and I do love him, even if he doesn't return the sentiment."

Greg's face fell. "God, Cordie. I should have been more attentive to you. None of this would have happened if—"

Cordie wrapped her arms around his neck and he held her tightly. "Just help me now, Greg."

⁂

Brendan took a relieved breath as the Avery coach finally started down his drive, taking his wife's mother and all three brothers away from Bayhurst Court. Thank God!

The night before had been one of the most uncomfortable he'd spent in his thirty-five years. Lord Avery glowered at him the entire time. The two officers constantly bickered with each other over one inane reason or another. His mother-in-law pouted non-stop. Rose was oblivious to her surroundings, wearing a look of exuberance, while Thomas quietly kept to himself. All of that was bearable, or would have been if his wife had been able to look him in the eyes. She hadn't, and his heart still ached.

With her family present, she'd successfully avoided him the entire night, never even retiring to her own room—something Brendan knew for certain as he'd waited there for her until dawn. Thankfully, she appeared on the front lawn to wish her family a safe journey. The sight of her nearly broke his heart. She'd smiled, gushed over her brothers, even wished her mother well—but pain was still reflected in her eyes, and Brendan berated himself over and over for putting it there. He wished he'd done things differently, told her the truth early on. He was at a loss for what to do that would return her to the joyful woman she'd been just days earlier—when it was just them, before the real world consumed them.

The coach rambled down the drive, disappearing from view, and his wife turned back toward the house. Brendan stopped her, with his hand on her arm. "Cordie," he said quietly.

"Yes, my lord?" she replied, her eyes locked on his cravat.

"Look at me," he implored.

"I'd rather not."

Brendan tipped her chin back with his hand, until her green eyes met his. Her anguished expression tore at his heart. "Oh, my darling wife, tell me what I can do to make you forgive me."

She wiggled out of his grasp. "There's nothing to forgive. You were protecting your family." She frowned, then turned her back on him so he couldn't see her face. "I do wish you'd told me the truth from the beginning. It wasn't necessary for you to marry me simply to get my assistance with this matter. The letters are yours after all."

"If you recall, you were not particularly warm towards me in the beginning." Not that it excused him from telling her the truth on the way to Scotland or even after they said their vows. But the letters had been in the back of his mind most of the time, his thoughts occupied by Cordie every waking hour.

"I suppose you're right." She heaved a sigh. "Courting me, making me fall in love with you, was the better plan." A light summer wind picked up her skirts and she shivered. Brendan stepped forward, but she moved further away, looking towards the path her family had recently departed down.

Brendan hated seeing her so forlorn, and he couldn't resist touching her any longer. He came up behind her and slid his arms around her waist, pulling her against his chest. "I fell in love with you too, Cordie," he whispered in her ear. "Almost from the beginning. I lost sight of mother's letters when I saw you chasing after Haversham. I wanted to tear the man apart every time you looked at him."

"I've never *chased* after anyone."

For the first time that day, he smiled. He'd become so accustomed to her contradicting him. It was good to know her spirit wasn't completely broken. "Of course not," he agreed amiably. "You've left swarms of heartbroken naval captains and wicked marquesses in your wake. I'm very fortunate to have caught you for myself."

"I don't find you remotely humorous," she said quietly.

"Oh, I know." Brendan chuckled and kissed the spot behind one ear. "If memory serves, you find me stodgy."

"And old" she grumbled.

"And old. How could I forget?"

Cordie turned in his arms, looking up into his eyes, causing his body to react in a most pleasurable way. "I do wish you wouldn't be charming. I'm quite put out with you, and plan to stay that way for some time."

Brendan caressed her back, apologizing with his eyes, pleading for her to see the truth. "I love you, Cordelia Clayworth. I never meant to hurt you, and I'll spend the rest of my days making up for it. Give me that chance, will you?"

The tiniest of smiles tugged at her lips. "The rest of your days? Is that all?"

"Well, that and my heart and soul," he vowed before lightly brushing his lips against hers.

He silently rejoiced when she relaxed in his arms and allowed him to deepen the kiss. He tightened his embrace until the soft mounds of her breasts pressed against his chest. She sighed against his mouth, and settled her hands at the base of his neck.

It was the sweetest victory he'd ever enjoyed.

Brendan mingled his tongue with hers, relishing the feel of her lithe body against his, the taste of sweet summer berries, and her light lilac scent. There was nothing more he wanted than to scoop his wife up in his arms, carry her to his room and sink deep inside her. "Dear God, I need you," he whispered across her lips.

Somehow that was the wrong thing to say.

Cordie pushed lightly against his chest and wriggled out of his embrace, a slight frown marring her pretty face. "I don't have anything else to give you."

Brendan stepped towards her, but she backed away, shielding herself from him with an outstretched arm. "I—um—well, I've decided to return to London."

London? But they were going to stay in Derbyshire, at least for a while. Enjoy each other, without the watchful eye of the *ton*. He was going to show her how much he loved her and do everything in his power to make up for hurting her.

"My friends are there," she continued matter-of-factly. "My life is there. I'd like to return to what I left behind."

The distance in her voice made Brendan's heart drop. "You're not returning without me," he told her.

She shrugged, walking towards the house. "I don't want you to feel you must accompany me. You have many things to attend to here, and I'm certain I can manage on my own."

She wanted to leave him. She didn't want to give him the chance to make things right between them. Brendan's jaw tightened. She wasn't going back to Town or anywhere else without him. "You are *my* wife, Cordie."

"I don't think I'm in any danger of forgetting that, my lord."

Before he could respond, she escaped into the house, abandoning him to his vacant front drive.

Thirty-Five

CORDIE'S heart pounded as she stomped back inside Bayhurst Court. At least she knew where she was going today. She'd roamed the corridors the night before and now had the layout fresh in her mind. She hadn't intended to do so, but after Brendan had escape into her room, she hadn't had much choice. She wasn't up to seeing him. She still wasn't.

She made her way to the music room and sat down at the piano, gently running her fingers over the keys. She wasn't as accomplished as Livvie in this realm, but the music did soothe her a bit.

One would think she'd become accustomed to being alone since she'd been exiled from Livvie, but she hadn't. And her loneliness had never felt so pronounced as it did now.

Most marriages were arranged to the mutual benefit of both parties, the merging of lands or fortunes or connections. However both participants knew from the beginning what they each brought to the table. They both knew the situation they were getting themselves into. Cordie hadn't been offered that. She'd been misled from the onset. How could she believe anything he said to her now?

Only a fool would do so.

Cordie had never been a fool. Other than when she believed he loved her. Other than when she'd lost her heart to him. She didn't intend to make a habit of continuing to be foolish however.

"You play very well," said a timid voice from behind her.

Cordie looked over her shoulder to find Thomas Reese leaning against the doorway. He bashfully hung his head when their eyes met. Despite the pain in her heart, Cordie couldn't help but smile at the shy boy. "Thank you. Do you play, Thomas?"

He shook his head, still not looking directly at her. "No. But Uncle Brendan says my mother did."

"I hear she was very lovely." What did one say to a child who'd never met his mother?

Thomas shrugged. "You're not leaving because of *me*, are you?"

Cordie's mouth fell open and she shook her head. How did he know she was leaving? Had Brendan already told everyone? So much for his wanting her to stay at Bayhurst Court. "Of course not. Why would you think such a thing?"

He winced. "I know I'm not... Well, I'd understand if you didn't want to live here with me. But I'm supposed to attend Eton this October. Uncle Brendan has other properties he could send me to until then."

Cordie thought her heart might break, which was something of a feat as she didn't know there was any of it left. She rose from her bench and started towards the boy. "Thomas Reese, please believe me. This has nothing to do with you." She touched his shoulder, and his blue eyes pierced her soul.

"I've just never seen him happy like he was when you arrived," the boy explained. "I don't want to be the reason he's sad again."

Cordie brushed a tear from her cheek. She'd been happy when they first arrived too. She desperately wished they could go back to that day. Before she knew what Brendan really wanted from her. When she believed he truly loved her.

Thomas' eyes widened in surprise. "I didn't mean to make you cry. I—"

"Tom!" Brendan's voice came from the top of the hallway.

Cordie looked up to find her husband walking their direction and wiped away her remaining tears. She didn't want him to ever see her cry.

Too late.

His brow furrowed and his pace increased. He was before her in seconds, offering her a handkerchief. "Please." He turned to his nephew as she blotted her eyes. "Excuse us, will you, Tom?" he asked.

The boy nodded woefully. "I didn't mean to, uncle."

Brendan ruffled Thomas' hair. "I'm certain it wasn't you. Do go on. I'll find you soon."

When Thomas was out of earshot, Brendan grasped Cordie's elbow and led her back into the music room. "It wasn't his fault," she said weakly.

"No. It was my fault." Brendan drew her into his arms and held her tightly. For a moment, it felt so comforting to be back in his arms. She couldn't stay there for long, but just a moment or two couldn't hurt, could it?

He kissed the top of her head. "Cordie, I know you don't believe me, and I suppose you have every right to doubt me. Would that I could do it differently, I would do everything in my power to keep from hurting you."

She pulled back to look at him. He did seem sincere. She wanted to believe him.

"I love you with my entire being, and hate that I have done this to you." His face was drawn up tight, and Cordie *hated* to see the pained expression in his eyes. Brendan looked away from her. "I've thought of nothing else, Cordie, but how to make amends to you. Your happiness is most important to me. If being my wife truly makes you miserable, if you cannot be happy with me, with Bayhurst Court, then I'll grant you the freedom you've so desperately wanted."

Cordie gasped. Did he intend to divorce her? Have their marriage annulled? She couldn't find her voice. Both prospects were equally horrifying. It just wasn't done.

He seemed not to notice that she was in utter shock. "Since I first met you, gaining your freedom, doing as you pleased and with whom was all important." His twilight eyes pierced her. "I can give you that, Cordie. My heart will break if you leave me, but it will break if you remain here. I can't watch you live in such misery. One of us should be happy."

"What are you saying?" she whispered, her heart barely beating at all.

Brendan turned away from her, his hands clutched behind his back. "You have my name, the safety that comes with it. If you're dead set on London, on returning to your friends, and whatever else... Then go. I won't keep you here, miserable and wretched. I love you too much for that."

Cordie's knees threatened to give out. She stumbled against the pianoforte and clasped the edge to keep from falling over. "You'd give me my freedom?" she whispered in disbelief.

He turned back around and rushed to her, ushering her to a small settee. "Isn't that what you want, Cordie?"

Was it? She blinked at him. Suddenly she wasn't sure. For so long she'd hated being dictated to, forced to submit to her mother's will, having no choices of her own. He was offering her the complete freedom she'd craved and struggled to achieve. "You'd let me leave? You'd let me make my own choices?"

He sat beside her and responded with a tight nod. The pain in his eyes was deeper than before and Cordie's heart constricted even more. "Why?" she whispered.

Brendan took her hands in his. "Because I don't know how else to show you that I love you. I *want* you to be happy, Cordie. I had hoped you could be so with me, but if you can't..."

She threw her arms around his neck. She hadn't wanted to. She'd wanted to be strong, but she couldn't help herself. He seemed to hurt as much as she did. The Brendan Reese she'd known would never have given up his claim on her. She'd expected him to fight her every step of the way. He'd told her that he wouldn't keep her from her friends, but he'd always maintained his right to dictate to her as a husband.

If he was truly willing to give all that up, simply to make her happy... It was the most selfless act she'd ever witnessed.

His arms wrapped tentatively around her. "Do be careful, *ma minouche*. If anything happened to you—"

Cordie touched her lips to his. Brendan moaned and Cordie cupped his jaw, pressing herself against him. His arms tightened and she relished the feel of her breasts crushed against his chest, the urgency of his mouth against hers. She didn't want him to ever stop holding her, to ever stop kissing her.

But he did.

Brendan lifted his head. "What are you doing?"

Cordie snuggled against him. "Would you *really* give me my freedom?"

"I'll do anything to see you happy," he said softly. "Even let you walk away from me."

Cordie closed her eyes and breathed him in. No one had ever loved her that much. "I don't want to walk away from you," she admitted. "I don't want to be plagued with my family. I don't want there to be phantom letters. I just want you, Brendan, for things to go back like they were mere days ago."

He sighed, stroking her back. "I want that too, love. But you do have a family and there *are* phantom letters. And—"

Cordie pressed her lips against his, silencing his words. She didn't want to think about all that was wrong in their world. Not right now.

She moved her hands to his waistcoat and slid one button through its hole. Brendan pulled back from her, surprise alighting his eyes. "Here?"

Life was too complicated to worry about the whens and wheres. Cordie nodded, undoing another button. He groaned, leaned forward, and claimed her mouth. His tongue brushed against her lips and Cordie ran her hands along his chest. His muscles tense at her touch, making her yearn for more.

He felt it too. Brendan's quick hands unclasped the fastenings of her gown and it soon hung loosely about her shoulders. His lips sought hers and he eased her back on the settee, settling his knee between her thighs as he rose above her. He pulled the gown beneath her breasts, sliding the fabric against her sensitive nipples. He teased one peak with the rough edge of his fingertip. It tightened, sending a rush of ecstasy to her core.

One leg dangled over the edge of the settee, opening her to the cool air. Cordie thought she might come undone. She arched against his knee, wanting him closer. He nipped at her bottom lip and tugged at the hem of her gown. Then his hand slid up her leg, sending warm shivers racing across her skin.

Brendan lifted his head only to smile at her. "My adventurous wife." Then he freed himself from his trousers and nudged at her slick entrance. "Say you'll never leave me."

She shook her head, pledging herself to him for all time. "I'll never leave you."

He entered her in one thrust, and Cordie clutched tightly around him. She never wanted this to end. Brendan's lips found the tender skin at the base of her neck and she couldn't help but moan beneath him.

He nibbled at her neck, teased her nipples with his tongue, then blew against them. Feminine power raced through her blood and her core pulsed around his length. He began to saw himself into her over and over, causing the music room to spin around them. Cordie closed her eyes and he delicious pressure built inside her.

"Ah, love," Brendan whispered. "That's it. Let go, Cordie."

His words unleashed the last hold she had on her sanity. The room stopped spinning and she dissolved into a million pieces.

Lost in her own state of bliss, Cordie fell limp as Brendan emitted a guttural groan and then collapsed upon her. He nuzzled her neck and pulled her tightly to him. "Cordie, I love you."

She sighed, running her hands over his back. She loved him. She'd never stop and she'd never leave him. "Me too."

Thirty-Six

A SENNIGHT passed, then a fortnight, but there was no word from Gregory. Cordie tried not to think about the letters that were just waiting to destroy her happiness. Though neither she nor Brendan mentioned them, their existence still loomed in the back of her mind. And while there was no word about *those* letters, Cordie found herself awash in other correspondence.

> *Dear Cordie,*
>
> *I am so, so, so sorry. I do not even deserve your forgiveness. This is all my fault. I did not mean to tell your brothers where you were, but the lieutenant is a terrible, ruthless man and he was relentless in his search for you. The man actually threatened my person and I was so frightened, everything just spilled out of me. I am the worst sort of friend, and I will never forgive myself for your current predicament.*
>
> *My only hope is that you will find happiness with Lord Clayworth. Captain Avery says you seemed happy when he last visited and I pray that is true.*
>
> *I suppose you will not return to London until next season. Please know that my thoughts and prayers are with you.*
>
> > *Your unworthy friend,*
> > *Phoebe Greywood*

Cordie shook her head as she reread the letter. No one had ever called Tristan a terrible, ruthless man before. It was hard to imagine. He must have really scared poor Phoebe. She sent back a quick note, assuring her friend that she held her blameless and that, all things considered, she was quite happy with her circumstances.

My dearest Cordelia,

Please tell me you are well. Ever since Caroline wrote me of your elopement, I have been so worried about you. I still cannot believe that you ran off with Lord Clayworth, of all people. I will not rest at ease until I hear from you. If you are in trouble, my door is always open to you, my dearest friend.

Alexander and I have chosen to stay in Hampshire for the remainder of my confinement, away from the vindictive eyes and wagging tongues of society. Sometimes it is hard to realize that I once considered so many of those people friends. I have a new outlook on life.

Though this is not the path I would have ever imagined for myself, I am not sorry for the outcome. It is good I did not have a choice in the matter, or I would have done something foolish and honorable, and been positively unhappy with my lot. Alexander is everything I never knew I needed, and I would never trade him for respectability.

I am certain you have heard disturbing things in regards to my household, and I assure you they are all true. It is shocking, I know, but I truly could not be happier. My step-daughter, Poppy, is a delight, and I do not know how I would have survived the last few difficult weeks without her.

All I wish for now is to see you again, to relieve my mind of your circumstances. Please do not delay in your response. I am on pins and needles, awaiting your reply.

Your devoted friend,
Olivia Everett
Everett Place – Brockenhurst, Hampshire

Livvie was pregnant? What wonderful news. Though Cordie wasn't necessarily surprised. The duke didn't seem capable of keeping his hands off her. It was a relief to know that despite everything Olivia had been through, she'd found peace in Hampshire. Perhaps she could convince Brendan to make the trip to visit her friend. It would be so nice to see Livvie again. However, no trips to anywhere would be possible until Rosamund's wedding plans were solidified.

Her sister-in-law begged nearly every day to be taken to London to fill her trousseau, to which Brendan would rub his temples as if to stave off a headache. Cordie could understand the girl's desire, though. Every young bride wanted everything to be just so. Rosamund was no different. After enduring the girl's relentless pleas, Cordie finally agreed to talk to Brendan herself.

She found him in his study, a full glass of whiskey in front of him, looking as if he'd just lost his dearest friend. His shoulders slumped forward and his brow was drawn tight.

Cordie closed the door behind her and rushed to his side. "Brendan, what is the matter? You never drink in the middle of the day."

He closed his eyes and pushed a letter across the desk towards her. Cordie snatched it up and read.

Clayworth,

I am sorry to inform you that the letters you seek are not at Rufford Hall. The estate has been tirelessly scoured from top to bottom, but there is no evidence of your family's perfidy in Nottinghamshire. Likewise, I have traveled to London to search Avery House, with the same unfortunate result.

I do wish, for my sister's sake, I had better news to offer you. In the event that someone else finds the evidence you seek, I do hope that you will take Cordelia's well-being under consideration. You should send her to me so that I can look after her. If you are found out, only distancing yourself from my sister will save her.
Avery

Short, concise, and filled with just a touch of condemnation. Cordie sighed and looked up to find her husband regarding her with pain-filled eyes. "I won't ever send you to them. I'll figure something else out."

She dropped the letter and knelt at Brendan's side. "There's no need to send me anywhere. My place is with you."

"Not at the gallows," he barked. Then he winced and caressed her cheek with his fingers. "I didn't mean to yell."

Cordie ran her hand along his waistcoat. "Brendan, this means nothing. Marina has been gone for half a decade. Don't you think if she gave the letters to someone intent on doing you harm, they would have already used them? Just because Greg can't find them doesn't mean it's the end of the world. We can't live like that."

"Cordie," he said, as though he carried the weight of the world on his shoulders.

She shook her head. "Let's leave for a while. Rose is anxious to go to London and I'm sure Thomas would like the adventure. We could go to the theatre and shop and—"

"Pretend that none of this is happening?"

"Nothing *is* happening. Only in our minds."

His face softened a bit. "Do you want to go to London?"

"I'd like to make Rose happy."

"And what about you?"

She grinned at him, hoping to lighten some of his burdens. "Well, I would certainly love to show off my husband. I will be the envy of every woman in London to have caught the elusive Lord Adonis."

He groaned, but it was playful and not of the pain-filled variety. "You know I hate that."

Cordie giggled and ran her fingers up his chest. "Poor Brendan. It must be such a trial to be so handsome and sought after."

He clutched her fingers in his hand. "I only care for you."

"Then take me to London. It will be good for all of us to change our scenery, if only for a little while."

"As you wish." He smiled at her, warming her soul.

"And after Rose's wedding, I'd like very much to travel to Hampshire."

He laughed. "I thought after Scotland you were ready to give up travel forever, love."

"Well, I've heard from Livvie. Brendan, she's expecting. Isn't that grand? She and Kelfield are spending her confinement at Everett Place, and I do miss her dreadfully."

He leaned forward in his seat and cupped her jaw. "Whatever will make you happy, my lovely wife."

Watching Rose bound up the steps to his Mayfair home did bring a smile to Brendan's face. Thomas dashed out of the coach and followed Rose into the house on Hertford Street.

He supposed he should have brought them to London before now, if only to see the sights. The two of them had excitedly chatted nearly the entire way, while Cordie slept on Brendan's shoulder.

His wife had been fairly weary as of late and he was starting to worry about her. He gently touched her cheek to rouse her from her slumber. Cordie blinked her eyes open, then yawned. "Are we here?" she asked, stretching one arm above her head.

"We are indeed," Brendan said with a frown. "How are you feeling, love?"

"Just a bit tired." She leaned forward and kissed his chin. "I know that look. Please don't worry about me."

"It's not even possible for me to stop," he mumbled, climbing from the coach and offering her his hand.

Cordie smiled at him, brightening the dreary, overcast day above them. "I've never been here. I can hardly wait to see it."

"Only the new green parlor is worth seeing, according to Caroline. Feel free to refurbish as you see fit."

He followed her into the house and nodded curtly to Higgins, who held out a silver salver. "Your correspondence, Lord Clayworth."

"How is it even possible we already have invitations?" he grumbled.

Cordie laughed. "I did write Lady Staveley to tell her we'd be arriving."

Well, that explained it then. Brendan scooped up the pile of invitations and handed them to his wife. "Decide what you'd like to attend, love, and let me know."

"We're only here for shopping, Brendan."

"Not if you've already forewarned Caroline. We'll have to attend something, or we'll never enjoy a moment's worth of peace."

⚜

He was right about that. Cordie looked from one invitation to another. The most respected families in London requested their presence in one form or another. It wouldn't do to ignore them all. She was lucky they wanted to have anything to do with her, after her scandalous elopement. Lady Staveley, it appeared, had been quite busy.

She stopped when she opened a card bearing the Astwick crest, nearly dropping the invitation to the floor once she read it. Heavens! Well, they couldn't ignore this particular soiree. Both Ladies Astwick were hosting the event in honor of Lord Clayworth and his new bride. All of society would undoubtedly be in attendance.

She would have to face the same people who made such a fuss over Livvie's marriage to Kelfield, the same people who'd made her friend's life nearly unbearable. Panic began to set in and Cordie's stomach turned queasy at the thought. Perhaps hiding out in Derbyshire wasn't such a bad idea.

Thirty-Seven

"HAVE you heard from Rob?" Chet asked as they took their seats in Astwick's box at Astley's Amphitheatre.

Brendan shook his head, a bit distracted by his wife's health. He'd wanted to cancel the outing with his old friend, but Cordie had insisted he and Thomas attend since Chet would have his two step-sons with him. She also promised she would feel better in the morning. He wished he believed her. Tomorrow he would insist Doctor Watts pay her a call.

"Well," the marquess' voice boomed. "It seems Lydia is expecting again."

That got Brendan's attention. "Little Laurel is only a few months old."

"Three children in as many years," Chet agreed with a grin. "Our old friend is making up for lost time."

"Apparently."

"Carteret seems to think he won't stop 'til he gets a son."

Chet's youngest step-son sucked in a breath. "Ya promised Mama ya wouldna say anything about Uncle James anymore."

The marquess ruffled the young boy's hair and winked. "This time it wasn't anything unkind, Ewan. Now turn around or you'll miss the show."

All three boys sat forward in their seats, and Brendan enjoyed seeing the enthusiasm in Thomas' countenance. He'd try to make sure his nephew got the most out of the evening. "You promised Hannah you wouldn't say anything else ruthless about her brother?" At one point it had been his favorite pastime.

Chet shrugged. "I suppose he's grown on me, and he does love his sister and our boys."

Brendan shook his head. He had brother-in-law troubles of his own. "I would trade you Lord Carteret for Lord Avery any day of the week." At least Carteret always had his sister's best interests at heart, misguided as he may have been in the past.

Chet settled back in his seat, smiling indulgently as Ewan squealed with delight when the first horses and riders entered the amphitheatre. "That bad, huh? I didn't know anyone would be willing to take Carteret off my hands."

The marquess' oldest boy looked over his shoulder at the two men and Chet chuckled. "All right, Alasdair, there's no need to tell your mother about that last one." Then he refocused on Brendan, his light eyes more serious than usual. "So, is it the brother you object to? Or the sister?"

Brendan snorted. Only Chet would dare ask him that question. It came from years of playing the role as his older brother. "Weren't you the one who spread our romantic tale throughout Town?"

"Aye, that's why I'm asking."

With a sigh, Brendan met his friend's eyes. "Cordie is perfect for me. I am much more fortunate this time around. She is the wife I always should have had."

Chet nodded. "I am glad to hear it. And she has pulled off quite the miracle, your wife."

"Oh?"

"Mother adores her. I had been worried the girl was the devil incarnate to have garnered such blind loyalty from the old dragon."

Brendan grinned. Lady Astwick was a bit of a dragon, though she saved most of her barbs for her only remaining son. "Is that why she and Hannah are hosting this soiree?"

"I didn't have a prayer of stopping them. Ever since Caroline told them you were coming back to Town, they've been making plans and sending out invitations and—"

"What if we'd sent our regards?"

"You would never ignore a summons from my mother."

True, no one would. Still... "I think something is wrong with Cordie."

The three boys cheered wildly at an acrobatic stunt Brendan had somehow missed. He turned his attention briefly to the center of the amphitheatre where a woman stood on the back of a horse, her arms outstretched towards the audience.

"Why do you think something is wrong?" Chet asked.

"It's her health. I think she's hiding something from me." He'd catch her in pain, but whenever she noticed him, she'd feign a bright smile and pretend as though everything was fine. "It's maddening."

Chet chuckled. "Welcome to the world of marriage, my friend."

Cordie leaned back in her chair and closed her eyes. It would take Rose another five minutes to decide which card she wanted to play in their game of piquet. Her sister-in-law hummed lightly to herself and Cordie wished her headache away. She hadn't felt right ever since Greg sent his note informing them he couldn't locate Brendan's lost letters.

A light scratch sounded at the door, and she sat forward, opening her eyes. "Come."

Higgins pushed the door open. "Lady Clayworth, you have a guest."

"A guest?" she echoed, rising from her seat to retrieve the calling card.

The Earl of Ericht glinted off the heavy vellum. Cordie couldn't help but smile. Haversham. She did owe the marquess a thank you, but perhaps another time. Brendan would be furious if he knew Haversham had visited, using an assumed name, and tried to call on her. "Please tell Lord Ericht I am not in, Higgins."

"Very well, my lady," the butler replied, leaving them alone.

As Cordie resumed her seat, Rose regarded her with confusion. "But, Cordie, you *are* in."

"Not for Lord Ericht. Besides, I am not feeling up for visitors at the moment, dear."

Rose sat forward. "But you'll feel up to seeing the modiste again tomorrow, won't you?"

For their final fittings. Cordie smiled at her young sister-in-law. Oh, to be free of worry. How she envied the girl in that way. "You know I'd never miss that, Rose. Now I believe it is still your turn." She pointed to the card on the small table between them.

Rose dropped her hand to the table and stared at Cordie. "Richard says you changed Brendan's mind. About the wedding."

"I'm certain your brother would have done the appropriate thing without my help." Though she was not certain of any such thing. He was quite stubborn and set in his ways, but the decision was made and there was no point in wondering what might have been.

"Thank you," Rose said with a hushed voice, though there was no one around to hear her. "I love Richard. I do not know what I would do if Brendan had said no."

Cordie squeezed Rose's hand. "Well, that didn't happen. And next week you'll be married and..."

The room began to spin slightly and Cordie grasped the table to steady herself. Rose rushed to her side. "Are you all right?"

She blinked her eyes, then nodded. "I don't know what came over me."

Rose touched Cordie's brow. "Brendan is worried about you."

She shook her head. Her husband didn't need something else on his plate. She wasn't feeling well, but she'd be fine. There was no use getting him upset over nothing. "Brendan is always worried about something. Let's not tell him about this little thing, all right?"

Rose frowned at that. "I don't want to keep a secret from him. He would be very angry with me if he knew."

Cordie caressed her sister-in-law's hand. "It's not really a secret, dear. I'm fine. He has so much on his mind at the moment, I don't want to add to it. If I'm feeling badly tomorrow, I'll tell him. I promise."

"Promise?" Rose asked, gnawing on her bottom lip.

"I do. Now, dear, it is your turn."

The game dragged on for hours, and Cordie felt herself in danger of dozing off more than once. But when Thomas rushed through the doors of the parlor, gushing over the show at Astley's with Brendan in his wake, her game of piquet finally came to an end.

♦

Damn if his wife didn't look even paler than she had before he left for the evening. Brendan had enjoyed such a nice time with Thomas, Chet and his boys, but he should have been home with Cordie. What an awful husband he was to have left her in this state.

He rushed Rose and Thomas off to bed, then turned his attention to his wife. She looked tired too, her dark hair down about her shoulders and circles under her eyes. "Time you crawled into bed too, love."

"My thoughts exactly." She smiled at him, though he knew it was forced. The image pained his soul.

Brendan slid his arm around her waist and led her up the stairs towards his chamber. Her foot faltered before her own door. "I thought you wanted me to climb into bed."

He ushered her forward. "I'd like to keep you with me tonight." So he could keep a close eye on her.

"Brendan," she chastised. "You snore. I'll never get a restful sleep."

He snorted. He most certainly did *not* snore. At least she'd never complained about it before now. She was doing poorly and trying to keep it from him. That was obvious, and her machinations only made his determination stronger. "Then I'll stay awake and watch over you."

"Brendan!"

He opened his door and directed her inside. "This room faces the west. The sun won't wake you in the morning."

"My room faces west as well," she grumbled under her breath, though he caught it. "My nightrail."

"I've played your maid before, Cordie. Now stop being difficult." He pulled the bell-pull, unbuttoned her gown, and when a maid scratched at the door, he asked the girl to bring the countess' nightrail and wrapper to him.

In no time he had her dressed and tucked into his bed. He refused to let her protruding lower lip make him feel guilty. Something wasn't right with her and he'd shadow her every move until Doctor Watts put his mind at ease on the morrow.

Brendan shed his own clothes and slid under the counterpane with this wife, pulling her into the cocoon of his arms. "There, isn't that better?" he whispered beside her ear.

She interlaced her fingers with his and took a deep breath. "You make it very difficult for me to remain put-out with you, you know."

"That is the plan." He kissed her hair and closed his eyes, breathing in her sweet lilac scent. "Try to sleep, love. You look very tired."

"Hmm," she agreed. "And Rose has me running all over Town tomorrow."

Brendan shook his head. "You're not going anywhere tomorrow, Cordie. Not unless Doctor Watts says it's all right."

She gasped and turned in his arms. "You sent for Doctor Watts? But Brendan, I'm fine, I'm—"

"Staying in bed until the doctor says otherwise."

❧

Brendan paced his parlor for what felt like an eternity. How long was Doctor Watts going to stay with his wife? It must be bad. The man was very busy. He wouldn't stay to simply chat.

Rose pouted in the corner that her trip to the modiste was postponed, though Brendan ignored his sister's childlike behavior. She could fall on the floor and pound with her fists like a toddler for all the good it would do her.

What was keeping the bloody doctor? He was just about to stomp from the room to find out when Doctor Watts appeared in the doorway. The old man smiled warmly, which didn't put Brendan at ease in the least. He rushed forward. "Well, out with it. What's wrong with her?"

"Congratulations, my lord. There is nothing to worry about. Lady Clayworth is in perfect health—"

"She's *not* in perfect health. I know my wife, sir." He'd always had the utmost respect for Watts. Apparently that was misplaced.

"You didn't allow me to finish, my lord. The countess is in perfect health for an expectant mother. She'll need her rest, of course, and she'll need to eat well, even if she doesn't feel like it. But all in all she is quite healthy indeed. Now I would suggest—"

The air whooshed out of Brendan. He didn't hear the last of the doctor's instructions as he raced down the hallway, up the stairs, and into his chamber. Cordie lay against the pillows, her pretty dark hair fanned out beside her. A radiant smile graced her lips.

He stopped in the doorway like a fool, simply gaping at her.

"He told you?" she prompted, her emerald eyes dancing.

Brendan rushed forward and plopped on the bed beside her. "Did you know? Why didn't you tell me? I've been going out of my mind—"

"I didn't know," she assured him. "I thought it was all from the worry and—"

"No more secrets, ever." He kissed her cheek. "I want to know what's happening all the time. Don't spare my feelings, love. I need to know that you're comfortable and safe and—"

"I promise," she said softly.

Brendan placed his hand across her belly, staring at her in wonder. His child. Their child was there and growing. He'd never felt such elation.

He'd never had so much to lose before.

Thirty-Eight

CORDIE stared at her reflection in the mirror. Her dark hair was half swept up and adorned with a slender silver cord and diamond hairpins. Her new silver gown shimmered and clung to every curve, much more daring than the virginal dresses she'd been forced to wear for years. She remembered coveting Livvie's new, stylish wardrobe months ago, and now wondered how much longer her new gowns would fit her.

She rested her hand against her flat belly and smiled. "You know, little one, by the time I'm able to wear these new dresses again they'll be out of fashion." Not that she was complaining. The idea of holding Brendan's child in her arms made her heart sing.

"You'll be just a few months younger than Livvie's babe. I'm sure you'll be the best of friends. I do wish the Kelfield's were closer. We could experience all of this together." Just like she and Livvie had done everything else.

She sighed. Brendan would never agree to a trip to Hampshire now. Tomorrow morning, they'd head back for Derbyshire. Rose's wedding would be a week later. After that, she and Brendan would spend her confinement at Bayhurst Court. She wanted that, of course, she just wished that Livvie could be part of it.

"Breathtaking," Brendan said from the doorway.

Cordie spun on her heel, grinning at her husband. "Flatterer."

He crossed the room and slid his arms around her waist. "If you're not feeling up to this, we'll stay home."

She laughed. "You just finished telling me that I was breathtaking."

"You are."

"I may never get the chance to wear this gown again."

"Well," he began, rolling his eyes, "heaven forbid I stand in the way of fashion."

"Besides," she told him, "I don't think it would be at all wise to ignore an invitation from Lady Astwick."

"Hannah will understand."

"The dowager will not."

He sighed and she knew he'd given in.

♦

They just had to get through this miserable soiree, and then they could return to Derbyshire. It's just one night, Brendan kept saying to himself. He scoffed when he saw the line of carriages in front of Astwick's large Mayfair home. This was not a soiree, it was something on a much grander scale than that. It wasn't even the damn season.

He grumbled under his breath, but stopped when Cordie squeezed his hand. "We'll just stay long enough to see and be seen," he said.

Cordie laughed. "For heaven's sake, Brendan. I won't break. Who knows when we'll return? Enjoy the evening."

Their coach stopped in front of the mansion. The footman opened the door and lowered the steps before Brendan climbed out into the night air. He held out his hand and helped his wife to the ground, then led her up the stone steps.

They managed to navigate the swarm of people until they reached the ballroom, where their names were intoned, "The Earl and Countess of Clayworth."

It seemed as though all in attendance took the same collective intake of air as Brendan led his wife over the threshold. In no time, the dowager Marchioness of Astwick was upon them. "My darling Cordelia Clayworth!" the old woman gushed. "You are positively glowing." Then she linked her arm with Cordie's and said to Brendan, "You may go visit with my son."

He'd been dismissed, and it was never wise to argue with the woman. Brendan bowed. "Wonderful to see you again, my lady."

Her eyes actually twinkled. "It's wonderful to see you, my boy. Happiness looks good on you, Brendan."

"Thank you, madam."

"Now go on, so that I can talk to your beautiful bride."

Without another word, the dowager directed Cordie away from him and Brendan found himself alone in a sea of familiar strangers. Then a hamhock of a hand smacked him on the back and he turned to see Chet's light green eyes regarding him. "Come along and help me test my newest collection of whiskey."

Brendan grinned at his friend. "Collection?"

⸗⸎⸎⸎⸑

"I am so glad you came to your senses, Cordelia," the dowager marchioness said to her as they strolled the ballroom.

"Came to my senses?" Cordie echoed, noticing that not one person looked at her with condemnation. They'd managed to somehow avoid censure.

"A man like Brendan Reese only comes along once in a lifetime."

Cordie couldn't help the sigh that escaped her. "Of that I am well aware. I can't thank you enough, Lady Astwick, for smoothing things over with society. You are a blessing."

The old woman laughed. "You are the only one who thinks so, my dear." Then she stopped in her tracks. "That son of mine," she grumbled. "Does he truly intend to escape my soiree?"

Cordie's eyes flashed towards the door to find Lord Astwick and Brendan's disappearing forms. "I'm certain—"

"I'm certain that he's mistaken," the dowager growled. "Don't disappear on me, Cordelia."

The marchioness dropped Cordie's arm and started after her wayward son, and Cordie bit back a smile. The man was nothing like his mother at all. She had no idea how the two were related. Of course, she was nothing like her mother either, whom Cordie was glad to note that she did not see in attendance.

"There you are," came a deep voice from behind her, one Cordie knew well. "I worried I might never see you again."

She looked over her shoulder into the light blue eyes of the Marquess of Haversham. He was still dangerously handsome, though he seemed different somehow, in a way she couldn't quite pinpoint. More stoic, perhaps. "Lord Haversham." She smiled at him. "I cannot believe that Lady Astwick invited you."

He winked at her. "I've never let that stop me before."

"I am so glad to see you, my lord." She owed him so much.

"What happened to Marc?" he asked huskily.

"There are so many answers to *that*, I don't even know where to begin." She laughed.

"Will you dance with me?" His eyes focused on her with such intensity, she had to look away towards the couples on the dance floor.

"I don't think that would be appropriate, Lord Haversham."

He stepped closer to her and lowered his voice. "And since when are you appropriate, angel?"

Cordie turned to face him. She owed him at least that. "I suppose since I became the Countess of Clayworth."

Haversham winced at her words. "Indeed? So has his priggish demeanor rubbed off, then?"

She wanted to swat him across the chest, but that wouldn't be at all proper, not with half the eyes of the *ton* on her. "That's not a terribly complimentary thing to say about my husband."

"He can hang," Haversham growled, causing her to gasp. "I think I made a mistake letting you go, Cordie. Ever since you left—"

"Don't." She frowned at him, meeting his icy eyes. How dare he say such a thing? "Don't say another word. And don't come to visit me as Lord Ericht or as yourself. I won't see you."

He rubbed his brow. "So you're happy, then?"

"Ecstatically."

Haversham nodded. "When you're *not* ecstatically happy anymore, send me a note. I'll be waiting."

"I wish you wouldn't," she whispered. "You'll be very disappointed, my lord."

He smiled sadly. "I already am, angel."

At that moment, Lord Brookfield approached them and Cordie sucked in an anxious breath. Russell's words about the viscount echoed in her ears. *Opium eater.* The thought made her cringe. She slid her arm through Haversham's and smiled up at him. "You don't owe me a thing, but please don't leave."

His eyes shot to the penniless viscount and his features hardened. "Brookfield," he said dangerously.

The viscount jumped at the sound of his name. "Ah, Haversham, I didn't see you there."

"Don't know how you could possibly miss me. I do hope you haven't come to bother Lady Clayworth."

Brookfield's dark eyes raked across Cordie, and icy chills raced down her spine. "I just wanted to offer my felicitations."

"Then offer them to her husband. He's the fortunate one." Haversham steered Cordie away from the viscount, onto the dance floor, joining the already waltzing couples.

"I shouldn't be dancing with you," she said, looking at his neckcloth for fear of what she'd find in his eyes.

"I just saved you from Brookfield. I'd say a dance is the least you can offer me in return."

He was right, of course. "He makes me uncomfortable," she admitted. "Thank you for taking me away from him."

Haversham scoffed. "It wasn't Brookfield I'd hoped to take you from, angel."

Finally she raised her eyes to meet his. "I am sorry, but I do love my husband. That won't ever change."

He sighed and looked above her head. "Clayworth's face is an interesting shade of purple." Cordie tried to glance over her shoulder, but Haversham led her in a turn towards the other side of the room. "He'll have you back soon enough. This is *my* dance."

⚜

Without a doubt, Brendan was going to kill Marcus Gray. The question was did he dare do so with so many witnesses looking on? And would any of them care?

How dare the man whisk Cordie out onto the dance floor? And why the devil did she go with him? He kept his eyes trained on his wife's form, but every moment she was in that cur's clutches, Brendan's anger mounted even higher.

He started to move towards the pair, but Chet's hand on his shoulder stopped him. "Don't make a scene. It's what he wants."

"I'm going to kill him," Brendan growled.

"Perfectly understandable," Chet agreed, "but not with an audience.

It'll reflect badly on your wife."

Brendan ground his teeth together, knowing his friend was right, and biding his time until he could knock the smug look off Haversham's face. A footman approached Brendan and handed him a note. "This is for you, my lord."

Brendan snatched the note and tore it open.

Clayworth,

Scandal is so unfortunate, especially for a man such as yourself. I knew one day this opportunity would present itself. How fortunate that you and your new countess have returned to London. Unless you'd like the world to find out about Lady Clayworth's unfortunate past, you will pay me ten thousand pounds *to keep my mouth closed.*

No signature. No direction. Brendan's heart stopped.

Thirty-Nine

CORDIE cringed when she spotted Brendan's ashen face just a few feet away. This dance had been an awful idea. Blast Haversham for forcing it on her. As soon as the waltz came to an end, before the marquess even had a chance to bow, Brendan had snatched her elbow in his grasp and began escorting her towards the exit.

"Brendan," she tried to explain.

But his jaw was tight and he looked like a man possessed. "Not here," he growled.

He pushed her through the throng of people and out the doors to his carriage, which was still out in front of the Astwick's home. He hauled open the door and though he was furious, he took great care in helping her gently into the conveyance.

Cordie settled to the far side of the coach and within seconds Brendan was beside her, pounding on the roof with his fist. The coach set off with a lurch and Cordie swallowed uncomfortably. Of course her husband was angry, but surely he could listen to reason. "Brendan, I am sorry. I didn't really have a choice."

"I don't give a damn about Haversham."

Cordie gasped. He'd never used such language in front of her before.

"I-I mean I do care about it and I'll deal with him later, but right now we have bigger problems."

She touched his leg and tried to see his face in the darkness of the coach. "What's wrong?"

He took a staggering breath and scrubbed a hand across his face. "Someone knows about mother's letters, Cordie."

She was certain her heart had stopped. That didn't make any sense. Why would someone wait until now to use the letters against Brendan? "How—"

"While you were with Haversham, I received a blackmail note. Though there were no instructions as to where to pay the funds, the writer did ask for a sum."

"Bow Street," she whispered, only to hear him snort.

"I can't go to the authorities, love. I can't really explain about the letters to them, now can I?"

Of course not. She felt so inept, so incapable of helping him. "What do we do?"

His arm settled around her shoulders and Cordie sighed. Whatever was to be done, they'd do together. She took strength from that. "I have been thinking about this possibility for some time," he told her, sounding very distant to her ears.

"You have a plan?"

He held her tighter. "I'll take Rose and Thomas back to Derbyshire and as soon as she marries Lester, I'll send Thomas along with them for the time being. The vicar owes me."

On their honeymoon? Cordie tipped her head up to see him better. "Wouldn't it be better for him to stay with us?"

He shook his head. "There's no us, Cordie. You have to leave me."

Her heart lurched. She must have misheard him. "Leave you?" she gasped.

"Avery was right about that. Distancing yourself from me is the only way to keep you safe."

"No!" She shook her head. "I won't leave you. I promised you I never would. Brendan—"

He touched a finger to her lips. "Ah, my love, it's not just you anymore. You have to protect our child. Promise me you will."

Her hand instinctively fluttered to her belly. "I can't leave you. Ask me anything else."

Brendan pressed a kiss to her head. "You know it's best. I won't see you thrown in Newgate because of me."

"You've done nothing," she protested.

"I don't believe the home office will see it that way. Now you need to listen to me, we don't have much time."

"You want me to leave *tonight?*" This couldn't be. They had to have more time than that.

"Shh. Now I've put your dowry in a trust. My solicitor is Leland Birch with Amherst and Birch. I have his direction at home. Write him and he'll see that you are provided for. I've done the same thing for Rose, and Astwick will see that my orders are followed through."

"Does he know?" she couldn't help but ask.

"No. He lost a brother on the battlefields. I'm sure he will not be happy to assist me, but he's already given his word as a gentleman. Above all else, Astwick is honorable."

"Brendan, you're scaring me. Why don't you just pay whatever the blackmailer asks and we'll pretend none of this ever happened?"

He sighed and seemed to breathe her in. "It doesn't work that way, Cordie. Blackmailers are never satisfied. They always want more until there's nothing left—"

"Then give it to them," she hissed. "What does money or anything else mean without you?"

Brendan moved so he could see her better and Cordie cringed at the determined set of his jaw. "They would take everything and in the end still turn me over. Now, I need you to follow my directions to the letter. I am going to find those letters if it kills me, but I need to know that you are safe, that the baby is safe. Can you do that for me?"

She somehow managed to nod.

"Good girl." He kissed her gently. "Now if things go well, I'll write you and I'll come for you, and we can forget any of this ever happened. But if not, the world needs to believe that you've left me. Put as much distance between us as possible. I won't write you and you can't write me."

Her heart was breaking. "Brendan—"

"I know it will be hard, Cordie. But we can't risk it. The only thing that will make this bearable for me is knowing that I've protected you from my fate."

Cordie swiped at the tears that streamed down her face. How would she go on without him? "I can go home to my family," she offered, though it was the last place she wanted to be.

Brendan shook his head. "No matter what happens to me, love, I'll never let you live under the same roof as that woman ever again."

Cordie closed her eyes. She loved him so desperately. The idea of being away from him was the most painful thing she'd ever contemplated. He wrapped his arms around her and held her tight. "I'm so sorry, Cordie. I can send you to stay with Masten for a while. God knows he owes me."

Cordie shook her head. "I'll go stay with Livvie. She won't ask any questions."

"No."

"Why not?" she asked, glancing over her shoulder at him.

"I don't want you anywhere near Kelfield."

"Brendan!" she chastised. He knew how important Olivia was to her.

His hold tightened. "It's not the duchess. It's not even Kelfield. But Haversham is a friend of the duke's and I'd rather he not be around you."

Foolish man! Cordie turned in his arms and pulled his head down for a kiss. "Brendan Reese! You are my life. That dance didn't mean anything. He was keeping Brookfield at bay, is all —"

"Early on you fancied him," he said sourly. "And when he thinks you've left me —"

Cordie kissed him again. "It won't matter," she vowed.

His arms tightened around her waist and she wished they could stay like this forever. "I won't see you hurt, Cordie, not ever. Even if I'm...*gone*, you can't trust the man."

"Leaving you hurts," she told him.

"I'll find the blackmailer. I'll find the letters. I swear it."

❦

The trip to Hampshire was a blur. Cordie kept remembering the look in Brendan's eyes when he said his last goodbye and shut the carriage door, sending her off before dawn broke. It would be a miracle if her quickly scrawled noted reached Livvie before she did.

She watched the landscape pass outside the carriage window and drew herself up into a ball. She'd never felt so alone, and she'd never prayed so long or so vehemently about anything in her life, but the journey to Brockenhurst had been a long, one-sided conversation with God. There was nothing else she could do. Being powerless was unnerving.

When their speed slowed, Cordie peered out the window again. A large baroque mansion grew nearer with her approach. When the coach pulled into the drive, she spotted Livvie and Kelfield waiting out front and Cordie almost burst into tears. With nowhere else to go, she prayed again that Everett Place would be a safe haven.

The coach rambled to a stop and the door opened. Instead of a footman standing before her, Cordie was surprised to see the Duke of Kelfield holding the door himself. He smiled, though it didn't quite reach his eyes, and concern was etched across his brow. "Lady Clayworth."

She nearly choked, hearing her name, hearing her husband's name. "Your Grace," she answered, accepting his offered arm. Before she'd even gone two steps, Livvie threw her arms around her neck.

"Oh, Cordie! I'm so glad to see you. So glad you've come to stay with us."

Cordie hugged her back for all she was worth. It was the first relief she'd felt since before the Astwick soiree. She stepped back, smiling at her friend. Livvie looked healthy and happy, but different. And the hug had been different too. Cordie glanced at the duchess' abdomen. "Good heavens, Livvie! You're showing." Something she could very well be facing alone, if things turned out poorly.

The smile that spread across her friend's face stretched from ear to ear. "We're very happy," Livvie gushed, linking her arm with Cordie's.

Both of their lives had changed so much in the last year. It was amazing they even recognized each other. Cordie blinked back her tears.

Do let me show you around," Livvie said as her hazel eyes met Cordie's.

She knew. They'd known each other every day of their lives and Livvie knew there was something wrong. Cordie shook a head at her own foolishness. Of course Livvie knew there was something wrong. She'd traveled all night alone and had shown up at the Kelfields' home uninvited. The simplest of simpletons would know.

"That does sound lovely." She forced a smile to her face and stood up straight. Brendan expected more from her, and she couldn't fail him in the only task he'd given her.

Livvie linked her arm with Cordie's and lead her towards the side of the house. "My mother-in-law breeds sheep dogs. Can you believe it?"

"Heavens!" she gasped. Her friend was deathly afraid of dogs, always had been. "How do you bear it?"

Livvie smiled as they approached a small garden. "I'm trying to be a bit more brave. My step-daughter adores the creatures, and she's only five."

They stopped and Livvie bent forward to smell a rose bush that came to her waist. Then she glanced back and assessed Cordie silently. She saw a number of questions cross her friend's face.

Cordie smiled tightly and took a deep breath, searching for something to say. "Have you heard anything from Phoebe?"

Livvie nodded. "She does not particularly care for Tristan, which is hard to believe. He's always been my favorite of your brothers."

"Apparently he terrified her," Cordie replied, relieved that Livvie didn't seem anxious to delve into the reasons for her impromptu visit.

Livvie giggled. "I can't imagine him terrifying anyone."

"Mama!" a little raven-haired girl called, running up the path towards them. Then she hurled herself against Livvie's legs.

The duchess smiled indulgently at the girl and smoothed the hair from the child's face. "Poppy Everett, how may times have I told you that running is not ladylike?"

"Thirty-five?" the girl asked innocently.

"Make it thirty-six." Livvie dropped her hand to the child's shoulder. "Let me introduce you to my dearest friend, Poppy. This is Lady Clayworth. She's going to stay with us for a while."

Poppy's silver eyes widened, then she dropped a very clumsy courtesy. "Hello, Lady Clayworth."

"Hello, Poppy," Cordie answered. "I understand you like sheep dogs."

The girl's face broke out into a wide grin and she nodded eagerly before turning her attention back to Livvie. "Grandmama says she thinks a new litter is coming. She said I had to ask you if it was all right for me to stay with her."

Livvie furrowed her brow. "Poppy," she began.

"Please, Mama! I want to see the puppies."

"All right," the duchess sighed and then laughed as the girl took off at a run in the other direction. "Poppy, no running! And do listen to your grandmother."

The humor of the exchange did not escape Cordie. "Thirty-seven times now."

Livvie laughed. "She's so like her father."

Cordie linked her arm with Livvie's. If she couldn't be with Brendan, she was glad she was here. "She calls you 'Mama'?"

"Would you believe her own mother abandoned her and ran off to Italy? Poppy's such a sweetheart, I can't imagine how anyone could do such a thing. I can't believe that her mother loves her or she never would have left her in the first place. So I don't mind that she calls me, 'Mama'. Someone should fill that role for her."

Cordie touched a hand to her belly. Dear God, she'd left her husband. What would she do if Brendan couldn't retrieve the letters? What would she do if she lost him forever?

Forty

NINE days.

It had been nine days since he'd seen her pretty face. Nine days since he'd kissed her. Nine days since he'd held her in his arms and promised her that everything would work out. They were the longest and most torturous nine days he'd ever suffered through.

Brendan slumped down behind the desk in his London study and leaned his head against the large leather chair. Nothing made sense anymore. After traveling to Bayhurst Court, walking Rose down the aisle, making certain Thomas would be looked after, and returning to London, all Brendan could think about was how much he missed his wife.

And the blackmail notes.

Four of them, including the original, were spread across his desk, each one more confusing than the last. They were all written by the same hand, he was certain, but they contradicted each other and none of them told him where he was to deliver the money. What a strange thing for a blackmailer to forget.

Clayworth,
Send me fifteen thousand pounds or the world will learn Lady
Clayworth's secrets.

Clayworth,
I am patiently waiting for your funds. I am not anxious to reveal
the countess' scandalous past, but you are not leaving me much of
a choice. I await your twenty thousand pounds.

Clayworth,
You owe me money! You have taken everything from me, and I
will not hesitate to retaliate. If I do not have twelve thousand
pounds from you by the end of the week, Lady Clayworth's secrets
will be on display for all to see.

Brendan scrubbed a hand across his face. He was no closer to finding the damn letters or his blackmailer than he was the morning he sent Cordie to Hampshire. A scratch came at his door and he sat forward. "Come."

Higgins peeked inside the study. "My lord, Lady Staveley is here to see you."

Brendan closed his eyes. He couldn't deal with Caroline today. He shook his head. "Please inform her ladyship that I am not available."

Then he heard an indignant huff and scrambling on the other side of the door and before Higgins could disappear, the study door burst open. Like an angry queen, Caroline stomped into the room, but stopped short when her eyes landed on him. He looked bad—he knew it. She'd never seen him unshaven and unkempt. It was no wonder her eyes nearly popped from her head.

"Good heavens, Brendan!" she gasped. "It's worse than I thought." She rushed forward, tugged her glove from her fingers and touched his brow. "Well, you're not ill."

"I'm not up to seeing anyone, Caroline."

"Well, you'll see me." She sat on the edge of his desk. "Darling, you know you mustn't pay attention to the society rags. They're wrong as often as they're right."

Dear God. He hadn't even looked at any of those. Who knew what they said. Brendan leaned back in his chair. "Please, Caroline, I have a lot on my mind at the moment."

"I'm certain you do." She nodded fervently. "I didn't even get a chance to speak with you at the Astwicks, but I did see that dance and I can understand you being upset. But I can't imagine her up and leaving you over it."

"Caroline, I'm not going to discuss my marriage with you."

Her bottom lip thrust out in a pout. "Brendan, you need to go after her."

"I don't even know where she is," he lied.

She leaned forward, grinning like a cat who got into the cream. "Oh, well, if that's all that's stopping you, I know where she is."

Brendan cursed under his breath. Of course Caroline would have done her research before visiting him. He scowled at her.

"She's visiting Olivia and Kelfield in Hampshire."

"I'm not going after her," he growled.

"But, darling, she's miserable too. Livvie is terribly worried about her. Just take a tiny little trip to Hampshire to see her. I'm sure if you're in the same room together you can work this all out. There's no need for all this unhappiness."

If he was in the same room with her, he wouldn't have the resolve to stay away. Brendan heaved a sigh, letting her words sink in. Cordie was miserable. His soul ached for her, but her safety was of the utmost importance. "I don't want your help, Caroline," he said firmly. "This will either work itself out or it won't. But keep your pretty nose out of it."

"But, Brendan—"

"No!" he barked, pushing away from his desk and towering over her. "I don't want to discuss it. I'm not going after her. Leave it be."

She slid off his desk, her face twisted in surprised annoyance, which was an unusual look as she always got her way. "If you'll just—"

Outside his door, "Clayworth!" was bellowed.

"Heavens," Caroline gasped. "What is that about?"

Brendan paid her no attention as he stalked to his door and hauled it open. Before him stood the Marquess of Haversham, glaring at him. "What the devil did you do with her?"

Brendan itched to send the bastard crashing into a wall or out a window or down a flight of steps. But that would make him appear jealous and he needed to remember that distancing himself from Cordie was the best thing he could do to protect her future. "I don't know what you mean," he said with a calmness he didn't feel.

"You really are an imbecile," Haversham growled. "Cordie spent the entire waltz gushing over her love for you, which irritated me to no end.

If she felt half that much for me, I'd—"

"Apologies, Haversham. I have an appointment." Brendan brushed past the marquess, unable to listen to any more. He did need a bath and clean set of clothes. Once his uninvited guests left, and his house was quiet again, perhaps he could think clearly.

⚜

Marc gaped at Clayworth's departing form. He'd never imagined the man wouldn't put up a fight over his wife. She was, after all, someone to fight over. It wasn't until he heard the ruffle of skirts that he turned back to the study to find Caroline Staveley watching him with her wide hazel eyes.

"You really did cause them quite a bit of trouble," she said, folding her arms across her chest. "I hope you're satisfied."

Loyal to the last, even when Clayworth was acting the role of a dim-witted bastard. Marc shook his head. "It's hardly my fault. I came to talk some sense into him."

Lady Staveley snorted. "Everywhere you go, carnage follows, Lord Haversham. Forgive me if I don't believe that you have anyone's interests but your own in mind." She stepped around the desk and a piece of foolscap fluttered to the floor in front of her.

She stopped to scoop it up and she stumbled backwards when her eyes landed on the page. Marc rushed forward and caught her elbow to keep her from crashing to the carpet. "Are you all right?"

She clutched the paper to her chest and nodded.

For all that she was an excellent schemer, her ashen face and surprised eyes failed her this time. Marc pried the paper from her grasp and scanned the note. What could Cordie have done that would cost twenty thousand pounds to keep quiet?

"He's being blackmailed," Lady Staveley whispered.

"It would appear that is true," Marc agreed, while his mind tried to make sense of the revelation. What sort of trouble was Cordie in? His pulse pounded viciously in his ears. He spotted three other notes by the same hand on the desk behind the viscountess and quickly read them.

"He's asked for different amounts and I don't see where money is to be sent," Lady Staveley said at his side.

"Most strange," he added. "I can't imagine what she could have done..."

"I've known the girl most of her life. The most scandalous thing she's ever done is run off to Scotland to marry Clayworth."

There had to be something else. Something that wasn't public knowledge. Maybe something to do with that enormous dowry. Marc placed the note back on Clayworth's desk and quickly scanned all four one more time. "I'm going to find out what it is."

"To what end?" Lady Staveley frowned at him. She'd never thought highly of him and his next words weren't about to change her opinion, not that he cared.

"To kill the bastard who's trying to hurt her."

Lady Staveley nodded solemnly. "That does sound like a good plan."

Marc reared back from her, his mouth open wide. He would never have thought of Lady Staveley as the blood-thirsty type. She smoothed the letters back in place, as though they had never been touched. "Where do you propose we begin?"

⚜

Cordie was certain she was an abysmal guest. Livvie had been very understanding over the last fortnight. She hadn't pushed for information, and for that Cordie would always be thankful. She climbed out of bed, unable to sleep, and thought that perhaps an old, boring tome from the library would help her fall asleep.

Silently, she padded to the first floor and down the main corridor.

"I'd like to go straight to Town and hand Clayworth his ass," the duke's voice boomed from inside his study, which immediately caught Cordie's attention.

"Alex!" Livvie chastised. Though she couldn't see her friend through the closed door, Cordie imagined the duchess standing with hands on her hips, frowning at her husband.

Cordie shouldn't listen, but she'd been eavesdropping since she was a small child, and some habits were harder to break than others. Besides, they were talking about Brendan. Had something happened?

"What's he done to the poor girl? She doesn't even seem like herself."

"I know," Livvie sighed. "It kills me to see her like this. She was always the strongest one of all of us."

"Do you really not know what he's done?" her husband asked.

"She hasn't said, and I haven't asked. She'll tell me when she's ready, at least I hope she will."

Guilt washed over Cordie. She hated putting Livvie in this situation. Kelfield grunted something she couldn't understand, so she pressed her ear to the door to hear better. After all, if being at Everett Place wasn't going to work out, if they didn't want her here, she needed to know sooner rather than later.

"She's *enceinte* too," Livvie said softly. "She hasn't told me, but I can tell."

Cordie's heart lurched. She thought she'd hidden that fact so well.

"God damn it!" Kelfield snarled, breaking into her thoughts. "Give me one good reason I shouldn't track down that bastard. At this rate she would have been better off with Haversham."

Livvie snorted. "Please."

"You didn't see him," Kelfield protested. "I was there, Olivia. Marc was brokenhearted when she left. He still is."

"Impossible. He doesn't own a heart."

There was a long pause, and Cordie imagined Kelfield leveling his wife with the intensity of his silvery glare.

"This is neither here nor there, Alex. She chose Clayworth. She loves *him*, and still does, despite whatever it is he's done."

"What kind of man lets his expectant wife leave him? Travel across the country alone?" Kelfield growled. "Do you know how furious I would be if it was you? And Marc is convinced she's in some sort of trouble."

"Then I'm so glad she's come to us," Livvie's calm voice filtered through the door. "I can't imagine she would have any peace with the Averys. And I don't want you to push her, Alex. She needs a quiet, safe place to stay and I need her to have it here, where at least I know she's all right."

"Of course I'm not going to push her. She's the only one of your friends I actually like."

"She's really the only friend I have left," Livvie replied.

"Oh, I'm sorry, sweetheart. I'm sorry that being my wife has cost you so much."

"Alexander Everett," Cordie could hear the smile in Livvie's voice, "*you* are my life and I wouldn't trade you for anything or anyone in the world—certainly not to have hordes of fraudulent friends at my disposal."

"It'll get better," he promised.

It sounded like he kissed her, and Cordie stepped away from the door. Eavesdropping was one thing—spying on her friend's intimate encounters was something else entirely. Besides it made her miss her own husband more than she already did.

Cordie sighed. She shouldn't have come to Everett Place. If Brendan was revealed as a spy, would things be even worse for Livvie for offering her shelter? She'd have to write Mr. Birch tomorrow and ask for some funds. She couldn't rely on the Kelfields' generosity for much longer.

Forty-One

CAROLINE Staveley looked across the carriage at the Marquess of Haversham's profile as he kept a keen eye on Clayworth's residence. How strange to have made an alliance with the man. It was rare, indeed, for anyone to surprise her, and yet Haversham most assuredly had. In all the years she had known the marquess, which was not all that well as he lived on the outside of propriety, Caroline had never imagined him to concern himself with anyone's welfare other than his own.

"A messenger," he said, nearly pressing his face against the glass to get a better view.

Caroline peered out her window toward the mews behind Clayworth's home. A young fellow in grey and crimson livery approached the servant's entrance. "He belongs to Astwick. I'm not certain who Brendan's blackmailer is, but I do know that he is not Astwick. They're like brothers."

Haversham relaxed a bit against the leather squabs while Caroline kept her eyes focused on her friend's town home. She felt the marquess' gaze on her before he spoke. "Again, Lady Staveley, I am quite capable of conducting this bit of espionage on my own. Don't you have luncheons or garden parties you should be attending?"

Keeping her eyes trained on street before her, Caroline sighed. "And

263

if I did so, you'd be following a fellow in Astwick's employ and leaving Clayworth House completely unguarded."

"All right, you win." He shifted on his bench and the coach moved beneath his weight. "I don't have the desire to fight with you."

Caroline smiled to herself. It had been that way all of her life. Men never did have the desire to fight with her. "Tell me, Haversham," she began, "why are you doing this? Troubling yourself with the Clayworths?" She glanced back across the coach at him , curious at what she could read in his eyes.

Honestly, he looked a little weary. Drained might be a better word. "I wouldn't let anyone hurt Cordelia, not if I could stop it."

"Why?" she breathed out.

The marquess smiled wistfully. "I think she was the one, Lady Staveley. I just didn't realize it until I let Clayworth have her."

"The one?" she echoed. He couldn't mean what she thought he meant. Men like him didn't believe in such notions.

Haversham nodded. "I love everything about Cordie. Her penchant for trouble. Her joy of life. Her pretty smile." A hardened look crossed his face. "I was a fool not to keep her while I had the chance. Though she's not mine, I won't let any harm come to her."

Caroline smiled at him. "I do believe, sir, that I was wrong about you."

He winked one of his light blue eyes at her, appearing the rogue she'd always known him to be. "No, Caroline. I'm certain you were right about me from the beginning—a scoundrel to the very last."

She tilted her head to one side. Perhaps the gentleman doth protest too much.

⚜

While she watched, one of Kelfield's maids packed her trunk and Cordie released a nervous breath. She was doing the right thing. She couldn't stay at Everett Place any longer. To do so would cause irreparable damage to Livvie, and she couldn't bear the guilt of that. After receiving word from Mr. Birch that he had located a nice place in Bedford Square if she'd like, Cordie made up her mind to move back to Town. Brendan wouldn't be happy to learn she was returning to London, but she needed to be closer to him. Even if she couldn't touch him or speak to him, it would help to be in Town near him.

A knock sounded on her door, breaking Cordie from her thoughts. "Come," she called.

Livvie opened the door and a frown marred her face as her eyes landed on the packing maid. She turned her attention to Cordie. "I do wish you wouldn't do this."

Cordie bounded off the bed with more energy than she actually felt. "I will be fine," she lied.

Livvie sighed. "Join me for tea, will you?"

"Of course."

They left the maid packing and started down the hallway toward the set of cantilevered stairs. "You know you can tell me anything," Livvie said, grasping the railing to steady herself.

But not this. Cordie nodded. "Of course. You are my most trusted friend."

She followed Livvie down the steps and into a small, modestly appointed yellow parlor. For all that Livvie was now a duchess, she still wasn't accustomed to all the pomp and circumstance that went along with the title. After Livvie rang for tea, they both settled on a pale yellow damask settee.

"Can't I convince you to stay?" Livve asked, clutching Cordie's hand. "I'm worried about you being all alone. You may stay with us for as long as you need."

Livvie would help her to her own detriment. Cordie shook her head. "I know, Liv. But I can't. Everett Place should be returned to you. I can't be permanent guest."

"But—"

"I need to adjust to my circumstances," she pressed on. "Tell me you understand that."

Livvie didn't respond as the parlor door burst open and Kelfield stood before them, silver eyes wide in amazement, his mouth slightly open. It was a look Cordie had never seen on the striking duke before, and the sight immediately put her ill at ease.

Livvie pushed herself off the settee. "What is it, my love?"

His strange look was replaced by a charming smile for his wife. "Nothing to worry you about, sweetheart." Then he turned his attention to Cordie. "You have a guest. But if you don't want to see her, I'll be more than happy to throw her out on her ear."

"Who?" she asked, completely confused by his demeanor.

"That dragon. That awful Astwick woman."

Livvie sucked in a frightened breath. "The dowager?" she asked.

Cordie blinked. Why was Lady Astwick here? "Where is she?"

"I told the old bat she'd have to wait in the corridor."

"Alexander!" Livvie scolded.

Cordie rushed to the door and down the hallway towards the front entryway of Everett Place. What was the dowager marchioness doing here? She slid to a stop when the old woman came into view. Lady Astwick's frown was firmly in place and she was rapidly tapping her cane against the marble floor in agitation.

Cordie swallowed nervously. "My lady, whatever are you doing in Hampshire?"

The old woman's frown deepened, which Cordie hadn't realized was possible. "You've left your husband to come live in *this* den of iniquity? I hadn't thought it of you, Lady Clayworth. I'm thoroughly disappointed."

The name Clayworth tore at her soul, but Cordie refused to cry. Brendan would expect better than that. "Have you come all the way from London to chastise me for visiting my friends?"

"Friends!" the dowager muttered sourly under her breath. "Fiends is more like it. Do you know what that man said to me?"

"Kelfield?" Cordie asked.

"That blackguard said that if I couldn't be civil to that wife of his, he'd throw me out on my... Well, I don't like to say the word."

"Ear?" Cordie prompted.

Not *ear*, Lady Clayworth," the old woman snapped. "A man like him uses derogatory terms."

Cordie was fairly certain she knew the word in question. With a placating smile, she stepped towards the dowager and held out her hand. "I'm certain His Grace would do no such thing. He's very protective of his duchess is all, and she hasn't been treated warmly by the upper echelons of the *ton* as you well know."

"Humph!" Lady Astwick grumbled, though she allowed Cordie to maneuver her towards a nearby sitting room. "That is what happens when one associates with men such as him."

Cordie resisted urge to growl. It would only make matters worse. "As

Her Grace is my dearest friend, I'm certain you don't mean to impugn her name, especially in her own home."

Who knew what the dowager had said to make Kelfield so agitated? Cordie was certain she didn't want to know, or she too would be tempted to throw the old woman out on her *ear* as well.

"I had such high hopes for you, Cordelia," the old woman complained as she settled onto a white settee. "What did Clayworth do to drive you away?"

"Many spouses live apart, Lady Astwick," she replied evenly, proud that her voice hadn't cracked. Then she sat on a chintz chair and faced the old dragon.

"Bah!" the dowager barked. "The man was utterly devoted to you. He would never have left on his own. Now, tell me what he did." She pounded her cane on the floor as an exclamation point.

Perhaps she should have let Kelfield toss the old woman out in the first place.

"Cordelia Clayworth!"

Cordie sighed. "We discovered we didn't suit." She forced the lie out, the one Brendan made her promise to say. "No one is to blame."

Instead of getting angry as she expected the dowager to become, Lady Astwick blanched and looked suddenly frail. "What is it, my dear? I can see that you're in pain. Why are you lying to me? I'll help if I can."

Cordie thought she'd been doing so well. If she couldn't convince Lady Astwick, how was she ever going to convince anyone else? "I'm not lying," she whispered. "Brendan is focused on finding something right now, and that makes it impossible for us to be together."

"What is he looking for?"

Heavens, she was as persistent as a Bow Street Runner. "Something that belonged to his mother. That's all I can say."

"Dear God, *the letters*?" the old woman asked, pain echoed in her voice.

Cordie's eyes flashed to hers, and she realized too late she'd given Brendan away. Defeated, tears finally fell from her eyes. What was she to do now? Lady Astwick knew of the letters? All was certainly lost. How could she get word to Brendan? There was still time for him to flee. She'd never see him again, but he'd be safe. He'd be alive.

The widow heaved a sigh. "This is all my fault."

Cordie brushed away some tears and stared at the old woman. "I beg your pardon?"

"I didn't know he knew about them."

"How do *you* know about them?"

Lady Astwick continued as though Cordie hadn't said a word. "When Marina gave them to me, she said it was for safekeeping. She didn't say Brendan knew of their existence."

"Marina gave them to you? *You're* blackmailing him?" It was hard to believe and didn't make any sense at all. The dowager seemed to adore Brendan.

"Blackmailing him?" the old woman paled even more. "What are you talking about, Cordelia?"

"Someone sent Brendan a note at your soiree, threatening to expose Lady Clayworth's past if he didn't pay a large sum of money."

"*You* are Lady Clayworth," the dowager reminded her.

Cordie choked on a half-laugh. "Only the most recent one. My two predecessors had ugly pasts, not me."

Lady Astwick frowned. "Why does he think this has something to do with Jacqueline's letters?"

"He's been looking for them since before Marina died. She taunted him and said he'd never find them. She said, 'The lion holds your secrets.' He thought that mean the Avery crest, that we had the letters. It's the only reason he courted me in the first place."

"That was hardly the only reason," the old woman grumbled. "I've never seen a man so besotted. Brendan Reese would have chased after you, letters or no letters."

Cordie wasn't certain if that was true or not. It didn't even matter anymore. Regardless of what brought them together, she had no doubts that Brendan loved her now. And here was Lady Astwick, in possession of the letters. "Brendan isn't a traitor, my lady. Please return the letters to him."

The old woman leaned forward in her seat. "I'm afraid that's not possible, Cordelia. I don't have them any more."

Cordie's heart dropped. "Who does? Please tell me."

"No one does." Lady Astwick shook her head. "I burned them. All of them, when I realized what they were."

Cordie gaped at the marchioness. "You *burned* them?" she echoed.

Lady Astwick frowned at her as though she was the simplest of fools. "I didn't see any reason to hold on to them. If they fell in the wrong hands Brendan would have been carted off to Newgate. Marina made the fatal flaw of entrusting them to me." There wasn't a note of regret in her voice. "She thought that since Walter, my middle son, had died fighting the French that she couldn't have found a more formidable ally. She was wrong."

"I don't understand," Cordie managed. Brendan himself was convinced Astwick would turn on him when the truth was revealed.

Lady Astwick shrugged slightly. "I was duped by Jacqueline. She always called me a lioness, protecting my cubs from danger. Brendan, I suppose, is one of my cubs. A more noble man you'll not find. He shouldn't be punished for his mother's sins. I was the one who eased Jacqueline's entry in society. If anyone was to blame for her meeting the right people, it was me." She shook her head in disgust. "No. I would never let harm come to Brendan, not if I could help it."

"You burned them?" Cordie repeated, her emotions a jumble, her mind racing. "Are you certain you had them all?"

"I am. Marina was enraged when I refused to return them."

"Then why is someone trying to blackmail Brendan? And what evidence do they have?"

Lady Astwick blinked at her. "That is a very good question, Cordelia. I, for one, plan to find out. Have you sulked enough in Hampshire? Are you ready to return to your husband and face whatever this is together?"

The idea of seeing Brendan again sent her spirit soaring. Besides, he had to know that whoever was after him didn't have his mother's letters as a weapon. What else had the previous Lady Clayworth done? "Yes. I plan to return to London today."

"Excellent." The marchioness clapped her hands together. "You can ride with me."

Forty-Two

Clayworth,

I have grown tired of waiting, and so I have come for you. There is a hack waiting for you out front. If you do not have the funds I've requested, all of London will know of Lady Clayworth's exploits on the morrow.

BRENDAN stared at the letter in his hand, his heart pounding viciously in his ears. This was the moment he'd been waiting weeks for. And he had to act with precision. Pocketing the letter, he strode to the front parlor and glanced out the window. Sure enough, a hack did wait in front of his steps.

"Higgins!" Brendan bellowed as he returned to his study. Then he opened the safe behind a portrait of his mother and began retrieving stacks of pound notes.

A moment later his butler stood on the threshold and cleared his throat. "My lord?"

"Please bring me my black traveling valise."

Higgins took in the scene before him, the money on the desk and Brendan's disheveled state. "Do you think this is wise, sir? Going out with that amount of money on your person?"

Of course it wasn't, but Brendan didn't really have a choice. He wasn't even certain how much his blackmailer actually wanted from him. "The bag will be empty, just for show. I'll need my greatcoat as well." Brendan wasn't a fool. Whoever his blackmailer was could cosh him over the head and abscond with valise, never relinquishing the letters and blackmail Brendan all over again. Thankfully, his overcoat had more than enough space in its interior pockets to stash the stacks of pounds inside.

Higgins still looked dubious, but he rushed to do Brendan's bidding anyway.

After filling his coat with the money, retrieving a pistol from his desk drawer, and snatching up his empty valise, Brendan exited his home, dashing down his front steps to the awaiting hack. He looked at the driver, who made no attempt to conceal his identity, a usual looking fellow garbed in grey and a shabby hat. "Where are we headed?" he asked the man.

The driver gestured southward. "The bloke said to take ya to the Whitehall stairs fer ya ta catch the ferry."

The ferry? That didn't sound appealing at all. Who knew where he'd end up? "You don't by chance know who this bloke is, do you?"

The driver shook his head. "Nah, 'e said ya needed a ride is all."

Well, it was worth a shot to ask the question. Brendan took a deep breath and stepped inside the conveyance. What other choice did he have?

◄◄◄✦✦►►►

"Whitehall stairs to the ferry?" Marc hissed, relaying the information to Caroline Staveley as his coach followed Clayworth's hack.

"The ferry?" she echoed.

"If I was a wagering fellow…"

"Which you are."

"Which I am," he agreed with a smile for his new compatriot. "I'd say Clayworth's blackmailer is awaiting him at Vauxhall Gardens. That's what I'd do in any event. The place is teeming with people, plenty of places to hide along the walkways and go undiscovered."

"I'll take your word for it."

Marc grinned. He couldn't help himself. Caroline was simply delightful as a partner in, if not crime, the prevention thereof. "Lady

Staveley, are you telling me you've never engaged in an assignation in the pleasure gardens?"

She sat up a little straighter and met his gaze like a regal queen. "I am a proper lady, Lord Haversham."

A proper lady who ran around Town and did whatever she wanted, never answering to her husband. A proper lady who was married to a royal bore. "Why, even proper ladies should experience at least *one* little assignation, my dear."

"Indeed? And how *little* are we talking about?" she returned, a playful glint suddenly lit her eyes.

So much for a proper lady. Marc coughed in his fist. "No one has ever called me such a thing, I assure you."

"Of course not," she replied. Then Caroline glanced out the coach window, watching Mayfair as it blurred past them. "How will we follow him in the ferry without detection?"

"I don't think that will be possible, dear."

Her eyes flashed back across the coach to him. "It *has* to be possible, Marcus. We can't let him face whoever this is without us watching out for him."

Of course they couldn't. They hadn't spent weeks watching Clayworth's residence to let him go this last bit alone. At the same time, things had become much too dangerous to let Caroline continue on this journey with him. Still, she was certain not to like Marc's opinion on the matter or the plan he would have to put into effect, so he simply smiled what he hoped was his most reassuring smile. "Do you trust me, Caroline?"

She seemed to consider his question before finally nodding. "Against my better judgment, I suppose I do."

Most women usually did. "Then don't worry your pretty head about it. I'll think of something."

Just then the carriage slowed to a stop. Marc peered out the window and saw Clayworth descending the Whitehall steps to the Thames landing. "Stay here," he whispered. "Let me see what he's doing. I'll be right back."

Marc hopped from his coach, shut the door, and quietly slid a metal pin into the lock. Then he rushed to the driver's box and ordered his man to return Lady Staveley to Lord Clayworth's residence to await him before bolting toward the steps Clayworth had already descended.

As the coach lurched forward, Caroline pounded on the door, cursing him loudly. He smiled to himself as he reached the river's edge, the murky water reflecting the moonlight above. Lady Staveley wouldn't be the first woman to curse him after discovering she'd been duped, but this time it was for the lady's benefit. If he didn't watch himself, he'd end up heroic in some fashion, and that would be a travesty, indeed.

Before Marc, Clayworth was just about to step onto a ferry when he heard Caroline's commotion above them. The earl turned his head toward the sound and caught sight of Marc behind him. Fury lit Clayworth's his face. "You!" he growled, before hurling himself in Marc's direction.

Belatedly, as he fended off his one-time rival, Marc realized Clayworth must have mistaken him for the blackmailer in that instant. Perhaps he should have put more thought into his plan, but he hadn't had a lot of choice in the matter or the timing. "Damn it, Clayworth!" Marc ducked as the earl swung a black valise at his head. "I'm trying to help you. Will you listen to reason, you dolt?"

Cordie rushed up the steps to Clayworth House, the dowager Marchioness of Astwick quick on her heels. It felt so good to be home after the ride from Hampshire. She could barely wait to throw her arms around Brendan and tell him his worries were unfounded, at least in as far as his mother's letters were concerned. Whatever else, they'd face together.

Higgins stood in the threshold. His old eyes bulged slightly at the sight of her. "M-my lady!"

Lady Astwick directed Cordie into the home, the two of them brushing past the elderly servant in their haste. "Tell his lordship that his wife has returned, Higgins," the dowager ordered in her most commanding tone. "And tell him she awaits him in the green parlor."

The butler cleared his throat. "B-but, madam…"

Lady Astwick frowned at the old man. "I've never heard you stammer so much, Higgins. Now don't dawdle, bring Clayworth to us at once. We have had a long journey and we are tired."

But Higgins shook his head. "I—well, I'm not certain where he is, my lady. He went… out."

"Out?" the dowager barked. "Certainly he told you where he was going. Send a man to retrieve him. Are you deaf?"

But Cordie could tell from Higgins' panicked expression that he didn't have the faintest idea where Brendan was. She sighed. After the weeks they'd spent apart, a few more hours wouldn't kill them. Besides, he'd be back soon, most likely. "We'll await his lordship in the green parlor, Higgins. When my lord *does* return, please send him to us."

"Let me out this instant!" came a woman's cry from somewhere behind them in the street.

Surprised, Cordie spun on her heel and her mouth dropped open when she recognized the Marquess of Haversham's coach, now parked right in front of Lady Astwick's traveling conveyance. "What in heaven's name?"

The entire coach shook as someone pounded on the door from inside. "Let me out, I say!"

"Is that *Caroline Staveley*?" The dowager peered around Cordie to get a good look through the open doorway. "In *Haversham's* coach?"

Was that Lady Staveley's voice? As soon as Lady Astwick said so, Cordie knew she was correct. What was she doing with Marc? Was she in some sort of trouble? Cordie dashed down the steps and raced to the carriage, and ran right into a hulking driver who stood sentry in front of the door. "Out of my way or I'll call the watch!" she commanded.

"I have my orders, my lady," the man replied, but he shuffled his feet uncomfortably as he did so.

Cordie folded her arms across her chest and glared at the man. "Indeed? A kidnapper, are you? Either move out of my way, or I'll see you sent to Newgate."

"But Lord Haversham—"

"Can deal with me," Cordie finished for him. Then she shoved at his hulking frame to make her point. He moved just enough that she was able to see that a metal pin kept the coach door locked, but he held his position, refusing to move another inch.

"Good heavens!" the dowager grumbled behind her. "What a bunch of nonsense." Then the old woman poked the driver in the groin with her cane, sending the man cursing as he dropped to the ground like a sack of flour.

Cordie took the opportunity to pull the pin from the lock and open the carriage door.

Caroline Staveley stumbled out, putting a hand to her disasterous coiffure. The viscountess glared at the driver, still rolling on the ground just a few feet away. "How dare you?"

"Lady Staveley!" Cordie's hand flew to her chest. "Whatever has happened to you?" Truly she had never seen the woman look so disheveled. The viscountess had always been the picture of calm perfection.

At that moment, Lady Staveley glanced around at the scene before her—the moaning coachman, the dowager marchioness still threatening the man with her cane, and Cordie—as though suddenly realizing she wasn't alone. The viscountess stood her tallest, pushed back a fallen lock of her hair, and flashed her most charming smile at the two ladies. "Thank heavens you're home. We must get to Vauxhall right away."

"Vauxhall?" Cordie echoed. Had Lady Staveley gone mad during Cordie's sojourn to Hampshire?

"As fast as we can." The viscountess nodded her head vigorously. "Brendan's in trouble."

Forty-Three

BRENDAN dropped his valise and clutched Haversham's jacket with both hands. "Are you following me?" he hissed.

Haversham surprised him by nodding. "Aye. I've been watching your home for weeks now. Waiting for you to finally get contacted by this son a bitch."

Brendan's mouth fell open and he released his grasp on the blackguard's jacket. "I beg your pardon?"

Haversham sighed, stood tall and smoothed his hands over the front of his jacket to remove the fresh wrinkles. "Caroline and I discovered your notes that day we ended up in your study."

Good God! Haversham had seen his blackmail notes?

"You got another one, didn't you?" the marquess pressed. "You are headed to meet whoever is threatening Cordie?"

Threatening *Cordie*? Hearing his wife's name on Haversham's lips made Brendan's jaw tighten. But he had to respond to the bastard. Why did he think the blackmailer was threatening Cordie? Because the notes simply said *Lady Clayworth*. Haversham hadn't put anything else together, thank God. Brendan breathed a slight sigh of relief. "I can handle this on my own."

"I'm sure you can. But you're not going to." Haversham nodded toward the ferryman. "Besides, no one will ever think we're working together. Our distaste for each other is well established."

"I don't want your help."

"Well, you have it nevertheless. So stop wasting time and tell me what you know or what you suspect." Haversham stepped onto the ferry and said to the boatman, "You are to take us to Vauxhall, are you not?"

The ferryman blinked. "The man said there'd only be one o' ya."

Haversham tossed the man a satchel of coins. "Well, there are *two* of us, but no one else needs to know that, do they?"

The ferryman grinned a toothless smile. "No, sir. Yer secret's safe wi' me."

Haversham took a seat on the ferry and patted the spot beside him. "Come along, Clayworth. We don't have long."

Brendan snorted as he stepped onto the ferry. He wasn't quite certain how Haversham had appropriated this affair with the blackmailer, and he wasn't quite certain he even wanted the man's assistance. He certainly didn't want the blackguard to learn about his mother's letters, which meant he was going to have to be extra vigilant as they met with the villain, but Haversham was correct in that no one would ever believe the two of them would ever work together. "Why are you so dead-set on helping me?"

The marquess shrugged as the ferry started down the Thames. "Because I would never see Cordie hurt if I could help it, even if that means working with you."

"Well, I suppose that makes two of us then." Brendan finally took the spot beside Haversham. "How did you know we were headed for Vauxhall?"

"It made sense. A number of places to hide, the ability to blend into a large crowd. The bastard could wear a mask and no one would think anything of it."

Perhaps having Haversham along was a blessing in disguise. Brendan's mind just didn't work the same fiendish way. "He could be watching the ferry, you know? If he sees you here as well, he could get suspicious."

"He won't see me," the marquess promised. "I've a talent for getting into and out of places without anyone being the wiser."

"Just so long as it isn't my home," Brendan grumbled.

AVA STONE

"Not for lack of trying. But your wife is devoted to you, Clayworth. No idea what she's done to bring this trouble on your heads—and I'd rather not know—but you can rest easy on that matter. Cordie is devoted to you, and you alone."

Brendan didn't doubt that in the least, but he supposed it was nice of Haversham to say. "So," he turned his eyes to the southern edge of the Thames, "when we arrive, I'll depart alone."

"I'll watch from the river and see if anyone follows you. Then I'll follow myself, at a safe distance, of course."

"Of course," Brendan muttered. Assuming the blackmailer followed him and Haversham brought up the rear, how would he keep the marquess from discovering the reason he was being blackmailed? Haversham was willing to help, believing Cordie was in trouble, but Brendan couldn't let him learn about his mother's treacherous activities. The marquess might be a lot of things, but Brendan had never thought him a traitor. "Keep a watchful eye on yourself, too. There could be more than one of them."

Haversham chuckled. "That would explain the variation in the letters. The amounts made no sense whatsoever."

Brendan sighed. "Don't remind me. I'm not all that thrilled you and Lady Staveley took it upon yourselves to rummage through my desk."

"Just be glad you're not going it alone."

But it would be so much safer for Brendan if he was going it alone, if another set of ears weren't listening in this evening—a set of ears belonging to a man who would waste no time in trying to steal Cordie away from him if given half a chance.

The ferry slowly floated up to the pier leading to Vauxhall Gardens, and the sound of lively music drifted to the shoreline. Brendan rose from his seat, tipped his head in the direction of the ferryman, and disembarked. He didn't look back to see if Haversham followed, as that could give away their ruse. He started down the main path toward the revelry as though he didn't have a care in the world.

People passed him going both directions and Brendan scanned the crowd, searching for a familiar face, wondering who was waiting for him. Then he felt something hard at his back and a voice hissed, "Make a sound and I'll pull the trigger."

278

Cordie closed her eyes, shivering a bit from the chilly air on the Thames, and willed the ferry to move as fast as possible. Though Caroline Staveley had explained in great detail how she and Lord Haversham had discovered notes blackmailing Brendan and then kept an eye on Clayworth House until the villain made his move, nothing really made sense to Cordie. If the blackmailer didn't have Jacqueline Clayworth's letters, what was he after? But most importantly, she needed to see her husband again, to tell him he was safe from the gallows and that they would face this fiend, whoever he was, together.

A hand grasped her elbow, and Cordie opened her eyes to find Lady Astwick's light gaze focused on her. "We will get to the bottom of this, Cordelia."

Cordie nodded, thankful for the woman's strength as she had so little of her own any more.

"We can cover more ground if we split up once we reach the gardens," Lady Staveley suggested.

But the dowager marchioness waved the suggestion away with her hand. "That sounds like a perfectly good way to get us each killed, Caroline. No, we'll stick together."

"But the gardens are so vast."

"I have no intention of ending up with a knife in back this evening. So we'll stay together."

Lady Staveley sighed but agreed with a nod of her head. Then she smiled at Cordie. "Are you all right, darling?"

As all right as one could be under the current circumstances. So Cordie nodded in response. "I just want to find Brendan."

As soon as they disembarked, the trio bounded up the steps and started along the main path to the gardens. Loud music filled the air, as did the laughter of the assembled crowd. Cordie remembered attending events here in the past, how she loved the fireworks and the dancing and the general reverie. She would never be able to attend Vauxhall again without a feeling of doom settling in the pit of her stomach.

"Caroline!" came a cheerful voice from the dinner boxes.

The three of them looked up to find Lady Juliet Beckford waving wildly in their direction. "Oh, bother," Caroline grumbled. "I can't put off my sister-in-law. She'll be suspicious."

"Go on then," Lady Astwick ordered. "Find us if you are able."

Caroline Staveley waved back to her brother's wife and started toward the dinner boxes, leaving Cordie and Lady Astwick by themselves.

"Where do we start?" Cordie asked, only because the dowager seemed to have command of the entire affair.

"If I was going to meet someone here for a nefarious purpose," Lady Astwick began, "I would be along the darkened hedgerows."

Which made complete sense. "My thoughts exactly," Cordie agreed. At that moment, a shot rang out in the night and then the sky lit up, full of color. Cordie placed a hand to her furiously beating heart. For a moment she'd thought it was a weapon, not the fireworks. "That just took off a year of my life."

"This way," Lady Astwick pushed toward a garden entrance with Cordie quick on her heels.

Again the night sky lit up and illuminated the gardens below. Cordie's heart stopped once again when she spotted a figured slumped on the ground against a hedgerow. "Dear God!" she breathed out. They were too late! She raced across the walkway as fast as her slippered feet could carry her. "Brendan!" she yelled.

She dropped to her knees beside the fallen man, and somehow managed to turn him part way, enough that she could tell the man was not her husband. "Marc!" she gasped.

"Over there!" Lady Astwick yelled. "A fellow just darted into the shrubbery."

"Damn ferryman," the marquess mumbled, his eyes still closed.

❧

Brendan was almost certain he heard his name. He started to turn toward the sound, but his blackmailer pressed the barrel of his gun harder into Brendan's back.

"I said go *forward*," the villain hissed.

Where the devil was Haversham? Shouldn't he be bringing up the rear? Brendan shook the valise in his hand. "There is no one here, why don't we make the trade right now?"

"Trade?" the man said, abandoning his whisper, and Brendan almost recognized his captor's voice. He must have taken the man by surprise for him to finally speak aloud.

"Yes, trade. You give me my letters and I'll give you your money.

Then we can both be on our way."

A maniacal laughed escaped the villain, then the man circled Brendan from behind, finally stopping directly in front of him. Brendan barely managed to keep his mouth from falling open. "Brookfield?" he whispered. His eyes were dark rimmed and he looked slightly mad. *Opium eater.* Captain Avery's words echoed in Brendan's ear. Brookfield clearly wasn't in his right mind. How long had he been like this and Brendan had missed it?

"Let's get one thing clear, Clayworth," Lord Brookfield spat. "You're buying my silence, but nothing else."

But Brendan had to get his mother's letters, especially from this madman. "I'm afraid I must insist on the trade," he replied calmly, hoping to alleviate the man's obvious agitation.

Brookfield looked at him as though he sprouted horns and a forked tail. "You'll give me every farthing I want, and you'll continue to do so until every penny you stole is returned to me."

Stole? Brendan shook his head. "I've never taken anything from you, Brookfield."

Exasperated, the deranged viscount blew a lungful of air from his chest. "I wouldn't have cared if she wanted to carry on with Haversham if that's what she wanted. I only wanted..."

"This is about *Cordelia*?" Brendan frowned at the deranged man. "All of this is about my wife?"

"She should have been my wife! I needed her...and y-you don't."

Needed her? Or needed her dowry? Things were starting to make a bit of sense. "I am sorry, old man, but she chose me. I'm certain however..."

Brookfield scoffed. "She chose *Haversham*. I saw her sneaking around to see him more than once. I saw her leave Sunderland's ball in his company. But you covered up for her, always the hero."

Brendan's head spun just a bit. He hadn't thought anyone other than Averys knew the truth about that fateful evening. How long had Brookfield been keeping an eye on Cordie?

"And if you don't pay me, everyone else will know it too," Brookfield growled, his wild eyes darkening with the pronouncement. "And we both know the ever-heroic Clayworth will never let scandal touch the perfect Reese family name."

"Brendan!" Cordie's voice reached Brendan's ears. Dear God! He hadn't imagined her calling him earlier. It really was her! What was she doing here? She should be safely ensconced in Hampshire, away from the unhinged Brookfield.

"Cordie!" he yelled back. "Stay wherever you are! Don't come any closer."

Of course she didn't listen to him. His reckless wife rounded a hedgerow and froze in her spot when she realized Brookfield's gun was trained on Brendan. "He doesn't have them," she called.

The letters. She'd somehow discovered that piece of information and thought to save him. He could see it in her anxious countenance. No, Brookfield didn't have the letters. It was too bad Brendan hadn't realized that before. "What in the world are you doing here?"

"Looking for you," she replied softly.

"Well, do come closer then." Brookfield gestured her forward with his pistol.

"This has nothing to do with her," Brendan said calmly. "Tell me how much you want and I'll give it to you."

"This has everything to do with her!" Spittle flew from Brookfield's mouth.

Brendan spotted Haversham, a little worse for the wear, rounding a hedgerow from the opposite direction. About time he showed up. The marquess, pistol in hand, lifted his finger to his lips, warning Brendan and Cordie not to say a word.

"I want every farthing that should have been mine." The viscount scowled at Brendan. "Or I suppose I could shoot you and then marry the grieving widow after all."

Brookfield must have heard a sound behind him because he spun on his heel and gasped when he discovered Haversham just a few feet away. In surprise, Brookfield fired his pistol and Haversham stumbled back slightly. A red stain on the marquess' left shoulder quickly began to spread as he fired his own weapon, hitting Brookfield squarely in the chest.

Cordie screamed and threw her arms around Brendan's neck, burying her face against his chest. He held her close, not certain if he would ever be able to let her go. After the weeks they spent apart and then Brookfield threatening their lives, Brendan wanted to keep her in his arms forever.

⌒⋆⋅⋆⌒

Cordie should dry her eyes, but she didn't want to let go of her husband. So she held on tighter even as Lady Staveley and Lady Astwick came upon the scene. Then the viscountess dashed across the garden and she threw her arms around Marc's neck, sobbing. "You foolish, foolish man!" she heaved. "You nearly got yourself killed!" Then she seemed to remember herself and released her hold on him. Caroline Staveley swiped at her tears and then began beating his broad chest with her fists. "And how dare you lock me in that coach and send me packing, you awful scoundrel!"

Marc grinned like the rake he was reported to be, snaked his good arm around Lady Staveley's waist and drew her back against him. Then he lowered his head and captured her lips in a searing kiss that even took Cordie's breath away from where she still stood within Brendan's arms.

"Heavens!" Cordie whispered, her mouth agape.

Brendan cleared his throat and Lady Astwick harrumphed. Loudly.

Finally, Marc lifted his head, his light eyes twinkling devilishly. "Now, my dear Caroline, you may say you've enjoyed a proper assignation in a Vauxhall walkway."

Lady Staveley ripped herself from his grasp and slapped his cheek, though the sound was drowned out amidst the blast of more fireworks overhead. "Don't you *ever* come near me again, Marcus Gray!"

He winked at her and nodded his head in acquiescence. "Not to worry, I never do kiss a lady more than once, my dear." Then he turned on his heel and disappeared into the revelry of the night, his left arm hanging limply at his side.

"Well!" Lady Astwick declared. "I think you handled that rather well, Caroline Staveley."

The viscountess still seemed to be trying to catch her breath. A dark blush covered every inch of skin Cordie could see. Then Lady Staveley touched a hand to her cheek as though to determine her own temperature. "I can't believe that just happened."

"As I said, you handled that rather well, Caroline," Lady Astwick continued in a softer tone. "You know how foolish men can be. I think there's no reason to mention any of this to Staveley or he'll feel compelled to defend your honor and you've already done so, quite wonderfully, yourself."

At that moment, a constable rounded the hedgerow and took in the scene before him. "An injured gentleman just sent me this direction."

Brendan whispered in Cordie's ear, "Go to Caroline, *ma minouche*." Then he closed the distance from their group to the constable. "I'm Clayworth. That fellow there," he pointed to Brookfield's now lifeless body, "threatened my wife and myself, then shot the Marquess of Haversham, who defended himself by firing back. Fortunately, Haversham is a better shot, and I believe he's gone to find a surgeon for his own injury."

"Aye, that's what the man said," the constable agreed, then he sunk to his haunches to take a closer look at Brookfield. He grunted unhappily. "Just what I needed to make my day complete." He glanced back up at Brendan. "Clayworth, you say?"

"The Earl of Clayworth," Brendan clarified.

"Well, my lord, why don't you see these ladies home? I'm sure we'll be around to get your statements later."

Brendan nodded. "I'll look forward to speaking with you."

Cordie snuggled against Brendan in Lady Astwick's traveling coach. It had been so long since she'd seen him. So long since she'd felt his arms around her. She closed her eyes and breathed in the scent of him, silently vowing to never be away from him again.

As soon as Caroline Staveley departed the carriage and the remaining trio started for Clayworth House, Lady Astwick sighed loudly. "I am so terribly sorry, Brendan. Had I known you were searching for Jacqueline's letters I would have told you they'd been destroyed."

"It's hardly your fault." Brendan ran his hand up and down Cordie's arm as though to keep her warm.

"Still, I wish I had something. I didn't know you knew is all, and I didn't want to tarnish your memory of her."

He laughed sadly. "I just can't believe it's over. I can't believe I can stop looking for the things."

"You can now enjoy the happiness you should have always had, dear boy." Then the dowager cleared her throat. "But if you ever send your wife off again, you won't have to worry about the Home Office. I'll hang you myself."

Brendan chuckled and the sound warmed Cordie, inside and out. "Not to worry, my lady, my days of espionage and subterfuge are over. I can't wait to retire to Bayhurst Court with my wife and never let her leave my sight."

"That might be a bit extreme," the old woman declared. "You don't want to make a nuisance of yourself."

"Within reason, then," he promised.

Cordie sat up a little straighter and stared into her handsome husband's eyes. "I was so terrified when I saw his pistol. I thought..." But she couldn't finish that statement.

"It doesn't matter." He pressed a kiss to her forehead. "It's all over, my love. But do tell me you don't have any other deranged fellows hoping to still marry you. This Captain Seaton fellow is of the reasonable variety, isn't he?"

He hadn't been reasonable about Cordie's friendship with Livvie, but Cordie couldn't imagine the captain brandishing a pistol or trying to blackmail Brendan. "I believe you are safe, my lord."

"Thank God," he replied with a charming smile upon his face.

Epilogue

July 1815 – Bayhurst Court, Derbyshire

"I KNOW you were behind it, Cordelia Clayworth!" Livvie embraced Cordie on the front drive.

"I don't have any idea what you're talking about," Cordie giggled, so happy that the Kelfields had finally arrived to spend the rest of July in Derbyshire.

"Hmm." Livvie grinned. "I suppose the dowager Marchioness of Astwick inviting me to her house party next month is just a coincidence then?"

Of course not. Cordie had finally broken the old woman down, begging her to ease Livvie's way back into society. "I'm sure you charmed her all on your own."

"I'm certain," Livvie replied drolly.

A squeal from Poppy Everett caught their attention as a little sheep dog knocked the child to the ground. Thomas Reese doubled over with laughter.

"I can't believe you rode all the way from Hampshire with a *dog*." Cordie smiled at the scene on her front lawn.

"Watch what you say about me in front of my children, will you?"

286

the Duke of Kelfield bounced his son in his arms. The tiny Marquess of Brockenhurst cooed and chomped on his father's finger.

"I will try to watch my tongue," Cordie teased. Then she gestured to the estate behind her. "Do come inside, I know Clayworth is eager to see you both."

"Eager to show off his heir, you mean, if his letter is any indication," Kelfield corrected. "Though I completely support his doing so."

"So generous of you." Livvie rolled her eyes.

"Well, I'd never begrudge him what I plan to do myself."

"You are indeed noble, Your Grace," Cordie laughed as she turned back to her home. She ushered Livvie and Kelfield into a sunny yellow parlor where Brendan sat on a settee holding their sleeping son, Julian Reese, the tiny Baron Bayhurst.

"Shh," he whispered. "The little lad just barely dozed off." His eyes however, twinkled with love and affection as they landed on Cordie and she felt it all the way to her toes. If she lived to a hundred she'd never tire of that look.

"Only Brendan can get Julian to fall asleep."

"My wife has always professed that I'm old and boring." Brendan winked at her. "Apparently our son agrees."

"You are awful. I haven't said that in ages."

Livvie laughed as she linked her arm with Cordie. "Do you suppose Brock and Julian will be as good of friends as we are?"

Cordie nodded. Of course their sons would be friends. They would know each other all their lives just as Cordie and Livvie had done. "I'm certain the Kelfields and Clayworths will be close for generations."

"I'm certain you are right, my love," Brendan said.

"Always wise to agree with one's wife." Kelfield smirked.

About the Author

Ava Stone is a USA Today bestselling author of Regency historical romance and college age New Adult romance. Whether in the 19th Century or the 21st, her books explore deep themes but with a light touch. A single mother, Ava lives outside Raleigh NC, but she travels extensively, always looking for inspiration for new stories and characters in the various locales she visits.

Feel free to visit her at:
www.avastoneauthor.com
www.desolatesun.com

17537299R00172

Printed in Great Britain
by Amazon